when Fenelon Falls

Dorothy Ellen Palmer

Coach House Books, Toronto

first edition

Published with the generous assistance of the Canada Council for the Arts and the Ontario Arts Council. Coach House Books also acknowledges and appreciates the support of the Government of Canada through the Canada Book Fund and the Government of Ontario through the Ontario Book Publishing Tax Credit.

Although the places in *When Fenelon Falls* are real, the characters are fictional, the product of the author's imagination. Any resemblence to real people, living or dead, is coincidental – except for Yogi the bear, who really did live in a cage in Rosedale, Ontario.

Library and Archives Canada Cataloguing in Publication

Palmer, Dorothy Ellen, 1955-
    When Fenelon falls / Dorothy Ellen Palmer.

ISBN 978-1-55245-239-4

    I. Title.

PS8631.A449W44 2010   C813'.6   C2010-904980-2

To my good witches of the north, Dale Nevison and Marianne Froehlich, and to the wonderful wizard who is my daughter, Severn Nelson.

If you cannot get rid of the family skeleton, you may as well make it dance.

– George Bernard Shaw

It was a wind with a woman's name that caused the trouble ... Hazel, fickle and frantic, had come to call with all her fury.
– CBC Archives for Hurricane Hazel, October 15, 1954

Now many moons and many Junes have passed since we made land. A salty dog, this seaman's log: your witness my own hand.
– 'A Salty Dog,' Procol Harum

ALONG CAME JONES

In the summer of 1969, I ran full speed into a bear cage – one complete with bear. But don't break out the bagpipes. That August 17 at 4:37 p.m. was one clean moment in an otherwise down and dirty summer, a heat of error, envy and malevolent stupidity. There's no easy explanation and little excuse. I was a kid; I was sick of being blown around by my baby sister; I had to put someone out of her misery. All true, but not all the answer you deserve. The only answer my reckless teenage self could see was a dancing bear. So I partnered one.

The tale is forty years and counting, years I've spent asking, 'How do I begin?' Jordan would have called that 'The Seminal Question, Pun Intended,' but I lack her wits and her wit. I'm kiltless, so bear with me. Unless you count the impersonal sagacity of Scottish proverbs, this memoir has no wardrobe of family lore to dress the scene. I own no letters tied with ribbon, no journals from front or farm, no family Bible that survived a perilous Atlantic, Gaelic motto intact. For these beginnings, there's nothing to do but pull up your stool and sit down.

We'll make do with living memory. With the sound of a cowbell ringing on the night of the moonwalk, Sunday, July 20. With a sunset on Balsam Lake, one rude day's end that left my sister on the dock, her feet in the water, her back to the path. Like her, you'll have to make do with me. Me at fifteen. One year her elder and an easy foot taller. Straight black hair, bone thin and criminally self-important. What am I doing? Memory has me fetching her, running from the cottage in a flickering of shadow like one of my father's home movies. I'd call myself her less-than-dutiful errand boy. Her legs man. Her second pair of worse-than-useless shoes. But when memory isn't lying outright, it leaves things right out. There's always a more inclusive truth, and here it is. That night and any other day? Same difference. I was always out to get her. It was the hallmark of that silver summer. My lone hunting season.

That's pathos you're hearing, not self-pity. And good intentions, but President Kennedy was bang on when he said we all know where that paving leads. For me it leads to our dock, to the moment where for once I arrived in time, just as the sun melted into the bay beyond. Flame encircled my sister's head. When she turned to me, I was blind and she was beatified – a corona of wild copper, a Medusa ablaze. Do myth and martyrdom seem improbably entwined, this early in the story? Good. This is a yarn of tangled tale ends, unravelled by me, a classic tail-ender. Ghastly puns? A snock-snarled lore of mixed metaphor and multiple beginnings? Welcome to the clan.

'C'mon! It's almost time to walk on the moon!' No reaction. 'It's safe, kiddo. They're acting like nothing happened.' In the slightest of movements, my sister lowered her head. Cicadas answered for her. Impatience answered for me. 'Can it, BS! I won't miss Neil Armstrong just because you're slower than molasses in January.'

Splashing stopped. A spine slumped. Corkscrew curls drooped red on worn grey boards.

BS? Short for Baby Sister and the obvious – terms more than synonymous in my book. And molasses in January? Perhaps it flows faster the other eleven months of the year. In any event, here's your first taste of Marchspeak, my family name and mother tongue, and the first tinge of regret. Mine, that is – yours comes later. Truth be told, twenty-plenty awaits us both.

The cowbell commanded a second time. Still in Sunday best, BS pulled off her glasses and scoured them on the hem of that stupid yellow sundress. Like they held all the dirt on the planet. Twisting it like a length of rope, she knotted her hair. She sighed, coaxed a reluctant left foot, struggled into shoes. A clear moment to stop for sorry, a gift I didn't take.

She stood, gained her balance and shrugged. 'Lead on, MacBluff!'

'What? We've been counting down for weeks and on *the night*, you don't care?'

Her answer took eons and was, of course, another question. 'Guess what Leonardo da Vinci called the greatest engineering device known to man?'

'What? The rocket? Something he invented? The helicopter or the submarine?'

'Nope. The human foot.' She hefted one of hers. 'See?' The heavy black leather of her new corrective oxfords caught the last line of sun. 'It's imperfectly perfect.'

I didn't know what to say to that. None of us did. Never at a loss for words, my family has no language for loss. So I got snarky. 'Well, Miss Imperfect, it's the twentieth century. Leo would be far more impressed by us, by our feet on the moon! Now that's perfect.' I figured I'd topped her. For once. She let me gloat the length of the path. More would have been illusory.

'*Our* feet? Really? And who is this *us*?' She'd clomped each stair for matching emphasis, but turned on the landing. 'And just exactly what will a dirty footprint or two on a dead and distant celestial body actually change? *For us*, I mean?'

'Don't be a retard. It changes everything!' I beat her to the door.

'Sure thing.' She pushed past me. 'Presto! It'll heal the lame. Presto encore! It'll find the lost and free Yogi. And presto miraculous! It'll turn Aunt May and MC into – '

'Jordan May March!' MC's stilettos announced her arrival from the addition. She folded her *Toronto Star* under one arm to retie the silk bow on her pink sweater. Combat-ready, her orders followed: 'Speak when you're spoken to. Do what you're bidden. And for goodness' sake, come when you're called! If you want to join us, Missy, you'd best be silent.'

'Roger Wilco, Mother Control!' Jordan saluted her. 'Per-Mission Controlled. Maintaining radio silence, as per standing orders. Private Almost March over and – '

'Enough, Little Miss Trench Mouth! Never run faster than your shoes.' MC smiled. 'Last time I checked yours, dear, you were *probably* a girl. Please consider acting like one.'

Jordan fired me a glance that said, 'See?' She turned, wound her arms into a hostile pretzel and levelled Mom a look that yelled, 'So?'

'Fix your face right now, Missy Sourpuss. No one here's at war but you.' MC grabbed her *Star*, rolled it tight, and tapped high heels forward. 'One ridiculous little girl determined to be her own worst enemy!' Newsprint swatted flies on Jordan's head, 'You march, March! No TV till KP.' 'KP'? A wartime expression: Kitchen Patrol. And 'march, March'? All the aunts and uncles used that one. Perhaps it had been marginally clever the first time.

MC's flyswatter morphed to cattle prod, administered in jolts to Jordan's back. 'Get a move on, Missy, and do us all a favour: drain that sarcasm with the dishwater.'

'Really, Mother? Aren't you afraid I'll pollute the lake?'

'Hmh ... Flatter yourself, Gypsy Sue, and no one else will.'

'Hmmmh ... No one else will anyway.'

Mother slapped a rolled-and-ready baseball bat into her palm. 'Dawted daughters can bear little. So, no, I've never coddled you. You can thank me later. For now, try being more like those other March girls, the ones in that blankie of a book you're forever carrying about. They did their chores cheerfully. Please consider your imitation the highest form of flattery.'

Jordan sniffed. 'Please consider My Book to be mine.'

'No, dear, I read *Little Women* too – when I was a child.' MC flattened bat to sword and thrust it. 'Here, stick this and yourself in the swamp. And don't come back into *my* house until you're ready to clean up your act *and* the dishes.' She smiled. 'Use that overactive imagination of yours. Pretend to be any March you like – Meg, Jo, Beth or Amy – but get out the tea and cookies. Let's use the Good Melmac, shall we, sweetie?' 'Melmac'? Don't ask. Indestructible post-war plastic made of God-knows-what-and-won't-be-telling.

'Don't be a retard!' Jordan mimicked as she clomped past me. 'Everything! It changes everything!' But march she did, straight to the swamp and back to the suds.

Thus passed One Giant Leap for Mankind, the defining step of a warring century. It left little impression on our own perfectly imperfect Tokyo Rose broadcasting cheerfully from the kitchen sink: 'Sea of Tranquility, my asp! Drain that sarcasm, Sweetie Snookums. Good one, Smarmy Marmee! What were you thinking, Cinderella, hm? I said, *hmmmhh!* Of course the likes of you can't go to the Moon Ball!' We ignored her. She dropped a stack of the Good Melmac – a fine Canadiana Green as opposed to the everyday Canadiana Brown – held her nose and intoned, 'Houston, Inequity Base here. The Melmac has landed!' Dad and I broke rank and laughed at that one. Come on, we had to. You would have too. But when MC squinted in our direction, 'Who brings a staff to break his own head?' we caved right quick. We knew which side our bread was buttered on and who held the knife.

Literally short on stand-up, my sister leaned on the counter switching feet like a wounded flamingo, alternately hooking one heavy shoe and then the other over the calf of the standing leg. Then she caved too. We heard the soft rasp of a wooden stool on linoleum. Mom used it for dishes, but at four-foot-eleven, Jordan was still too short to do so. When she tried, gravity laughed at her. Dirty water cascaded in twin waterfalls down her elbows to the floor.

'Excuse me, out there – I don't believe I heard a question!'

Jordan yelled the sigh with the reply, 'Arrrrrr-Mother-may-I-please-use-your-stool?'

'You may, Missy Lazybones, but don't you dare drip water on my clean floor unless of course you want to wash it too. Just stand back up for each dish.'

Jordan blasted into a far less tuneful version of last summer's dirge from Mr. Lightfoot, no doubt hoping that, on her own black day in July, a quick launch into singing badly would keep her from saying worse. My parents did what they always did when their daughter sang: they turned up the TV. Loud. Louder than necessary. With no other flight path, Jordan did what she always did when they ignored her: she pounded pots and pans and herself into the domestic order of silence we called home. There's no place like it. No one heard her questions about peace and brotherhood that night, despite her strident finale, half sung, half screeched and wholly ignored. Why not? As Jordan sang it, because the hands of this have-not keep landing in the sink.

Up the road slept a bear in a cage, her have-not black hands clamped over her eyes. I bet you weren't asleep. I bet you remember it exactly. Where you were standing and who stood with you, as you lifted your eyes into the night sky. Too young? Perhaps your parents remember. Had they met? Were they even born? Then ask your grandparents. Yes, it's getting to be that long ago – lifetimes. If you've got someone to ask, you're lucky. You can catalogue chaos, locate yourself in the tumbling of time and space. About family history, about the times before our time, we rely on the telling of others. We become what we tell ourselves.

So when you look up, dear gazer, up from this book or to consider the heavens, do be careful what you wish for, because every wish defines its opposite. Name your heart's desire and with only the slightest of figuring, the universe learns your heart's despair. If Yogi woke when her captors cased the moon, then she paced the seven steps of home entrapped, back and forth in cave painting – the raw pads of her feet imprinting the concrete pad of her cage with blood. Bear feet are so human. Curved one-inch claws print like five little toes. That's one small step for ursine kind – too small a step for ursine kind. There's nothing kind about it.

For me, that marvellous night for a moon dance marked the end of all things marvellous, and that Summer of Love proffered little or none. It still sings in my head, a haunting Top 30 countdown, the lyrics of mistakes and malice, a libretto laundry list of soiled moments, sour notes I couldn't sing true. It's the muzak to the soundtrack of my mother's voice, hammering home all too many of her maxims, tossed off as if in and of themselves they explained all things, as if they were undemanding lessons. I didn't know she spoke in proverbs. I thought she made them up, thought her wise until years later when I realized a plagiarist is afraid of her own voice. But beggars can't be choosers and if wishes were horses, beggars would ride.

Because that summer our wishes cut to the crux. Not romantic, birthday-candle, coins-in-a-fountain, wishing-well wishes. Not the song Jiminy Cricket kept on singing and Pinocchio kept on believing until he became a real live boy. Not Cinderella's song, where her heart makes wishes when she's fast asleep. What bloody good is that – to you or anyone else – a wish stuck in dreams? No, our wishes were possible and probable, ones that could have and should have come true. Unfortunately, most of us are more like Pinocchio. We wish for the improbable – wooden, waiting and stuck, expecting some god somewhere to pull some strings.

Except Jordan. She hated Pinocchio, considered him more kindling than kin. She'd have kicked him in his knotty little ass or, worse, chased him with an axe. It wouldn't be the first time. She'd holler, 'Quit yer quiddling, pea brain!' She'd smack him down and not let him up until he got it: 'Sure you've got strings, but you've also got a tongue and opposable thumbs. Ergo, you're both; you're Puppet Boy. Don't ask permission. Dance if you bloody well feel like it!' She'd say the same thing to him as she'd want me to say to you: 'Wishes *are* horses. So don't be a stupid beggar, *jump on and ride!*'

And if Jiminy doffed his ridiculously oversized hat, slithered to Pinocchio's shoulder to whisper blasphemy in his ear, if that meddling cricket tempted anyone in my sister's hearing with the lie that being a real live boy would be better than being his true hybrid self, well, Jordan would squash that bug for what he was – a snake.

EVERY DAY WITH YOU, GIRL

Jordan's wish that summer – the one that started it all or, depending on your perspective, ended it – seemed at the time of its uttering both unlikely and harmless. Dare I say it? Toothless. Made back at another beginning, June 29, Kronk Sunday, a title I'll explain later. That afternoon we were halfway up our freshly laid gravel road, anticipating the moment of money in our pockets, thanks to the first pop bottles we'd find on the first trip to Mrs. Miller's General Store, when we heard shouting, the clanging of metal and the roaring of a bear. Not entirely unexpected sounds, for where our gravel met their highway stood a rusting homemade bear cage, home of Yogi the Bear.

Now before you get all Michael Jackson on me, thinking how jazzed you'd be to have your own personal zoo next door, you should know straight up that Yogi did not belong to us and that neighbouring a captive creature taught us but one thing: bears should belong to no one but themselves. Her very existence brought us shame, an edge that sharpened in our teens, a jab that March adults either did not feel or did not speak. Same difference.

At twelve, when Jordan tried to share it with Mom, MC had shrugged. 'Steel walls do not a prison make, nor iron bars a cage.' Jordan looked her bang in the face and said that was, bar none, the stupidest thing she'd ever heard anyone say about an imprisoned bear. Of course bars make a cage when you're the one in it. MC had smiled. 'A fool may ask more questions than a wise man can answer, dear. Stupid is calling your mother stupid.' That's the first time BS got sent to bed sans supper and the last time she went to MC with anything real. For once, Mother and the family March agreed. In their collective shrug, the alpha birthed the omega: March became Yogi's saviour and the agents of her demise. Hear it all before you judge us harshly.

In the spring of '64, Grayden, our eldest cousin, had been hunting deer up in MacIsaac's back bush when he accidentally shot a black bear. 'Accidental' is the term he used when he discovered it to be illegal. He came upon her cub bawling like it had just lost its mother, which of course it had. Gray diapered it up in a hunting tarp, plopped it in the crib of his pickup and sped home. Somehow – I never got this part of the story straight – Kronkowski, the drunk who ran the all-but-defunct bait stop at the top of our road, convinced Grayden to hand the cub over, explaining that he'd raise it right there in Rosedale and Gray could visit anytime he wished. My cousin, no doubt seeing 'his baby' as some kind of animated trophy – one that guaranteed him equal if not greater bragging rights without the mess or bother of having to have it shot, eviscerated, stuffed, mounted, financed or dusted – agreed.

A bullet to the brain would have been kinder. The only thing worse than watching a living creature fade is watching human beings stare at suffering and refuse to call it by its name. Killing with kindness – it's not just an expression. First Kronk erected a makeshift cage. A concrete slab, fifty feet of chain-link fence taut around four iron poles, and Yogi became the slave of no domain, trading the wilderness for seven paces in any direction. In a calculated generosity, Kronk gave his newborn a toy: he ran a yard of chain through an old tire and drilled it to the crossbeam. Now, dangling centre stage, Yogi had a swing, or more accurately a sway. It didn't have much of an arc. Jordan said the same thing, word for word, each time we passed it: 'Hold me back Brother Mine! I'm seized by a sane desire.' I took that bait only once. 'Okay, BS, what sane desire?' She'd grinned. 'The need to push.' I asked if that was sane, what did she consider insane? She'd shrugged. 'Doing nothing.'

Out on the highway, in red, in the all-too-Canadian tradition of flexible public spelling, Kronk posted a homemade plywood sign, its letters perpetually dripping: SEE YOGI BARE.

If you ever drove up Highway 35, you'll remember her. If you veered north at the turnoff to Fenelon Falls and drove another twelve minutes over the Trent-Severn canal bridge between Cameron and Balsam Lake, then you drove right into our hamlet of Rosedale. With a gas station, a marina, a bait store and a bear cage, our Rosedale bore no resemblance to the affluent Toronto neighbourhood of the same name. Ours began its life in the previous century as Rosadale, but the locals rechristened it for their ease. As we did Yogi. For Yogi was a she, a girl with a boy's name. And for our ease, and our entertainment, we put her in solitary for life.

And that cage changed everything. It caged a changeling, a bear in form, one who dimly remembered being a baby bear, but who'd been forcibly transformed into Almost Bear, Display Bear, She Who Never Belongs, She Who Must Pretend. In short, One Majorly Pissed-off Ursa. Yogi became what we called her: a cartoon, an animated inmate, lacking birthright or any right to define herself as a wild female bear. And we stared – as easily as the well-fed denizens of Toronto's Rosedale might do at yet another bag lady. And we laughed – until Yogi reclaimed her birthright in a manner natural to bears but with consequences unnatural to the rest of us. To quote MC: Give a dog an ill name and you may hang him. Enough said.

Initially, the opposite appeared true. Rechristened with a celebrity name, our Yogi became a yogi and for a few short years our blink-and-you'll-miss-it gas stop became a tourist mecca, where pilgrims participated in the vicarious recapturing of one small resident of the Great Canadian Wilderness. Recaptured on film, that is. Like that other 1960s yogi, the one with the next-to-unpronounceable name venerated by Beatles, our Yogi built a transient following, one that measured its weekend great escape from Toronto in minutes to and from her cage. The usual chant, 'Daddy, are we there yet?' became 'Daddy, are we at Yogi yet?' The most devout stopped twice, making offerings both times. Of crap. Non-stop crap. Edible wampum. Demeaning the purchase and the purchaser, exchanging worth for worthless.

Now I understand it and admit it: as a kid, I was fascinated. Every morning, as much as an hour early, Jordan and I would head to the top of March road to await the mail truck. We'd nuzzle in close to Yogi's cage, hand-feeding her dandelions and Pablum-soft branches, mesmerized by long pink tongue and ivory triangle teeth. We'd hunt down nests of tent caterpillars and shriek as she crunched them like Smarties. But we were kids, excused by definition. The worshipping fools who pulled off the highway in droves were grown adults, at least chronologically. Repetitiously insane, each had the same scathingly brilliant idea: 'Hey! How 'bout a shot of you/me/Grandma/Uncle Bertie/Baby Susie feeding a real live Yogi bear! Bobby, get the Instamatic!' So Yogi ate junk all Friday on the crawl up, and all Sunday on the exodus down. Did Kronk bother to feed her weekdays? Who knows. Her weekend worshippers never stopped. Such bare-fisted photographic bravery: Yogi licks ice cream from outstretched cones, Yogi nurses Orange Crush, one long-tongued baby. One shot left? Chips! Little fingers fit right in! Good one.

Did Kronk foresee the danger? Of course. He profited from it. Who else could look at a cub and see Jack Daniel's? Our Kronk: Rosedale's unreasonable facsimile of Donald Trump. A man with a plan. Research: Drive to Fenelon. Scout day-old baked goods. Purchasing: Acquire the cheapest. Ignore mould. Logistics: Unwrap, place in wicker fishing basket. If tourists notice the smell, tell 'em Yogi likes it. Marketing: Make sign: 'Yogi's Pic-a-nic Basket. Stolen from Jellystone Park.' Operations: Sell each deathly stale Ding Dong and doughnut at triple cost. Sidelines: Overpriced film and trinkets. Hours: To paraphrase the theme song, Yogi 'might sleep till noon but before it was dark she'd have eaten every picnic basket in Rosedale Park.' Employee Morale: If bear is sluggish, find hose. Soak her till she earns her keep. Bookkeeping: Unscrew peanut-butter jar. Profit Management: Buy booze. Security: Put jar, basket and rifle in old Coke cooler with the bait. Look for the GD keys. Employee Benefits: Don't be a retard. It's a bear. Big live bait for big fat fish. Health and Safety: Frogs on the doughnuts? Scrape 'em off. Year End: Never. Sell Christmas trees. Tell 'em Yogi likes snow.

I can't forget the butter tarts. Kronk called them homemade, declared them his and Yogi's favourite. It was half true: Yogi loved them and Kronk loved to show off how he'd trained her to appreci-ate them. He'd stand beside the cage, swinging the box back and forth. Pendulum arms, with his flat round face as the clock. She'd match him, moaning, tossing her snout in anticipatory pleasure. Rifle cocked between his knees, he'd unlock the padlock, stand in the doorway, raise his arms and twist the box around in the air, 'Dance for it, baby girl! Dance for it!' An obedient if ungainly balle-rina, Yogi would rise up, clasp claws overhead and stomp in circles. You could all but see the tutu. I'm sure Kronk saw it. He drooled.

At his drunkest it slid out in one wet slur, 'Dansfuritgurlie! Dansfurit!' When he tired of her, he tossed the gooey mess in her face.

Now, I grew up watching Dancing Bear on *Captain Kangaroo* and never once asked myself why a kidnapped, captive bear would want to dance. Today I wonder what kind of sadist looked at the muzzled and starving and saw entertainment for toddlers. Today, at the sight or scent of butter tarts, my stomach heaves. You can't blame Yogi. Sweet and syrupy, they were as close to honey as she was ever going to get. You can't really blame Kronk. Yogi got him as close to the big-city gravy train as he'd ever get. 'So who is to blame?' you ask. Good one. That's your Seminal Question. Remember it. If you don't, who will?

The March clan certainly didn't. We took our lead from the three monkeys: what evil? Our Yogi didn't even have a cautious Boo Boo sidekick to keep her from hoovering every goodie in sight, let alone a Mr. Ranger to step in and take it away from her. Even Grayden quickly forfeited his *in loco parentis* status. For a summer or two, he exercised his visitation rights. He went right into the cage to play. When baby gave her daddy a bear hug that broke ribs and ripped an incision down his back that sent him into Fenelon for twenty stitches, Grayden became a deadbeat dad. No one admonished him. Not word one.

Now in her sixth year, our teddy bear on permanent picnic barely resembled her cute baby self. Bored and bloated, she wept from a permanent sore on her left eye, one inhabited by flies. Did this stop the tourists? Give those turdists a moment's cause for pause? Of course not. When preconceptions rule, human eyes don't stand a chance. They couldn't see what they were looking at: a sick, sad, overfed, aging bear, one trapped in permanent babyhood in a glorified playpen. No one saw bloody footprints. They saw 'a real live bear!' They said, 'He's sooo cute!' Do bears get cavities? Do bears on a Ding Dong diet become diabetic? I don't know. I know she got lethargic. She learned to snarl. She abandoned her swing and cowered, rubbing her weeping eye against the wire, making it worse, perhaps deliberately so.

Why did no one come to her rescue? Even Mr. Ranger is always more concerned with the property of tourists than the well-being of one he has sworn an oath to protect. MC would say: Once a thief always a thief. Little beggars don't choose their own nourishment. (You march, March! You shut up, suck it up and be grateful that you're fed!) As Yogi's Mr. Ranger, Kronk viewed his charge likewise, saw himself as her benefactor, noblesse oblige. In the wee hours he'd sprawl over the picnic table, munching tarts and lullabying at the top of liquored-up lungs: 'Now if I had the wings of an angel, over these prison walls I would fly! I'd fly to the arms of my poor darlin', and there I'd be willing to die.' Sometimes persons unknown called the police. When the local constabulatory arrived, they found no crime beyond country music and lawn vomit – both of which should be indictable offences, but sadly are not.

In typical March, the last word got rendered without words, with family, tourists, locals and the law complicit: Kronk had saved a motherless child. He could raise her or kill her as he pleased. Only you can prevent forest hires, and back then we didn't even try. Back then the almighty tourist dollar turned more than one wild beast into a sideshow attraction. Take Overall Boy, a case in point. He was a local and our neighbour, one of farmer Hezzy's sons, not the one who delivered the mail, but the one we called OB for reasons obvious. He bred a whole hockey team of coons. Kept them in a roadside pen at the Fenelon turnoff.

When a car pulled over and a window rolled down, OB tapped his chest until a kit poked her nose out of the big front flap of his greasy overalls – a trick that wowed 'em every time. He sold those babies down the river or anywhere else, no questions asked or offered, five bucks a pop. Canada's first drive-thru, eons before Tim Hortons. If the new owners drowned the kits next week or put them down once they got uncute or bit little Janie, so what? Plenty-twenty where they came from. Last summer, at Jordan's insistence, we'd turned one of our Saturday morning meanders through Fenelon into a forced march, hoofing it all the way from the dairy, over the canal, past Hanley's Lumber, to the Rosedale-Fenelon turnoff, all to ask OB to stop.

'But city pissers like it,' he'd grinned with brown teeth, 'and I doan like them.' When Jordan looked dubious, he moved his plug from left cheek to right and frowned. 'Lookit, girlie. Us locals have a right to make a buck offa tourists. Yer daddy'd agree. Ask him.' When Jordan shook her head he spat over it. Spittle showered her hair. When she suggested raccoons had rights too, a brown blob grazed her cheek. 'What are ya anyway, one'a them there hippie tree huggers?' When Jordan said maybe, he spat on her shoes. 'Git lost, girlie. Now! Unlest y'want me to whistle for m'dog. His name's Calvin and he doan like yellow.'

So we were used to cages and all they stood for, and specifically used to all manner of sounds both ursine and human being broadcast from the top of our road. But that first Sunday afternoon the hullabaloo was neither tourist nor intoxicated, at least not on booze. It was a greener version of Gray: his youngest brother, cousin Derwood. Our feet built little speed on the fresh gravel, but crunching round the last bend we saw him, still in church clothes, crouched prostrate and preying: firing handfuls of gravel bullets scatter-force into the cage. Most found their mark: Yogi, curled in fetal whimpering, little black-gloved fists clenched into her eyes.

Jordan's wish? It cuts near the wood: 'I'd give everything I am to free her!'

I lost mine by yelling it: 'You dirty little bastard! I'm gonna shove you in that cage!'

It only alerted him. Proving what Grandma often said in his direction, that a bully is only as brave as his unfair advantage, Derwood dropped his free ammo and took off, quickly gaining a safe lead on the all-too-public asphalt. He turned. Running on the spot, he stuck his thumbs in his ears, wiggled his fingers, jiggled his bum and stuck out his tongue. 'Na-na-na-na-naaa-na!' Such a juvenile asswipe.

Then he leaned toward my sister and did something far worse. He smiled.

GET BACK

You are maybe three years old. You have two sets of pyjamas. They stay the same, even when The House and The Family don't. When they're going to move you, they iron your yellow dress stiff, snap the silver locket around your neck and the silver lock on your red suitcase. For now it's empty, stashed under This Crib, and waiting for next time. Your pyjamas have lived here, safe in a drawer in This House, for more than seven sleeps: your soft green nightie with the bunny rabbit, your thick winter sleeper with snaps. It's yellow too. Tonight you are wearing it. Good. Sometimes snaps confuse him. Smile at the bluebird. She's how you know you're not in the hospital. She's like This Crib, baby blue. Hospital cribs are metal. This one has a happy picture pasted on its wooden head. This Lady has made it herself, a birdie cut from a magazine, perched in apple blossoms, bursting pink. Happy notes come chirping out of her tiny beak. You know only the first line of her song, 'Bluebird! Bluebird! Smile at me!' That's what This Lady sings as she drops off your bottle, 'G'night, baby. Kiss, kiss! Now close those eyes.' Bouncy brown curls all soft round her face, she pats your tummy, flicks light into night, and rap-tap-taps down the hall. You sit back up. You drink half your bottle. Never more. You crawl into the farthest corner. Press your back against the bars. Chant the alphabet – you know most of it. Just keep chanting. Hum. Sometimes when he hears how good you are at ABCs, This Man changes his mind. There's the slow crunch-thud, crunch-thud – his step in the hall. Sing louder. 'A-B-C-D ... ' There's the slower grind of doorknob. 'E-F-G.' Can't you see me? 'L-M-N-O-P!' He looks right at you and lowers the bar. Such a racket! Surely This Lady must hear it This Time? He yanks the bottle from your hands. He grabs your feet and drags you to him by the ankles. It hurts to kick him, but you try. A damp palm clamps your mouth, smothering 'W-X-Y and – ' 'Shut up, you little bastard!' He smiles.

For now, dear reader, let's stop for sorry. You see, in order to understand Derwood's smile, you had to see that other smile too. It needs to hang over your head and menace each moment the way it did ours. So later in this story, when you chastise me for reading Jordan's diary, please remember, so have you. It's a cruel violation of her privacy, but she left us little choice. I'd say no choice, but there's no such thing. You've opened this book in time and you've got plenty of it. My mistake? Thinking I did. At fourteen, unlike yours truly, Jordan already saw time like an adult, as a finite ball of yarn. To recast an analogy my crafty sister loved: 'Find fallen loops. Go back to knit forward.' To do so, you need to know that one of us could knit and the other never had a clue about loop one. Now, in this telling, I'm holding the needles, but back then I was the one with hands outstretched, watching the yarn unravel.

What's that? Narrators aren't supposed to admit to spinning a yarn, let alone recuse themselves for doing so poorly? Says who? Says the single best reason I did not become an English teacher: the decrepit Miss McElfiend. She who stood so ramrod straight at the blackboard my hockey buddies swore she'd rammed a goalie stick up her ass in an attempt to score the pickle. She who lectured with the wattles of her hairy neck in full pontification: 'Modern exposition craves artful invisibility! As Tarzan would put it, "Show good. Tell bad."'

Well, flow schmo. You won't convince Jane or Boy or even Cheetah that Tarzan was merely *in* the story – Tarzan *was* the story. Show a movie, a horse or your good side, but by definition, a story is told. The view contains the viewer; any artful dodger is still a thief. And as for invisibility, I'd bet everything I am that it's overrated. I'm always exactly what I appear to be: a fifty-something math teacher, an old dog with no body for new tricks. These are my lesson plans. This is my day book; it's written the way I teach. So, how does one teach math, particularly the hybrid skill of problem-solving?

For any problem, there are always an unlimited number of often tempting but incorrect answers. But, as I promise all my students, there's also one shining right answer, waiting. I can't just set a problem and stand aside. It's quackery to pose at the blackboard and silently show off how Mr. Smartypants Me gets that answer all sigh my belf. You have to get it, for yourself. If I slap chalk on the board, sit back and assign seatwork, I'm no teacher. A teacher revises each time. Out loud. By multiple examples. When my natural inclination is to speed up, I have to slow down, to go step-by-logical-step until I'm blue in the face, until you see both the answer and, more importantly, the reasons for it. Even math has a backstory. I tell and retell it, hoping to hit on the version that hits you, hoping to hear your Eureka Moment: 'Hey, I get it!'

Then to ensure you keep it, we do some metacognition, a.k.a. thinking about thinking. Both show and tell. Jordan would agonize each semicolon of this story; I just want it told. And I don't want you to forget for a second that it's being told by me, a teller with a very vested interest in how you hear, what you hear, and what you never hear. I struggle to knit the truth for myself, let alone the reading public. 'So why am I knitting Jordan's yarn?' you ask. 'Why knit, period, when you can't recast her holes?' Good question. Here are my reasons three:

Reason 1: Because I promised. Holes are the story.
Reason 2: Because BS can't be trusted. To quote Ms. Dickinson, she'd tell the truth but tell it slant, and you wouldn't be allowed to lean any way but hers.
Reason 3: Because BS Fundamentalism is born-again boring.

'Not *can* we squash ants,' she'd insist. '*Should* we?' The Should Question made all things relative – as in related to her – even A + B = C. For Jordan, they're sentient. This was one of the givens in her life that the likes of me couldn't see, so she elected to enlighten me. I can still hear her: 'You *should not* add A to B. Has A been consulted about the impending loss of her individual identity? Have you no conscience? To make this new C creature permanently schizophrenic! To rename the living! Who died and made you Noah? It won't work; they'll remember.' When I tried to tell her that sometimes a number is just a number, she shook her head. 'Nonsense. It *should* always be seen as a symbol, as a sum of final reckoning.'

So just because it's her story doesn't mean she gets to tell it. She'd lemniscate, word without end, no *amen*. When you're fourteen, everything's an outrage. When you're full of it, releasing it takes forever. Take 'Extemporaneous,' a BS invention in point: open dictionary, point and begin speechifying. Her kind of fun. I got to hold MC's stopwatch, to time BS BSing. Would you let that Little Miss Mouthful tell your life story? I think not. The driven don't make sympathetic narrators; you'd hate her by page two. In all probability, you'll hate me once you add it all up and ask yourselves, 'What's a bit of wind and a dead bear between friends?'

But till that final metacognition, dear ants, be grateful. At least my book is finite, bearable, able to be borne in hand. Hers would take a month of Sundays – that's five of them, from Moonwalk to Woodstock. See? I'm great at lists and dates, but can't pretend her insights into why. BS flashed from A to B to See so fast she damn near teleported. Or here's a better image, one she'd have enjoyed: like a tesseract from *A Wrinkle in Time*, her mind instantly folded all distance between any two points. My mind's adrift on MC's 'slow boat to China.' This math teacher can't add things up. I eventually see, but there are twenty-plenty brackets first. This is memory, importunate but imprecise; it's wrinkled but it's not time travel.

Too bad. We could sure use a Wavelength Acceleration Bidirectional Asynchronous Controller – a WABAC machine. Remember it? Jordan's favourite part of *Rocky and Bullwinkle*: 'Peabody's Improbable History.' Something I guess in hindsight she knew more than a little about. It featured Mr. Peabody, both a genius and a short white dog – probably a Westie – who time-travelled upright, sporting horn-rimmed glasses and a bow tie. To right the small events that caused colossal wrongs, he'd say, 'Sherman, set the WABAC machine to the year 1969!' Dials would be twisted, heroes would arrive and, presto, wrong would be righted. Instead, we're stuck with the imperfect machine of memory. You're stuck with me, Jordan's far-from-perfect Sherman: Mr. P's adopted boy, a mostly useless sidekick whose only real contribution was to be amazed by bespectacled genius and shout, 'Gee willikers!' Sherman lives a day late and a dollar short, blindsided at the end of each episode by yet another of Mr. P's atrocious puns. He never learns. He runs to the rescue only to find that genius is always

26

faster. That's me in a sidekick nutshell. So don't get too attached to me. Enough said.

In your binder – the one you're knitting right now, purling pages in your head – cast on seven tabs. You've met Tab A: the bear. You'll need Tab B: the hurricane, Tab C: the families, Tab D: Polk Salad, Tab E: the diary, Tab F: the bastard and Tab G: the ghost. Odd tabs for a math binder? Correct. This math-English hybrid requires a recalculation of Ye Olde Leap of Faith to sum up the ever-popular Willing Suspension of Disbelief. Assumptions about right and wrong, fact and fiction, good and evil – suspend those too, or you'll be jumping to some pretty inaccurate conclusions. Expect some seriously difficult multiple-choice questions – my favourites. And yes, the answer's in the back of the book, but that's always cheating. I'll take some questions, but this Sherman is too busy to stop for every hand. There are uncountable holes in this knitting. We have to go Way Back to pick up the fallen. We have to carry Way Back and Back Then and Now, all in our heads at once. And bear it. Like she did.

If you can't knit, you'll learn. This is your yarn too. You're as finite as the rest of us. Grab a loose end and set your needles clacking. I'll set the dials for the year 1954. One windy autumn. For Tab B, wind yarn over index finger, insert finger, turn page here:

HAZEL #13

Mumsie sat me down on her visit last Sunday and told me point blank that Walter was the best I'd ever do for myself, especially now, so I should quit playing Missy Nose in the Air and put his ring on my finger right quick. Janie tried to stick up for me, saying she'd only accepted Kevin when she felt good and ready, but Mumsie interrupted, saying it was all very well for pretty girls to wait, but not a plain and getting plainer girl of twenty-three with a dainty younger sister who's already tied the knot. 'Beggars can't be choosers.' She looked right at me as she said it. 'And damaged goods is exactly that – *damaged for good.*'

She's right. She's right. I know she's right. Walter is a good girl's dream. Short but darkly handsome (if you like pomade and thin moustaches), and forty is young, to be Accounts Manager that is, and the bank is so stable. Mumsie's always saying if Granny'd had half a brain when she got off the boat from Inverness, she'd have done what she set out to do and gone straight to the city to marry her fortune instead of falling for a penniless boy farmer before they shouted, 'Land, ho!' (Mumsie knows something about penniless boy farmers, having fallen for one herself.) She's always said that the only way her girls will make the same mistake is over her dead body, insisting that we should find a good catch in a bank or an oil company so we won't have to have to get our hands dirty all day long like she does.

Kevin works his dad's farm weekdays (Janie would never move to the city like me), and weekends he drives an oil truck. Not usually one for compromises, Mumsie approves. Kevin gave her a big felt banner, red and green with white writing. Mumsie said it looked just like Christmas! It had a smiling gas attendant in a smart uniform tipping his hat, 'BA: The Largest Oil Company Owned by Canadians.' She tacked it over the kitchen cupboard with the very best teacups and gave Kevin permission to marry her baby. Walter's job is better than Kevin's, so what am I waiting for? Her equal approval? Hell won't ever get that cold.

Maybe if I put it down on paper, maybe then I'll get some sleep.

I used to love writing in this diary, but here it sits, untouched since the night before: Thursday, October 14, 1954. 'Tomorrow is payday. At lunch I'm going over to Eaton's and I'll buy those cream gloves with the sassy pearl buttons. See if I don't! And a new umbrella, too, since Mr. Bad News (that's what Mumsie calls the radio) predicts showers yet again. A girl mustn't look bedraggled if she wants to get engaged!' How pathetic! The *Star* says over 4,000 homeless and more than 80 dead! I should quit my quiddling. In that hurricane, I was one little puff of wind.

It had been raining off and on for days. I left without my breakfast and, to my eternal regret, without saying goodbye to Gladys. I was double guilty; I'd borrowed her locket without asking. I trudged up the hill from Pleasant Valley already drenched, vowing to get an umbrella and cursing, for the umpteenth time, at being so far out in the west end that it took a ridiculous forty minutes to get to work. I remember reminding myself that Gladys and I were in her grandmother's trailer rent-free and that I should be grateful. (Yes, I should be.)

Despite the rain, the Long Branch streetcar arrived on time, but at Union I had to wait forever for the Yonge car. I know I should have taken the subway. It's been open since March, running safely for a full six months. Mumsie scolds me for a fool but I can't do it. I'm not going underground so the planet can collapse on top of me. I'm just not.

When Walter saw the sodden lump that was me, he said, 'Late again, Miss Johnston? You're not a Country Bumpkin anymore, my dear. Get a watch!' I know he only said it to keep up appearances. Some tellers were in hearing distance – tellers are always in hearing distance – because later, during dictation, he reached under his desk and squeezed my knee. (Mumsie says to smile and let him. Once, but never twice.)

At lunch I headed over to Eaton's. I could barely see the curb. I slipped, and out of the blue, who do you think appeared like Superman to save me? Angus! He said he was in town to check out a building on Yonge Street he'd be bricking next Monday and was on his way to ask me out to lunch. (Mumsie always says that what a man don't know can't hurt you, and besides I wasn't officially engaged yet and that was Walter's fault, not mine.) Angus was an old flame, but he was still my roommate's brother, so we ducked into Eaton's cafeteria, just like old times.

On the way back, the storm was much worse. He had to hold me up, and even then I nearly fell, three times in fact (and only once on purpose). When we reached the bank he asked if, considering the weather, I'd like a ride home. He had another errand and then would be heading west to see Gladys and drop off some of their mom's preserves before heading north and home himself. A ride to my own door sounded heavenly. (It almost was!)

Walter kept me late. Around 6:30 he tipped his fedora and told me to be careful, saying it was 'Positively heathenish!' out there. (Mumsie says I should appreciate his education and stop wishing he talked more like normal people. Janie says I'd better keep him away from Kevin, who'd laugh in his face.) But there was good old Grade 10 Angus in the lobby, happily chatting up a Boy Scout peddling his wares for Apple Day. Angus saw me, grinned and loosened his tie. His pants were bulging.

We had to shove full force against the big bank doors and, once outside, could barely hear each other. We decided to go to Fran's for a coffee until it let up. I made it up for him the way he likes it: three cream, no sugar. As impossible as it sounds, the rain got even worse. And the wind! It took forever to reach his car. (Back in high school, I called it Nessie, the Long-Lost Scottish Behemoth. I'd tease Angus, asking how a car that weighed a trillion stone could move at all!) I was so eager to get in that I sat on his mother's strawberry-rhubarb jam, ripping the note to Gladys attached. I transferred it to the back seat and took its place. That big old front bench, as welcome as my own bed. That's when Angus decided to tell me he had only one working wiper, and it was on the passenger side. He leaned over. 'I can drive with my head in your lap, can't I?' He only said it to break the tension. When I pushed him off, he laughed.

We headed on to Lake Shore, and it was some slow going. And dark. (Black as Mumsie's warning card, the Ace of Spades.) We talked a couple of times about getting off it, but were strange roads were any better? I know the devil you know is still a devil, but we couldn't stop, not with only thirteen cents between us. There was a beat-up green Packard with tartan seats behind us that must have decided the same thing; he'd been there awhile. Angus called us a Celtic Crappy-Car Caravan. I smiled. So we kept going, slower than snails. We were all but home. (But I could hear Mumsie: 'Forget close! Close only counts in horseshoes.')

We got to Mimico Creek. We could hear water snarling beneath the car. In the flash of a second, you could see things floating by. It wasn't my imagination. A hockey stick. A garbage can, then some boards and a bicycle. A furry thing. A man's fur coat? A big fuzzy pillow? Angus said he thought it was a sheep. I said, 'That's ridiculous! The storm's getting to you, Farmer Boy.' That's my nickname for him, the title of our Grade 4 novel, one of Laura Ingalls Wilder's Little House books. He grinned and played the part, 'If'n you say so, little lady!'

As we crossed the bridge, the wind tensed like a wolf pack, poised to pounce. From behind us came a growl, then a crack. I turned. It was a tree, and I mean a full-sized maple tree, not a limb, careening after us, a tree on a hungry brown wave, licking the car behind us. Angus gunned it. He veered up the embankment and punched the emergency brake. Behind us, the tree swept south and disappeared, sank with a Packard caught in its crown. I screamed. I fought to open the door. Thank goodness Angus held me down until I came to my senses!

When he turned Nessie off, I kept begging him to put the headlights back on. I knew I was being a baby. It wasn't entirely dark. For some inexplicable reason random lights flashed about like homeless fireflies. But Angus said no, it would drain the battery, better to use the army flashlight. Before I could stop him, he was clinging to the doorframe, inching back to the trunk. Mud lunged at his knees. When I pulled him back in, he graciously draped a blanket over my shoulders. Ever the gentleman. Huddled warm and safe, clutching a torch so big I had to use two hands, I remember thinking, 'Thank God for country bumpkins.' (How many city slickers keep Hudson's Bay blankets and army flashlights in their trunks as a matter of course? We were raised to respect weather. We had to. We'd seen it kill. So much for us rubes. We weren't drowning in their stupid subway.)

I don't know how long it took. It felt like hours. I might have slept a little. The floor flooded. Angus said if it got any higher we'd have to take our chances on the roof. It got as high as my ankles would have been if they weren't tucked into his lap. Then, in the dead of night, the wind and the water dropped. Angus murmured, 'Thank goodness for small blessings!' That's when I cried. It's one of the few things I ever remember Daddy saying. He said it about me. (Janie understands, but it's the one part of this whole thing I could never tell Mumsie. I heard my daddy in his voice.)

Eventually we could see the embankment again. Less than twenty feet away, in water the ugliest shade of brown, things were still churning by, most of it unidentifiable debris. When it passed the wide beam of our flashlight, you wished you hadn't seen it: a pressback chair, a baby's crib. The worst was the dog. We heard him before we saw him, a spaniel surfing along the edge of the water, clinging to a set of stairs from someone's front porch. Without thinking, Angus opened the window and whistled, 'Here, boy! Come, boy!' The dog jumped in, so close to the edge we were sure he'd make it, 'You can do it, boy!' A brown wave swept him under. 'I killed him,' Angus mumbled. 'He's dead because of me.' What could I say to that?

At some point, we ate the apples. I remember wondering about the Scout, hoping he'd made it safely home. The water had all but receded when we saw a light in the east. Angus read my thoughts and said he hoped these wise men were bearing whisky. We giggled even harder when we saw it was a boat. Imagine rowing down the middle of Lake Shore Boulevard! They tied up to a telephone pole, expecting us to board, but Angus said no, he wanted to drive. They looked at his boat of a car and agreed to help him try. I paddled the accelerator as our Good Samaritans got sprayed with mud, rocking us from behind. (Just like the snowdrifts between the house and the barn, I told myself. Should be as easy as Mumsie's Five-Minute Pie!)

We headed the last few miles skiing through swamp, driving right up over sidewalks and front lawns. Any path in a storm. I don't think we ever said her name. (We should have figured that any hurricane that could wipe out bridges and swallow Packards could do a great deal worse to a rickety old trailer, but we were so cold and tired and just plain done that we weren't thinking, period.) It was almost light and we were almost there when Angus joked that Gladys, being Gladys, had no doubt made a pot of hot chocolate, drank the whole pot, and made some more. We could all but taste it! That's why the police cordon at the foot of Brown's Line took us so much by surprise. Fire trucks. Ambulances. A policeman who said no, we couldn't go farther. Angus jumped out. 'Of course we can! She lives there,' he yelled, pointing back at my face in the car. 'She lives there with my sister!'

I'll always remember the even look in that officer's eyes. His voice so soft and slow as he gripped Angus by the shoulder, 'Not anymore, son. Not anymore.'

He took us to the Red Cross truck. A nurse gave us coffee. I was taking my first sip when the officer said the storm had decimated the trailer park and all the little cottages around it and handed us a survivor list. No Gladys. We read it three times. No G. Campbell. He said the injured had been taken to St. Joe's Hospital. No sister on that list either. No roommate. No best friend since kindergarten. But Angus stayed calm. Clear. Efficient. He gave his mom's number, his work number, Mumsie's number and my work number. He gave a description: Age twenty-three. Blond hair, five-foot-four, hazel eyes. Distinguishing features: Green cat's-eye glasses. A chipped tooth, earned smiling all the way to the ground riding a two-wheeler for the first time, age nine. Occupation: Student, Lakeshore School of Beauty. He asked me what she weighed and I lied. (Mumsie told me later not to feel guilty, said it was the least I could do for poor Gladys, who'd always been a wee bit porky.) Angus shook the officer's hand. And then he just stood there, looking out at the first silver rays of dawn. I had to call him back to the car.

Then he drove. Fast. Wild. Much wilder than necessary. To God-knows-where-but-I-don't. Not home. To some back street in Mimico, some deserted factory parking lot too near the creek for my liking. He slammed to a stop and began to shake. He wouldn't meet my eye. He jumped out, stood there lost, then opened the back door. I waited. Then I joined him.

Blood? Blood on his hands? No, preserves. He was eating it with his fingers. All five of them. Scooping sweetness as if he were starving. I wished he'd say something; I wished I could. He held out a finger, 'Try it.' I licked and he crumpled his mother's note in his other hand. Then with two hands, he tore it to pieces. Jam looks even more like blood on paper. He began to cry. So I held him.

I held on when tears turned to kisses. When kisses deepened, I returned them. When his hands, hands that had been so professional on the steering wheel, so calm writing his sister's name, so respectful shaking the officer's hand, when those hands got mean, ripped my blouse and tore my skirt, I'm sure I asked him to stop. Sure but not certain. All I'm certain of is that as light crept into the car, not ten feet away, a shape slowly shifted clear. What's that line in the Bible? 'And the void became substance, became words.' Something like that.

Maybe the floating shape had been a sheep because this shape was unarguably a cow, a very dead, very bloated cow, upside down in a factory parking lot in Mimico, a beast on her back with two feet pointing skyward and two broken beneath her. With jelly brown eyes, she watches me. When I should be sleeping, I watch her watching me. Dead eyes quiver with each thrust.

And this place isn't any better. The only decent person in here is the night cleaner, an older man with the musical name of Carmelito Trigliani. At night he comes into my room, pats my hand and says notta to dwell on dark things. He says the sleepawalking comes froma da dark things. Thatta a wedding is justa da ticket! There's a'nothing like a bella bride to cheera us up! (He talks like that, in exclamation points with anna accent!) He put his hand on my shoulder before the nurses wheeled me from my big red brick building to the small red brick building, the one with a rubber floor, 'Trusta him, the doctore. He knows whatsa best.'

When Mumsie heard about the electroshock, she said, 'Good, if we're lucky a few thousand volts will solve all our problems.' But I overheard her complaining to Janie. Mumsie kept insisting that it's not her fault, that even a good cow may have a bad calf, that at least she got one daughter right. To my face she says that women have nothing but their bodies to bargain with, and now that I've played all my cards, the only sure bet is to put that ring on my finger, right quick. Janie nods. They're all so certain they must be right. They're all so right they must be certain. They take me on walks by the lake. To see water. The stupid cows.

But hurricanes have eyes. And that Hazel, she was one smart cookie. She took one look at Toronto the Good and what did she do? She flooded the subway. One of their precious tunnels collapsed. They think if they repair it quickly I'll forget, but I wasn't born yesterday. I was reborn in a hurricane; I've got second sight. I'm plugged into the quivering universe. She will be a girl. I will give her Gladys's locket and Granny's name. Will she ever see Inverness? I hope so. See, I'm not crazy; I don't claim to know everything.

Here's what I do know. As nasty as the rushing water of a hurricane is, it's exactly the colour of the coffee we put to our lips every day. Dirt brown. Hurricane Hazel Brown. The taste of Angus – three cream, no sugar. Last week when he finally came to see me, and I got brave enough to ask him what happened, he looked at the ceiling. When I started to cry, he stared at the floor, 'For Chrissake, my sister died. That's it. That's all. Enough said.'

So, I can swallow that for the rest of my life or I can spit him out and start clean. I should have said, 'Angus, you taste just like what you are – plain old country cow shit.'

Mumsie says nice girls don't swear, but I no longer qualify. I'm about to be a married woman. And Walter, when he proposed at my bedside yesterday, his hand thumbing my knee, assured me that grown-up wives with aspiring bank manager husbands to instruct them don't have to listen to their Mumsies (especially not to Maladroit Mummified Maters like mine).

GOOD OLD ROCK 'N' ROLL

The drive that got us to the cottage that summer of '69 was, much like the family in the Ford, a day late and tender short. It occurred uncharacteristically in broad daylight, on Saturday morning, the 28th of June. Had we followed the Departure Protocol, our car Tessie would have joined the Friday night diaspora of the last day of school. Ordinarily, MC rocketed around the house all afternoon, ordering Jordan about in a frenzy of cleaning and packing, both of them tripping over our springer spaniel, Balsam, who knew that barking makes women pack faster. We couldn't waste a nanosecond. MC's self-imposed countdown had us blasting off the second Dad engaged the screen door. But that night broke the routine. Jordan walked no farther than the triangle between couch, radio and TV, surfing our three U.S. stations. Mom'd start pouring cereal or powdered skim milk into mouse-proof jars, then find an excuse to join her.

'What earth-shaking event had transpired?' you ask. Not transpired, expired. Judy Garland – she died. A week of footage already: Judy dancing with Mickey, clanging trolleys and ringing bells. Judy singing 'The Battle Hymn of the Republic' after JFK's assassination. Judy, Judy, Judy. Just get over the bloody rainbow and be done with it.

Apparently not. Friday was her funeral, so of course they played *The Gizzard of Boz* yet again. I had to listen to BS redeclare it 'the number-one-all-time-best-possible-movie-ever-in-the-history-of-the-possible-world!' I had to watch Little Miss Chubby Pigtails outwit a twister and a witch, lions and tigers and bears, only to discover what most of us already know. When a network bulletin interrupted to announce a riot after a police raid on Stonewall, a men's bathhouse in Greenwich Village, and Jordan asked why didn't they have tubs, Mom snapped the *Gizzard* off and told her to go pack something. But when Dad got home, he found the TV on and them side by side on the couch blubbering at some clicking ruby slippers, snotty Kleenex snowballs piled between them. When he got out the camera, MC put the kibosh on that blockbuster with one slam of a bedroom door.

Next morning, Jordan held three things safe in hand, refusing to consign any of them to Tessie's trunk, especially not her Little Yellow Miracle. Last summer, on her thirteenth birthday, she got the usual, a little party and a little present: a bowling party for two, her standing request since nine, and her very own transistor radio. A Lloyd's, sun yellow, the size of a deck of smokes but thicker. It had two gold knobs, tuning and volume, and a plastic wristband, also yellow. I'd be surprised if the parents laid out more than five bucks, but when she opened it you'd have thought it was a brand-new Pontiac Firebird. She squealed. She actually hugged them and they even let her. 'It's perfect!' Queen for a day, she all but danced.

Later she told me it was the only time they got it right – that usually, after hours of deliberating (the kind of hours you have to spend when you're only getting one thing), she'd give them a page from the Eaton's catalogue with her wish circled or stand in the bargain aisle of Savette's and point. Come the 23rd of June, however, deliberation counted squat. She'd inevitably unwrap a close second, something almost but not quite the real thing: a cheaper version, the wrong colour or size. 'That's me,' she shrugged, 'always silver, never gold,'

The sight of her clutching her Miracle that day elicited my first act of similar kindness that summer. I won't say what kind. I leaned over Balsam, always plopped down on my half of the back seat as if he didn't need to share it, flicked the side of Jordan's head with my finger and whispered, 'You love a stupid little yellow box more than anyone will ever love you.'

A dead moment. A shrug. She asked MC for the car thermos, full as always of watered-down grape High-C, and with no help from me, poured it straight down the front of her yellow pop-top into a puddle on her new white shorts. I laughed. I said she looked like a walking exclamation mark, like one of the Riddler's henchmen. When we stopped in Manilla for ice cream, Dad moved to let her out, but MC reached back and locked the door. As we stepped away, we heard, 'Hey, all you CHUM Bugs out there! Here's your brand-new CHUM Chart, #648, Saturday, June 28, 1969!' And when we got back, she was still singing. Dad filmed her through the window, glasses on her head, holding the tiny print of it under her nose:

THIS WEEK	LAST WEEK	ARTIST	TRACK
1	1	Desmond & the Aces	Israelites
2	6	Three Dog Night	One
3	1	Blood, Sweat & Tears	Spinning Wheel
4	12	Oliver	Good Morning Starshine
5	9	Paul Revere & the Raiders	Let Me
6	15	Joe Jeffrey Group	My Pledge of Love
7	5	Friends of Distinction	Grazing in the Grass
8	26	Jr. Walker & the All Stars	What Does It Take
9	20	Andy Kim	Baby I Love You
10	10	The Buchanan Brothers	Medicine Man
11	27	The Winstons	Color Him Father
12	3	Henry Mancini	The Love Theme from Romeo & Juliet
13	2	The Beatles	Get Back
14	8	The Classics IV	Every Day With You Girl
15	24	Tommy James & the Shondells	Crystal Blue Persuasion
16	18	The Young Rascals	See
17	25	Motherlode	When I Die
18	4	Elvis Presley	In the Ghetto
19	21	Tom Jones	Love Me Tonight
20	30	Kenny Rogers	Ruby Don't Take Your Love to Town
21	29	Jerry Butler	Moody Woman
22	17	Bill Deal & the Rhondels	I've Been Hurt
23	0	Brian Hyland	Stay and Love Me All Summer
24	13	Marvin Gaye	Too Busy Thinking About My Baby
25	0	Booker T. & the MGs	Mrs. Robinson
26	0	Roy Clark	Yesterday, When I Was Young
27	0	Life	Hands of the Clock
28	0	Neil Diamond	Sweet Caroline
29	14	Sonny Charles & the Checkmates	Black Pearl
30	0	Cat Mother/The All Night News Boys	Good Old Rock 'N' Roll

If my Tin Roof was too good to share that day, if we all turned on her that summer, music was the only thing that didn't. And, man, how she loved it. The Miracle never left her side until she went in the lake. It lived on her left wrist where normal people wear a watch, attached by a disintegrating loop, now more duct tape than wristband, more dirty silver than yellow. In true sixties style, it rocked round the clock: on the dock when she went swimming, on the deck at supper, on the butt wad in the kybo, under her pillow long past sleep. Up at Mrs. Miller's General Store, Mrs. Miller set aside Miracle batteries at least once a week.

What was playing? For teens in the Toronto of 1969 there was only CHUM. (That's a.m. – f.m. was for old people.) If her radio played other stations I never heard it do so. It's no exaggeration to say that Jordan knew every word of every CHUM Chart hit that summer. She had a disgustingly eidetic memory, memorized whole songs at one hearing. She sang like a chainsmoker smokes, igniting the next with the previous. She kept her CHUM Bug card in her wallet where the rest of us keep our names. Come December, she pooled her babysitting money and took a toy down to the CHUM Christmas Wish. On New Year's Day, when CHUM played the Top 100, she sang every word. She sang the jingle: 'C-H-U-M, Ten-Fifty, Toronto.' She sang the ads. She knew all the DJs and all their time slots: Bob Laine from eleven to three weekdays, Jungle Jay Nelson, mornings from five till nine, and the all-important Top 30 countdown with Chuck McCoy on Tuesday nights. She'd sneak up to the pay phone at Mr. Miller's and part with a whole dime – she collected them – to call the 'Twenty-four hours a day, you say it and we play it' CHUM hotline. On the way she'd sing the phone number, 'Nine two nine, fourteen eleven.'

Between visiting Yogi, calling her CHUM and cashing in pop bottles, we hit the paved – read public – road several times a day, and whenever we did, she'd ambush me: 'Lyric Speak!' Another BS game. We had to converse in song lyrics and, in a rule I'm sure she devised to make me look like a total spastic retard, we could walk only when speaking. She'd get most of the way to the store reciting 'Love Child' by Diana Ross and the Supremes as if it passed for conversation. The day it knocked 'Hey Jude' out of Number 1 was the only hearts- and-stars day of last winter's calendar. That summer I came prepared –

she called it cheating – by repeating the chorus of the new Ray Stevens hit. This cowboy hero kept rescuing Sweet Sue from every conceivable danger, kept being tall, thin, long, lean, lanky and potentially heroic, until she added a no-repeats rule. She'd be yards ahead, 'Love Child'ing away and I'd be shuffling my feet like a midget-idget. I'd cave and walk normally. Of course, she never would. When I did, I had to spring for a Dubble Bubble. Jordan got a lot of gum that summer. She could have papered her room with Bazooka Joe.

How did she get weekly CHUM Charts up in the Kawartha Lakes boonies? There were none to be found in Fenelon, let alone Rosedale. Enter BS's small army of nerdy little browner girlfriends. Must have been a dozen girls mailing her charts. What'd she do with the extras? No such thing in March. She'd lay them out in chronological order on her bed, then in thematic order, by longevity, by unknowable Jordanian orders, until she'd made a CHUM Chart quilt. It's insufficient to say she memorized them; she scrutinized, cross-referenced and made projections from them. She could quote hits and stats with the same obnoxious accuracy that Derwood did from his extensive collection of baseball cards. I hesitate to think it, but it's true: they had something in common. Obsession knows no gender.

On weekday mornings, I followed Jordan up to our battered tin mailbox, the one connection to the city and our other life. It leaned precariously sideways on a splintering post across from Yogi's cage. We'd gather dandelions for her breakfast and then Jordan would lean against the cage and wait, sunshine-yellow thank-you notes to the Chart Brigade in hand, for Not Overall Boy, Hezzy's postal son, permanently rechristened in March as NOB. You raised the flag if you had mail for him and she always did. He'd drive up, open his window and exchange letters, but never a word. There was much discussion in March about whether or not NOB could talk. (He was a mouth-breather.) Derwood's father, Uncle G, said every village has its idiot. Grandma said whether or not the youngest Mr. Gale could speak, he could read demonstratively better than Uncle Gavin. Ouch. When she wanted to, Grandma could truly cut to the wood.

I remember the CHUM Charts so eagerly pulled from the mailbox at the start of that summer. All variations on a theme: a black-and-white photo of a DJ with coloured sound waves radiating from his head. Gary Duke, 'Boss of the million-dollar weekend,' emanated green sainthood. You could 'get Weaverized' with Hal Weaver in Easter purple, and a psychedelic orange Jay Nelson invited you to 'Bet your sweet bippy.' Jordan read them aloud on the walk home, made her quilt and eventually put them to bed in her improvised record case, an ancient round red suitcase that sported a red and white relief drawing of two red-slippered feet poised in pointe. Obviously born to hold ballet shoes, something Jordan would never own, it had been kicking around as a Barbie case, and then as a record case, for as long as I could remember.

For Saturday's drive north, it got stashed under protest in the trunk, nestled between Jordan's equally precious homemade diaries – two industrial-size binders, reclaimed from Dad's work at the order desk of BA Oil. Jordan worried the heat would warp her precious 45s. Her singles. In 1969 a single cost sixty-nine cents, that's sixty-six cents plus three cents tax, and I hoped the trunk would liquefy every cent. Let's cut to the chase. For a smart girl my sister had the musical taste of a puke Twinkie. Donovan, Simon and Garfunkel and Mr. Lightfoot had my grudging respect. But Neil Diamond, Tom Jones, the Cowsills and the bloody Bee Gees could improve the music scene only by contracting the Black Plague and popping their buboes in the face of every known fan and genetic relation. When I said her collection lacked seriousness, she played the Monkees, 'Daydream Believer,' her first single. She was twelve, but that's no excuse. The schlock remains the same. What the cluck did girls ever see in that scurvy midget Davy Jones? When I said no sane person could dig both Iron Butterfly and Bobby Sherman, Steppenwolf and Andy Kim, she sniffed, 'I can.'

Error. Teens live and die by their music. It's who we are and who we aren't. You know exactly who someone is when they say, 'I listen to *blank*.' If you like *blank*, you like them. Solid. If not, walk away. It's a matter of pride to be consistent. I tolerated folk, loathed pop and loved rock. I liked bands that weren't Canadian, the Stones and Procol Harum, but thanks to Canadian-content legislation and arts spending on Ca-na-da after our 1967 Centennial, I was also the first generation able to claim that most of my favourites were home-grown: Three Dog Night, Motherlode and Blood, Sweat and Tears. It's just plain dumb luck that I got to be a teen in the late sixties, when for a few short years they played the best music ever written.

Consider it: I still played my Christmas present every day, a little LP called *The White Album*. By June, Rocky Raccoon, Bungalow Bill, Sexy Sadie, Molly and Desmond and their barrow were all close personal friends.

But in the summer of '69, while Cat Mother and the All Night Newsboys sang 'Good Old Rock 'n' Roll' and David Clayton-Thomas belted out 'Spinning Wheel' and the Stones rocked down with 'Honky Tonk Woman,' I am embarrassed to this day to admit that the most-played record in the case, the song my supposedly intelligent sister walked around all summer humming and, yes, unabashedly singing, the one she subjected us to as Ford and family pulled out of Manilla, was 'Sugar Sugar' by the Archies. When I yelled, 'They aren't real! They're cartoons!' she accompanied her vocals with hand to armpit and rhythmic farting percussion. At that moment, I truly wished I'd come equipped with a gun to shoot off the hands of my rival. When she sang the 'do do do do – do do's,' I sang louder, 'I'll kill, kill, kill, kill – kill you.' Good one.

In her defence, BS could call a hit from one hearing. It wasn't just Burton Cummings's mojo that moved her to become one of the first card-carrying fans of some dark-haired boys from Winnipeg who'd seen their first and so far only hit last fall: 'These Eyes.' When their new song hit the CHUM Chart July 12, a week before the moonwalk, she predicted, 'It'll be a monster hit. Like the Canadian Beatles!' I figured she'd lost it. With that candy-assed little ballad? 'Laughing'? Who calls a song that? Well, Guess Who had the last laugh. It sat on the charts longer than a pregnant elephant. Her life-size poster of Burton the Beloved, bought in a special promotion from Sam the Record Man, right downtown on Yonge Street, that was her second hand-held treasure, wrapped in Saran Wrap, sealed against even her fingerprints.

Her final hand-held gem was a handmade Countdown Calendar. Hearts and stars encircled two days: the 17th of August, our Annual Balsam Lake Regatta, and 29th of August, when Burt and boys would play Galaxie, the revolving Coca-Cola stage at the Canadian National Exhibition. Another miracle was stapled to August 29: one GENERAL ADMISSION ticket.

After extended grovelling and a Cinderella's list of chores to earn the exorbitant ticket price of $7.50, after lectures about a fool and her money, after BS reminding Mom that when she was a girl she'd once gone all the way to Buffalo to see Glenn Miller, MC caved. She even drove Jordan down to CHUM at the crack of dawn to be one of 'the first fifty at 10-50' to get a special early-release ticket. In the margin of her calendar, in Jordan's usual immature open scrawl, was a proverb in tribute: 'A day to come seems longer than a year that's gone.'

But I don't think I ever believed they were really going to let her go. It was the principle of the thing. We always went to the CNE together. Well, more or less. Mom took us down. We'd do the buildings in the morning and for lunch she'd let us loose in the Food Building. We could have anything we wanted – anything that was free. In those days that was everything; we pigged out on Pogos and beaver tails and Tiny Tom doughnuts that left you smelling cinnamon the rest of the day. We saw the afternoon grandstand show with her, and then she handed us off to Dad, who met us after work at the Princes' Gate and took us to the Midway. And we did all of that in that order, every year, on the last day of the CNE, Labour Day, because no real March ever left the cottage until compelled to do so. What March would drive Jordan all the way down to the city for August 29th? Good question.

I'll admit to a certain shade of green. I was the one with good taste and she was the one with the meal ticket. How was that even remotely fair? The CNE would host every major Canadian band that summer – Lighthouse, the Five Man Electrical Band and Motherlode – but like the song says, Jordan only had eyes for Burton. Even rolled up, he smirked at me. With all that black hair he could have been a cousin or any paisano from Alderwood, except neither would be caught dead in his pansy outfit: purple bell-bottoms and a hippie-dippy shirt, paisley maroon with – get this – lace, hot pink lace on the sleeves. He lay in the back seat of the car, leering unbuttoned, sprouting chest hair down to his navel. Okay, so maybe I gave her elbow a little push. Maybe I was aiming for his face. Unfortunately, the High-C landed elsewhere.

But a reproof is no poison. Like ordinary siblings, BS and I could be at war one second and united the next. Take the car radio, a case in point. That's where we first heard it that Saturday – the song that sang summer, claimed summer, still is and always will be that summer. We loved it instantly; our parents despised it sooner. No small part of its attraction. At home, we'd negotiated a détente of door closing, but a three-hour ride renewed hostilities because the little yellow radio, Miracle or not, didn't work in a moving car. So over the years, the car radio ritual – who got it, how and for how long – had become quite the song and dance.

We'd ask before Dad's key turned in the ignition. Mom would say, 'Sure,' and turn it to CFRB, smiling into the back seat, 'Oh, that isn't what you meant?' We'd specify CHUM and she'd say, 'Hmmmm, you've got a friend on the radio? How nice. What's her name?' As if she'd been born a March, perfecting their tactics: deny, stall, blame. 'What radio?' 'Wouldn't it be nicer to sing? "Michael row the boat ashore ... "' 'Your father's too tired.' 'Surely you don't want to make him have an accident?' She'd make us play stupid licence-plate games and I Spy. Then finally she'd say, 'Okay, When Fenelon Falls. Win, and you can have that noise you call music.'

When Fenelon Falls was a family invention, a triumph of March-speak, a fact I didn't appreciate until I discovered firstly, that not all families played car games, and secondly, that even avid mobile gamers had never heard of it. Legend has it that it evolved from a discussion of autograph books, that Mom was explaining that when she was a girl you wrote stuff in them like: '2Y'S U R, 2Y's U B, I C U R, 2Y'S 4 Me,' girlie stuff that ended with 'Yours till Niagara Falls!!!' when Jordan asked, 'When Fenelon Falls, does he get hurt?' And that's all it took to get them falling all over themselves to show off their brains.

How do you play? Well, it sounds simple enough. Theoretically, we each had thirty seconds to add 'when' to any place in Canada so that it becomes personified. Swansea becomes 'When Swans See.' Port Hope becomes 'When Port Hopes.' Adding an 's' is permitted. But play any game in March and it gets complicated. As keeper of the stopwatch, MC clicks, I swear, at twenty seconds for any turn that isn't hers. 'You're out!' Repeat a name and you're likewise out. Foist a dubious construction in her direction and, well, you get it. Dad and I, we're always out. I suspect Dad knew I often took myself out because I was sure he did. Cut to the chase: BS and MC ruled the airwaves and we all knew it. They'd memorized the classics; they had new names at the ready. They hid Canadian atlases under their beds for nights when they were too busy plotting strategy to sleep. A good one, but no joke.

Mom always starts: 'Who names the new and learns the calls can stand alone when Fenelon Falls.'

We sound like this:

'When Brace Bridges.'

'When Saska Tunes.'

'When Moose Jaws.'

'When Green Would.' There are lots and lots of 'wood's.

'When Lind Says.'

'When Cobo Conks.' One of Mom's favourites.

'When Winnie Pegs.' Jordan insists that Winnie the Pooh could play cribbage.

'When Waska Peepees.' My favourite and, yes, there really is a Waskapipi River in northern Ontario. I liked to use it in a double-play with 'When Bummers Roost.'

'When Dale Leaks.' Dad loyally plays it after 'Bummers Roost.'

Mom unfailingly rules him out, and never gets the joke. 'It's Leaskdale, Tommy, not Leaks-dale!'

'So sorry, Caroline,' Dad says, winking into the rearview mirror, 'I just can't seem to remember that.'

Once we're out, Mom and MC only make triple plays. While Dad and I drive and get driven in silence, Ux Bridges, and Manito Baas, and Alber Taas. This favourite of Jordan's is much disputed by Mom. Jordan always insists that it's technically correct: a man named Albert, pronounced the French way, could say 'Ta ta,' the singular third person past tense being 'taas.' Mom scowls but relents. She wants to count her equally dubious inventions of 'When Stove Ills and When Picka Rings and When Victoria Corners.'

'When Peter Burrows and Sud Buries and New Found Land.'

'When New Markets, Port Credits and Cale Dons,' Mom counters.

Jordan smiles. 'When Prince Edward's Eye Lands. When Prince Edward, I Land. When Prints Edward Island?' Enough said.

That Saturday, all the classics had been played. Mom thought she'd won with 'When Court Ices,' which I'm sure she expected Jordan to contest. Instead BS coolly offered, 'When Vank hoovers and Sku Gogs and Skoota Mattas.' Boss, a new triple play. Mom had plenty-twenty time to match it but, as I bet Jordan expected, Mom began contesting 'Skoota Mattas.'

'Of course it counts,' Jordan leisurely explained. 'It's the Scoota-matta River. 'Skoota mattas' is 'Skooter matters' if you're from the Bronx. Skooter's a real name; she's Barbie's little sister, and 'matta' is like 'Wossamotta U,' the college on *Rocky and Bullwinkle*.' Good BS, BS. The ensuing debate exceeded thirty seconds. So Jordan proclaimed, 'I've named the new and learned the calls, I stand alone' – we all joined in – 'when Fenelon Falls!'

Mother nods. Dad flips to CHUM. A temporary victory, lasting only till in range of Lindsay's CKLY, when we'd have to suffer through the every-three-minute singsong ad for 'Lynnn-say Cleeean-ers and Dyyyyyers,' and hear Dad wonder yet again how a little town like Lindsay could employ so many people who dropped dead for a living. Mom would *shhh* us for the incessant updates on the floating whereabouts of the CKLY Courtesy Cruiser. That always pissed me off. Why did anybody need to babysit a thirty-foot yacht? But we were beggars, not choosers. The choosers contentedly sang along with Mitch Miller, Steve and Eydie or Bob Goulet. 'Just walk on by, wait on the corner. I love you but we're strangers when we meet.' Mom's favourite. That's what you hear when you're fifteen and haven't got a gun.

I remember the moment exactly. We'd just earned CHUM. We were sliding down Leaskdale Hill, passing the gold brick house with the blue plaque, the historical home of Lucy Maud Mont-gomery, author of *Anne of Green Gables*. On cue, Jordan was muttering 'That goodie-two-shoes, Anne with-a-stupid-E Shirley,' when Tony Joe White's grinding drawl invaded the car, thrusting 'Polk Salad Annie' like a giant tongue into my parents' primly closed mouths: 'Down in Louisiana, where the alligators grow so mean, there lived a girl that I swear to the world, made the alligators look tame.' Jordan smiled. Tony Joe grunted. He moaned. They who spawned me but wanted all to believe it happened like salmon, achieved without touching, shot *do something* looks at each other in the overhead mirror.

'Filthy,' MC announced, reinstating CFRB, 'like he's mating with a bullfrog.'

'Unsuccessfully, it would appear,' my father added.

'Thomas Cranston March, when you get to *your* church tomorrow, you'd better kneel down and pray for a cure for that nasty hoof-in-mouth disease!' Dad tried to make a joke of a proverb, to say, 'Every man to his taste, said the man when he kissed his cow,' but proverbs were no joke to MC and she talked right over him. 'Please attempt to remember that any little pitchers attached to the big ears in the back seat are yours.'

That crack about *his* church? Attending summer service in Rosedale, in the tiny green-and-white church where Grandpa had been minister, was both the prime directive of March and an order MC refused to follow. Annoyed now at the children in both the back and the front seats, she turned the radio off and a frown out the window. Silence: the sound most likely to be perfected by a March. Insert it here.

As we crossed into Cannington, passed Woodbridge, and the Argyle General Store, to swing down Glenarm Road from shoulder to wrist, the only one making any noise was Tessie. At the turnoff, Mom didn't join in for the requisite refrain: 'This is Fenelon Falls all right, so pitch your tent where the fishes bite!'

One hill past Cameron – as always, just past the spot where legend had it a suicidal cow jumped right through the barn wall – Jordan peered through the trees and called it: 'I see Balsam Layyy-ake!' As we sighted the canal bridge and neared the green highway sign, she threw herself over the front seat to plaster her hand against the windshield and claim her victory in sing-song: 'I'm the first one in Rowws-dale!'

March litany dictated that Dad should immediately turn to her and intone what I've always considered the most nonsensical of family sayings: 'Don't get excited. Don't turn pale. We didn't go to Harvard, we went to Rosedale!' But before he could speak his lines, MC upstaged him. Insert MC's moment of kindness here: 'Excuse me, Little Miss Hooligannie!' She shoved the interloper into the back seat. 'Are you my daughter or a changeling abandoned by gypsies?'

Jordan slouched down and into her hair. 'Both,' she whispered in my direction. 'And don't we all know it.'

HAZEL #17

When I finally made it down to the lobby, no one was there but the Boy Scout with his bushel of apples still half full. That darn Walter had kept me so late that Angus had given up and gone home. Can't say I blame him. I did feel sorry for the Scout; he'd been there since lunch, so I stopped to buy an apple. I was fumbling with my gloves and change purse, encouraging him to go on home, and he was saying he couldn't because he'd promised his Akela not to quit his post until all his apples were sold. That's when I felt a hand on my arm.

'Excuse me, miss,' said a thick American accent. 'Perhaps I can offer some assistance?'

I turned. He took off his hat. A tall man with wavy red hair and a crooked smile, sporting a beautiful blue cashmere overcoat and a dark paisley scarf, silk. He turned to the boy. 'Son, I was a Scout myself, and you're absolutely right. A promise is sacred, especially one made to your Akela, your commanding officer.' He reached into his pocket. 'So, had you sold all your apples today, how much would you have made?'

The boy just stared. 'Perhaps a good ten dollars?'

He nodded. 'Right. So I'm buying these fine apples, all you have left, please.' He peeled an American ten from a gold money clip, then added, 'And if it's all right with you, I'd also like to buy this fine basket to carry them in?' He passed him another ten. I thought the boy was going to pop! 'Now do as this kind young lady says and get home safely.' With that the boy burst into *Thank you, sir*s and exploded out the door.

We laughed. I smiled, 'Yes indeed! Thank you, sir. That was most generous of you.'

He smiled, 'Don't thank me, miss. I only thought of it because I saw you doing it first.' He held out the basket. 'So, how do you like them apples?' We laughed again.

We chatted and he introduced himself, by first name only, though I thought nothing of it at the time. He said he was in town to check on a family business interest but since his return to the States had been grounded, he'd been advised to stay at a place called the Royal York. Could I point him in the right direction? I was going that way myself, so off we went.

Once we got outside, the wind was so strong he had to move his arm from my elbow to my waist. Again, I thought it nothing more than a gentleman's courtesy to a lady. It should have taken us only a few minutes but he walked more slowly than I expected. Of course, he was fighting the wind with that huge, heavy basket. Since the storm rendered conversation all but impossible, I waved goodbye at the front door and stepped away to cross over to Union Station. He gripped my hand and spoke into my ear, 'Please, miss, a moment more?'

A doorman in red, complete with gold braid and a peaked cap, opened enormous brass doors. We climbed a mahogany staircase to a marble lobby and plunked down in two deep velvet chairs. Chandeliers! Five of them! I counted seventeen fur coats without even trying! It seems the Torontonians with the nicest homes to go home to were the first to give up on getting there.

'Excuse me a moment,' he said, rising up slowly with an involuntary hand to his back, which he covered by leaning forward with a smile. 'You wait right there.'

Too embarrassed to ask, I spent his absence wondering how to get him to say his last name. Even if I'd heard it, I doubt it would have registered. Remember, this was 1954; he was only a Junior Senator. Plenty of water under plenty of bridges since.

'See here,' he said when he returned. 'My father taught me to be forthright and I'm proud to be so. The wind out there is beyond any storm I've ever seen, and in the South Pacific I saw a few. So I've taken the liberty of securing a room for the night.' The look on my face as I rose to leave must have said it all. 'No, no, my dear young lady, your own room. On a different floor than mine, in fact. Please forgive me.' So I sat back down. He smiled, and when he handed me a key I took it. And my darling daughter, I'll tell you why.

One: I was soaking wet and frozen stiff. Two: I was dreading the prospect of going back out there at all, let alone forcing myself downhill to the lake from the Long Branch loop to the trailer. Three:

I'd just been offered a room in the Royal York, the hotel I'd fantasized about my whole life but had never, ever expected to stay in. Four: I'll admit it, he was a most handsome man. I know what you're thinking, dear. I knew it then too.

He suggested that we take an hour to freshen up in our separate rooms, emphasis on 'separate' with a grin, and then he'd meet me in the dining room. I'd had my bath and was in a panic trying simultaneously to do something with my hair while ironing the sodden brown lump that had been my tweed skirt. I was thinking, 'Bank clothes! You're going to dine at the Royal York in bank clothes? You'll be a laughingstock. Better make a run for it!' when there was a knock on the door. It was a bellhop, complete with that funny little chinstrap – a bellhop with a dress box! A dinner dress, black velvet, sleeveless: 'For the Apple Lady.' Where he got it, I'll never know. It fit perfectly. I'll admit it, this Cinderella was glowing.

The rest of the evening? I can share some of it, dear. We had dinner. We talked. You would probably want to know that he never actually lied. To paraphrase Emily Dickinson, he told the truth, but he told it slant. Said he came from a large New England family and shared some funny stories about his brothers. He didn't want to talk about the war; I didn't want to see his wedding ring. After a few glasses of wine, he asked me to come up with some good ideas about things a man could do in bed and winked! Explained he was facing a back operation next week for an old injury and would be bedridden for months. What could he do with himself during his convalescence? Any suggestions?

When he summoned the waiter and asked for *the special*, the chef wheeled in a dessert cart and lifted the lid off a still-steaming apple pie. How we laughed! We toasted the Scout and agreed that everyone should have his sense of honour and courage. He said courage was something that interested him a great deal, having seen men with so much of it and also, sadly, with so little. I thought he meant the war. I said it's an ill wind that blows nobody good, so maybe he should use his recovery to write a book about courage? He called it a capital idea and ordered champagne. It got late. I'd never had champagne.

And the rest of that long-ago night is nobody's business, my dear one, not even yours. But today of all days, how I wish I could tell you!

Do you see it? Your father's charm saved my life. If I'd returned to the trailer I'd have been killed with Gladys and Angus. I long to tell you that no, your father was *not* a brick-laying bumpkin with a Grade 6 education. People just assumed it was Angus, once he was dead. If only I could hold you and tell you the truth! Today when I saw your sister bury her face in her mother's skirt and your brave little brother salute your daddy's coffin, I longed to find a way to tell them too. But of course it's not possible. They can never know they have a big sister. And you, you'll never know any of us.

Why did I never come forward? Shame. Pure and simple. No good country girl can be proud of a fling with a married man, even a now famous one. I could never hold my head up in town again. Mommy and Janie were barely speaking to me as it was. It was so much easier to let my boss play Sir Galahad, to burst into tears and confess that I'd been very, very foolish with Angus when I thought I was going to die in that nasty hurricane. I assured Walter you were a dead man's baby. He agreed to marry me on the condition that he wouldn't have to raise another man's child, so I had no choice. What good would it have done either you or your father to know the truth? It wouldn't give you a family. It would have ruined his career, not to mention his marriage. And it would have robbed the world.

Because, of course, he became who he was. For years it's been impossible to pass a newsstand and not see your father's face, or hers. Don't misunderstand – I didn't, and still don't, resent her. As impossible as it sounds, I don't bear her any ill will at all, his pretty wife. Do you know that she and I are exactly the same age? She doesn't look a thing like me though, so dark and fragile. Over the years, if I felt anything, it's been pity. The year I had you, she had a miscarriage. I had such guilt, fearing she'd miscarried because he'd told her about me. A year later, she had a stillborn baby and then, after your brother and sister, little Patrick, who lived only two days. I long to tell the world, to set the record straight: your father had six children, two alive, three lost to death and one lost to life. How could I hate her? We are so much alike, loving the same man's missing children, loving him despite his other women.

If I could tell you anything, my darling lost daughter, here's what I'd say. I'd tell you that I loved you when we made you and every day I carried you. I'd tell you he remembered. A year to the day, a Birks box arrived. How he got my address, I'll never know. It held a locket, pure silver, and a note with three little words: 'Remembering our hurricane.'

When Walter finally made me give you up, the last time I saw you, I put that locket around your neck. I hope they let you keep it. I keep his book – I like to think of it as our book – under my pillow, with his note tucked safely inside. He'd see my sacrifice as a true profile in courage: 'Ask not what your child can do for you. Ask what you can do for your child.'

My answer was to give you to the world. So today, when the known world mourns, I have in all my sorrow a place of secret joy. Imagine it! I alone, in all the world, know you are alive. My secret song. Who will you be, child of mine, child of ours, somewhere out in the world? Who will you be without us? Yourself, I hope, your one true self. That's everything your father and I could have wanted.

So, my darling, be brave. Be kind. Be nice to Boy Scouts. Because, sweetheart, you just never know who may be standing right behind you, longing to know your name. In my heart, that stranger will always be me. Know that I love you forever, wherever and whoever you may be. For every second of yesterday, tomorrow and especially today, Friday, November 22, 1963. Say goodbye, my darling. Wherever you are, put your arms around the television set and kiss your daddy goodbye.

COLOR HIM FATHER

I know it's merely Scottish superstition that a bad beginning seldom makes a good ending, but I often wonder if all the late and unappreciated arrivals in the early days of that summer added up to something so heavy that they pushed time out of joint, if we somehow jinxed the whole damn thing. Better late then never? Now there's a proverb never uttered by a March.

As we came over the Rosedale Bridge and pulled off the highway on to March Road, the crunch of new gravel under Tessie's tires announced the first thing we'd missed: the Rock Concert. That's what the uncles had taken to calling the laying of fresh gravel on our winding road from the highway into March. By dictum of the Arrival Protocol, it got refreshed each summer at the crack of dawn on the first Saturday. We look like this: Hezzy – you'll meet him in a minute – shows up with a load of gravel from Fenelon rock-'n'-rolling around in the flatbed of his ancient truck Bessie B. The uncles debate the division of the bill and pay him for it. Hezzy drives slowly with Bessie's crib open. All male Marches bigger than a shovel display their shirtless manhood, flinging gravel as if the swamp were gaining on them. The scrunch of stone, the scrape of metal shovels on metal bed, the bellowing of Bessie B, all makes for some decidedly discordant music. Dad played backup shovel and he'd left his band shorthanded.

So when we landed in Rosedale that Saturday the 28th of June, we weren't in Toronto anymore, but only Grandma was over the rainbow to see us. The rest of March, who probably liked Ms. Garland well enough but saw no reason why her death should change anything, had marched as ordered on Friday. They stood primly at attention beside budding red roses, glaring at our rusty brown Ford and radiating indignation. We'd better have a darn good reason. When they judged it, and us, inadequate yet again, they eyed Tessie's overflowing trunk tied half shut with binder twine. Tessie, named after Bessie, didn't know she wasn't a truck and obliged MC by hauling a rig's worth of cottage accoutrements. Knowing it would take us all day to unpack alone, knowing that the Arrival Protocol dictates that a March always helps a March settle in, they asked themselves if they owed that courtesy to a Johnny-Come-Lately March? Hmm ... Maybe not. Grandma hugged Jordan and kissed her ear. Aunt Elsbeth, who had boys but no girls, smiled at her and lifted a box or two until Uncle Gavin hollered at his wife to go back to their place to get him a beer. As uncles drifted off, they each had to remind Dad that he'd missed the Rock Concert. Dad's name got nicked by gravel that day; Uncles called him several versions of Lazy Bum, with commiserating eye rolls in the direction of the whip cracking in the kitchen.

One might expect forgiveness. One might even assume that spending all summer, every summer, cheek to jowl with every living member of March would produce a strong sense of clan, of identity and belonging. Good ones. Logical but wrong. Proximity is not intimacy. We drove north to face thirty-odd Marches with whom we shared little more than a last name, all shoehorned into our Group of Seven cottages, so many cousins we didn't know what to do. And we'd just done the one thing March could not forgive: we'd snubbed tradition. Again.

It goes way back. My grandparents came to Balsam Lake in 1921, before my dad, the baby, was even born. The local Anglican parish couldn't afford a year-round minister, but in summer, their ranks swelled with the owners of catamarans, they could. They offered my schoolteacher-minister grandfather a summer job on the condition that he accept in payment what was then worse-than-worthless: seven acres of undeveloped Kawartha lakefront. Hezzy's father, the farmer who offered it, had no use for it. It had no road, much of it was swamp, and he'd lost too many calves, some to snappers and some to the misguided bovine belief that their kind could swim across the bay and live to tell the tale. Grandpa quickly accepted.

He spent a decade burning bush and building March One, painting it in English Countryside like his church, snow white with forest-green trim. He planted the same cedar seedlings and English primroses around both, hardy and red. He put in a gravel road and spent a summer up to his neck in warm water, lugging much bigger rocks into a crib for his dock. The very day he mortared the last rock in the rustic stand-up fireplace, legend has it, he stood up, keeled over and died. Grandma's cottage had been hers alone for forty years. High on a promontory that jutted into the bay, surveying the lake from three angles and her vast Victory garden from the fourth, she had the coldest well and the best breeze.

And the rest of us? It was an era of romantic wood-burnt names, of letters blackened into slabs of heavily varnished yellow pine, sliced like thick bananas, still sporting bark: 'Kawartha Hideaway,' 'Rose of Rosedale,' 'Cozy-cat Cottage.' More signs than I could count stole Fenelon's nickname and proclaimed themselves 'The Jewel of the Kawarthas.' March disdained signs; we named by number or, as Jordan put it, only halfway joking, by rank.

Second in command, stationed just down the hill from Grandma, sat Aunt May's March Two, built like a mini Eiffel Tower, an exact but scaled-down replica of March One. Technically our great-aunt, Grandpa's sister and therefore Dad's aunt, Aunt May crossed the pond during the war to avoid the bombs. In double disappointment, not only did she fail to go back across the pond in time to get hit by one, she never returned at all. When Dad asked Jordan why she wouldn't call her 'Great-Aunt May,' Jordan looked him dead on and answered smooth as Brylcreem, 'But, Dad! The Reverend Southwell says a lie can imperil your immortal soul!'

In the fifties, Grandma's five children, now with their own growing families, planted their roses and their white-and-green cottages in birthright pecking order, all identically replicating the curve of the bay. From out in Grandma's canoe, we looked like teeth with spinach trim.

March Three was the only custom-designed cottage, home to cousins Grayden, Cranston Jr., Gavin Jr., Dexter and, of course, Derwood. Dad's only sister, Aunt Elsbeth, had 'married well' by 'snagging' Uncle Gavin, who made a fortune in post-war construction. I had visions of a big cartoon hook like the one that drags Snagglepuss offstage. Jordan laughed and quoted Mom: A rich man's wooing need seldom be a long one. She said the real hook was Grayden's birthdate. That Uncle Gavin had been a war buddy of Uncle Howie. That Uncle H felt sorry for his pal when he had nowhere else to go one Christmas, so Uncle H brought him home for turkey and his sister. Uncle G had been so grateful to marry into March that he became one. His last name wasn't his anyway. At ten, he'd been sent over from Wales to some farmer out in Belleville who'd used him as a hired hand and a punching bag, stashed him in the barn and beat him senseless on a nightly basis for no other reason than because he could. Uncle G flatly refused to give his kids 'that bloody bastard's last name.' So, presto, everyone in March was one.

In March Four, Uncle Percy and Aunt Evelyn had custom-made triple and quadruple bunk beds: the triple in the boys' room, the quad in the girls' – that's seven cousins and the first set of twins: Trent and Severn. Uncle Sloan and Aunt Penny in March Five had six cousins and the second set of twins, both named after Uncle Sloan's best war buddy: Alexander and Alexandra. The cottagette, March Six, had no cousins. It sat back on the road into Rosedale, empty except on weekends, reserved for Uncle Howie and *insert name of current squeeze here*.

Is this too much Marching for you? That's exactly how Jordan and I felt. At least you don't have to keep them all straight. Just know that there were litters and litters of them, all hanging with their sharp, genetic claws on the edges of our 'Almost' lives.

That's us, Almost March Seven, clinging literally and figuratively to the edge of March. Each summer, as MC walked in the door to survey what havoc wintering mice and raccoons had wrought, she sighed and said the same thing: 'Home is home, though it were never so homely.' A fitting saying for a squat pine box on cinder blocks squashed against a swamp. Almost had a view of duckweed. Almost had bedrooms the size of beds, a single couch in the picture window, a dining table touching the back of said couch and a kitchen you couldn't swing a cat in. But Dad could quite rightly and did frequently respond, 'Yes, a poor thing but mine own.' He'd built it all and had the film footage to prove it, of the framing, the wiring and the plumbing. He'd bricked the chimney and lived to film the flames.

Far from a haven, at best our cluster of cottages offered us a separate peace. That's Jordan's second favourite book, *A Separate Peace*, so I had to get it in at least once. And March was separate for certain, fanned around the bay a stone's throw from the lake and each other, hemmed in on one side by Peace's swamp, which separated our land from Hezzy's farm, and on the other by the water's edge that curved south from Grandma's, ran down the canal, past the trailer park at Lock 35 and into Cameron Lake. More than tourists but not quite locals, caught betwixt and between, we didn't live on the land, but neither could we see or hear Highway 35 as it tore past Yogi's cage in the tourist section of Rosedale. With a foot in each camp, you're traitor to both. There's no place like Almost.

But Almost didn't get its diminutive from being separate, smaller or shabbier. Dad had not married well. When he introduced Mom to Aunt May, thinking to break the ice, he proudly asked if Mom didn't look just like Della Street, you know, the TV star from *Perry Mason*. Aunt May, who nursed a none-too-secret spite for all things Scottish, replied, 'That aging sweater girl with the big cow eyes who has to type for a living because she can't get a ring on her finger? Why yes, Tommy, I do see the resemblance. It's almost as plain as the nose on her face.'

They married anyway. In 1951. There must have been a grace period – not one I remember, but I've seen the footage. Mom in a bikini and flip-flops, her curls swept up in a movie star head scarf. The uncles raising our roof. Mom planting lipstick kisses on a new washing machine. All of March on our lawn toasting the successful installation of our space heater, each with a beverage of choice in hand. Jordan's there with a bottle dangling. Incontestable cinematic evidence that Almost began its life in white and green as March Seven. It even had the requisitely prim roses. But a new broom sweeps clean, and in 1964, my mother grabbed one. Legend has it she got out of the car, grabbed a shovel, dug up Grandpa's roses and planted petunias before she even unpacked. She made Dad cut down the ancient hedge of lakeside cedars. She bought a second dog; nobody had two. Even if her second one was cast-iron and nailed over the door. It was still a Scottish terrier, known in March as a Rat Dog, a rat snarling bold white letters: 'Caroline's Clan.' To March it read 'Keep Out.' So they did.

Intent on further mutiny, Mom drove herself into Fenelon, filled her trunk with leftover poorly mixed paint from Canadian Tire and handed Dad a brush. Grey paint. Pink trim. Aunts pursed their lips. Uncles came over and told him to straighten up and fly right. They yelled, drunk and sober, insisting he paint it back. They offered to paint it back. They offered him good money to do so. When it became clear who wore the pants that held the wallet that paid the painter, they demoted our cottage, and our dad, to Almost.

That was 1964. Yogi's first summer. I was ten, Jordan nine. The separate pieces summer. For reasons I didn't understand until I read Jordan's diary, my parents had not wintered well and only my father managed to knock himself more or less back together. It took a frenzy of hammer and nail, a frantic effort to please Mom or to avoid her, God only knows. She spent most of that summer in her room; he worked alone and at night. It must have been odd without his brothers. Ordinarily, when someone proposed the building of anything in March, uncles discussed it, scrapped drunken plans and drew sober ones, got them approved – not by the township, but by Grandma – then built it together. That summer, none of them would have agreed to help had he asked, because everything my father built in 1964 amounted to one thing: a kick in the teeth.

It started with the dock. Low to the water, a mere yard wide, it gave a good swift boot nonetheless. No one had their own dock. We used Grandma's; Grandpa built it. Enough said. Dad said it was for Jordan, to make it easier for her to get into the water, but nobody believed that for a nanosecond. We all saw Mom slip into the waves at odd hours, now without having to walk past all those blooming roses. Her reason for digging up ours? 'March fecundity! Give them an inch and they'll plant a baby every mile! Time they got a bite of their own bridle.'

That explained everything. So Dad kept hammering.

He built an addition, not on the back where the uncles had obligingly put theirs, but at the side, a choice even more affronting than a dock. It made Almost bigger across its face than all of them, even March One. He built out to the swamp, so close he couldn't walk around it. He fell in trying. He waded out of the ooze and chased Jordan over the front lawn roaring like the Creature from the Black Lagoon. In the end, he had to frame the room square on the front lawn and tow it over rollers into place with Bessie B. He jacked the room on cinder blocks, glued it to the cottage and cut an adjoining door with his chainsaw. Mom cowered, clutching her ears, as the invading blade carved through the wall where the Welsh dresser had been. Despite Mom's protests, Dad let Jordan cut the last inch, his big hands over hers.

If March allowed my father the illusion that the paint, the dock and the addition were his ideas, we all knew the final kick at the clan – the deck – was pure Mom. A deck like those of the rest of March would, normally and logically, have faced the bay, good for dinner at sunset and the moon at night. But then March could see us eating. They could see what we ate. Could see us chew. 'And that,' said my 1964 mother, 'went beyond the pale.' So our, read *her*, deck got built on the far side, out of sight, cantilevered out from the addition over the swamp, like a nature walkway in Wye Marsh or Presqu'ile Bay. It stuck out like a sore foot. When snapping turtles caught their dinner, we saw fronds thrashing. Dinner died screaming. Truth be told, there were twenty-plenty dead things out there, and they didn't all die naturally.

Whatever other religious beliefs my father may have had, after his duckweed baptism of 1964, he clearly believed that from swamp we are born and unto swamp we shall return. He decided to help his God along, hurry him up a bit in the Firmament Department, so he made land for himself, from scratch, from litter, from any and everything he could find, terraforming long before *Star Trek*. If historians ever need proof of how the Depression marked my parents' generation, Almost is sitting on it. Simply put, there is no such thing as garbage. There is only landfill. Like offspring, it comes in two varieties: yours and not yours.

Anything ours, as in any item given to or paid for by my parents, endured a circuitous journey to its landfill destiny. No item ever deviated from this itinerary. It went from the store to the main floor of 26 Delma Drive, Toronto 14, Ontario. Once chipped, scratched or stained, it retired to the basement. If the rec room already held a similar item, the cheaper of the two got sent to the cottage. Note: not the older, more worn or broken – the cheaper. Even when something became unarguably unusable – defeathered archery arrows, a clock on permanent midnight – if the parents had paid 'good money' for it, it didn't qualify as landfill. That took years, possibly decades. That hibachi with a hole in it might be just the ticket someday. You never know when you might need an empty croquet rack or an empty crib. You can move it near its eventual grave, but you can't bury it. Treasures on their last legs got propped up in the pump house. No room? Make room. Only when the obligatory death watch had fully elapsed, only when Dad and MC regretfully released each other from the sacred duty to attempt an item's salvation, then and only then did my parents inter it or, perhaps more fittingly, grab it by the throat and drown it in duckweed.

The other kind of landfill, any offspringings not ours, as in anything not purchased by or for my parents, any item regardless of condition, quality or cost that someone else had paid their good money for and was subsequently fool enough to discard at curbside or into a public dumpster, those castoffs – praise the Lord and pass the ammunition – became landfill immediately. We tossed better stuff into the swamp than we used in the cottage.

So the swamp got filled with the expected trash, paint cans, tires and rusty lawn chairs, but also with the unexpected. Uncles were forever skulking over in the dead of night, when they thought no one was watching, to let fly some secretive personal refuse. In daylight, in reverse Conspicuous Consumption, they competed to chuck the most the most often. The undisputable winner, Uncle G, had contributed a cracked fibreglass canoe, two couches and a dead ride-'em lawnmower. Dad, intent on outcrapping them all, asked the existential questions: When junk is scarce and time is fleeting, why not take a truck and wander forth? Why not boldly go where no garbage picker has gone before? Carpe detritus!

And where do you find the best detritus to carpe? Dad circled one day on his calendar: Victoria County's Big Garbage Day. He borrowed Hezzy's truck, loaded up the uncles with a two-four of Carling Red Cap barley refreshment, and flew into Fenelon like a Bizarro Santa collecting presents: washers, dryers, freezers, fridges, couches. Ho, ho, ho, but no joke. In '67, Centennial Year, he snagged the Big One, the find he boasted about the way fishermen brag about the one that got away. His catch wasn't a muskie, but he did stuff it. Twenty double-wide red leather seats from a wrecked school bus, stuffed in the swamp.

Remember that crackpot artist in the nineties who wrapped a shoreline in pink cellophane to represent the intrusion of mass production on the environment? Dad's Centennial project had him beat by thirty-some years. Let's call his 1967 installation *When Chaos Meets Cottage* or *So You Think Life's a Movie?* For personal reasons, not the least of which is my undying love of the Muppets, I want to call it *It's Not Easy Being Seen*, but enough said. As Dad's personal outdoor theatre, the name that stuck was *The Rosedale Roxy*, but no matter how many movies he made, not one premiered there. Imagine raspberry-red seats pitched randomly off the deck like a giant set of Pick-up Sticks. They land helter skelter in a lime-green swamp: end to end, perpendicular, vertical, facing each other or face down. With no hope of a movie, the Rosedale Roxy immediately began its decent into obscurity. For a time it had patrons. Sunning snakes and turtles congratulated each other on finding such soft leather logs. Confident frogs leapt from one colossal red lily pad to another, and we got the scathingly brilliant idea to do likewise.

Unfortunately for us, but perhaps fortunately for the planet, Darwin's theories can't be accelerated by pubescent desire. Compared to frogs, we humans lose every time. We have little of their accuracy, none of their agility and weigh, what, a few thousand times more? Did that stop us? What do you think? In that uniquely teenage blend of stubborn, hopeful arrogance, we practised Olympic thishful winking. We kept jumping and, as it should have, the planet laughed at us. So did my father. His jumping films jump themselves, his usually steady hand bumping with laughter. He offered strategies, directed moves, even drew us a hopping map, showing how he thought it might be done. 'Don't show your mother!' He'd cheer us on until he heard her coming. We never told her, but for reasons obvious, stilettos on a wooden deck are like a machine gun – you heard her aiming for you every time. Leaving us the courtesy to be reamed out in private, Dad would film a few more seconds, snap his lens cap and vamoose.

Our amphibian aspirations were likewise short-lived. While we might pretend to be frogs, the seats refused to be lily pads. They met our far-from-graceful landings with lurching indignation. They chortled, they tipped us into the big green swim. There's no quicker cure for pride than the suck of swamp slime in your shoes. We should have known better. Renaming fools no one, especially not the renamed. Ask Yogi. Ask Jordan. Those bus seats asserted their identity, registered a protest, and then like all things consigned to a swamp, they sank.

But spite floats. And apparently it winters well. It was late Saturday night by the time MC finally signed us off as being officially unpacked as per Arrival Protocol. We'd heard cousin laughter for over an hour – the first summer game of hide-and-seek. Never planned or discussed, at twilight we all simply materialized before the big cedar at March One. Last to appear was It. Uncles joined in. Jordan and the aunts watched from kitchen windows doing dishes, because bad legs and ill wives should stay home. For me, missing hide-and-seek was bad enough, but now the Saturday bonfire was well underway, and to miss both was treason.

Every Saturday night, and I do mean since 1921, March held a bonfire, a ceremonial burning of bush to mark the further wresting of habitable land away from the maw of godless wilderness. Attendance compulsory. All the Whos down in Marchville, the large and the small, metaphorically joined hands. My father, no doubt grudging every cubic inch that went up smoke instead of down in swamp, smiled his lips shut. But Mom wouldn't play the Make Nice game. She who may have once looked like Della pouted a Grinchy pout. Legend has it that she once tottered into the bush clinging to Dad's arm, announced that the slime was ruining her shoes and made him take her back. Her heart did not grow three sizes that day or any other. She issued standing orders that light supper makes long life, and forbade us to touch the Who Feast of toasted marshmallows and swampwater. No, of course we didn't drink swamp. It's a hybrid concoction of double sugar: half root beer, half orange Freshie. Once Mom pulled the addition curtains, Auntie E always passed us a cup and Dad always filmed us drinking it.

So whether it was an apology, another broom, or a thumbed nose saying I-can-be-as-late-as-I-bloody-well-want-thank-you-very-much, when MC broke her own protocol that first Saturday night, produced see-through snap-on boots in the shape of high heels and tugged them over hers, we just stared. She unfolded the impossibly small see-through emergency raincoat she kept in her purse, put it over her pink silk ensemble, got out to the fire under her own steam and sat down on a dirty overturned stump. No one spoke. Not word one. Until Uncle G pointed a smoking marshmallow stick in Jordan's direction and casually asked, 'So, Caroline, you all settled in? You and your little Almost family?'

'Enough said, Gavin.' Grandma shot back, 'Jordan became a March, just as you did. At least she didn't have to pay for it.'

I imagine even Grandma never saw the irony in that statement until it was far too late. But I repeat: we should have known better. We were sitting in a swamp. A swamp with rules – how March is that? We all knew what belonged there, and who didn't. Mom stood up.

'I'm sorry, Caroline ... ' Grandma started, but she didn't know how to finish it.

ATLANTIS

S o there was a lost world down there, way down below the duck-weed, but unlike the Donovan song, I doubt it was anywhere you'd want to be. I often wondered what the snapping turtles thought of their not so brave new world, if they rolled their eyes at the random crap we so indiscriminately chucked into their habitat, if they had the good sense to take their shells elsewhere while the swimming was good. Probably not. Like most of earth's creatures, turtles are both stubborn and shortsighted. I bet death surprised them.

The frogs were a little smarter. They moved out ahead of the overcrowding, creating their own housing crisis deeper in the swamp: too many frogs, not enough pads. Jordan loved it. You see, once she got her feet in place and gained her balance, she was March's undisputed Frogging Queen, particularly good at hanging on to bait frogs, those tiny baby leopards that squeezed out of larger hands. Must have been the manual dexterity of all that writing and knitting. She would have won every Frogathon had Dexter and Alexander not cheated. Seventeen that summer, and so inseparable that Uncle H did their already similar nicknames of Dex and Der one better by calling them Ching and Ching, the boys simply combined their catch. They resented the fact that when Uncle H wanted bait he went to Jordan first, that when it should have been a nephew, a niece went fishing with him in his boat, *Excalibur*.

Should we have been in the swamp at all? Ask me no questions, I'll tell you no lies. All I'll say is that any future archeologist would have a field day, X-raying our ex-swamp. It held a career-making Ph.D dissertation: *The Cultural Anthropology of Illicit Mid-twentieth-century Refuse*. Pun intended. I'm sure my father's exuberant landfill practices violated every known dumping code, even back then. Was any of it toxic? Let's hope the oil drums were empty. Let's hope they were oil drums.

Whenever a patch of swamp solidified into chunky duckweed stew, Dad would whistle for Balsam. He'd say the same thing every time: 'Gotta see a man about a rock.' A few days later there'd be a familiar threatening sound, a mechanical growl that by the time it reached us sounded like some fool firing a machine gun at a tank, a din that only got worse until Mr. Eustache Hezekiah Gale cut Bessie's engine and she dropped her load.

Jordan dropped whatever she was doing and ran. She loved Hezzy. The rest of us kept double distance. It's not kind but it's true: he looked like both of them, Popeye and Olive Oyl. Short and muscular, he had the longest arms I've ever seen; brown and bandy, he carried them curved like a ready gunslinger, hanging to his knees. But he also had slicked-back black hair and tiny black eyes set much too close together. He had a chipped right front tooth that had turned equally black. He shaved on Sundays and on the other six days had a face full of Brillo pad. Jordan would launch into his arms and he'd say, 'Here's a girlie wants to be tickled pink!' He'd swoop her up and give her a whisker rub that could've scraped paint. She'd sit in his lap and ask yet again how he got his name: 'Well, girlie, it seems I got me one grandaddy from Kee-bec an' another from In-ver-ness. My mama, she called me after the Frenchie one, but I stuck with the one that wouldn't get me beat up after school.'

Hezzy knew where to dump without having to ask. He'd cut the ignition of his rust-green 1930s pickup, get out and lean on the door. He'd slip his key, that's key singular, not keys, into his overalls chest pocket, trading it for his Buckinghams and a book of matches from the Pattie House, his watering hall in Coboconk. Then he'd pat his best girlie's ass and say, 'Good one, Bessie B.' Twice the size of the putt-putts we call trucks today, Bessie Behemoth would call a Hummer 'junior'; she hauled rocks enough for a personal mountain. And Hezzy had one. Thanks to a glacier that paused and took a dump between Cobie and Rosedale some uncountable number of years ago, creating a rock face that still stares at you as you're driving up Highway 35, local farmers had more rocks than they could ever use. The first settlers, many of them rock-savvy Highlanders, tried. Better bend than break. You can still see stone houses, stone fences and old stone roads. But there are only so many ways to bend a rock, and a century has dated their usefulness. Hezzy saw them as vermin, as big obstinate bugs. He was as happy to be rid of them as Dad was to get them, but they both stayed framed in the same scripted dance of distance. A good-old-boys flick, two aging cowpokes who'd known each other forever, but, beyond hat tipping, don't know each other at all:

Dad: So, buddy boy, what do I owe you?
Hezzy: Tommy, it's rocks. Himself owns 'em. Hain't a selling what I don't own. It's illegal, see? I tol'ja finishin' school wouldn't make you smarter 'n me.
Dad: That you did, pal. So can I pay for your gas then, and your time?
Hezzy: Nope. I'm gettin' a field 'n' all you're gettin' is a buncha disappearin' rocks.

I like to imagine Hezzy's response to the fact that forty years later people part with big bucks for big rocks, that they're a hot commodity in newfangled stores called garden centres. I can just hear him, 'Garden what? City pissers are dim, I'll gran'cha that, but y'gotta be a special kinda stupid t'pay for rocks.' He'd be slapping his knees and coughing. He'd suck on his Buckingham and try again, 'Whatcha going to sell 'em next? Water?'

His kind has all but passed from the planet, but his settler common sense plays a central role in these pages. Hezzy didn't call a spade anything; he was too busy digging. He figured folks had more use for lawn than swamp and he was quite prepared to look the other way to help us get it. Hard to ignore the stove top jutting through the duckweed? Not to mention the helter-skelter Rosedale Roxy? Not for him. 'Don't go a-huntin' guilty,' he'd say. 'It'll find you just fine.' Or, 'When a ewe's drowned, she's dead. And folks? Same difference. We're all just walkin' fertilizer.'

To solidify the rocky patch, Dad drove into the Canadian Tire in Fenelon and ordered a load of gravel to be followed by a load of soil, both of which – insert sigh here – you have to pay good money for. He skimped, surprise, surprise, because after a heavy rain we'd get up in the morning and discover that the swamp had belched up a tire, a distasteful lawn chair or an indigestible chunk of couch. Jordan and I would run on deck shouting, 'All Hail the Swamp

67

Vomit!' We'd lean over the rail chanting our version of Donovan's song, also from Centennial Year: 'First there is a bedspring, then there is no bedspring, then there is.' Or 'First there is a toilet, then there is no toilet, then there is.' We sang in an unstoppable loop, the way a bus of kids will shout themselves hoarse at 'Ninety-nine Bottles of Beer on the wall.' And then we had to end it properly.

'SNAFU,' she'd pronounce seriously. 'FUBAR,' I'd respond with equal gravity. We'd pause, nod and shout together, 'Sayonara, SNAFUBARRR!'

Dad couldn't criticize. He'd been the one to tell us, privately of course, what SNAFU and FUBAR meant. Seems in the days of wartime rationing, you could even economize swearing. It had, of course, been Jordan's creative economy to combine them. Dad had grinned, until he heard high heels, at which point he shook his finger in Jordan's direction, gripped his shovel and force-fed the unpalatable back down the swamp's gullet. As I guess you've figured out by now, Dad was too busy feeding the swamp to raise us and too busy filming the script of our lives to help us write it, so MC pretty much directed the show. She plotted as she wished, but the universe was listening, so she also got its opposite.

A case in point: take the review of the Summer Protocol that MC launched into once we came in from the bonfire. Accentuating her points with the hairbrush as she made Jordan's night braid, she ran through her expectations and came to Kronk. 'What cannot be cured must be endured. Boozers are bums. Avoid him.' Well, that would have been pretty hard to do because Jordan was, in fact, his business partner, the main supplier of the baby brown leopard frogs he sold for bait. When he'd been mean to Yogi, we'd repay him in his own coin. We'd sell him a dozen little baiters one day, swipe them out of his Coke cooler at night, and sell them right back to him the next: two dimes a dozen. For Jordan's collection. Other denominations went straight down our gullets via Mrs. Miller's General Store. MC should've listened to herself, to what she said often enough about her daughter: forbid a fool a thing and that he will do. Us fools figured what she don't know couldn't hurt us. So assuming one of the things MC might have wished for was obedient children – ones who didn't consort behind her back with the local drunk to make under-the-table cash for better treats that she was willing to provide – she didn't get it.

Did she deserve our deception? Good question. One, I never asked. When you're a hungry kid, any notion of just desserts for adults flies out the screen door. MC fed us the way she fed the swamp, with reluctance and resentment, and wouldn't let us be fed any other way. Enough is not as good as a feast. There was no long table sit-down, no Who Pudding and no Rare Who Roast Beast. We ate alone. And that pushed us another fork length away from March, busily potlucking each other's cottages. In Almost, the purchasing, preparing, consumption and clean-up of food was pure Protocol, never pleasure. Monday: bangers and mash. Tuesday: Salisbury steak. Wednesday: chicken potpie. Thursday: Spam or Spork. Friday: fish and chips. Saturday: bubble and squeak. Sunday: roast beef and Yorkshire pudding if you'd been good. If not, Spam tastes just as good reheated. What we ken first we know best.

For years, I honestly believed every family ate like mine, believed that all mothers buttered their kids one slice of day-old white bread each and plated portions in untouching triangles: potatoes mashed or boiled on the right, canned vegetable on the left and meat below. Food got served on Melmac green or brown, and you ate it. All of it. No questions asked. No Biafran children necessary. No Oliver Twist audacity. The very concept of asking for more, of more existing to be asked for, never occurred to us. Mom's special spatula had already scraped every morsel, drop and crumb. It rendered the question of sharing moot. Those who never learn generosity at the family table are unlikely to offer it to others. They never extend it to themselves. Here's what they ken first and best: they don't deserve it.

More turtle stubborn than I ever was, BS kept trying to do so. She began that summer by attempting to rewrite the menu of the Summer Protocol. Probably not good timing, given MC's singeing at the bonfire. Not wise to pick the moment when your mother is raking your head with a metal hairbrush. They sounded like this:

'Can I sleep out in one of the cousins' big tents this summer? Ouch!'

'No dear, that'd be a waste of good sheets.' Good twenty-year-old sheets.

'Could cousin Marianne have dinner, owww? Or maybe cousin Dale sleepover?'

'We'll see, dear. It depends on how good you are. Only time will tell on that score.' Jordan's version two imitated that line later, adding its translation: 'No, you selfish little brat, because we'd be obliged to return the favour. If you sleep there, then said cousin will want to sleep here. We'd have to feed them breakfast which isn't possible because a box of eight Muffets and one box of Alpha-Bits in pre-measured one-cup servings lasts this family exactly five breakfasts. You only get bacon and eggs on the weekend if you follow the rules.'

In real time, Jordan sighed. 'Time, tide and turnips. I'm never good enough for you.'

Mom snapped a hair elastic and played dirty. 'Fine. You win.' When *maybe* gleamed in her daughter's eyes, MC shrugged. 'I don't care if all of March learns you wet the bed. But you might.' When Jordan's retort included the word 'damnation,' she got to burn the midnight oil writing this poisonous little reproof a hundred times: 'The intelligent have vocabularies sufficient to any task. Only the vulgar and unintelligent resort to profanity. Which are you?'

Now don't misunderstand. British vernacular and war lingo – those were encouraged. We could say 'bloody well' all we bloody well wanted. Given Grandma's working-class roots, she often uttered words learned well before she married a minister. If the occasional imitative 'bollocks' and 'shite' left our mouths, she'd say, 'Well, I'll be buggered, that's Lizzie the Q's second language!' March found it charming. But we never swore. We were never profane. Not even Derwood. The words I hurled at Yogi's stoning were every swear word I'd ever uttered. You'll find that hard to believe, I'm sure, but it just wasn't done. Even when I swore in my head, it was laughable by today's standards. 'Tough titties,' now that was bad-ass. Alone, BS and I would try, 'What the cluck!' and 'Kiss my asp!' and 'Chuck you, Farley!' We'd even risk 'Puck off!' 'Piss off' was rude; we said 'P.O.' We'd call Derwood an asswipe and feel like James Dean. But that was as foul as we got. And had we been in ear's reach of a familial adult, they'd have replaced our Dubble Bubble with a bar of Sunlight. And scrubbed.

So that first Saturday night, MC got her way and BS got hand cramps. But win by emotional blackmail and no one wants to give you anything else. MC should have listened to herself: he's the slave of all slaves who serves none but himself. When you cannot give, you'll little get. Penny wise and pound foolish. Deny your child and she ceases to be your child. So Queen MC got her pink-trimmed castle, her royal purple petunias, a gangplank dock, a chuck-you-Farley-March deck and got left royally alone. She presided over mosquitoes, snappers, skunks and an inquisitive gaze of raccoons. Yes, that's exactly what you call a bunch of OB's little caged friends.

But MC did give us something else, a gift she never intended. As the minister-grandpa I never met might have put it: 'The last shall be first.' Unlike Marches One to Six, veiled by sacred cedars and rose hedges no one but a sky pilot would call a bush, we had eyes. We could gaze out. If you stared past the garbage and breathed past the smell, Almost had the very best of sunsets. Bannocks are better than no bread. Our little finger of a dock got washed at each day's end by the rosiest light of all. When Jordan sat there – well, you remember.

HAZEL #21

She's such a liar. She's done it all her life, just for the attention. Needs to get everyone around her cooing, 'Oh Hazel, you poor hard-done-by-brave little thing!' Well, this time she's gone too far. If I have to pick between my sister and my Kevin, it's no contest. When that lying smut came out of her mouth, I reached for my rifle, said I'd be out hunting rabbit. Said by the time I got back, she'd better have a better story and she'd better have made Mumsie believe it. Because I knew. Spat it right in her face, said I knew how she really paid for that fancy-dancy apartment in the city. Said if she didn't know which 'fancy man' it was that had got her in the family way, if she didn't even know his name, well, that was just too damn bad! She could flip the bloody phonebook, for all I cared. My rifle pointed itself in her direction. 'But if you ever say anything so filthy about my Kevin again, I'll be hunting you.' She didn't even look up. She hunched on the parlour couch, hand at her throat, clutching her version of the matching lockets Daddy gave us. She was still there when I came in, jabbing a needle into the ripped seam of an old doll's dress. Eyes blank as a cow, mending yellow silk with red cotton. Like there was nothing wrong with that. Like nothing had happened, certainly nothing that could make one sister hate another. Every rabbit I shot at looked like her belly.

GRAZING IN THE GRASS

But familiarity is not the same as family and we all know what it breeds. The Sunday after the first family bonfire, it also bred a lie.

When Aunt May spoke, she spoke for God, a burden she shouldered freely and often. Cousins held the collection plate. Derwood did it for years until he got caught making offerings to his pocket. Miss Minnie McKelvie plays the organ. Plenty of keyboard cousins, Jordan included, could have done a more musical job, but Minnie's real qualification was her preternatural ability to keep in sycophantic sync with Aunt May's erratic singing. Jordan said Minnie was short for 'minion.' The elders, a.k.a. the uncles, convened once each spring for the sole purpose of listening to Aunt May read a list from her purse dedicating each Sunday to a family of 'historical Christian standing,' also known as wealth. We won twice: March Sunday always came first and Grandpa's Founding Minister Sunday always ended the season. The only exception to that bookend tradition was that summer, when God whispered in her ear that, just this once, March Sunday could fall a tad later in the church calendar and land on the same day as that less auspicious occasion: the moonwalk. I have no idea which worthy family officially got that first Sunday. For me, Sunday, June 29, was and always will be Kronk Sunday.

I'd always watched him. When I should have been reciting the Creed or the-Venite-found-on-page-thirteen, I'd mutter his name. Top Secret. My secret. There were only three on planet Earth who knew it, and I wasn't supposed to be one of them; I'd heard it by accident last summer. Reverend S. had the kind of transparent skin and Vaseline blue eyes that only men with receding ginger hair are blessed with. When he talked he looked at your feet. All five feet of him looked beyond ridiculous as he shook Kronk's whopping, hairy paw. I only heard the secret because I was standing right behind them when Kronk's handshake dislodged the Rev.'s all-too-pretty gold-rimmed glasses. That's probably why he let his cover slip and said, 'Bless you, Stankus, my son.' (What's in a name? Ask the guy named Stankus.)

'Why was he even there?' you ask. Doesn't seem the type, does he? Saturday-night benders wound down around three a.m. and Aunt May roused him at seven to wash and shave and make himself otherwise churchy. Why'd he put up with it? Because it was his place. Or, more accurately, because his place wasn't his. His store and Yogi's cage sat on March land – technically, they were ours. Aunt May, and in truth most of March, considered it freeloading. It galled them no end that he lived rent-free in return for tramping around the cottages over the winter, leaving footprints to ward off a would-be Kawartha Sasquatch or Trenter vandal, that he did no more than the odd summer chore, like taking down dead trees for his woodstove.

Various March contingents had appealed to Grandma to make him cough up some rent, but she wouldn't budge. She said that in the hard years Mr. K. had been a different man, a godsend. She told them they could stop being Nosy Parkers because her husband and their father had given a minister's word back when they were wet behind the ears and in diapers, and she wasn't going back on it just to take a few dollars from a broken man. When Aunt May kept lobbying, Grandma smiled, 'Mention it again, May dear, and I just might get the urge to tell the family a little story about you and Mr. Kronkowski. Something about a Coke cooler?'

So Aunt May clamped her jaws tight and exacted payments by other means. She decided that driving Herself to church was a summer chore. Oh no, she couldn't possibly ride with one of the uncles like Grandma did with us. She deserved a personal chauffeur. She posed in Kronk's sputtering Packard, as if it were the Popemobile and she Her Holiness. It put her one notch above her cronies, the also aged and unmarried Miss McKelvie and the Missies Peace, (the one who ran the library and the one who didn't). These sisters, so refined in their peach and lilac dresses with straw sun hats and shoes to match – who swapped ensembles each week so we might be fooled into believing they each had two – they walked to church. This was no small feat, pun intended, for the frail and deaf not-librarian Missy Peace, who at damn-near eighty shuffled over the swing bridge from our half of Rosedale bent over two canes. Last summer, when Derwood told her she looked like a monkey on cross-country skis, she smiled, 'I knew your mommy when she was your age, honeybunny. And don't you look just like her!' When HRH drove past her lady friends as they inched their way home each Sunday, she also smiled. She even waved, then rested a weary regal hand on Kronk's arm.

On Kronk Sunday morning, the lucky recipient of Aunt May's one-woman temperance crusade didn't seem much tempered. When the church bell rang, Kronk wasn't just hungover; he was still fully Stankus. And he clearly hadn't washed. He escorted Herself to her pride of place, slunk into a back pew and fell asleep. Nose to the ceiling, he snored. He began to drool. Not normal human drool – St. Bernard drool. A glistening stalactite tobogganed right down his greasy green tie and hung poised to drip from his belt buckle. Then, smack in the middle of the sermon, the spirit, or the spirits, smacked him. He snorted, leapt to unsteady feet and began belting out a less-than-accurate version of 'Onward, Christian Soldiers.' And like my parents' diversionary soundtrack, he turned it up loud. Delightfully louder than necessary.

Unable to preach or to punch him, Rev. Southwell, who had his mouth already open, decided to model Christian charity and sing along. In energetic sign language, he motioned for his sheep to do likewise. Initially reluctant, the flock eventually rose to their feet to baa along. And that's when my pal Stankus, deep in the throes of religious ecstasy, leaned out a touch too far, lunged at a pew only to have his reach exceed his grasp. As he fell from grace, his greasy head bounced off the pew in front of him. He crashed into the aisle, out cold. Hymn on hiatus.

The uncles, all four of them, grabbed one limp limb apiece and carted him out. We watched through the open windows. As they stashed him in the Pukemobile, Kronk sat up and anointed the seats. Uncle H jumped, but his alligator shoes still got barf-basted.

And the rest of Kronk Sunday? A total anticlimax. I stayed pumped for a while, rewinding his belly flop, wondering if he'd done it on purpose to be fired from the escort service. If so, he didn't know my Aunt May, who was no doubt rehearsing her 'No Rest for the Wicked' speech. The service droned on likewise. Here it was, only Sunday One, and the biggest thing likely to happen in church was over, or so I figured. There'd be men on the moon, but I'd still be stuck in the kiddy choir. Younger cousins, even Derwood, sat in family pews sticking tongues in my direction. We couldn't join the congregation because Dad never got us conscripted, as MC called it. We figured she wouldn't let him. So I stood and sang the Kiddie Hymns, 'All Things Bright and Beautiful' or 'Jesus Bids us Shine,' nose out of joint and a ridiculous head and shoulders above the rest. I particularly hated the one we sang that Sunday, 'When He Cometh,' all about Jesus collecting the souls of dead kids: 'Like the stars of the morning, his bright crown adorning, they will shine in their beauty, bright gems for his crown.' That's sick. If I ever had to be a dead child I wanted to be buried in the ground like everybody else, thank you very much, with my soul in heaven if there was one, not perched on Jesus' head as a little extra twinkle in his thorny miner's flashlight.

All right, I'll quit my quiddling and get back to that lie. By tradition, Aunt May sifted through the after-church crowd dispensing invitations to the elect. In summers past, she sounded like this: 'Please do drop in. I call our little family compound Marchport, after the Kennedys' Hyannisport. My little joke.' But that Sunday, watching the fantasy of her beau chauffeur reduced to vodka vomit, she felt a need to improvise. Grandma caught her trying out this face-saving rendition on Rev. Southwell at twice the necessary volume: 'You, my dear Reverend, may call at Marchport. Our family compound. Exactly like the Kennedys'!'

Grandma grabbed Aunt May and yanked. 'Honestly, May, like Hyannisport? More like Jalna! And you! You're more like Adeline's nasty parrot than Jackie. Go home. Now.'

Aunt May sallied over and joined the crony contingent as if walking home with them were her idea, a great gift she Herself deigned to bestow. Grandma glared until she was gone. Aunt May may have herded us around with the cattle prod that was her tongue, but we all knew who the real Mistress of March was. Grandma didn't put her foot down often, but when she did, nobody picked on NOB, Kronk lived rent-free and Aunt May's lies got shushed.

We were back in the addition. We'd worn ourselves out doing Kronk falls, and been handed our every-Sunday lunch, bologna-ketchup sandwiches and Junket. Once She Who Buttered Our Bread left, I asked, 'Jalna?'

BS rummaged through the book trunk for a worn paperback. A redhead in scarlet. Ouch. Even I knew they shouldn't wear red, knew what it meant if one did: this scarlet woman had cans like twin volcanoes, juttin' and ready for ruttin'. Sorry, the hockey voice comes out of my mouth unbidden, and as my buddies would put it, that Jezebel was absolutely asking for it.

'See this?' Jordan moved her thumb, deliberately voiding the view, 'A Jalna novel. Canadian bestsellers. Historical romance. All the aunts have 'em. Just like they all have several copies of this thing – for all the good it does them.' Beneath the novel she'd spotted Mom's battered copy of Dr. Benjamin Spock's *The Common Sense Book of Baby and Child Care*, its blue and gold cover held together, like Jordan's Miracle, with duct tape. She held it up and without opening it, intoned its opening line: 'You know more than you think you do.' She snorted. 'And still do nothing!' BS tossed the good doctor and picked Twin Peaks back up. 'This *Jalna*? They're good at making babies, not raising them. Lots of petty bickering about who's a true Whiteoak and twenty-plenty sneaking around. Yep, sounds just like us.'

'What? Who are you accusing of sneaking around?'

'None of your beeswax.' When I stepped in her direction, she clarified, 'Don't get excited. Don't turn pale. I just meant Uncle Howard bringing girls to Rosedale.' She smiled at her smug replanting of one of the family's oldest chestnuts.

But I knew a fast cover when I heard one. I also figured that was all I'd get out of her. On land, anyway. 'So what did Grandma mean then, something about Caroline and a parrot?'

'No, Adeline, the main character, a spirited red-haired beauty.' I snorted. 'No, I'm not making it up,' she pointed at the cover. 'See? And my hair is auburn, not red,' she sighed, 'but I suppose I can't stop you from thinking me a beauty.' I chucked a pillow at her. 'You'll be happy to know she ends up a bitter old biddy, left with a pathologically overprotective parrot.'

'Ouch. Grandma can certainly deliver the chops.'

'You don't know the half of it. Enough said.'

At Sunday dinner, we said nothing about the afternoon stoning of Yogi or the morning fall of Kronk. Roast beast and Yorkshire Pudding got hoovered in the usual silence until Dad asked for the Marchport Horseradish and Mom said yes, if he'd pass the Marchport Margarine. He must have let her in on it that afternoon. When she announced that regretfully, she had just crushed the Marchport Fly with the Marchport Flyswatter, BS hoped to make hay while MC shone. Jordan got her diary, found a fresh page and tried Marchport New Math, drawing circles for Marchport Muffets to prove that the one she didn't eat by staying over at Aunt Irene's could go to Emma or Rachel on another Marchport Morning.

Élan left the building. 'Who do you think you are, Missy, the Madam of Marchport, spending your father's hard-earned money like a drunken sailor?'

'Lately, Mother, when you say "dear," I hear "deer," as in venison, as in dead meat.'

MC closed Jordan's diary and pointed at her bedroom. I muttered, 'Go directly to bed. Do not pass dessert. Insert my double peach pie here. Now that's some tasty math.'

When it got too dark to hide or seek and I reluctantly came back in, Elvis was coming out of my sister's room non-stop and I don't think it was my imagination that it got louder than necessary at the bit about the mother not needing another hungry mouth. Were we ghetto poor? No. Mom was that Scottish. And don't get yer kilt akimbo saying it's 'Scots,' we said 'Scottish.' '"Scots" sounds like "Scotch." That is an inebriant,' MC explained, 'and I most certainly am not.' And so at bedtime, when our Scottish mother relented, just a little, maybe it was less than medicinal, but maybe it was much as she knew how. She opened Jordan's door. 'Get your diary, dear. Let's add "Marchport."'

That summer Jordan had two diaries and naturally she brought them both. Part journals, part scrapbooks, they began their lives as industrial-size bookkeeping binders from Dad's work. Now dried flowers, cards, leaves, ribbons and newspaper articles all jostled out at the edges. The elder of the two, earnestly re-covered in lace and pink velvet, spanned five years, from age nine to this June. When it got impossibly full, she started her current one, less girlie but also resplendently ugly: harvest-gold wide-wale corduroy ugly, pink-

and-lime-green felt flowers ugly. She'd made the same title page for both. With uncharacteristic shyness, she'd shown me the old version and a more skilled one, on the morning we left for the cottage. A verse from 'Desiderata,' reformatted to fit on a page, inscribed in free-hand calligraphy, illuminated like a medieval prayer book, in silver leaf:

> You are a child of the universe,
> No less than the trees and the stars.
> You have a right to be here.
> And whether or not it is clear to you,
> No doubt the universe is unfolding as it should.

What had I said when she held it out to me? When I barely glanced at it? When I knew it was important to her? I said, 'Great! You'll have a useful skill when you become a nun.'

The ensuing flash of regret? Unfortunately hers.

The only entry she shared with Mom was the Marchspeak Concordance, a three-tab compilation of meticulously annotated family idioms, christened in homage to Newspeak in George Orwell's *1984*. Jordan held pen and paper and got the last word on wording, but they did collaborate. In *Marchisms*, they split hairs between 'twenty-plenty' (a lot of things) and 'plenty-twenty' (a lot of one thing). In *Holy Writ* they recorded the unbreakable laws, how at a cottage door, Marches do not demean themselves by knocking, they yell, 'Knock, knock! Anybody home?' and the congregated respond, 'Nobody home but us chickens!' Or when a little cousin is ready to jump off Grandpa's dock for the first time, all of March chants in witness: 'One two three and a bumble bee and the rooster crows and awaaaay she goes!' Jordan's favourite tab was *Moribund March Madness*: When a girl cousin shows less decorum than necessary, aunts sing: 'Put chur shoes on, Lucy, doncha know you're in the city? Put chur shoes on, Lucy, you're a big girl now!' And they keep singing until she figures out how to straighten up and fly right. And you can bet your bottom dollar they don't stop until she does.

If someone is feeling sorry for themselves, or isn't trying hard enough to fly right, you already know what we yell. For decades, I thought 'quiddle' pure Marchspeak until I came across it on a trivia calendar: 'either wasting time in a trifling pursuit, or undertaking a useful pursuit in an indifferent or superficial way.' We used it both ways at once. Equally enough said. That night, let's just say that 'Marchport' got added by a quiddling lexicographer who personified the term. And the following evening, Monday, June 30, when she added herself late to the tree, demanding to hide and be sought with the rest of us, she was as welcome as a raincoat. But March was watching. So under their breaths as they ran past her, our chicken cousins called her every foul name Marchspeak had ever given her. And a few new ones.

Now we all had nicknames. March aptly rechristened all speakers of its mother tongue. It gave us cottage monikers. At Christmas the cousins answered to stiff and distant city names: Garrett, Susanna, Sylvia, Terrence, Emma, Rachel, Sarah, Laura, Nicholas and Jamieson – I'll stop for saliva. But at the cottage they went slumming as Gargoyle, Banana, Squeak, Toad, Empress, Cha-cha, Kay-Sara, Lippy, Nine-doors and Yollies. But BS, she got rechristened more than the rest of us put together. Why? Good question.

Cousins got one nickname, usually a derivative of their given name, but BS kept getting derived. Only Grandma called her Jordan and that begat the problem: it was a boy's name. And worse, when Jordan asked where it came from, she got told from nowhere. Bollocks. Every March was named after someone, dead or living, or both. So whether it was true or a bone they threw, they told her she was named after MC's favourite actor, Louis Jourdan. That appeasement went over like ye proverbial lead dirigible: 'Cousins get pretty girl names and I get some foreign guy's ugly last name?' So she improvised. 'I'm named after Jordan in *The Great Gatsby*, another Almost!' Nobody got it or pretended not to, but complaining cost her.

Uncle H took to calling her BM, subsequently claiming it stood for Brainy March, Big Mouth or Brat Monster. If he had bodily alternatives in mind, he didn't share them. Dad called her Pooch, Pumpkin or Peanut. Mom called her Trixie Pixie when she liked her, a name Jordan quite liked as it reminded her of Trixie Belden, a girl sleuth like Nancy Drew, and Gypsy Sue when she didn't, a name BS despised. Uncle G called her Fluffernutter, after the sandwich. Cousins called her Jo-Do, born of a baby cousin's poor pronunciation. We went through a backwards phase, so she still got Od-Oj or

Nadroj Hcram: a swell moniker, if I don't say so myself. Better than the one Mrs. Miller contributed. 'You can't fool this old lady. I've heard your lovely mother call you Missy with my own two ears!' Given her curtain of hair, cousins had recently taken to calling her Cousin It, after the hirsute little goblin from *The Addams Family*. Jordan obliged them, shaking it over her face and dropping to her knees. I threw my towel over all but my hand and chased her, an equally obliging Thing.

Usually our nicknames made a jovial laugh track to each day's finale, our mass game of hide-and-seek. We all wanted to spot Cranston: 'I see Crotch!' Always funny. Still is. But don't break out the bagpipes. Nicknames don't end name calling; one spirited game together didn't make us Kennedys. When Jordan got grass stains, she sure didn't get them playing collegial family football. Call it what it was: an exercise in evasion. And it wasn't just because she came late to the game; they'd have done it anyway. Jordan got made It and stayed It. When cousins called her by a different name each time they beat her home, they knew it hit home. Jordan lost both again and anew each time. On his runs home, Derwood faked a limp and still beat her there in the last split of a second. Cousins laughed. The game ended early. And next morning, on Dominion Day, when elders weren't watching, or if they were, shrugged, seeing nothing but monkey business, that's when the pecking crew cranked it up a notch.

'Nobody home but us chickens,' the game that wasn't one, originated when Jordan was nine, in the summer of her first walking cast, 1964. Cousins would scream it at a moment's notice, precisely to spoil a moment when we'd all been playing croquet or sunning on the dock. They'd stop, drop and run. Many bullying hands make light work. And instead of doing the one thing that might have made them stop for sorry, instead of ignoring them, Jordan tried to run too. It made them laugh. It made them meaner. Snickering over shoulders, they'd chant, 'Go, go, Jo-do! Watch her go, go, go!' Yes, it's another cartoon on *Underdog*: *The Go Go Gophers*, complete with this lovely Injun English theme song:

Out west in Gopher Gulch lived Indian tribe,
Then came the pioneers, pushed them aside.

All Indians leave but two; they vow to fight.
What can two Indians do?
Go, go Gophers! Watch them go, go, go!

Colonel Kit Coyote and his sidekick Sergeant Hokey Loma were likewise 'relocating' the last two remaining First Nations residents of Gopher Gulch because to them, these varmints were vermin: part gopher, part Indian. How nice. Chief Ruffled Feathers led the resistance. His sidekick, Running Board, communicated only in a gesticulated Neanderthal grunting. Extra nice. Squat and dumpy, they ran like drunk Keystone Kops, falling, bumping into and knocking over all in sight. That's how they saw her. How they wanted her to see herself. They may not have wanted her dead, but they wanted her going, going, gone. And on that Tuesday, July 1, they wanted to make sure she stayed gone for the summer. So they took their long-legged selves through the dense bush of the creek bed edging Hezzy's back pasture, past the trailer park and right down Mac Isaac's tricky stone road, 'No, no, Jo-Do! No hide-and-seek, no!'

When they got too far ahead of her, they slowed down. Knowing he might be the next victim didn't stop Derwood from screaming the loudest, 'See! Nobody home but *us chickens*!' Dex, who ordinarily despised his brother, threw an arm around Derwood's shoulders and swooped into the swamp. A wolf pack of nimble white running shoes ran down a fallen log my sister could navigate only in dreams. They waited on the other side, howling.

I can still see her shoes on that log, her stiff new black-leather oxfords. As we all knew she would, she fought for balance, lost, rolled an ankle, screamed, and landed both shoes in the swamp. Of course they laughed. When Jordan pulled her feet out and her shoes stayed stuck, she laughed back. What choice did she have? Calling 'Olly-olly-oxen-free'? Running home free? Telling her lovely mother? Good one. They left her there. On the other side of an uncrossable barrier. To fish out her fetid shoes alone. And to wear them home.

Jordan missed the Dominion Day fireworks that evening. If the aunts wondered why the cousins were clucking, they didn't ask. And when it rained on Wednesday and a bevy of them flew into March One for long rounds of Rumoli, pretending within earshot of our grandmother that all us cooing doves were birds of a feather, let's call that inclement intimacy what it was: the insincerity of rainy-day friends. I know it well. When the sun shone, or once it set, or when they just plain felt like it, my cousins, older, tougher and fleeter of foot, ran off in packs. The wolf might lose his teeth but never his nature. Let them go. It was better than being run away from. Better than being a finger-pointing freak show. Better small fish than none.

So when the pack tired of Rumoli and demanded Cousin It and Thing, we performed on cue. Why not? Cousin It and Thing – they're faceless. Who knows if they're smiling? Who cares enough to ask? I'm sure that as she pranced in circles on her knees, while bystanding cousins whooped and hollered at the hairy girl-beast before them, no one yelled, 'Dance for it, baby girl! Dance for it!' But sometimes the things we hear in our heads echo longer and louder than the spoken word.

IN THE GHETTO

It led us to spend an extra long time with Yogi on the grey morning of Thursday, July 3, feeding her ferns long after NOB and the mail truck had come and gone. She liked to bend the sprays in half, roll them in her paws and pop the lacy green bubblegum into her mouth. As we re-entered March, I finally thought to ask Jordan what she'd told Mom about her shoes.

'Nothing. I went round the back way to Grand's.' She grinned. 'Amazing what a little elbow grease and shoe polish can do, isn't it?'

When Uncle G saw us alone at our picnic table, he hustled over. He came at Aunt Elsbeth's urging, ostensibly to invite us to Derwood's birthday the next day, but in truth, he'd been waiting to get us alone to treat us to a winter's worth of Wop Stand-up: 'Hey, Wopico kids! Didda ya hear abouta the woppa who went to the garagea for anna oil changea and said, 'Whaddaya mean, itsa notta for my haira?' Whaddaya call an Eyetie girl with a moustache? A no-boppa woppa.' He found every 'joka' funnier than the last. If aunts rolled their eyes, they never told him to stop. Privately, MC told us not to say 'wop' outside the family, because it made us look coarse. So whenever Uncle G got wopped up, Jordan would just out-March him.

'Hey, Uncle Paisan! You're whatta we see when we haven't gotta a gun!'

He thought she was kidding. The word 'bigot' wasn't in anyone's vocabulary back then, and to qualify as a bully you had to be a fat and stupid twelve-year-old boy in a red-and-white-striped T-shirt. So maybe Uncle G wasn't both. Maybe his Wopico jokes were just his way of reminding us that we were the Poor Cousins. The ones who didn't go to Bishop Strachan and Upper Canada College, who didn't have sailboats or riding lessons and hadn't been to Paris – that's Paris, France, not Paris, Ontario – and who certainly didn't live where Grandpa had, in the real Rosedale in Toronto. Out in the far west end of Etobicoke, the tiny wartime bungalow that was

26 Delma Drive didn't even blip on March radar. In 1952, it cost all of $11,000. We'd put Jordan and a rec room in the basement, making space plenty-twenty for me, but to March we violated the cardinal rule of real estate: location, location, cachet. Once again, we sat on the border of a swamp, a city cesspool – one infested with Italians, known as Mimico.

I didn't see the problem. Thanks to post-war planning, our square block of Alderwood had every amenity our little hearts desired. Sir Adam Beck P.S. stood across the street, so close I could watch Gumby and Pokey in the morning, Albert J. Steed and Sebastian at lunch, hear the bell and hop MacCallums' fence, all before the big green 'BOYS' door closed. I got home well in time for the Big Puppet Three: to hear Friendly call Rusty, watch Suzie the Mouse learn French *Chez Hélène* and help Mr. Dressup open the Tickle Trunk for Casey and Finnegan. And as we got older, we had swings, slides and monkey bars, two baseball diamonds, a skating rink, a swimming pool and BS's real home, the Alderwood Public Library. When finally, at ten, BS mastered a bike without training wheels, MC let us ride north up Brown's Line to Lapenna's Groceria, which had more penny candy than I've ever seen in one place: ropes of red and green licorice sold by the yard, rows of that nasty nickel-a-box Lucky Elephant Pink Popcorn that she loved. But what Jordan really wanted was south, and that sent her into the swamp.

If you coast down the cobblestone hill of the Long Branch loop, you can dismount to watch the waves of Lake Ontario break on the shores of Marie Curtis Park. I never understood her unwavering fascination. Pretty flat and boring to me. But BS did a project on Hurricane Hazel in Grade 5 and we were still hearing it blow: 'In 1954, 400 people lived here in 140 trailers. All were destroyed or condemned. Seven people died. One family gave their baby to rescuers and when the crew came back for them, their house was gone. All but the baby died.'

She'd climb the chunk of pink granite that held the plaque, face the waves and recite it: 'On October 15, 1954, Metropolitan Toronto experienced wide-spread devastation and extensive loss of life from Hurricane Hazel. Many people acted very bravely in their attempts to help and rescue their fellow citizens. This plaque is to commemorate those that lost their lives and those that displayed such acts of courage and heroism in this area.' Then she'd stare, saying nothing. For whole afternoons. I think MC let us bike there only because she was fed to the teeth of being asked to drive there and because, as the crafty one pointed out, it was technically still in Long Branch, solid Anglo terra firma, not Italian bog.

To my mother, the fact we lived on the northern side of that *West Side Story* war zone was a face-saving distinction. Mimico, only a stone's throw closer to the lake, was somewhere, as ridiculous as it sounds, I'd never been. There the Mafiosi lay in wait. A long knife with my name on it glinted on the other side of the Long Branch loop. Ours was a dying WASP neighbourhood, but it wasn't going without a fight. As the Singletons, Townsends, Doyles, Burlings and Campbells moved out, the Forgiones, Moremiles, Violas, Cazzarellis and Passarellos swarmed in. If MC preferred them to stay on the south side of the Maginot Line in her head, then they, in increasing numbers, preferred otherwise.

We got Eyetie neighbours so fresh off the boat they didn't know what a backyard was for. The Triglianis dug up every square inch of theirs and planted tomatoes. I'll bet dollars to doughnuts Dad envied a man who never got nagged to mow the lawn, and I suspect MC had a grudging respect for their economy. But when they dug up Mrs. Whitton's prize-winning roses, when BS went sans supper for pointing out that Mrs. T hadn't done anything to roses that MC hadn't done first, when they planted corn in the front yard, MC called City Hall. When she called again about their porch, I can't say I blamed her.

Wrought-iron porches are reserved for two things: special guests and baby carriages. That's why they're black. Always and only black. The Trigianis painted theirs a fruity day-glow lavender, so the old wops in wife beaters, swilling rot gut and wailing about the old country until two in the morning, could get as pizza-pie-eyed as they pleased but avoid Kronk's fate by grabbing a rail before they fell off and smashed their even greasier wop heads. Wop wives were worse. As unintelligible as Running Board, those black lace tablecloths flew up to St. Ambrose in gaggles, three times a day, screeching at us Anglese mangia-cakes. If Colonel Kit Coyote had come riding into town and made them go, go, go back where they came from, Uncle G wouldn't have been the only one cheering. Yippee ki-ay and fungoo to you too.

Are you shocked? Such language is shameful now and should be, but wasn't then. We said 'wop' like we said 'retard': without knowing better. That's what our elders called them. And because ours was the endemic post-war racism of the day, we believed them. We knew we were tainted. That we'd caught wop cooties. Proximity was destiny. Uncle G put it quite succinctly that day: 'Why doa you smella so funny? 'Causa wop women beena pooping bambinos onna your lawn!' We'd heard it before: he who sleeps with dogs may rise with fleas.

Maybe I'm reading too much into it. Maybe the cousins were too old for us and we were just too young for them. Back then, plenty-twenty separated fourteen from seventeen. Before the pill, when you had to be of age to buy condoms – love could be expensive. Jordan and I were still innocent, and cousins like Dex and Der most definitely were not. They'd snickered through Rumoli, making comments both veiled and swaggering about sneaking out at night to the trailer park to do God-knows-what-but-we-didn't. We figured they drank and got high. When they bragged about getting it on with Trenters, with wasted Trenters, we told ourselves that it wasn't that the cousins looked down on us but that we looked down on them.

If you looked up 'Trenter' in the Marchspeak Concordance you'd see this: 'The retard wops of the Great White North. Turdist excreta of the Trent Canal who wash up on the shores of the Rosy-dale Trailer Park at the foot of the dam road. Girls in putty-blue eyeshadow and pinched pink halter tops. MC sniffs past them muttering, "Skimpy Pimpy," not quite under her breath. The male of the species labours under the woppish misconception that wife beaters are T-shirts. Like all wops, they tuck switchblades into the back pockets of their tight black jeans. They sport ducktails like Elvis, but manage only to look like juvenile delinquents attempting to impersonate him. And worse, most Trenters are Yanker-Wankers, a.k.a. Americans.'

That Thursday, making the excuse that we needed batteries and walking away from Uncle G as fast as Jordan could, leaving him without applause or an answer about Derwood's party, we ran into Trenters twenty-plenty, all getting a patriotic day's head start on tomorrow's July 4th drunkenness. Littering our Government Dock with star-spangled towels. Screeching at each other, even when said other lay flopped on a towel, nursing a beer, a mere foot away.

'Perhaps in the next life they'll take a micro step up the Great Chain of Being and actually be seagulls.' A great line. One I double-dared her to repeat to one of their Trenter faces as we reached the store. She shook her head, 'Discretion is clearly the better part of valour when encountering such simian devotees of Manifest Destiny.' After my 'in Normal, please' look, she translated, 'No way, man. D'ya think I wanna get pounded?'

I stayed outside while BS re-energized her Miracle. Yeah, a Trenter would hurt a girl. The ones I watched on the dock that day were real Marlboro men. They had no interest in the things you'd expect a tourist to come to cottage country for. They didn't fish. They didn't swim, unless you count the strokes it took with your right hand, holding a smoke aloft in your left, to find the dock after one of your Trenter horde had pushed you off it. They drove God-knows-how-many hacking miles to be near the water but never in it, to sunburn on a splintery public dock that afforded them a fine view of the concrete underbelly of the Hwy. 35 canal bridge. They came north for one thing: bragging rights – those found on a catamaran or next to a cage. They smoked up to the flashiest boats, scouting the joints until the owners left for ice or bait, and then jumped on decks for shots of themselves at the helms. As we left the store, they swarmed past us and beat us to Yogi. In a torture as predictable as Derwood's, they fed her their national cuisine, a burger and a can of beer, and then in a move particular to Trenters, stuck a lit cigarette in her mouth, snapping a photo to prove it matched the one in theirs.

'Quite necessary,' Jordan nodded. 'Without photographic evidence, no one would believe the simultaneous presence of both a smoking bear *and* the missing link.' She grinned and held an imaginary microphone under her chin, 'Come nightfall, these feral creatures slink back down the Damned Road into the valley of trailer park. They leave lipsticked Camel butts and Dr. Pepper bottles behind, in stinking piles known as Trenter scat. This is your *Mutual of Omaha* host, Marlon Perkins, signing off from what truly is the Wild Kingdom.'

So let's cut to the chase: monkey see, monkey do. We all followed Uncle G's lead. The cousins distanced themselves from us because we were no better than wops, and we reviled the Trenters because then at least we were the Top Wops. And that left us two little Almost gophers looking at each other. But don't get the wrong idea. We had twenty-plenty city friends, and Jordan had the CHUM Charts to prove it. All winter, I hung out with my hockey buddies and she disappeared into whatever it was she did in Gifted. But come summer, we recombined. We shared 'Polk Salad,' frogs and the lake. After lessons last winter, paid for only at the insistence of her surgeon following her latest cast, BS swam pretty well for a girl. And compromise has its uses; one beats the bush, the other catches the bird. If I'd listen to her read, she'd time my morning run. I'd climb the tree house and call down to her, and she'd write down everything I saw. She'd catch the bait; I'd catch the fish. And a good tale never tires in the telling. If I asked her to tell me, yet again, about how great Burton's August concert would be, she'd ask me again about beating the school's best runner, Mark Worthington. I'd happily recount how thanks to her reading me *The Loneliness of the Long Distance Runner*, I'd let Mark run rabbit, and then passed him once he got winded.

But there's something more, something I haven't gotten across properly yet. Some kind of cold knife edged between us and them, a pervasive detachment, a severing. Ill wishes and mixed messages that got telegraphed in code to our cousins got received by us in three little words: you deserve it. So we stayed apart together. Did that explain our sibling bond? Don't hatchet your counts before they chicken. None of my friends stuck in the asphalt of Alderwood had ever seen a cottage, let alone owned one, but if something's always been there, it's like air – it's only human nature to take it for granted. As we left Rosedale glaring at Trenters, we couldn't rescue Yogi or turn down March Road without being recaged ourselves, so we simply headed out into Hezzy's fields. We took for granted what we didn't have in the city, accepted as normal what I now recognize as extraordinary: gentle paddocks have long ties. We were the last generation to have true freedom of movement, to live beyond the lawn.

Consider it: we roamed Rosedale, the docks and acres of cow field at will, left after breakfast, returned at lunch, showed up for dinner and reappeared at dusk, all without wearing a watch or being asked where or with whom we were going or when we'd return. If Balsam came with us, he ran ahead, behind, beside and anywhere he wanted. We'd left his leash in the city. If MC wanted us, she stuck a hand out the screen door and rang the cowbell, because just as we were the last free children, mine were the last worry-free parents. Someone who'd hurt kids? You don't consider a question you see no need to ask. Maybe in the States, or Mimico, but certainly not in the True North Strong and Free. Pardon my sarcasm. It's so damned ironic. Physical freedom is not the same as being free. Making like the three monkeys does not make you safe. Consider what we didn't see whenever we heard the Arrival Ritual.

I didn't mention that seminal bit of BS Protocol, did I? Perhaps I've been repressing it. It's such an obvious clue to miss, the sight of my sister conjuring up a haven, trying to make like a turtle and carry home in the book bag on her back. Whenever Tessie pulls in, no matter how much MC yells to get back here and unpack first, Jordan – limping after the long ride that put her feet to sleep – makes her halting way down to the water's edge. Reverently, she opens the Book of Summer. Reads the spell that raises her girls: Meg, Jo, Beth and Amy. Casts her words upon the water: *Little Women*, by Louisa May Alcott. Chapter One: Playing Pilgrims:

> 'Christmas won't be Christmas without any presents,' grumbled Jo, lying on the rug.
> 'It's so dreadful to be poor!' sighed Meg, looking down at her old dress.
> 'I don't think it's fair for some girls to have lots of pretty things, and other girls nothing at all,' added little Amy, with an injured sniff.
> 'We've got Father and Mother and each other,' said Beth contentedly, from her corner.

By 1969, I'd listened to the saintly Marmee and her daughters a full five times; I'd have gleefully eviscerated them. Instead, I had to play them. BS got to be all four sisters; I got to be Theodore Lawrence, their neighbour, only boy, and pansy-ass kiss-up. At least when *Little Whimin'* was done, she read better stuff and when she didn't, I had Almost listening down pat, just like my dad. And when she put the Book of the Day down, the Miracle had songs to play. We had bait to catch, a bear to feed, bottles to collect and dimes to earn and spend.

So what if Trenters were too crass and cousins too fast? So what if it was more than a knife's edge or an arm's length, more like being forced to play a game that, like hide-and-seek or hockey, had been rigged against my sister right from the get-go? What the cluck. Nobody home but us chickens here at the back of the Almost bus, trapped in pecking order behind able-bodied heirs of March and as Almost wops, barely holding on to our one seat in the swamp ahead of Trenters. So bloody what. Just play the hand you're dealt. To quote Grandma when Jordan answered her at their daily tea later that Thursday afternoon, saying yes, sadly, she would be attending Derwood's birthday party tomorrow: 'Well, child, it's little consolation but it's also true – whatever doesn't kill us keeps us chopping.'

HAZEL #23

I have the coaster. Plastic. Hospital green. They know I have it. I let them see it. I even let them use it but only with clear glasses holding clear liquid, like water or 7-UP. Okay, sometimes apple juice, but no china, no Melmac, no coffee, no tea. I need to be able to see the letters at all times. After lights out, I'm compelled to touch them. I reach under my pillow to check their impressions again and again, a blind woman who both clings to and resents Braille. I check it each morning too. If the large letters in the centre still say: *C.N.E. 'SAFETY PAYS' 1954*, and the small letters around the rim still say: *Factory Inspection Branch, Ont. Dept. of Labour*, and I can turn it over to check the tiny letters hiding along back rim: *Johnston Co. Plastics Div. Toronto – Plastics Machinery and Equipment*, then I can relax. It's my proof. My insurance policy. How can they tell me it's all in my head when it's all right here in my hand?

We left the bank later than we should have and drove along Lake Shore until we couldn't drive any more. We couldn't see for the rain. We couldn't hear for the wind. There must have been a foot of water rushing under Walter's little Morris Minor convertible. It finally gave up the ghost in front of the Princes' Gates. Out of habit I looked up for the winged victory with a maple leaf, to check the cornucopia and the beehive, the pylons for the man at the wheel of industry and my favourite, the woman with the stalk of grain. 'Be proud,' Ma always said. 'See? Farms are nothing without farm women.' When I was little, I thought it was the Princess Gates because my daddy said I was one. Not this time. Walter grabbed my arm and screamed into my ear, 'You have to trust me. Try not to fall on top of me, please.'

We ran. I remember sheets of water. I remember hitting my head. I thought I'd be sucked out to Lake Ontario, but he caught me by the belt of my skirt and hauled me inside. Once I got my bearings I turned on him. Most indignant I was. 'The Horse Palace? You say to trust you and then you bring me to the Horse Palace?' He smiled.

'I've slept here before. All soldiers have. It was the demobilization centre for all of Canada and it's as safe as the back of my hand. So yes, trust me. It'll be warm and dry and I bet I can find some blankets or at least some nice dry hay. What did you expect, Missy, the Royal York?' I had to laugh at that one. 'Besides,' he added, 'didn't you once tell me the CNE felt like home?'

I had told him that. Ma used to bring Janie and me, every year, before her bad years. She always won or placed with Granny's blackberry-peach pie and, as she often reminded us, before the fools dropped it, she'd won the sock-mending competition five times. 'And,' Walter smiled, 'didn't we have our first real date here? Or was that some other girl I kissed on top of the Ferris wheel?' Right again. I'd begged Ma to let me go. 'That Sexhibition,' she called it now, since they'd had the nerve to flaunt that Bazoom Girl on the midway. But I promised her my new boss Walter had no interest in smut. I was sneaky. I let it drop that he made good money, more than Angus. She made it look like she took her time deciding, but she didn't.

We toured the whole fair hand in hand. Saw the Avro Jetliner and ate at the brand-new Food Building. He had to pull me away from the best exhibit, a full-size cow and her calf just as real as back in our barn, but carved out of butter! Next summer the same artist has promised to carve a full-size horse and not just any horse, Trigger! You had to feel safe around him. I reminded Walter we'd also been right here only a month ago – it seemed like all of Toronto had been here – when that brave little swimmer Marilyn Bell reached the CNE shoreline and won $10,000. And guess who gave it to her? Roy Rogers, Dale Evans and Trigger! I figured if a sixteen-year-old girl could swim Lake Ontario all by her lonesome I could soldier through one lonesome night in the Horse Palace with Mr. You-Aren't-Good- Enough-for-the-Royal-York.

So we searched stall to stall, found blankets, enough hay to feed a hundred Triggers and even an old kerosene lantern. We found a display case full of coasters. 'Look,' Walter said. '"Safety Pays" on the front and my last name on the back. Two good omens. Keep it. It'll bring you luck.' We made a hay mattress, spread the blankets, started a fire in one of the braziers and pronounced ourselves snug as bugs in a stinky horse blanket.

Around here they say it's because I hit my head. Because I was thinking of Trigger and in the Horse Palace, but that's nonsense. I'll admit that, earlier, Walter had tried to, shall we say, take advantage of the situation? I can't blame him. As Ma says, 'Men will be boys.' But I said waiting for the wedding meant just that and he accepted it. I pushed him off and went to sleep. So no, it wasn't Walter. Even Walter says it wasn't Walter. It was a horse. Not Trigger, a *bad* horse. A sweating, snorting horse that refused to hear me screaming, a steed that mounted me from behind in the dead of night. His hooves carved into my shoulders. His teeth biting my back. If I ever smell hay again, I'll – Why do they all keep saying it must have been Walter? That any other story I tell myself, I'm making up catch as catch can. They're wrong. Walter is my boss. My fiancé. A gentleman. I'll spend the rest of my life with him. Once we're married, then and only then will I have his children. I'm a nice girl, Ma. A good girl. I really am.

Around here they try to make me admit otherwise by all kinds of tricks. Today Dr. Swift tried the Pragmatic Approach: 'Upon admission you were wearing a striped shirt dress with twenty-three buttons and undergarments which covered your full torso: a waist-cincher bra with seven hooks and an Even-Pul girdle with a five-inch waistband. Be sensible, my dear. Lacking opposable thumbs, exactly how could such apparel be removed by an equine?'

City people don't understand animals. I'll show them when I foal this summer. I can see her now. Long legs and a glorious chestnut mane. Ma will be so proud! Safety Pays Johnston. No, it's not a strange name. It's a name for a princess and I'm going to lead mine right through the Princes' Gates. I'm going to show my baby off at the Horse Palace of the Exhibition where she'll take the blue ribbon and the gold medal hands down. That is, if she doesn't cut me apart with her hooves being born.

RECONSIDER ME

There's one more thing before we can get back to that smile. Not about Tabs A, B or C – about me. Where did I stand in this snock-snarl of Almost? Good question. Some of us who play second fiddle long for first chair. And smart is not the same as strong. If it makes its own deceptive strength, it also makes enemies. Judge for yourself. After tea that Thursday, July 3, we were having a snooze on the dock. I'd been humming Otis Redding and wondering who Wendy Torrington, who'd let me cop a feel before we left the city, was consoling herself with, when out of the blue of the western sky comes not Sky King but this missile of a missive: 'I know you hate me because I hate hockey.'

'BS, that's ridiculous. I don't hate you.'

'But I'm rude about it. I'm mean to you about it. All the time.'

That was true. She'd never been to a single game. 'One would have to be quasi-simian to strap knife blades on one's feet and chase a ten-cent piece of Melmac with a stick. Only a total cretin would freeze his butt off to do so. Those fool enough to pay good money for displays of such brazen, chest-beating inanity should be euthanized before they accidentally reproduce.' I knew she'd rehearsed it.

But truth be told, I harboured no resentment on that score. As unlikely as it sounds, her contempt for what I loved most in the world made perfect sense to me. I'll admit to this day that I never got most of what made my sister tick – I found her brainy, girlie or just plain weird – but her hockey hatred, I got it. I absolutely got it. If you couldn't skate, never had and never would, you wouldn't want it rubbed in your face all winter either. You wouldn't feel like you belonged in Canada at all. You sure wouldn't want to sit in a freezing arena listening to fans cheer a sibling who was really good at it. Not when you were afraid to climb stairs. Not when, despite the committed athleticism that took, few noticed and none applauded. Those who noticed? They looked away. Or laughed.

'Look, BS, you've got your reasons. Enough said.' That's as close as I dared come.

'Yes, and most of them are coming this way with fishing poles.'

I turned my head to see uncles H, S, P and G approaching. As they opened their tackle boxes, they joked, as we all did, about landing Biggie, the giant bass as old as Grandpa. But once hooks had worms, they began baiting Jordan. Talking Leafs. Something even I didn't do in front of her. Even I could see that she was fed to the teeth by how the March boys behaved on the subject. I'll go on record as saying they should have been ashamed. They weren't.

The uncles' team, the Toronto Maple Leafs, had won Lord Stanley's Cup only two years back, in Centennial Year, and they'd been extra gung-ho ever since. That summer, when BS first said she hated hockey, they laughed, and their attempts to talk her out of it were teasing and jovial. But when she held her ground, they ceased to be so. At bonfires or birthdays, uncles would mysteriously break into animated, self-congratulatory, show-off-my-stick ranting whenever she arrived. As if she should pretend not to notice, let alone be hurt by it. As if it were their brawny right to publicly reinforce her limp with every virile word. As if her only choice were to join in, to pretend to be whole. Ya can't beat us so ya bloody-well better join us.

I kept my eyes closed. They kept the penalty box open. For a good ten minutes, as if BS and I were both invisible. How the Leafs would probably, definitely, win. How probability was definitely on their side. Jordan groaned, 'Time out, already. Probability CAN'T be definite!'

'Oh, look who it is, Little Miss Ratfink. You know, boys, the little girl who ran to her grandma to ask her big mean uncles not to talk hockey in front of her this summer. Boo hoo.'

Jordan's eyes snapped open. 'I did no such thing. If Grand asked it, she did so alone.'

'Sure, sure,' the uncles hooted. 'You couldn't fight your own battles, could you?'

'I can,' she answered. 'Tell me, uncles, would you discuss music in front of the deaf?'

Uncle H snorted, 'Sure! How the Sam Hill would some deaf guy know anyway?'

They found that especially clever. Of course it was – a clever Gopher-Avenger ambush.

'So, Uncle Sloan.' She looked right at him. 'I suppose that means you'd also rave on about hockey in front of your best war buddy. You know, Alex Anderson. The one you named the twins after, the one who had his legs blown off. Both of them, right?'

Dead silence. Then Uncle S spat back that Little Missy Sour Grapes shouldn't poke her nose into things that stupid little girls knew nothing about. They packed up and revved up *Excalibur*. But before they left, they went back to talking Leafs as if their fraternal back-patting were her problem, which, in retrospect, it probably was.

'Speaking of probability,' Jordan offered minutes later. 'Teachers say it's just as probable to roll, say, a six, three times in a row, as three different numbers. That's never sat right with me. It isn't just about rolling *any* number at *any* time, where chances are obviously one in six, but what is the probability of rolling *the same number* in series over time.' She yelled, 'That's it! It's four-dimensional, not three. We've all been asking *the wrong question!*'

Okay, she was smart, but in this case wrong. Numbers were my game. As I explained her error, somewhere in the back of my brain I suspected that she thought a lot, probably too much, about things that my limited knowledge of the species suggested other girls weren't overly concerned with. Wendy probably didn't know the meaning of the word 'probability,' and if she did she'd probably be smart enough to pretend she didn't around me. But Jordan wouldn't play the Girl Game. Last summer there were times when she seemed to want to. When she'd look longingly at a bevy of girl cousins in a knot on the dock, perfecting their suntans, reading magazines in hot pants and pop tops, doing each other's hair. But if she sat with them a while, she'd come away, stick her finger down her throat and make barfing noises.

'They talked for an hour about Slickers.' When my face said, 'What?' and my mouth said, 'Raincoats?' she laughed. 'No, midgit-idjit, a new kind of frosted lipstick.' She tossed her hair like a ditz and sang the commercial: 'Slicker under. Slicker over. Slicker alone!'

Whatever consciousness was being raised by the sisterhood in places like New York and San Francisco that summer, Grandpa's dock wasn't having any of it. Only my sister got razed there. A gaggle of girls wandered on to the dock after the fishing folk had left, and when they saw Jordan, they didn't need sticks. The girls, pardon the pun, were slicker, asking about boyfriends they knew she didn't have, about makeup they knew MC wouldn't let her wear. And, in a crueller version of hockey rapture, they waxed orgasmic about the latest trend: platform shoes. When they tired of her, they did what they always did: they tossed giggles in her face, linked arms and flocked off. When I asked why, Jordan shrugged and said what she always did, 'They developed an urgent need to iron their hair.'

It may have been her refuge in the city, but Gifted was no gift up north. Especially for a girl. Now I don't dispute the need to do something to recognize her brainy weirdness, but I wish Sir Adam Beck P.S. could have supported the former without exacerbating the latter. I don't give a rat's asp about her test scores. My parents agreed because that's what you did back then, but as a teacher I simply cannot fathom why so-called professionals pushed a girl already tiny and frail to skip Grade 1 and accelerate Grades 3 to 5 in two years. I'm not saying she couldn't do it; I'm asking the Should Question. I'm saying they shouldn't have pushed her on any more than we should have pushed a bear into a cage.

Before accelerating, you should make sure the whole car can stand the strain. Watching Jordan with the girl cousins was like watching Herbie the Love Bug up against sleeker and far more experienced Alfa Romeos. Since neither hide-and-seek nor the Girl Game were open to her, our little Herbie revved up and over-compensated at the School Game. She read non-stop, Miracle dangling from her wrist, on the kybo, at the table, under covers with a flashlight. Assigned a novel, she'd read every book by said author. She claimed it was for context but I knew better. After me you come first. She had to come first at something. Was it worth it? You tell me. She'd worn out her eyes. Needed new glasses every year. She had insomnia and walked in her sleep. She caught every germ going: bronchitis and pneumonia twenty-plenty. Last fall, she had pleurisy so bad she lost half her left lung and nearly died. A winter of swimming lessons helped, but she still got easily winded. When she got excited, she wheezed. Hell, that brain was the only part of the kid that worked.

Somebody should have done the math. Some semi-simian adult should have sat down and done a moment's metacognition. She was two full years younger than her grade and a year younger than her already young accelerated classmates. You can bet the cousins loved that. In high school at twelve, she'd graduate at sixteen. And then what? Live on her own? 'Maybe that's the point,' she offered once. 'MC realized how much sooner she could be rid of me.'

Finally, and please note I did leave it till last, there was a little something left out of the equation entirely: me. My baby sister was a full grade ahead of me. That's some serious SNAFUBAR. She'd entered Alderwood Collegiate two years ago and I, her must-be-a-total-retard older brother, started last September. Like Lucy, I had some 'splaining to do. But if you did what I and the cousins couldn't and put the animosity aside, her obvious mental gifts became clear in five seconds. Consider that day's case in point: on Thursday, July 3, Jordan gave me the ride of my life, sent me water-skiing against my will, slalom no less, in an electrical storm. And, in the process, she outed Uncle H and MC.

Uncle H is the Bachelor Uncle, the cottagette uncle, the one who breaks all the rules and is forgiven every time. The one with a new car, a new boat and a new squeeze each summer. The Uncle in Advertising. His latest toy, one of the three he picked up that Thursday morning, the one that all us boys were itchin' to ride, was a sleek turquoise half-cabin racer with an eighty-horse Evinrude inboard-outboard. It came with fancy aluminum skis, replacing unwieldy wooden ones. They caused a short a territorial war in March over whether the old ones should be landfill or firewood. Uncle H pitched one in each direction. His third toy, also brand spanking new, also came with the boat and, as Dex announced to Der, most likely in it.

Hearing a car at lunch, MC had glanced out the back window and announced, 'Hmmm, it seems this month's model is the Bottle Blond.' Exiting his car was a pair of the biggest cans I'd ever seen. Even better, when we ran to meet her: red lips, red nail polish, bursting white halter top and, best of all, her name was Bitsy. She peeled off her clothes, revealing a teeny-weeny red bikini and obligingly fell asleep tits up in a lawn chair. When Uncle H came back from fishing, he gassed *Excalibur* back up and took the itsy-bitsy and the cousins skiing.

BS and I kept watch as usual, spotting from the back of the boat. It was our job, when a cousin fell, to point at their bobbing orange jacket so Uncle H could circle round and effect rescue, our job to haul in the tow rope, hand over icy hand, keeping it clear of the motor. The sky was a warning grey when we started with Grayden, and darker by the time our captain had run the ranks down to me. Uncle H turned around to ask Jordan what she thought.

'Well, Uncle H, thunderheads like flying Brillo pads, churning grey with a venomous tinge of green. Cumulonimbus praecipitatio for sure.'

That prompted Bitsy. 'Howie, what did she say? Is she kinda slow or something?'

To which Jordan shot back, 'Elementary, my dear Bitsy. Give a dog an ill name and you'll hang her for sure.'

I caught the smile Uncle H tried to swallow. His question had been an attempt at a graceful exit. I didn't care if he did as he'd so often done and made up some stupid excuse to stop before our turns. Not in that weather, not whit one. But when instead he squinted in our direction and gave little Janie a turn, Uncle Sloan's Janie, who was a full year younger than Jordan, BS widened a tear in her life jacket and began flicking its innards over the side.

Uncle H cut the motor and docked. 'Out of gas means all out. You march, March!'

Bitsy pinched his cheek. 'Oh, Howieee, you're so funneeee.' That one entered Marchspeak immediately.

A half-hour later, Jordan looked up from her diary, 'Here, I like this version much better. I wrote it for you because you didn't get a turn. In first person in fact, as if I were you. My experiment in being a boy. What d'ya think?'

> 'You march, March!' The bimbo with him thought it was original, the silly boobs.
>
> Uncle H looked back at my sister. Jordan hadn't budged. She stared at him, as hard as necessary. 'Hmm ... you know, Uncle H, I just might get the urge to tell another funny story – the one about you and my mother? Something to do with a houseboat?'
>
> In one smooth movement, Uncle H pulled a ski back and handed it to me. 'What's a little rain, eh, son?' I must have looked dubious. He snapped Bitsy's namesake bikini. 'Hey, Bits, here's an even better joke. This kid wants to water-ski but he's afraid of getting wet!'

So up I went. I could ski slalom, one handed, backwards and with the rope between my knees. I was the only one who could ski as well, or maybe even better, than Uncle H, which may have explained things. But on that day when he threw *Excalibur* – he called all his boats *Excalibur* – into full throttle and carved into snarling whitecaps, I knew I was going to die.

I couldn't breathe. I couldn't see. Spitting needles of rain and spray lacerated my legs. I had to close my eyes. My left foot, usually secure in the glove of the ski, kept jumping out as I bounced on the pounding whitecaps. Uncle H took a larger circuit than his usual once round the bay, far beyond Peace's Point, halfway to Grand Island. As each spear of lightning forked the waves, I felt a raw tingle travel up my spine from the metal skis into the metal-handled tow rope. Somehow I kept standing. Uncle H was an excellent pilot. But then, nearing the dock, nearing the point where I could let go and glide to safety before the assembled, pride intact, he banked a hard left and gunned it. I wiped out on the wake, lost my ski and flew.

Jordan, still spotting, told me I'd launched myself some twenty feet, spun two full somersaults through empty air and landed head first a foot from the dock. I have no memory of it. I remember the bottom, remember lying there flattened and puzzled, nose to nose with Grandpa's rock crib. I remember ricocheting to the surface, hoovering air.

Cousins, dazzled by my prowess, put fingers in their mouths and whistled. Their splashed-down astronaut waved obligingly – with my left arm, I couldn't move my right. They pulled me out and carried me over their heads. I'd landed on my ski. The bruise ran the length of my arm, giving me Freak Master status for days, fading from purple-black to yellow-green. Cousins tell the story still. My only regret? In Dad's camera: black-and-white film.

What could I say to that? What would you have said? 'Pretty good BS, BS.'

She reached for it back. But she'd started it on the back of another entry and had to flip the page in order to line up the holes for her binder. Of course I looked: 'Gold Medal Winners of the Cross-the-Bay Swim at the Balsam Lake Regatta,' a dated list of names and notations, that went back at least a decade. The rings clanged. The binder slammed shut.

'A list of winners? What the Sam Hill do you need that for?'

She shrugged. 'Some people make history, some people write it down.'

But you'll miss the point if you let her end it there. In her version, I looked the conquering hero. I was older and bigger, a full-blooded March, an able-bodied, athletic boy. But the pedestrian truth of it? She was the history maker, the historian, the boat, the motor, the gas, the tow rope and even the bloody storm. No fifteen-year-old boy wants to admit to being a BS sidekick, but if you're going to get the rest of this, I have to. Watson to her Holmes, Robin to her Batman, Moose to her Squirrel, Sherman to her Peabody – use any brawn-to-brains analogy you wish. Same difference. I got pulled along by a strength way out of my league. The force of nature that was BS sometimes made me look spectacular and, I'll admit it, often produced results for which I took undeserved credit. Was I resentful? Duh! Did her enormous brain fool pretty much everyone, including me? Did it give us all the perfect excuse to leave her alone and lonely to fend for her Little Miss Smarty-pants self? What do you think? Seeing really is believing, and I saw what my cousins saw: the competition. Compared to Little Miss Maestro, the rest of us were all fiddling around ineffectually in the back row. And we knew it.

So in Nobody Home But Us Chickens, I played the monkey in the middle – ahead of her, behind them – running with one foot in each camp. Jordan can see and be sighted. I'm telling myself I'm bloody Switzerland – but of course there's no such thing as neutral. Ask Yogi. By definition, a bystander stands by and lets it happen. And when push came to shove, that's exactly where this chicken stood – right beside her. But I was even slicker than the girls. Insert green here, the final and unfading colour of my true-blue sibling bruise.

SPINNING WHEEL

As we lay splayed out to dry on the morning of Derwood's birthday, Friday, the 4th of July, BS returned to her preposterous theory of probability as four-dimensional. So, Almost listening, I became preoccupied by two electric blue dragonflies mating an inch from my nose. Never one to be upstaged, she announced, 'What goes up must come down. He'd have killed you. Probably speaking.'

I replied, 'Naa, if that dragonfly tried that on me, I'd swat him bloody-well dead.'

'I'm talking Uncle H. I'm talking March Jalna. I put what he did to you in my story because he's never forgiven Dad for taking Mom away from him. So he takes it out on us.'

'Whoa there, Flicka! Down to a slow trot, girl. Uncle H dated Mom? That's retarded. Correction: that's disgusting.'

'Paradoxically,' she paused to let me fully appreciate the Word of the Day for the fourth time, after 'paradox,' 'paradoxes' and 'paradoxical.' 'It's also true.' She grinned. 'Go back for fallen loops and maybe even you can knit forwards.' I reached down to splash her so she caved, 'All right already! Uncle H met Mom first. You know the story, when the houseboat her mom had rented for a painting holiday ran out of gas at Peace's Point?'

'Yeah. Uncle H met Mom when he towed them to the marina. So what?'

'So then they kept company for about a year.'

'They did not. Correction two: *you're* disgusting.'

'Did too. They were engaged. He's never been engaged since, has he?'

'Well.' I jerked my third finger in and out of a coiled other hand and sniggered. 'Guess that depends on your definition. I'm guessing he's been engaged to Bitsy plenty-twenty.'

She slapped my visual aid away. 'Get your mind outta the gutter.'

I gave my stock reply. 'Why? Is it crushing yours?'

She ignored me. 'Mom must have met Dad at the same time, must have known him all the time she dated Uncle H, especially coming up here so often. But here's what you don't know. More March Jalna. Dad, he was Best Man, and I guess he took it literally, because he snuck into Mom's room the night before the wedding and they eloped. Absconded to Niagara Falls. Disappeared in the dark and came back married!'

Say nothing. Stare. She stared back, her best yes-I-am-dead-serious look. I wasn't buying. 'Double-triple-cross my heart and hope to die.'

I waited for the 'Gotcha, sucker!' It never came, so I caved. 'So how come you know all this and I don't?'

'Ask me no questions, I'll tell you no lies.' She lay face down and began spitting through the biggest crack in the dock, counting hits on the Saliva Stone. The record was eighty-seven. My record. I had to kick her to get an answer that wasn't one: 'Hey! I don't cease to exist when you're not around. I do my own stuff. For example, what time do you get up?'

'Jordan, don't change the sub– '

'I'm not. Humour me.'

'Fine. As late as you'll let me.'

'And then you go for your run.'

'Yes. Seventy minutes every morning, but – '

'And you've never noticed I'm always up first?'

'Yeah. No. So what? I don't know and care less. Cut the crap, BS!' My fist crashed down on the dock and the dragonflies zoomed off, miraculously still suctioning love.

She ceased spitting, my record intact, and sat up. 'Has it ever occurred to you that maybe you're not the only one with a morning routine? I get up at five-thirty.'

'Bollocks! You're up at five-flippin'-thirty? In the bloody summer? Are you insane?'

'Ask me what I do.'

'Jordan, get with the words right now or I swear – '

'I'm trying to. You see, I'm working on ... I'm going to ... ' She squinted at me, hard. I saw decision flicker past her eyes, 'I go and help Grandma work in her garden. Afterwards, to warm up, we have tea. We talk about stuff then. That's when she told me.'

'See this leg? Pull the other one right off while you're at it. That's royal BS, BS. Mom has to threaten to confiscate your precious Miracle to get you to pull a single bloody weed.'

Jordan pulled her towel tighter and whipped one braid behind her. 'Believe what you want. Mom's not Grand. You'd both be surprised what I can do when I try. You should come with us ... Or on second thought, no, you wouldn't want to. In all probability, that is.'

'All right, I'll bite. Why not?'

Jordan began unravelling her other braid. This was no simple task. Its ends lay swivelled asleep on the dock. Wet curls wound into knots. She watched me a moment. 'Because we have our own routine, a *private* routine.' When I showed no signs of chewing, she frowned. 'When we're done gardening, we go swimming.' I closed my eyes. She flicked the wet end of her braid in my face. 'Naked, that is. We go skinny-dipping.'

'You filthy little liar!' I threw her off the dock, jumped in after her and in the tried-and-true method of sister taming, used her braid as a noose and lynched her under water. That mouth needed some serious cleaning. In my defence and for reasons that will become eventually obvious, I want to point out that I left her towel dry and docked. As I held her under, I wasn't out of control although I sounded so: '*You fix your face right now, Missy Smutmouth!*' I know. I know. I sounded just like her.

Jordan laughed before she hit the water, laughed underwater and surfaced laughing. She swam to the beach, tied her braids behind her back and strolled up the lawn. And she didn't turn around, not glance one. Was she pushing my buttons? She was a good enough actress to do so; God knows she'd done it before. But it rang true. BS and Grandma, they were tight.

Last summer Jordan carted Grandma's birthday present around with the Miracle: Maya Angelou's brand-new book, *I Know Why The Caged Bird Sings*, in which Grand had written, 'And so do you.' Over the winter, Jordan spent whole weekends at St. Clair and Bathurst in Grandma's pseudo-Tudor apartment: the kind with dark floors, darker panelling and tiny black-and-white tile on the bathroom floor. For me, a short Sunday visit was plenty-twenty ointment and old lady. But Jordan would play the baby grand for her Grand until MC pried her hands from the keys. Once I bet BS that she'd never heard the words 'I love you.' I meant from a boy. 'Of course I have,' she'd snapped back. 'Grand says it all the time.' It never occurred to me to ask why she hadn't heard it elsewhere. No place like home.

But Grandma was also one tough broad. Grandpa died with no life insurance, in the Dirty Thirties, when Dad, the youngest of five, had just turned seven. She traded their Rosedale home for a small apartment and spent as many months as possible in Rosedale North, a most unreasonable facsimile, wherein she cooked and heated with a woodstove, raised Sloan, Percy, Elsbeth, Howard and Thomas with a garden, hand-pumped water and a hand-shovelled latrine. Now in her sixties, she looked a decade younger. (Whose grandma wears lumberjack shirts, wellies and overalls? Mine, but don't tell.) And forget a Granny haircut. She wore it long, as long as Jordan, in two thick braids around her head. (No midget-idjit, not like Princess Leia, around her head, not her ears.) Black turning grey turning white. She'd tuck it up in Grandpa's chopping hat to cut kindling. Did I mention the axe?

In the tradition of Carrie Nation or Lizzie Borden, you'll find an axe-wielding woman in the most-repeated of March legends. We all had a favourite version of the following: back in the days of the Great Depression, Grandma would say, 'Gotta see a man about a turtle.' She'd take the canoe and two paddles deep into Peace's Swamp. Why two? She was hunting snapper. A full-grown adult snapping turtle, two feet across. She'd track it and tease it, smacking its spiky ridge, goading it to attack. Once they clamp on, snappers – stubborn and stupid as fridge magnets – never let go. She lashed paddle one to the stern and paddled back with number two, turtle rudder in tow. She'd drag that sucker clear out of the water, up the path and onto her lawn. What does a full-grown snapper weigh, some fifty pounds? Stupid thing. It didn't even retract its retard head in that last split of a second when it saw the axe come hurtling down. A little kindling, a little fire and presto: turtle soup. Complete with shell.

That Grandma, she would go skinny. Silly me, confusing her with those grannies who wear frilly aprons and do nothing more strenuous than bake cookies, the kind who, if they hit their thumb with a hammer, assuming they ever wield or even own one, might say, 'Oh, dearie me!' My grandmother yells like the British bloody blue blazes. The lake isn't cold, it's 'colder than a witch's tit.' My grandma, upon slugging her frequently blackened thumb, yells, 'Bugger face!' So yes, it was probably true. But being true doesn't keep something from being revolting. Or just plain wrong. Would I confront Grandma about her wanton ways or Uncle H about the probable violation of my mother? Not this little turtle. See no paddle, hear no paddle – what paddle?

HAZEL #36

The silly goose of a girl insists she heard bagpipes. Getting pregnant must have turned her tiny head. Of course I don't believe it. She swears it wasn't the storm, swears she saw her Da, piping just as she remembers him, marching double-time through the back cornfield, says she ran out to tell him how happy she was that he wasn't dead. She says he took one look at her all growed up and that's when it happened. I tell her she needs more Dr. Chase's Nerve Food – it clearly isn't working. I tell her that, like that movie girl, Dorothy Gale, she must've got herself banged on the head in the storm, because he's no more alive than the Wizard of Oz. But she's sticking to her story, all smiles, wearing the locket he gave her. She's telling everyone it wasn't Walter or Angus. It was her Da come back from the dead. And what does she say to me? 'Momma, it's déjà vu.' No. She can't possibly remember. I was pregnant with Janie. She was three. When I came in from the barn, he had her flat on her back on the butcher's block. I picked up her panties. Once he left, I told them both he was dead. I probably should have killed him. But he cried and I couldn't. So if there's any chance it's true, if he's alive and back for more, it's my fault. And my cross to bear, because God forgive me, I'll say it once – I'd give anything to see him again! Lordy, how I've missed that man! So if that little tramp has tempted him yet again, then it's her own damn fault. No, she'll tell the agency some other story, if she knows what's good for her. Oh, damn it all anyway! Why am I even bothering with this little yellow dress? The child will be born an imbecile or a monster.

ONE

Since it's about to be his birthday, and now that you've purled Tab B, the hurricane, and Tab C, the families, we should probably get back to that smile. Even when he smiled – especially when he smiled – Cousin Derwood looked like a ferret. This wasn't his fault. So did his parents. Auntie E resembled a bottom-heavy seal and Uncle G could have passed for the love child of an ill-conceived – if not conceptually impossible – union between an orangutan and a raccoon. His pointy face beamed rodent and his body ... well, enough said.

Between them, they bred five testosterone-laden variations on the ferret theme: sleek, black-haired and tubular. Derwood could have body-doubled for Beaker on *The Muppet Show*. His face folded back vertically giving him a nose like a prow. Ice-blue eyes slanted backwards into his skull. Did he have any redeeming qualities, like, say, a personality? No. Not unless you counted a fanatical devotion to Boy Scouts and a knack for blowing things up. He got his start as a kid sticking firecrackers into clams. Then he graduated to frogs. Any orifice would do. He had the timing down pat. He'd cage the impaled frog in his hands until the last split of a second, then free it with a well-timed toss. It exploded exactly at the end of its arc into freedom, spattered just as it touched what it thought was the safety of swamp.

You disapprove? Of Derwood or the firecrackers? Probably of both. Yes, he was a jerk in progress, but remember, this was a time when firecrackers, particularly ladyfingers, the tiny ones, could be had by anybody at any time, purchased quite legally just up the road at The General Store along with penny candy. You could leave the cottage penniless, pick up three discarded pop bottles along the way, cash them in for six cents and head home with any of the following: a giant gumball or a black licorice pipe with red sprinkle smoke or two baby chocolate bars, or five firecrackers and a book of matches.

We thought nothing of it; saw nothing wrong with selling them, buying them, having them or using them. Saw nothing wrong with the kids as young as ten who lit them. We had no problem with frog splatter. Boys will be boys. It was a naiveté of normal, a time before publicized perverts, when no one knew what everyone knows now: a boy who begins torturing animals grows up to be one sick puppy.

Next to Jordan, Derwood had the most nicknames. His Mummie called him Derwie. None of the others were remotely fond or flattering. He could have been Woody but wasn't, as it could have been construed as a masculine compliment. He could've been Der the way his brothers Dexter and Grayden were Dex and Gray, but Der and Dra were taken by the twins: Alexander and Alexandra. His kindest moniker was Blackhead, doubly earned for his typical March flat-top, soot black and buzzed straight as the 401, and the uncountable pustules that littered his pointy face. He answered to Dimwart and Deadwood, but attacked if called Wittle Wuwu. That one haunted him from the days when Gray and Dex tried to make him say Little Lulu so they could laugh at his speech impediment. Too young to know the difference between being the source or object of humour, he toddled happily behind them singing the cartoon theme song without any l's, 'Wittle Wuwu, I wuv you-hoo, just da same!' Until they threw stones at him, which he did understand.

When we were little ones, our attitude may have been unfair, a mimicking of siblings' disdain, a barely conscious desire to be seen to be on their side against him, but once the bullied grew into a bully, he brought our enmity on himself. Chronologically, we should have been allies. He was the closest cousin, born right between us: I was January 29, 1954; he was July 4, 1954; and Jordan was June 23, 1955. But it bears repeating: proximity is not intimacy. We loathed him and nobody and nothing could change our minds.

Aunt Elsbeth tried. Like most rich women, she figured the poor, they are always with us and, thank goodness, they can always be bought. Do you think I'm too harsh? Perhaps the truth lies somewhere between her heartstrings and the strings attached to her gifts. Whenever she went into Fenelon, she'd get treats – the good kind, not the day-olds Mom would buy if she got there before Kronk did – and send Derwood over with an invitation. Our response never varied. We'd follow him through the front door, scarf down the bribe – the chewy chocolate-chip cookies or still-warm Chelsea buns from Bell's Bakery, the Kawartha Dairy ice cream, hopefully Tin Roof – in maybe two silent minutes, rinse our dishes, set them carefully on her counter, chant, 'Thank you, Auntie E,' and leave out the back door without him.

It only made Aunt May try harder. As Jordan explained, it was thanks to her orders that Derwood and I got identical Christmas presents, believing in the simple-minded way of adults that identical toys make identical boys. Elaborately wrapped parcels arrived a week beforehand. They asked for an immediate ripping, all but begged for it. My favourite? No contest. Age ten, my Johnny Seven. A gun the size of a small child, an easy yard long, housing seven different projectiles including a grenade launcher, 'armour piecing bullets' and a cap gun. Hey, it's all good fun, especially when someone loses an eye. Unfortunately, Derwood kept his.

If I ended up with some halfway decent stuff, I want to go on record: I never kissed up to any of them to get it. Zitwood, on the other hand, was a totally classless act. As valedictorian of the Eddie Haskell School for the Obsequious, he was Aunt May's favourite. He would have been anyway, being named after her fiancé, the Dearly Departed Derwood who expired from a wound in France rather than the slow death of marrying Aunt May. Privately, we called our Almost Great Uncle Dearly Departed Deadwood and Clearly Desmarted Deaderwood and Done Defarted Deadestwood, but Aunt May kept on loving her Derwie-kins.

Twice a summer, she made the long, demeaning walk down to Almost, the might-as-well-be Mimico she only visited when armed and dangerous: in mid-August, clutching her regatta program, and on Derwood's July 4 birthday, when she invariably showed up with a wrinkled five-dollar bill for Jordan. No bow, no wrap, no card, just a bill. She'd toss it at Dad, 'Give it to the girl, Tommy.' Always with a wink. 'Mind you, only if she's worth it.'

Each year he'd say something pale like, 'Thank you, Aunt May, but Jordan's birthday was a week ago.' She'd wave it away with an impatient gloved hand. 'Beggars can't be choosers. Tell the girl to write a thank-you note. Hogs and Fishes to her Great-Auntie May.'

So we were braced for her 'Knock, knock!' at the door that day. Given the March dictum that you can judge a summer by the first knock at your screen door, we shouldn't have opened it. As usual, Dad spoke up like a man. 'Nobody home but us chickens.' Aunt May spent five-felt-like-fifty minutes chastizing our lateness yet again, and never touched her purse. Mom didn't ask her for lunch, but called us to it. I went to wash my hands.

As Jordan re-enacted it, when his aunt moved to go, Dad actually showed some balls and asked her if she'd forgotten something. Aunt May shook her head, 'No, Tommy, nothing worth remembering.' She patted her purse. 'I'm putting my money on Derwood.'

BS pulled off imaginary gloves and began to purr. 'My, my, Tommy, you've caught your Great-Auntie May red-handed!' She reached into her purse and pulled out a boys' birthday card with hockey players on it. 'I wanted to announce it at church, but – ' she snapped her gloves into her carpet bag – 'some drunk ruined that.' She sat uninvited, poured herself tea and patted Mom's hand. When that hand slid away, she didn't notice. She opened the card. 'So I'll announce it at Derwood's party today. Such a lovely surprise! Our two Little Men, I've signed them up for that swanky hockey camp in Lindsay! It's frightfully dear, hundreds of dollars dear, but well worth it. Mr. K will drive us. Not to worry,' she winked at Dad, 'it's arranged.'

I'll admit to temptation – for about a heartbeat. But Jordan had me down pat too.

'A whole summer with Wuwu? You want to let a whole team of decent guys know my hockey star brother is actually related to Derwood? He can't even skate!' She grinned at me. 'I knew you'd see right through her. She figured you'd jump at the chance to ditch me.'

She was right. Sweet as it was, that was one bribe I wouldn't swallow. What'd she take me for, a big stupid dancing bear on skates?

Apparently MC had answered in one typical MC word: 'We -can-provide-for-the-family-just-fine-by-ourselves-May-thank-you-very-much.'

Dad kept clearing his throat but only got as far as 'Maybe– ' when BS butted in.

'Where we come from,' she announced, 'in Mimico, anyone stupido enough to wearra da skates inna da summer getsa one througha da backa da head! Capiche?' She grabbed the card, ripped it in half and stuffed in back in the old bag's purse.

Mother held the screen door for a sputtering Aunt May. 'Embarrassments! Ingrates! You can take the family out of Mimico, but – ' Shrapnel precisely timed and volume adjusted to hit Mom once Dad was out of range. MC slammed the door faster than necessary. It bounced off our guest's ample rear end, but unfortunately failed to knock her to her knees.

So no hockey for this little player. But the look on my sister's face as she told and retold the story, so worth it. No other present ever materialized, except this one from me.

'You did exactly what I would have done,' I told her. 'Except I'd have done what the door didn't. I'd love to watch her try to pick gravel out of those hams!'

'Good one, Brother Mine. Most excellent.' So don't say I never stuck up for her.

MEDICINE MAN

BS answered MC's third call to change for Derwood's party by yelling back that Derwood would be in his uniform, so she was going in hers too. Armed with a pile of CHUM Charts, she came out her yellow sundress, the first dress she'd ever sewn, age nine. With smocking and puffy sleeves, it looked more like baby-doll pyjamas than a dress. And to my mind, especially when worn with her incongruous heavy black boots, she was more than asking for it. When cousins called it a baby dress, she said thank you. On regatta day last summer, when it got ripped by Derwood, who claimed he was swatting a horsefly – with a stick, a stick that just happened to get caught under her hem – Jordan cut up one of her paisley headscarves and declared that patches were high fashion.

MC took one look at her and said what she always said: 'That belongs in the swamp.' She sighed. 'Really, Trixie Pixie, I know you're proud of it, but it makes you look like secondhand tatterdemalion.' To which Jordan shouted, 'Eureka!'

After cake and ice cream, Aunt May insisted on giving her Derwie-kins his first present and handed him a postcard, a shot of the falls in Fenelon, all but obscured by a giant blue bow. He read it far louder than necessary: 'It's your birthday! Make any wish you like!' He immediately wished for a kayak, a racing kayak. It made perfect sense to me that he'd ask for a one-paddle boat, the perfect conveyance for the solitary pursuit of dressing up in his Scout uniform and heading into the swamp to earn whatever obscure badge he hadn't yet.

'Perhaps a Pervert in Training badge?' you ask. Don't be so quick to judge. Yes, he's fifteen and still in Scouts. That looks like a warning sign, doesn't it? In 1969 it was normal, even laudable. Children were allowed childhoods. Boys moved up from Cubs to Scouts to Venturers, and many stayed for Rovers. Uniforms didn't scare us then. We saw the fleur-de-lys on Derwood's hat as a symbol of peace and purity. Before the darkest days of Vietnam, before My Lei or Kent State or Iraq, we had a much different reaction to young men in uniform. They made us uniformly proud. In 1969, World War II wasn't ancient history. In March, it was barely yesterday. My uncles had enlisted willingly, eagerly and early. Even Dad, who had to lie about his age to do so. The War was one of the reasons they hated Yanker-Wankers. As Uncle Sloan put it, 'They came late to the party and then tried to run the show.'

Once each summer, they'd remember; they'd break out their uniforms to serve roast beef and lumpy mashed potatoes at the Veterans' Supper at the Legion in Coboconk. Hezzy wore his uniform full of medals. Uncle Percy and Aunt Evelyn both wore theirs – hers was for CWAC: Canadian Women's Army Corps. Only Uncle G had to leave his coat hanging open. Sometimes, when Saturday bonfires were but glowing coals, when women and children had all been sent to bed, when they all forgot that Jordan's window right next to the swamp was open, and when they'd imbibed just the right amount of Red Cap, my uncles would bivouac, smoke their Buckinghams and talk – haltingly, in fits and starts and silences – about the War. About buddies they'd lost. About bombs in England. About how the greatest man to ever breathe air was Winston Churchill. About how their Leicester aunts and uncles had been forced to send their cousins into the country so they wouldn't starve. About Hitler and how he'd fooled so many for so long. They held the door open for Uncle Sloan – as the eldest, he'd been gone the longest. He landed at Dieppe. He took part in the liberation of Holland. He'd talk about that a little, but the word 'beach' never came out of his mouth and we all knew better than to ask. To them, to me, to all of us, a Scout looked like a soldier, and a soldier looked like my Uncle Sloan, always a hero and always one of the good guys.

So if Derwood wore his full Scouting regalia to his party, that was entirely normal. If he spent the party alone, don't blame his uniform. And don't waste air feeling sorry for him; he derived enormous comfort from his uncountable number of toys, because – cut to the coins – Uncle G was loaded. His custom-built house in North York held a sprawling twelve rooms, including a separate games room that was not the same room as the swimming pool. Worst of all, it backed on to E. P. Taylor's horse farm. It galled me no end to think that the likes of Derwood could wander out his back door and pet Northern Dancer. Unfair is so foul.

And Jordan was having none of it. For March birthdays, various members of the shirtless gravel-shucking crew were reassigned to score everyone's picnic tables and bring them together in one long tesseract on the birthday front lawn. That evening, Jordan pulled out a lawn chair, refused both burger and cake, and sat with CHUM Charts in front of her face while Derwood opened his presents. But she peeked. I saw her several times, as he got showered with some really choice stuff: a racing pair of remote-control speedboats, an autographed baseball bat in a velvet-lined case, and one very expensive guitar.

That guitar. A Fender Stratocaster. The axe of John Lennon and Jimi Hendrix. Derwood kept trying to show it to her that night, but Jordan refused to learn its name. She kept asking him if his Fender Bender had been fixed, if his friend Fender had stopped drinking, if his Tender Sportscaster was too shy for his job. Derwood deserved it. He acted as if simple possession of said instrument made him the next Mr. Lightfoot. He perched on top of his picnic table, sheet music in Aunt May's adoring hand, strumming for the only captive audience he'd ever get in front of him. Repeatedly glancing Jordan's way, first he mangled 'Abervagenny.' Discovering no genetic advantage there – if you remember, Uncle Gavin was Welsh – he then massacred Desmond Dekker's 'Israelites': 'Mock Havana Geela, Josie's hobo, I really want to be just like Bonnie and Clyde.' The party died as quickly. But Derfoot kept strumming until Uncle G yelled at him to quit playing that 'humping monkey music' and get on out to bed.

Yes, he had his own private bunkie, set behind his parents' cottage. 'Proof even they can't stand him,' Jordan noted. To spite us, he'd nailed a horseshoe over the door, claiming it came from straight from Winfield Farms, that he'd been right there when they pried it off Northern Dancer. Instantly, the bunkie became the bunko. We never set foot in it.

On the day after his Yanker-Wanker birthday, a calm early morning the fifth of July, we opted for a cleansing dip before our first Saturday trip into Fenelon, only to be ambushed by the Birthday Boy, who snuck down to the dock and dropped a frog bomb into our eyes-shut, upturned faces. It singed Jordan's left eyebrow. It took forever to get frog guts out of her hair.

Why'd he do it? Perhaps to do what all of March wanted to do: punish us for arriving late. Perhaps for ending his fun with Yogi, or for staring at a CHUM Chart instead of at him. Who knows? Same difference. It was an escalation. One that could not go unchallenged. He hightailed it back to his picnic table and sat there smiling and strumming like a scotch mint wouldn't melt in his mouth. That singing bear-baiter had to go down. We owed him twice now: once for Yogi and once for the frog frappé. The only question was how.

To answer it privately, we trekked through Hezzy's pasture and sat beneath the tree house. 'Is Clearly Deaderwood an asshole because we treat him as one, or because he is in essence assholian?' Jordan posed this philosophical variation of nature vs. nurture for good reason. He wasn't the only one with firecrackers. But the worst thing I ever did was stick them in cow patties. I'd light them and run like stink, yelling my favourite phony and verboten book title jokes: *Rusty Bedsprings* by I. P. Nightly and *Shit Spots on the Wall* by that great Chinese writer, Who Flung Poooooo! Don't ask why, I just did. And every time I found it as funny as the explosion itself. But Derwood's bombs did real damage. The frogs were merely weapons' casings. He'd placed the doomed-to-die in weird places before, boasted of test spatter in the kybo, the pumphouse and Uncle H's beer fridge, but this time he'd aimed at a human being. Ratting, telling his parents or ours, never occurred to us. Revenge – that occurred to us.

'I ask about assholian,' Jordan continued, 'because if it's a case of nurture, if we could reform him by treating him kindly, then perhaps we have obligation to do so?' A moment passed. 'Nnnaaaaaa,' we said in unison, then jumped to, 'Jinx on you, jinx on you, no talk-backs. Jinx on you, jinx on you ... ' As always, I caved. Jordan ended it with punch to my shoulder. 'Ya owe me a root beer. Again. You can buy it when I come up with a plan.'

We heard the cowbell – Mom's 8:25 summons for our 8:30 trip into Fenelon – and double-timed it back to Almost. I was eager to get into town, to explore it, to see what changes winter had wrought, but first we went straight to Stedman's where, miraculously, they had one single serving of Polk Salad left. We willingly shelled out the sixty-nine cents and carried it around town in its frail paper sleeve with the round centre cut out so you could read the name of the song. After some debate, we rechristened it the BMW: the Bullfrog Mating Witual. We all but wore out its grooves and CHUM played it almost as much. It became the most persistent and perhaps the most unlikely hit of the summer. Jordan's CHUM Charts record its debut at #30, on July 5 and a steady rise to #3 on August 30, bested only by 'Honky Tonk Woman' at #2 and, of course, that 'Sugar Sugar' abomination with its summer death clutch on #1.

From that Saturday on, we made sure the parents ate Polk Salad plenty-twenty. We strung five extension cords end to end, packed Annie up in the red suitcase and moved her to the dock. Everybody knows how well sound carries over water. You had to walk the planks carefully or the needle of the record player would skip. Not that it was cheap – it was the only first-class object BS owned and, no, the parents hadn't bought it. Jordan won it in 1967, in the Grade 8 speech contest: Centennial Year – What One Hundred Means to Me.

Her intro is forever stuck in my head: 'Ladies and gentlemen. Pioneers and *coureurs de bois*, soldiers and missionaries, French and English, European and Indian, orphans and elders, it took a hundred combinations of the human spirit to build homes in the mountains and prairies and forests of our nation. Hundreds were tested and hundreds were found true.' Everyone stood up, even MC, eventually. They didn't stand for everyone, just for her. So she won the player. High-fidelity. Stereo sound. It played both LPs and singles with a built-in centrepiece for 45s that lifted right up from the turntable so you didn't need to fiddle with those stupid red or yellow plastic inserts. If you're reading this and don't know what I'm talking about, lucky you. Enough said.

Once we bought the BMW, we didn't tour much of Fenelon that day. BS visited Missy P at the library, then headed straight to what was normally our last stop: the green bench across from the Roxy Theatre. Usually we'd admire the movie posters and debate what we'd seen and wanted to see. That day our bench might as well have been the rock at Marie Curtis Park – a place to stare. I waited. Although neither of us knew Dorothy Parker's remark that revenge is a dish best served cold, we knew it was a tall order. We needed the devious energy of Gophers. A scheme as smooth as those sexy, black-clad

Avengers, Emma Peel and John Steed. 'That's it!' BS said suddenly. 'We'll be both. The hybrid best of both: the Go-Go Avengers.'

She sat on it the first full week of July. Hatching, cross-pollinating, metacognating, call it what you want. Her brain at work. Not much else happened during it. Just the usual shenanigans. Dex and Der got caught drinking Red Cap, but once they paid Uncle H back for swiping it out of his beer fridge and paid for a lock on said fridge, the uncles found it funny, though they said otherwise for the aunts. Balsam dug up something Dad didn't bury deep enough and got sprayed by a skunk. Grandma arrived with jars of homemade tomato juice and got the usual speech about how BS had wanted to call Balsam Chocolate Sundae, after one of her Little Golden Books, *Mr. Moggs' Dogs*, where a guy with a litter of puppies gets the scathingly brilliant idea to name them all after ice cream. Grand kept smiling and kept scrubbing. Now that is love. And playing innocent.

Jordan waited until both the scent of skunk and any whiff of revenge had abated, until Derwood stopped being guarded, until Aunt Elsbeth bribed us yet again, this time with huge banana Popsicles. Jordan took one look at hers and, once she was finished, cheated both the bonfire and the swamp by putting the stick in her pocket. In the middle of the night, I heard her open her sock drawer, heard her cutting the wood with her nail file. I knew better than to ask.

On Saturday, July 12, I began to wonder how much of Fenelon I'd see that summer. Again, once Jordan visited Missy P, she benched us, this time smack-dab in front of a huge poster of Paul Newman riding Katharine Ross on the handlebars of his bicycle. There, in the shadow of Butch Cassidy and the Sundance Kid, she whispered, 'Fools look to tomorrow; wise men use tonight.' Whispering was hardly necessary as it was raining, a stubborn spitting that rose with dawn. We were the only ones turtle-stupid enough to be out in it. When she outlined the whole shitty business, I choked. Don't misunderstand, I wasn't yellow and it was a boss idea. It was the smell. One whiff and I toss my cookies. BS had no sense of smell, not whiff one, and mine was keen enough for two. 'Don't worry, Mr. Pansy Nose. I'll carry it myself.'

So on that night, Saturday, July 12, with only crickets to hear and the moon to see, Jordan proved you didn't need to be a Scout or a boy to be prepared. Even the weather co-operated; at midnight the rain gave up the ghost. She tapped on my wall. Safely outside, she murmured verse two, 'Two little Indians. No others near. Now let's just see what two Indians can do!' We whisper-chanted all the way to bunko, 'Go, go, Avengers, watch us go, go, go!'

Why did she embrace a song used to humiliate her? Here's what you need to know about the Gophers: appearance isn't destiny. Despite their physical shortcomings, their bungling ineptitude was a clever Columbo facade. No one expected an ambush. No one saw a bushwhacking coming. So they won every episode, foiled every plan of Colonel Kit Coyote and Sergeant Hokey Loma, who had ostensibly obliterated the rest of Gopher-Indian kind. Ruffled Feathers and Running Board – they weren't going anywhere. Like Yogi, they were smarter than the average bear.

We reached the bunko, thankfully without encountering an uncle with a nocturnal commission. At that bit of shtick, we got the giggles. Then it got worse. Derwood snored in Z's, rhythmic comic book ZZZZZZZZzzzzz's. Jordan took tongue in teeth and slid her sharpened Popsicle stick – thank you very much, Auntie E – into the frame of his wooden screen door, lifting the inside hook from the eye that held it. Three steps in, empty-handed, became three steps out, Fender in hand. Good one, Sister Mine.

We slipped into Hezzy's pasture stopping only to grab the Gym Bag Gopher Avenging Kit we'd secreted in the woodpile, eventual pun intended: flashlight, clothes peg, garden spade, plastic gloves and knitting needles. Jordan knelt, wound her night braid into a bun and ran it through with the needles. Backlit by the moon, she looked like a worshipping Wilma Flintstone, complete with hair bones. She popped the peg on my nose, muttering something I didn't get about how finally Amy March was good for something, and grabbed the gloves, liberated from one of the many boxes of Auburn Sunset hair dye that MC hid unsuccessfully under the kitchen sink. Then we hesitated. The moment must be marked. 'Here beginneth the lesson.' Jordan opted for Dad's grace, the only one ever heard at MC's table: 'Over the lips and past the gums, look out stomach, here it comes. Praise the Lord and pass the ammunition!'

When we stopped laughing, I held that curvy baby down and spread its strings; she spooned it full of cow shit. For good measure, we rolled it in fresh cow patties until every square inch of Fender was buttered baby-shit brown. By then, despite the clothes peg, my face, already ghostly, had turned beyond the pale.

True to her word, Jordan carried the fecal Fender back alone, thrusting it out in front of her like the collection plate at church – one awful, offal offering. (Sorry, but I figure you're rock-star lucky to get even one opportunity in life to make a triple play like that and you're a damned fool not to take it.) We hung it from the door frame of his bunko simply by tossing his Northern-Dancer-My-Asp horse-shoe into the swamp and tying his broken G string to the convenient nail. We left that Fender bending in the wind, a giant rank piñata.

Next morning, Aunt May's sleepy little man walked right into it, face first. He yelled. He raised his hands to smear off his eyes and lunged at the piñata, which swung obligingly away from him. And then, no more able to alter the laws of physics than the sinking red seats of the Rosedale Roxy, the guitar pendulum creamed right back into his face. He screamed. He throttled it, wrestled it to the ground and stomped on it, breaking its neck. Then he wiped his eyes again. He plopped down on the grass. 'Fender? Oh no, I'm so sorry, baby, no, no ... '

He pulled off his pyjama shirt to wipe it down. He tried to piece the shitty broken bits of it back together. He gave up and began to cry. We almost felt sorry for him, the pathetic little asswipe, except we remembered what he did the last time someone cried: he threw more stones. If he was going to sow that wind, he could bloody well reap our whirlwind.

So that's what two little Indians do. This Rosedale Ruffled Feathers and Running Board showed their Gopher Gulch that you ruffled their feathers at your peril, that we weren't just whistling Dixie or running bored. At breakfast, as the parents' cereal spoons froze halfway to their mouths, Jordan stood, saluting at attention, and sang as loud as Gopher-Indian pride made necessary, 'Oh, Canada, our home on Native land. True gopher love, in all thy braves' command!' Emma winked and John tipped his bowler hat. Gave new meaning to the term 'shit-faced.' Power drunk. Insert Avenged here.

HAZEL #44A

Once I'm rid of the smelly little blighter, I can finally go home. This chilly outpost of civilization has been such a royal pain! (Pardon the funny.) I'm sure Canada's a lovely colony – if you're an Eskimo! I still can't get over how easy it was to pass myself off as a common farm girl. Dungarees and bad lip rouge and, presto, this princess becomes a pauper.

My stand-in has done a standup job, while I'm here on my diplomatic mission at 999 Queen. (Oh, aren't I just full of funny!) But dear Philip, he misses me dreadfully! He was right: my duty to God and the Country, pip, pip! But I felt a tad guilty, so I made that lackey Walter go out and buy a locket, anything to draw the eye away from that godforsaken little colonial face. As she grows up, she'll just have to lie still in Canada and think of England, because one look at Smelly's hideous red hair and the *Mirror* would have been intolerable. Like Bozo. Like a bloody red monkey at the Regent's Park Zoo. (No hair, no zoo. It simply will not do!)

I ordered the nurses to admit that I do so have a husband, a forgiving one, waiting for me across the pond. They look at me like I'm a wounded bird. So I show them my chart: birthdate April 28, 1926. That proves I'm exactly who I say I am, that I couldn't be anyone else, but with the unutterable banality of bovines, the stupid cows still don't believe me!

Oh, there's no place like home! The Q. M. will be over the moon to see me. Mater will take one look at my pretty figure and call for high tea. We'll pour it milk first like civilized British beings, in proper china cups, not these boorish, maple-leaf, Melmacian monstrosities.

Together, we'll sip it slowly, pinky aloft, and smile the secret: 'What bloody baby?'

Will she have Perry's deep-set dark eyes and black hair? It won't matter. It's not as if he's ever going to know. I told him I'd spent the hiatus up north with my Canadian aunt. He doesn't care enough to check. I told the hospital some ridiculous story about this hurricane they're all still yapping about almost a full year later because nothing but weather ever happens up there in that iceberg of a country. LA is sunny all year round. Just like me. Shooting resumes tomorrow and don't you worry, fans! Della Street will be on set and on time. Svelte and smiling. There are plenty of lockets in wardrobe, these two won't be missed, but your Della, she can't be replaced. She doesn't do diapers for any man, not even him. Your darling Della unbuttons her cardigan set one chaste button at a time. The matching locket will lie there, secret against her throat, and she'll be calm, giving all you fans her famous big-brown-eyed moue, her inscrutable drop-the-calf-and-run Mona Lisa smile.

YESTERDAY WHEN I WAS YOUNG

The shite hit the fan right after it hit Derwood. He ran straight to his Mummie and we got caught. By the rain – rain that makes mud, footprints in it outside his door and several of it inside. Footprints that could only be Jordan's. For reasons obvious. So the parentulas let us go to church that Sunday morning, but no further. Lock-up isn't the best way to start a summer, but it could've been worse. We'd speculated what they might do if we got caught. Jordan worried we might miss Thursday's choir practice. I didn't think we'd be so lucky. We both worried it might be a week without radio or TV, meaning we'd not only miss liftoff on July 16; but Apollo 11 altogether. They let us sweat and then at dinner sentenced us to three days in the addition. On Monday, July 14, when MC turned the key but left us the TV and the Miracle and the red record case – that was no sweat. Or so we figured.

We DJed that entire first day, creating our own CHUM Top 100, as if it were New Year's Day. We played, debated and rated every 45 in Jordan's suitcase, both the A and the B sides. Little Miss Show-off could sing both, so naturally she had to play both.

After supper we played TV. This required negotiation. If I agreed to *Bewitched*, she'd agree to *I Dream of Jeannie*. I liked to hear her say, 'Yes, master!' If I agreed to *Here Come the Brides* she'd agree to *Combat*. We both loved *Green Acres* and sang the song several times, complete with Jordan being yanked halfway across the addition the way Oliver Douglas yanked Lisa, 'You are my wife! Goodbye, city life!' We recreated Mr. Haney by imitating Hezzy, the farm hand Abe by imitating OB, and Mr. and Mrs. Ziffel's son, Arnold the Pig, by imitating Aunt May. For *Lost in Space*, I played Professor John Robinson, the evil Dr. Smith, the handsome pilot Don, the brainy Will, and best of all, the Robot. I slid along the carpet on my knees, cupping my hands into giant waving pincers: 'Danger, Will Robinson. Danger!'

Laugh-In required no negotiations. We never tired of 'You bet your sweet bippy,' or 'beautiful downtown Burbank.' Always funny; still is. Jordan did a halfway decent impression of Lily Tomlin as Ernestine the telephone operator, 'One ringy dingy, two ringy dingy! Is this the party to whom I am speaking?' She had child philosopher Edith Ann down pat, 'And that's the truth!' I wasn't half bad at making up stupid poems like Henry Gibson, but my real forte was leering like Arte Johnson's dirty old man. Lacking Ruth Buzzi's giant purse, Jordan obligingly smacked me over the head with the record case. She flatly refused to be the Sock It To Me Girl, so I didn't get to hit her at all, a deprivation I protested. The Flying Fickle Finger of Fate Award? Derwood won it hands down. Which finger? Good one.

Then she picked the *Smothers Brothers*. I liked it (who wouldn't like a show that featured the Doors singing 'Touch Me'), but I was tired of playing Tommy the Retard to her Genius Dick. When CBS cancelled it that March, she'd fired off impassioned letters, signed with pseudonyms, using some very choice nyms for network executives. But despite her one-girl resurrection campaign, Tom and Dick stayed dead. I teased her for caring but had to eat my words when on April 4, they cancelled *Star Trek*. So I suffered a few moments as Tommy Too-Dumb before Jordan got to be Uhura, the name of freedom, and I transformed into my true self: stud captain of the Starship Enterprise, James Tiberius Kirk.

On Tuesday morning, Jordan smuggled in her shoe box. She hid it under her breakfast tray, because if Mom had seen that Jordan was about to get crafty with the box from her brand-new oxfords, a box barely a month old, Mom would have taken it away from her and made her grovel for an older one. The new one was almost square, which was why Jordan wanted it.

It took most of the morning to cut out narrow bars on all four sides, and all of a pencil crayon to colour the remaining bars black. She left an inch at the bottom for grass and dandelions. On the front she pasted a dripping duplicate of 'See Yogi Bare' and inside sectioned off a sandwich-size square for 'Yogi's Pic-a-nic Basket.' She tied a Tinker toy tire to an old locket chain from her jewellry box and hung it over a Popsicle stick beam in the centre. Yes, the same Popsicle stick. As dioramas go, I had to admit that the perspective was quite clever. Like you were standing out on the road beside the sign and staring into the cage. Using drops of India ink to darken her beige Plasticine, she began the shape of a bear. What possessed her? The diorama deamon? Something far worse: a fiery need to win the St. John's Anglican Children's Choir Box Social.

Let me explain. BS isn't just for Baby Sister and the obvious. It's Jordan's game. Every Thursday, after practice, we went to one of the church ladies' houses with a sandwich in a paper bag. We scarfed down supper ASAP to get to the evening of games: Capture the Flag, British Bulldog or scavenger hunts. You can imagine how good BS was at those, how good we let her be: as referee, timekeeper and applause meter. But one Thursday night each summer was the Box Social, a competition with only one rule: decorate a shoe box to hold your sandwich supper. When you only get one game a season, you have to play to win.

Once Plasticine Yogi was set and swaying, out came the board games: Mouse Trap, Operation, Risk and Sorry. Then it got hot. Out the picture window, we heard cousins cavorting on the sunniest day so far, laughing far louder than necessary. BS sat with her Etch A Sketch, fiddling with the one working knob. Not to suggest I was gainfully employed. I was scouting old *National Geographics*, keeping, shall we say, abreast of parts unknown. Insert juvenile here. When BS moved to the big armchair and sat crossways, making loops on a needle.

It never ceased to confound me that despite having little interest in most girlie things, BS hungered after every kind of handicraft going. Mom taught her to sew, quilt, embroider, macramé, decoupage and tat. Probably the only time they didn't fight. That and when they talked Marchspeak or Scotland. When Mom taught her to knit, BS picked it up so fast we all got scarves for Christmas. Mine was great: Maple Leaf blue and white – her one concession to my game. When I teased her about caving, BS shook her head no, said a person should get the present they want, not what someone else wants to give them. Now she knit so fast you couldn't see fingers, but that afternoon her yellow loops kept unlooping, kept tangling into knots and tail-ends abetted by teeth. I offered professional assistance, 'Hey, reject, double your pleasure, double your fun. Even I know you need two needles.'

She threw me a glance that would have burned water. 'This, midget-idjit, is a crochet hook. And, as its name suggests, with it one does not knit, one crochets.' She aimed it at my head. I caught it enroute. Six inches. Metal. A thick grip narrowing to a small hook. Could be useful. I returned it with regret. She poked it into her yarn's yellow heart and stuffed the whole mess down her armchair. 'Let's play cards. Hearts or double solitaire?'

During Crazy Eights she started scribbling on the score pad. Random numbers. Big and small. Everything but the score. 'Good one, BS. I start winning and you stop playing?'

'No, I got distracted. I wrote 121 and well, it hit me that palindromes apply to numbers and to history. It got me wondering how many people have lived through a palindrome, how many a person could live through because it's getting harder to do so.' I glared with all the efficacy of staring down a virus – it's gonna run its virulent course whether you like it or not.

'A palindrome must have at least three letters, or, in this case, digits. Someone born in 101 AD, could live to see 111 and 121 and back then, maybe 131. That's four. For the first thousand years, palindromes are only ten years apart except at the century change when they're eleven, as in 494 to 505. As lifespan improves, one could live through seven or eight of them. Conceivably, that is.' BS grinned. 'At the first millennium and each successive one, we catch a break. Since 999 is so close to 1001, someone born in 919 could see eleven palindromes if they were born in 909 and lived till 92 in 1001. But then we hit years with four digits: 1001, 1111 and 1221 are 110 years apart. Nobody sees more than one. Most don't see any. But you and I might: 1991 and 2002. We'll be the first humans to see two palindromes in over a thousand years.' She shrugged and tossed a braid in my face, 'That is, if I let you live that long.'

I couldn't let her see it. The damn near worship in my eyes. In that one moment, she made me a math teacher. But I knew she was also, in her own sweet BS way, telling me something else. Numbers were supposed to be my game, and just as I was heroic only in her storied imagination, if she chose to play my game, then in all probability, she'd beat me at it.

'Well, BS, what can I say? The eights are looking pretty sane at this moment!'

My hand few out of my hand and chopped her nose, knocking her glasses to the floor. My only regret? That I didn't hold enough cards to make her play 52 Pickup. So why didn't I simply call her bluff? Yell that, smart as she was, she sure wasn't playing with a full deck? Well, a proverb in hand is worth two in the bush. When the shoe fits, only a fool beats a dead horse twice. BS would have squinted in my direction, thickened her second-generation Scottish brogue, and corrected me until I caved: A bird in the hand is worth ten fleein'. Ale sellers shouldna' be tale tellers. A wise lawyer ne'er goes to law himself. Burnt bairns dread fire. Enough said.

BAD MOON RISING

On the morning of the third day, Wednesday, July 16, we witnessed perfection: a burning sword thrust straight to heaven. At least that's how I saw it. I didn't realize I was holding my breath until I had to gasp for air. Dad grinned but left before Mom caught him fraternizing. He'd been trying to film the TV, but of course that was worse than useless.

Jordan fussed with her Box Social, resetting Yogi's bracelet-bead eyes, rethreading her torso through the tire. Unlike the real one, this tire swung right over the crossbeam. She flicked it until chain and bear were wound up tight. Not a push of sane desire. Her elbow hit some unused beads and sent them scampering under the book trunk. She pushed it from the wall and surfaced with a dusty black book. Lord only knows how long it had been there. Literally: *A History of the Catholic Church from the Renaissance to the French Revolution*, by Rev. James MacCaffrey, 1914. Light summer fare. A joy to read to your captive brother. Kill me now.

I figured I'd better look busy if I wanted her to keep her religious enlightenment to herself. Thankfully I had a plan, a Hardy Boys plan. When Frank and Joe get marooned in the woods, they find an isolated cabin and enhance the signal of a rickety ham radio with tinfoil and copper wire to get a rescue call through to their parents. Remember, this was the third day of stir-crazy. It seemed entirely logical. If it worked on a ham radio in a book, why not on our rabbit ears in the addition? I desperately wanted to be rescued from CHEX, Peterborough. We were the only cousins marooned in one-station isolation. Their tall antennas all got CBC and CFTO, channels 6 and 9 in Toronto, and, weather co-operating, WBEN, channel 7, Buffalo. So not fair. Maybe if I rolled the tinfoil extra tight and snaked the copper wire just so ...

'Hey, here's why MC kept this old book. It's about the guy they named Fenelon after, a real mouthful: Francois de Salignac de la

Mothe-Fenelon, born August 6, 1651, at Chateau de Fenelon.' I longed to give her a mouthful of BB de Fist. 'A scholar. Taught by his cousin, Jeanne de la Mothe Guyon, who wrote a twenty-volume guide to the Bible.

'And all twenty volumes aren't in the book trunk? Gee, what a cryin' shame.'

'Neither is the one they wrote together. On their theory: Semi-Quietism.'

'BS, that's ridiculous. It's like semi-dead. You either are or you aren't.'

'Ha. Ha. Profoundly clever.' Under her breath, I just caught it. 'Unless you're me.'

Five configurations of tinfoil later, I decided Joe and Frank were semi-quacked. Then my fully-cracked sister began to list Fenelon's books, 'The Inner Life or Christian Counsel on Diverse Matters Pertaining to the Inner Life and Spiritual Progression and –'

'Enough already with the retard titles. Who cares?'

'The church did. Fenelon believed personal prayer, said you could enter into the mystic and talk directly to God. But it's the 1600s. You wanna talk to Him, you gotta go through a priest.' She grinned. 'That's what the priests said God said. So Jeanne and Fenelon get arrested by Louis XIV, thrown in jail, and made to recant. But the rest of this sounds pretty tame: 'Righteous acts proceed from pure love without hope of reward or fear of punishment and all virtuous acts to be righteous must proceed directly or indirectly from charity.'

'I'm gonna donate you to charity!' I rushed her and the book went flying. We wrestled for it, but rather than let me win, she pitched it across the room. A clipping floated out, one faded yellow butterfly. I caught it and began reading despite myself. 'Too bad, Little Miss Know-It-All. Wrong Fenelon. The Fenelon Gazette says your bookworm had a brother, an older brother, I might add, missionary Abbe Fenelon, a Canadian explorer. Typical, eh? Baby stays home with her nose in a book, while her brave big brother conquers the real world.'

'The Glaze-ette? That's a rag, not a newspaper. A bunch of old biddies gossiping about strawberry socials and the Dearly Departed. I wouldn't trust a word of it. Not ever.'

It felt good, for once, to preach to her: 'In July of 1669,' I smiled at her, 'which is not a palindrome but is exactly three hundred years ago,' I kept reading, 'Fenelon became the first explorer to leave Quebec, to canoe through the Kawarthas and the Rouge River, and winter on the shores of Lake Ontario. Both Fenelon Falls and Frenchman's Bay in Pickering are named after him.' I tossed the clipping. 'So much for Missy Semi-Accurate. Brawn 1, Brains 0.'

As I boasted, she retrieved the book. She stuck out her tongue and recommenced at full volume, 'Give every truth time to send down deep roots into the heart, the main point is ... '

By then I'd reached the single I wanted. Yesterday she'd rated it second so her precious Burton could be first. Not today. Today I was Big Brother Born to be Wild, taming Jordan and the entire Canadian wilderness, me and Creedence Clearwater Revival: 'I see a bad moon arising, I see trouble on the way,' She threw the book at me but missed. Time to drown her out, her and Madame Whatever-her-Moth-face-was, 'Die witch, die!' I turned it up full crank and wailed: 'I hear hurricanes a blowing, I know the end is coming soon. I fear rivers overflowing. I hear the voice of rage and ruin.' She stomped in my direction and we screamed the chorus in each other's faces. Meaning every word: 'Hope you got your things together. Hope you are quite prepared to die. Looks like we're in for nasty weather. One eye is taken for an eye.'

We never reached the final chorus. The double racket brought MC on the triple. She ran to the player and reefed on the needle, 'Off and stays off.' Jordan kept singing. 'Cease and desist!' Jordan didn't. 'Now! Unless you want another day in here!' BS stopped. 'So Missy Misbehaving, exactly what do you think you're proving here?'

Jordan threw her arms open and stepped forward. 'The main point is to love. Digest every truth leisurely if you would extract the essence of it for your nourishment.'

Mom blinked. She grabbed Jordan's side plate, the lowly Canadiana Brown, its fading Maple Leaves all but transparent. 'Really? Here's another old saying: time, tide and dirty Melmac wait for no Smarty-Pants Gypsy Sue. You march, March!'

The only real punishment came that evening from an unexpected source. When Mom came in to retrieve the supper tray, she held the door wide. 'It appears you have a visitor.'

Auntie E brought her own little purse pack of Kleenex. She pulled one out and began to twist it into shreds. She headed for the couch and would have sat on Yogi had BS not jumped to rescue her from the certain death lurking under a round rear end. Auntie E perched on the couch as if the bear might bite. She looked at the ceiling, the floor and outside. Anywhere but at us. And then she actually said this: 'So, why can't we all just get along?' And, 'Did we think ourselves the Queen of England to rule on her boy like that? And 'What had he ever done to deserve it?' Plenty-twenty, we thought. But as I've said, we weren't ratfinks. I still wonder what a resetting of dials might have saved, had any of the Semi-Quiet March adults bothered to make some noise into Derwood's proclivities in time to change them.

But we kept silent and she kept sobbing. 'I can't defend you anymore! I'm sorry but I just can't. The horrid things the rest of the family says – you deserve them. They're all true.'

'I guess when the meek inherit the earth they won't be any nicer than the rest of us.'

That's the conclusion Jordan recorded once Aunty E left. The only charity of the occasion came from the same unlikely source a few beats later, when my sister looked up from her diary, 'But you know what? Good for her. It's time for some backbone. Who wants to be meek anyway? Not me. The meek shall inherit the hurt.'

HAZEL #48

On Friday, when I caught Walter with his hand too far up that nasty Darrah McKelvie's skirt to be fixing her garter belt like he claimed, I figured a hurricane had to be good for something. Who the hell does he think he is, replacing me with a teller? So Saturday morning I went straight to his mother, burst into tears and begged her forgiveness for what we'd done that night. She gave a sigh, almost as if she expected it of him. I said it was no excuse, but her son and I had figured we were dying for sure. We'd seen other cars get swept right into the Humber; we could hear folks screaming to Jesus to save them. She liked the sounds of that, so I told her I'd said a little prayer myself, one for her and Mam together, asking God not to leave our mothers alone. (Actually, there's nothing I want more. Since Janie got married, Mam's gone crazy with missing her. She sits by the radio all night waiting for *The Lone Ranger*. It's been cancelled since September, but she says that can't be right, it's always been on, always, since she was a little girl. She falls asleep in her chair and I lug her into bed. Stuck with that cow the rest of my life? Nosiree.) So I crossed my fingers and yes, the prayer clinched it. Mrs. J. dispatched Walter to the farm on Sunday, ring in hand. And then the feathers flew! He knows the baby isn't his, and he knows no one, including his mother, will believe it isn't. I point out that everyone at the bank will believe it's his once I say it is, so we'd best get married right quick or he can kiss his new promotion goodbye. He swears and says fine, he'll marry me, but only for appearances. Good enough, I say. Appearing married is married. He pulls something out of his pocket, says it's from his mother and throws it in my face. I pick it up. It's a locket. I toss it back and say I'll need more than cheap jewellery and he gets really nasty, screaming that cheap deserves cheap and he'll be damned if he'll raise another man's by-blow. I say two words: 'Barnardo Boy.' That shuts him up. I remind him that I know he was one, that he started out in his 'mother's home, not as her son but as a nine-year-old farm hand. Shipped there on a milk truck. Penniless and fatherless. His red face turns green. Says if I ever mention that again, ever, even once, he'll kill me. Says it'll be bad enough having a slut for a wife; he won't raise a slut's bastard. I made him put the ring on my finger anyway. Men say all kinds of things they don't mean. If there's not enough room in his misery for company, what's that to me? Engaged is engaged. After all, what kind of man would make his own wife give up her own child? He'll come round in a few months and if he doesn't I can always have another one. I can't wait to see Darrah on Monday. I'm going to flash my ring in her stupid cow face.

LAUGHING

'I've decided. It's time.'

'For lunch? Good one, BS. You get it, I'll eat it.'

'You want it got, Brother Mine? Then you go get it.'

'I will gladly pay you Tuesday for a hamburger today.'

'I will gladly pay you no day for a Spamburger no way.'

Yes, we were quiddling. We were supposed to be gardening. When Thursday finally came, an end to lock-up and the day of the Box Social, our excitement lasted about as long as it took Yogi to snort a butter tart – under two seconds. We were doubly disappointed. Once by the weather, a misty morning, and by MC who unlocked the addition only to hand BS the weed fork. 'A girl of words and not of deeds is like a garden full of weeds. So, Missy, there's a week of weeds that better get pulled pronto if anyone named March expects anything named lunch.'

By noon we were still at it, or more accurately, I was weeding and BS was doing what she did best, feeling wounded. At ten o'clock she'd asked Mom for a break to go up the road where three days of girlfriend news and CHUM Charts were waiting, and gotten the line about the grindstone. She condescended to pull a weed, only to throw it at me. When I didn't duck and it hit, she lit an imaginary pipe, 'Watson, your capacity to ignore the obvious never fails to astound me.'

'Okay, Sister Sherlock, I'll bite. What's so obvious to you this time?'

'Yogi.'

'No ship, Sherlock! Something the size of a bear is obvious. Next!'

'It's only elementary, my dear Watson. Yesterday your precious astronauts lifted off for the moon, so today we must follow their lead and get our plan off the ground.'

'My astronauts? Excuse me? I don't think *we* ever planned anything.'

She came out of character. 'Fine, Mr. Pansy Pants, I'll do it all sigh my belf. Again.'

'Good. Just don't do anything I wouldn't do first.'

And went back in. 'How unfortunate. I never took you for a coward, Watson.'

I let that one pass. 'Jordan, don't tell me you're actually considering letting that bear out of its cage? Somebody'd shoot her dead before she got past the mailbox.'

Jordan straddled the garden stool and twirled her fork in the air. A majorette with fangs. 'Yes, yes, my dear Watson. Naturally, I've thought of that.'

'Okay ... So that's that. Bad idea. End of discussion.'

She dropped the pipe, gave herself buck teeth and a bad Chinese accent. 'No. This Chinky find chink in that armour. Get better idea. Beginning of discussion. (It's wrong now. But that's the way we talked back then and I've sworn to tell it with all its warts and pimples.)

'Whatever you say, Confucius. Hmm ... Tasty. Rhymes with mucus.'

'You're Mucus, I'm Confucius. Get it straight!' She launched the garden fork at me but, as per normal, missed by a BS mile. She continued anyway. 'And Confucius say: in dead of night, on Sunday night, is best prayer for woolly bear, when she get best head start.'

I looked at her like she was from Alpha Centauri, which at that moment, despite the pidgin English, she damned well might have been. 'The best head start Kronkwise.' She rolled her eyes and assumed a tone of insincere patience that one uses to explain toilet training to a particularly obtuse infant. 'Kronk sleeps past noon on Monday because Aunt May has had him up at the crack of dawn to get her to the church on time when no sober man would. He gets rehammered once the tourists are gone on Sunday night. Ergo, we'll set Yogi free on Sunday night.'

I must have accidentally nodded or something because she thought she had leave to continue. 'We'll lure her northeast. If she goes south she'll be caught at the Gov Dock. East, she'll end up a rug on some Trenter's floor. West puts her in the lake; straight north keeps her too close to the highway. So, it's north by northeast, past Hezzy's and into MacIsaac's woods.' The very route the cousins had led her down, and now she wanted me to prove I wasn't a chicken either. 'See? The best idea and the end of discussion. Recursion. We take her home.'

'Aw, how very sentimental, BS! Emphasis on "mental." Bears don't have homes.'

'This one will. Depending on how fast you can run.'

'I repeat, "mental." As in 999 Queen Street mental. That's the only home you're going to have if you keep this up!'

Jordan gasped. She began pulling up carrots. She looked hurt but I wasn't born yesterday. Who'd take that one seriously? Every kid in Toronto used it. Her face was pointed down and mumbling, but I'd swear I heard her say, 'Fine. At least I come by it honestly. In for a penny, in for a pound.' When I said, 'Pardon me?' she said, 'Nothing.'

MC appeared, saying they who rise with the sun have their work well begun, so anyone who wanted to do so could nip up to the mail-box before Jell-O salad. I followed. 'What the cluck, Jordan! Tell me you aren't serious? You actually want me to run one step ahead of Yogi calling: "Sooey, sooey! Come eat me, I'm nice and gooey!" She grinned but I ruined it. 'If it's so easy to run from a bear, then you do it.' That was mean; we both knew it.

She let it hover. 'No can do. I'm too generous. I give all my best lines to you,' she nodded. 'Come on: "Exit, pursued by a bear"? Who wouldn't want to make that line live?'

'I'd rather live myself, thank you very much.'

'It's *obviously* Shakespeare, pea brain.' She paused. 'Who also said if it clucketh like a fowl, then forsooth, it's the truth.' And there it was again. The same old chicken button. The same old push. The one accusation I couldn't bear, pun irrelevant, and she knew it.

We reached the mailbox. She yanked on the metal door. It was empty. She put a hand in and moved it around. I teethed my tongue, so as not to utter the word 'obvious.' She closed the door, winced as she dropped to her knees, and began searching the long grass. I laughed, 'Me thinks thy false friends hath forsaken thee.' I turned, dropping the line over my shoulder at just the right moment, 'No letters, forsooth; you're friendless in truth. Three days is full proof.'

She shrugged. 'If you'd done it in iambic pentameter, I might have been impressed.'

Post Jell-O salad, Thursday, July 17, got really sticky. Cousins lay unmoving on the dock. When Jordan attempted to start a conversation by pointing out that our regatta was exactly one month away, they laughed. Somebody said, 'Why would you care, little girl?' They started laying bets on who would win the Cross-the-Bay Swim. Since Dex and Der had turned too old that year, Derwood got enough votes to make us want to hurl Jell-O.

And it got hotter. One of those days when July shows off before it fades to August, when your top sweats even when your bottom is standing in the lake. When forgetful frogs on sunny logs become crispy frog bacon. When breathing air is gone, replaced by soup. BS coughed non-stop. Being anywhere but outside was out of the question, and being on the dock had become likewise, but so was the exertion of real swimming. So we went clamming.

Now when it comes to clams, the word 'hunt' is more than a misnomer – it's hyperbolic. A clam, even an athletic one, vamoosing at the rate of a foot an hour, isn't going to require either a stalking or the skills of hot pursuit. You are not the great white hunter in search of a wily beast. A clam is no bear. With no skill or training, with basically no effort, you can bag fifty an hour. It takes no safari, no guide, no tactics and no gun. Thrills? Danger? Well, you could get a nasty sunburn on your exposed back. Balsam could scrape you with his nails as he dog-paddles beside you. You could get thirsty. You could get tickled by weeds where the north side of the bay is part lake, part spillover from Peace's Swamp. You're in the shallows, where it's less than three feet deep. Attach your mask and lie face down. Reach down, pluck clams from the sandy bottom and store them in the net bag tied to your waist. With a snorkel, you don't need to surface. Hell, you don't even need to swim. Just lie there. I lay there, suspended in the warm jelly of the shallows for so long I could easily have been an unlucky corpse doing a real dead man's float a mere stone's throw from shore.

Thankfully, only clams met death that day, but they did it in droves. We didn't cull the baby ones, only the big dark brown ones that had that white shingly-stuff like tree lichen on them. We'd catch, count and release, but leave a few out on the beach. At twilight, we'd lie dead still on the dock and wait for raccoons to nose out of the swamp and wash them for dinner. Sometimes we saw them and sometimes we didn't, but next morning without fail our offerings lay spread-eagled on the beach, their pearly walls scraped clean, mirroring the sun.

We'd been at it an hour, and the sheen had come off the shell. Time for fun. For me, anyway. I wore full gear: flippers, mask and snorkel – took to it like a second skin. Not so my sister, who was barely comfortable in her own. She'd come up with what even I had to admit was an ingenious plan and glued the frame of an old pair of glasses inside her mask so she could see underwater, at least sort of, but she couldn't fix the fact that flippers refused to stay on her feet. And the snorkel was not her friend. Because it limits your air intake, she got quickly winded and, although she'd never admit it, probably a little panicked. So she surfaced ten times to my one – a big advantage for yours truly. If I wanted to, I could beat her to a clam even if she was closer and saw it first. And on that hot day, I wanted to. I was tired of watching her bag every frog in town. Guess I had something in common with Dex and Der after all. I swept circles around her, practically yanked the last few from her hands. At the tally, she had twenty-three and I had over forty. 'As it should be,' I gloated. 'Bested by your better.'

When MC rang the cowbell, Jordan jumped up and dove for home. Box Social Time. We rounded Peace's Point and ran smack into Derwood. This was not unusual. In his own deranged version of parallel play, he'd often plant himself close enough to us to feel part of whatever we were doing and then try to do it one better. If we were fishing, he got out his fancy-schmancy retraction reel and began casting. If we got in Grandma's canoe, he launched his new racing kayak. If we sat on Mrs. Miller's concrete steps and read comic books, something she let us do because she liked us and, frankly, because March kept her solvent, Derwood would see what were were reading – *Batman* for me and *The Archies* for Jordan, so she could hum 'Sugar Sugar' and not get punched – and when we put them down, he'd pick them up, take them home and leave them out on his picnic table unread so we could be impressed by his superior buying power and graphic good taste.

That day, he got the scathingly brilliant idea to hunt crayfish. In typical Derwoodian sportsmanship, he decided to catch, count and decrease. Nothing like being stark dead. As we came by, he had a dozen future corpses in a sandbanked pool at the edge of the shore. He'd survey them, select one and methodically dismember it, removing its swimmerets and flipping them into the pool. Then he kindly set it down so its entire crawfish family could watch it drown. In final wickedness, to be sure they were really most sincerely dead, he tossed them overhead for batting practice. Lately he'd taken to carrying around his bat, much the way Jordan did her radio. Guts and carapace spattered his uniform. Good clean fun for our boy Derwood.

We kept walking. Our disapproval only fed him. Only Balsam growled. Once clear, we broke into 'The Derwood Song,' written in his honour not by us but by his lovely brother Dex, based on 'Felix the Cat': 'You'll laugh so much, your sides will ache, your arse will go spatter-splat, watching Derwix, the pimple-faced rat.' Goof one. The rock he batted missed.

'If he's gotta kill something,' Jordan suggested, 'at least it's only crawdads.' She screeched the word 'crawdads' like Granny on *The Beverly Hillbillies*. 'And not Yogi.'

Jordan collected her cage from its pride of place in the kitchen window. Mom was staring through it and chopping onions for meatloaf, the one weekly supper she got to have alone with Dad. She told Jordan she could try saying thank you for what was already made for her and in the fridge. When Jordan tried to fit said sandwich into Yogi's Pic-a-nic Basket, the wax paper kept popping open. MC watched her struggle and said nothing. To date, she'd said nothing about either box or bear. When Jordan opened the drawer for elastic bands, MC didn't even look up. 'Hmmm ... once a thief.'

Jordan frowned. 'May I have an elastic band?' The knife kept chopping. 'Please.'

MC nodded. 'And what do you say next?'

Jordan secured her sandwich. 'Thank you, Mother. So ... what do you think?'

Her knife never hesitated. 'I think you'd better bring it back. I've only got a dozen left.'

Jordan hummed all the way, even though it was Auntie E's turn to drive and the front seat held a Boy Scout who smelled of crusty death. Derwood kept his unfraternizing box in a brown paper bag, refusing to show to anyone. At practice, Jordan's hymns were an impatient half note ahead. Everyone noticed. Eagerness. That was her first mistake.

I forget which one of the High Cs we went to. That's what we called all the ladies who routinely hosted choir: Cornish, Covington, Carstairs, Cowan and Chandler. Our boxes milled sociably together on every available kitchen surface, the counter, the table, the floor.

Missy P set a numbered library index card beside each box so the judges could refer to them by number, not by child. A ridiculous precaution, since the judges had watched us set our creations down, but the sheer formality of it raised the stakes and our heads high.

As the rest of us stepped outside for the judging, Derwood insisted on unveiling his last and alone. When we returned, his number 27 wore a blue ribbon. Jordan's 23 was naked. Derwood whooped. He waved blue in her face 'So, retard, whatcha got to say to that?'

Jordan held out a hand. 'I say congratulations.'

Derwood refused to shake it. His eyes slid over to his box, and when Jordan's followed, she screamed. It had three decorations: a label, 'To See What He Could See,' some lumpy grass made of crumpled green CHUM Charts, and perched atop the lump, one perfectly executed Plasticine bear.

'That's mine! Those are mine!' She grabbed for his arm but missed. 'You dirty thief! You stole my Yogi *and* my mail, didn't you?'

The High Cs frowned. One said, 'Yours was nice too, dear.' Another said, 'Don't be a sore loser, child. You can't win every year.'

Maybe if it hadn't been so hot. Maybe if Jordan had stayed calm, they might have listened. Maybe I just want to believe they might have. Instead, she lost it, yelling that they should look at Yogi's legs, that they were twisted because her Yogi was a swinging Yogi not a walking Yogi. When that got her some pitying looks, she yelled louder and that cost her. Nice girls don't scream. Auntie E heard none of it. She was outside setting up games. Hoping to end false claims, one of the High Cs called out the window, 'Elsbeth, have you seen your son's winning entry?' She didn't get the answer she wanted.

'No, but I'm sure it's wonderful!' Auntie E entered smiling. 'Oh, Derwie, how clever! It's the song.' She sang it, 'The bear climbed over the mow-an-tain, to see what he could see!'

Jordan pulled on her sleeve. 'Auntie E, please look at it again. That bear – it's mine. You saw Yogi last night in the addition. Remember? When you nearly sat on her?'

To give her a little credit, it's hard to serve two masters, and at least Jordan's aunt gave Derwood's mother cause for pause. Auntie E squinted at her son. She opened and closed her mouth. Meanwhile, Aunt May's minion, Miss McKelvie, had been examining Jordan's box. 'No matter, Elsbeth. She's disqualified! The rules clearly say the children must use a shoe box, and look!' She smugly turned it over and pointed for all to see, 'Foster's Orthopaedics.'

Missy Peace's librarian expertise came to the rescue. 'Don't be an idiot, Minnie! It's a medical term. It's the kind of shoes the child wears.' The choir, grouped around the table giggled. 'Stop that! Look right here – it says Size Two.' They giggled some more. They'd been size two when they were babies. Missy P slapped the table. 'Enough! Those shoes,' she pointed, 'came in this box.' Given permission for once, everyone stared. Missy P realized her error. 'Eyes up, children.' She set the box down and smiled at Jordan. 'Of course it qualifies.'

The High Cs looked confused. 'Maybe they should both get a ribbon?'

Then Derwood's mother won out. 'That won't be necessary. I remember quite clearly now. My son and I discussed his idea at length the other day. In the car, on our long trip into Toronto.' She looked my sister full in the face. 'To pick up his new guitar.'

Missy Peace murmured, 'But if you didn't see him make it, then how can we – '

'I saw it,' interrupted Auntie E. 'Today in his bunkie. With my own two eyes.'

It made for a rather silent ride home in the back seat. I guess all Jordan could see was the other side of the same old mountain. When she attempted to hand over the elastic band, MC made her wash it first. Jordan dried her hands, got told to straighten the towel and went to her room. When she came out in her bathing suit, I agreed to a swim, mistakenly thinking that her brain would be as defeated as the rest of her looked and I could relax. Always a mistake.

Flopped out on air mattresses, awaiting the first breeze of evening, I was inches from the safety of slumber when the great white hunter launched her retaliatory ambush. She began in camouflage, in masquerade as the everyday and harmless.

'Whatcha thinkin', Lincoln?'

Disarmed, I responded on cue, 'Just fuzzin', cousin.'

So she took aim in Chinese. 'Confucius thinking Wittle Wuwu has my wetters and my most honourable CHUM Charts. Confucius say, I humbly request your help.' She turned her mattress face to face with mine. 'But Yogi first. I'm thinking maybe you could use your bike?'

Danger, Will Robinson! Danger! 'Not at the moment.' I gestured at the water. 'Bicycles tend to sink. As I suspect you remember.' This was a low blow. A much younger Jordan, insisting that she *could so* ride a two-wheeler, had borrowed cousin Severn's new ten-speed, intending to coast up to a bunch of cousins on the dock, and had instead ridden right through cousin Trent and off the edge. They'd never let her forget it. 'Go, go, Bike Girl ... '

'Ah, a funny! You made a funny. I am laughing so hard inside at your hilarious funny!' When I lurched up as if to come at her she added, 'I mean, you could lead Yogi on your bicycle, since you're too – ' I moved in. 'Too self-preserving to do so on foot?'

'What the cluck are you clucking about?' I closed my eyes. Of course, I knew exactly what she was talking about, and she knew full well that I knew full well, et cetera, et cetera.

'Is Mumsie's baby boy bwave enough to wide away fwum da fwearsome tweddy bear? Can snookums pedal his widdle feet fwast enough?'

I responded with predictable courage and tact: I capsized her mattress. She almost vamoosed, but I nabbed the end of her braid. I reeled her in hand over hand, looped that braid around her neck and lynched her underwater until she yelled aunt a second time. She broke the surface unbroken and yelling. 'Go off with your mail-stealing pal and drown something together! Unlike me, you're related to him.' So I noosed her again – if truth be told, for longer than necessary. She emerged limp, her lips blue. 'You're bloody well trying to kill me!'

'Bollocks! Go shoe the geese. Or better still, go tell it on the mountain.'

'No. This bear's climbing over it.' She retrieved her mattress, still struggling to breathe. 'That's the last time you'll ever do that. Do you hear me? *The last time!*'

'Yeah? And you and whose army's gonna stop me?'

If I thought aunt was aunt when she fell back coughing, I was mistaken. Aunt didn't last five minutes. 'Seriously, BB, hear me out. We'd tie something she likes – say, maybe, butter tarts – to the back of your banana seat. You'd ride up Hezzy's back pasture dropping them one by one. She'd follow the scent right into MacIsaac's. You'd be perfectly safe.'

I sat up, straddling my mattress like a saddle. 'Well, BS, even if this so-called plan made a lick of sense, which it doesn't, and even if I could condone the waste of perfectly good pastry, which I can't, aren't you forgetting something?'

'No, I don't think so. What? What have I forgotten?'

'Let's see. It's called a padlock. You can't just go up to Kronk and say, 'Hey buddy, can I borrow the key? See you later, man. I'm just taking your cash cow for a little walk.'

She snorted. 'The key? Who'd forget that? Kronk keeps them in the Coke cooler, but he's had Mrs. Miller make multiples because he's always losing them when he's drunk. She'll make any key for a nickel.' She swatted a horse fly. 'She made one last week, in fact.'

'Oh, man! Tell me you didn't ... '

'No, it fell into my sock drawer by accident.' I squinted at her. 'Oh, don't be a retard, midget-idjit. Of course I did.'

'Seriously? I figured you were just whistling Dixie.'

'No pucker here, man.' She knew I'd be goofing on that one so she did it first, improvising her favourite line from *Horton Hears a Who*, 'I meant what I said and I said what I meant. Your sister is faithful, one hundred percent. I've done my part. So will you do yours?'

'Let's see. Your part involves waving bye-bye, and my part involves going bye-bye. Likely by dismemberment. Hmmm ... No. And no, not sorry.'

'Fine.' She slipped off her air mattress. 'Don't help me get my mail back and don't help me free Yogi. It's not as if I should be able to count on you or anything.'

Wait for it. With all of March out catching a bit of breeze before hide-and-seek, she towed the mattress to her best advantage, pointed back in my direction and theirs, and began flapping and clucking – don't forget the clucking – like a chicken on speed. Damn her hide. Did they laugh? What do you think? It came out of my mouth unbidden, 'Damn! Damn! ... Damn, damn, damn!' If I sounded like Bamm-Bamm, like a petulant cartoon kid itchin' for a hurly-burly smackdown, then so be it. That's how a misty morning may become a clear day.

HAIR

Friday, July 18. Bedtime. Apollo 11 may have been en route to the moon, but my parents were ending this day like any other, with the *Toronto Star* in front of their faces and the CHEX broadcast a few feet beyond. Tea and cookies reduced to dribbles and crumbs. News of the planet reduced to Chappaquiddick, a name that opened some interesting anatomical possibilities for When Fenelon Falls. Seems Ted Kennedy, following in the steps – or should I say sheets – of his tomcat brothers, had dumped his latest fling, Mary Jo Kopechne, literally dumped her dead right off a dock. Presto! Another obscure little town becomes darkly famous.

Jordan sat tight against Mom's legs, the nightly position for her mandatory hundred strokes, because time, tide and snocksnarls wait for no man. Mom's wire hairbrush whipped on autopilot, deep and hard. MC scraped skull with her right hand and read the paper with her left. Between distracted and uninterested, she frequently smacked her daughter in the face. But if Jordan tried to beg off, Mom uttered the inevitable, 'Comb seldom, comb sore.'

That night BS left off uttering *ouch* every seven seconds and strained toward the TV. Compelled by all things Kennedy, she kept pictures in her room of JFK and the recently assassinated RFK, both surrounded by a funeral array of black crepe paper. When she dropped her magazine, some teen fashion rag, probably *Seventeen*, a bribe from Auntie E, it fell open to Twiggy. How'd I know her name? You'd have to live under a rock not to – the start of all the fuss. A boyish haircut and too skinny to be a healthy role model for young girls. At the time I figured, who cares? Was she good-looking? That's her Seminal Question. Hell no! The chest of a nine-year-old and hair shorter than the Beatles. Notta woppa, but stilla no boppa.

Mom glanced down at her and sniffed. Dad followed the sniff and said, 'Her again? She always reminds me of what Italian fathers did to wayward daughters during the war.'

MC cleared her throat and rattled her paper. Too late. Jordan sparked. 'Wayward, Dad? What's that? Lost?' She knew the answer, but wanted to make them give it.

Dad turned to Mom expecting her to answer for him, which of course, she did. She set her paper and the brush down and began braiding. 'During the war, Jordan, young women in many countries, not just Italy, dated American soldiers. British and Canadian ones, too,' she added. 'You know that. Many became war brides like Mrs. Whitton back on Delma.'

'Mother, if you don't want to define "wayward" I'm sure Uncle H will.' Good one.

'Trust me, dear. A girl who gets educated by Howard won't end up with a diploma.'

'So?' Jordan handed MC an elastic and twisted the belt of her dressing gown tight.

'Well, it was wartime, not that that's any excuse. But some girls, wayward girls, used it as one. They went too far.' She reopened her paper. 'They had babies. Out-of-wedlock babies.'

'Bastards,' I offered helpfully, but everyone ignored me.

'Your father was referring to an old custom. When an Italian family discovered their unmarried daughter was pregnant, they held her down and shaved her head.'

'Oh. But why? It's humiliating. Didn't she feel bad enough already?' She wrapped a protective hand around her hair. 'How could it possibly help?'

'It wasn't supposed to. It was a message, a symbol.'

'Short hair?'

'Yes. Back then, only ladies of the evening – '

'Who?'

'Prostitutes. Back then only prostitutes had short hair.'

'Her family turned her into a prostitute?'

'No, no. The family did it to show their daughter which side her bread was buttered on, to humble her, and to prove to the village that they didn't share her shame.'

'I see,' said Jordan. 'So they shamed her more. They made their own daughter look and feel like a prostitute.' She closed her magazine and began to roll it tight. 'If they did that to their own child, what did they do to the man?' Insert a silence most uncomfortable here. Newspapers slid back in front of faces, an insufficient shield. Jordan yelled it down. 'I repeat. *What did they do to the man?'*

Suddenly the parents couldn't take their eyes off a dead girl's little wet Volkswagen. Silence thicker than tree sap. Jordan took a deep, considered breath. Mary Jo Kopechne smiled. 'What if the girl was raped? Was it still her shame then? Was she forced to give the baby away? Would they shave her hair off then, if it wasn't her fault, or if it was as long as mine?'

Mom folded the paper wall and erected an impenetrable one. 'Bedtime, Missy Asks-Too-Much. *Now!* Not another word. Dishes and go. Good night.' She added just a hair's breadth too late, 'dear.' Jordan's lowered eyes never left the floor.

And then it was Saturday morning. July 19. Our third trip into Fenelon. Maybe we'd finally see some of it this time. We swallowed the last bite of fried tomatoes and cows' brains at 8:30 sharp, rose from the table and went straight to the car. The Grocery Protocol. We left at 8:30 sharp. Why? We were twelve minutes away, and the IGA opened at 9:00 a.m. Arriving at 8:42 ensured MC her pride of place as first in line. She said a cottager had to be first, to avoid those vile Trenter types who slept and shopped later than good common sense allows. The whole truth, however, included four more words: Getting There Before Kronk. Those stale butter tarts wouldn't go into Yogi if she could get them into us first. We didn't have to shop with her, but we had to be back in seventy minutes to help her load Tessie. As we pulled into the parking lot, MC clicked the start button, handed Jordan the stopwatch, and said what she said every time: 'Sixty-nine minutes, fifty-nine seconds and counting. Have fun.'

Out of sight, and eager to get her out of mind, we took that count for every second. Our Freedom March from March. Some Saturdays it seemed endless, plenty-twenty time to stomp through every store in town. After all, Colborne Street is all of two blocks long. At one end sat the Canadian Tire with room after room of surprises, up and down stairs with twists and turns like a rabbit warren. Cider's China Shoppe stood across the street, opposite in every way. We'd go in and pretend to be enamoured with the hand-painted teacups. Jordan would twist her uneven gait into the dance moves of the china ballerinas, just to see how nervous the blue-haired bunch could get.

None of them saw a tutu. They threw old-lady manners in her face and asked her to leave. Sometimes kindly; sometimes not.

We'd scurry across the street to Bell's Bakery, happy just to stand on the creaky wooden floor, inhaling the steam loaf and the Chelsea buns to watch how quickly Mrs. Bell could tie up the cake and cookie boxes with the cone of creamy string suspended from the ceiling. We'd stop at the butcher's to watch him write on the pink paper meat parcels with a huge black marker that I claimed smelled stronger than the meat. That Saturday was Stedman's Sidewalk Sale. BS hemmed and hawed over some yellow barrettes, picking them up and putting them down. In the end she set them down so hard – all but threw them – so I almost missed the sniffle. Did I catch on? Did I care enough to ask? Not me.

Our next stop was always the tiny Fenelon library where Missy Peace, resplendent in her navy polka dot dress and white gloves, was waiting. Smaller than our living room, her volunteer library proved the principle of super-saturation – every cubic inch sogged with mildew. She unearthed the heaviest tomes for my sister, who'd read everything else. Still, it inevitably took longer than necessary for BS to exchange her seven-book limit. It took longer than bearable for Missy P to dip her fountain pen into her brass inkwell and write a spidery 'Jordan May March' and the full date still a month away, 'Saturday, August 16, in the Year of our Lord, 1969,' a full fourteen times: once on the lender's list glued to each bookplate and once on the faded blue index card that Missy P removed from the envelope glued in the back. She squared the pile each time she added a card, put the pile in alphabetical order by title, then squared it again. She hunted down the Ms in the alphabetical clusters she kept in a sewing machine drawer, secured by elastic bands.

I often complained about how long it took – couldn't Missy P at least leave the 'Year of Our Lord' part out, or maybe write 'YOOL'? But Jordan said no, she loved to watch Missy P touch each book as if it were her child. Who needs those ugly, newfangled date stamps?

It may have charmed BS but it bored me silly. I'd slip out and walk the half block to the end of town to scout out the Roxy. Like most small-town Ontario theatres back then it played reruns, city movies from the winter before, because rural beggars can't be

choosers. That Saturday was still *The Love Bug*. Up next, however –
the poster was still there and likely would be all summer – was *Butch
Cassidy and the Sundance Kid*, a flick most definitely worth an
encore. We got to see three a summer. Last summer we saw *Planet
of the Apes* and *Charly* and the Boss: *2001: A Space Odyssey*. Could I
get BS's vote for *B and S*? Probably. I waited on our bench full of
thishful winking: maybe at Fenelon's next Midnight Madness
they'd show *Midnight Cowboy* or *Easy Rider* and just maybe –
according to cousins, it did happen – they'd turn a blind eye to age
restrictions, or wouldn't lock the back window.

Jordan caught up, plunked her book bag on the bench, and
snorted at the marquee. 'What do you want to bet Aunt May takes
her little Love Bug to see Herbie?'

'What do you want to bet he doesn't understand it?'

'Good one, BB.'

'Thank you, BS.'

'He could make a movie: Derwie the Unloved Bug.'

'Wouldn't see it. Would you?'

'Nope. Not me. Better Herbie than Derbie.'

'Yet another good one, BS.'

'Yet another thank you, BB.'

Having exhausted both our cleverness and the business section
of Fenelon, we walked down the canal to admire the huge cliffs of
greying granite that lined it, under the bridge to get misted by the
falls, then up to the dairy to watch boats rise and fall through the
locks. Dad had given us our Saturday dime, so we could buy a cone
and stand with the tourists, a long bovine row of them, all of us proving we could observe gravity and lick at the same time.

'I made a movie once,' Jordan offered between tentative jabs at
her Maple Walnut. Ice cream hurt her teeth. I snorted. When I said
Dad filmed everyone's first jump off Grandpa's dock but that didn't
count as a movie, she added, 'God's truth.'

'Sure, man, and I'm Mahatma Gandhi.'

'Cross my heart and hope to die, Mahatma.'

'Okay, Missy Movie Star, where and when?'

'When I was nine. In the basement of Sick Kids Hospital.' My
Tin Roof required diligent attention. I developed a sudden need to
iron my stare. She continued anyway. 'They put rolls of brown

paper on the floor. They painted the bottoms of my feet with India ink and then they filmed me walking on it.'

'Sure they did. And then they filmed Mahatma likewise.'

'There were three cameramen. One filmed my feet, one filmed me top to bottom and the last one, he filmed me from behind.'

'Wow! That's one hot blockbuster of a movie!'

'Actually, I was kinda cold.' She broke off a chunk of cone. 'I had no clothes on.'

'You and the emperor. Both in a fairy tale. That's some good BS, BS.'

'It is not! Ask MC. She was right there the whole time, chatting up the doctors.'

'Bull roar! D'you really expect me to believe that my mother sat in a chair and let three dirty old men film her nine-year-old daughter naked as a jaybird?'

She almost dropped her cone. 'Yes, that's exactly what happened. But don't put it like that – they weren't old.' She looked alarmed. 'And it wasn't dirty. It was for science.'

That answer had no BS, only pure baby sister, reminding me that, despite her adult brain, she really was so young. That alone should have made me stop. It didn't. 'Science? No way. That's just plain sicko dirty.' (Of course, the term I needed was 'kiddie porn,' another miracle of modernity that no one had ever heard of in 1969.)

'No, it's not! She said it was for medical research.' Maple rivulets mimicked dishwater and cascaded down her right elbow. She tossed her cone into the canal. 'She said I had to.'

Finally, I stopped for sorry. And at least I asked it. Something I'd always wondered. 'So what did the doctors say? About your feet. About how they got that way, I mean?'

'No room at the inn.'

'What?'

'Sorry, private joke. They said 'no room in the womb,' I misunderstood and asked why there was no room at the inn. Mom told Dad. She thought it was particularly funny.'

At least I said, 'It isn't, BS. It's not funny at all.' And I have the memory of her smile back, full and open in gratitude, 'Thanks, man. You're right.'

Sixty-nine minutes and counting, we ran for it. MC stood next to Tessie with the trunk open, tapping a pointy pink toe. Watching us hoof it double-time into the parking lot, she held out her hand for the stopwatch and sighed her I-expected-as-much sigh. Seventy minutes and seven seconds. MC noted that Missy Late-Is-Late had gotten ice cream in her hair and added, 'You know, dear, if you lifted those feet just a little bit faster, people probably wouldn't stare so much at those hideously masculine shoes. Maybe we should put pink laces in them, hmm?'

We hefted the overfilled brown bags into the trunk. MC took each one out and repacked it properly with, as any fool knows, the frozen food bags on the left, the cold stuffs in the middle and the room temperature bags on the right where the sun comes in the window. We rode a silent twelve minutes. Upon arrival, she criticized how many bags Jordan carried, the way she carried them and how long it took her to carry them. Jordan opened the freezer twice, when, as any idiot knows, the correct procedure is to pile all newly purchased freezables on a tray, to move said tray to the mouth of said freezer and then and only then pry it open once, thus minimizing the amount of cold loss by decreasing the maximum proximity of the freezer to all that which must be or must stay frozen. Enough said.

HAZEL #51

I asked Margaret Ann to cancel the shivaree, thought I'd spare Walter that much, but she said, 'Just how in the world do you expect me to do that? I can't possibly get a hold of everyone we know in one day!' So I stayed. One night won't matter. That's what I told myself. Margaret Ann had wanted me to leave before it. 'Shivaree be damned,' she actually said. She wanted me to stick it to Walter. I figured she'd have enjoyed being one of the well-wishers sneaking up the back stairs and into our bedroom in the middle of the night to beat on pots and pans to wish us newlyweds good luck, knowing all along that the bride had made her own luck and left him. I bet she'd have liked to watch Walter try to squirm out of that. But it just seemed too cruel, too public, so I stayed.

When he left for the bank the next morning, Margaret Ann drove me straight to Susie. I had two bags packed, one for my baby and one for me. Her things were all new; I'd kept them hidden for some time and I couldn't wait to show them to her. I ran up the walk to the veranda of her foster home. I rang the doorbell three times before a little boy with a bandage on his head and his arm in a cast opened the door. My alarm bells were ringing. I asked him if I could please speak to his mummy. He held the door wide and I heard her before I saw her.

'Go 'way! Naw innerested!' She tried to sit up on the couch as I entered and instead fell forward, banging her knee on the coffee table and knocking a half-filled glass to the rusty carpet. She swore and ordered the little boy to bring her another.

'Excuse me ... I ... I'm just here for Susie, my baby.'

She grinned. She tried to light a cigarette and dropped it. She laughed. 'You're late. Too late. A day late and a baby short. Too bad. So sad.' She turned her face to the wall.

I turned to the little boy. He shook his head. 'Mummy's sad because my baby sister Debbie doesn't live here anymore.'

I didn't want to frighten him. I got down on my knees and smiled, 'It's Susie, honey. Her name is Susie. So where does she live then, dear?'

Her face crumpled. 'No, it's Debbie and she had a car crash. She went to live with the angels.'

I slapped him. So much harder than necessary. So hard I knocked him down. I ran to the car and told Margaret Ann to drive. Just drive. Anywhere. It didn't matter where. Nothing mattered. Nothing would ever matter again. My Susie was dead.

In the end, I made Margaret take me back to Walter. It's exactly what I deserve. When your heart stops, it's only a matter of time until the rest of you dies too. I might as well get a head start on hell. And for that, there's no place like home.

GOOD MORNING STARSHINE

We'd been wandering through Hezzy's fields, popping milkweed pods and letting the sun melt the chill of MC's freezer, when Jordan made me an offer I never refused: 'Wanna see a man about a rock?'

That was her standard invitation to wait for me while I climbed the tree house, a giant balsam on the edge of Hezzy's lower pasture overlooking the bay, one of my haunts, but a place she'd seldom frequented even at the tree-climbing stage. She'd sit on the step-up rock, coincidentally also pink granite, a scaled-down replica of her Marie Curtis boulder. Legend has it rolled up against the tree by Grandpa for his kids to climb when they were the little ones. I'd call down to her as I reached all seven platforms. Each was nothing more than a few boards strung by uncles, but for the shirtless, gravel-shucking boys of March they measured our manhood. We knew how old each of us had been when we reached platform three, or five or seven. Most of the girls gave up at five and of course one of them never made it to one. Or so we thought.

At platform three, maybe some thirty feet off the ground, there's a large hole, sometimes inhabited by birds, and often used by cousins. By habit, I stuck my hand in and checked it out every time. Usually there was nothing, but over the years I'd found a jackknife and a Duncan top, and once even some firecrackers. This incendiary device was a bright yellow envelope, one with a wolf's warning where my name should be:

> Balsam Lake may be compared to a wolf's head with the long muzzle pointing southward as South Bay, two long ears pricked up into Northwest Bay and the Gull River estuary and the neck half represented by West Bay. It is a large lake and only the wolf's snout projects down into Fenelon Township.
> – Watson Kirkconnel, *History of County Victoria*

Despite the fact that I stood a good three storeys off the ground, the first impulse of this hero was to run. It had to be pure serendipity. One very lucky guess. She couldn't possibly have hunted me. She couldn't possibly see me as wolfen as Dex or Der. I thought of myself as better. When I hunted Trenters, all I did was watch.

And if I'd been served evidence and indictment, why the Sam Hill did she want me to read it in a tree? The answer hit me with the question. Because it was a guess. Because up here, I was caged and on display. Because then she could stand by and stare and laugh, as she watched me swallow whatever crap she'd cooked up. No thank you. Not this little bear cub.

I'm sure it was because I'd been goaded. I'm sure it was because it was hot. I know I'm not crazy. But as I watched my runners land confidently on each limb on the climb down, I suddenly saw her shoes. I heard the chicken chant and this time it was meant for me. As angry as I was about what she'd just tried to do to me, it was nothing compared to what she'd risked doing to herself. New leather, so slick on one fallen log, just one, had already dumped her into the swamp. And to deliver this piece of mail, she'd had to balance on even thinner appointed rounds, on branches that swayed in the wind. Had she fallen, it would have been a bloody splashdown.

So when I glanced down again, I saw more than danger. I saw my feet in her shoes. I blinked. I shut my eyes and counted to ten, but I couldn't shake them off my feet. I had no choice but to descend as she had. Confidence left the tree. I felt each branch repel each shoe, as if the tree itself was taunting me, eager to see me fall. I clung like a frightened newborn monkey. With each unstable footfall, I saw my ankle snap and heard myself scream. By touchdown, I was shaking. If the rivulets on my face felt like blood, sweat and tears, I couldn't let her know it.

I pulled the yellow flag from my pocket, held it aloft, leaned in her face and hollered, 'What the cluck are you trying to prove, you absolutely ridiculous little girl?'

She pushed her nose into mine and yelled back, 'Probability. My version of it.'

'Really, BS?' I pointed at her shoes, if only to be sure they were on her feet not mine. 'The only probability here is that you could have killed yourself!'

Jordan smiled. 'You think I wore my Go Go Gopher boots? To climb a tree?' She shook her head. 'I'm melodramatic, not messianic. I took them off.'

'Jordan, that's utter BS. Without your shoes you can't – '

'Don't get excited. Don't turn pale. I used a climbing map like the one in Rosedale.' I blinked. 'You know, like the jumping map Dad made us for the Rosedale Roxy.' She fished another sheet out of her shorts, this one in notation: LH3, Left Hand 3rd branch, RF1, Right Foot 1st branch, RH4. Yes, she'd numbered and annotated every limb. All the way up.

'It's paper!' I crumpled it and tossed it at a cow patty. 'Are you seriously telling me that you think putting this – this stupid list – on paper kept you safe?'

She shrugged. 'Yes. Anything you put on paper keeps you safe. At least for a while.'

'BS, BS!' I walked back to the rock and sat down. And then I added it up. 'That is, assuming you actually did this yourself?'

'Fine. I didn't. I paid a Trenter. I bribed Derwood. I hired Rocket J. Squirrel. I hijacked the WABAC machine. It doesn't matter how I did it. What matters is that you get the message. So read it already.

Set stopwatch. Open sock drawer. Find ugly red socks. Remove screwdriver from left sock. Remove screws from window brackets. Put brackets in left sock. Pull crochet hook out of right sock. Pass hook through screen, snag frame and pop the window free. Good one. Much better than Dad's army knife. No tell-tale scars. Store hook in sock and socks in drawer. Close drawer. Check silence. Remove screen. Stash screen under pillow. Sweet dreams. With back to window, sit on dresser, lean head and arms through. Reach up, grab basketball hoop. Swing feet over ledge. Right. Left. Hang. Drop to picnic table. Hush Balsam. Check silence. Black as black. Tiny moon. Few stars. No uncles. Operation Starshine: good to go.

New gravel crunches, avoid it. Edge the swamp by back porch light. Step into the mystic, running blind. Fifty steps past Tessie, hit the road, Jack. Straight for three hundred. Bend left for twenty-three. At cottagette, bend right. Take the

156

quick centre curve in seventeen. Two-hundred-eighty-three strides in a slow left bend to the bear cage. Grab pole, swing a sharp right. Hit pavement and head out on the highway. Count lights. One: Kronk's. Two: the store. Three: the Gov Dock. Four: the bridge. Five: the dam. Breathe for the hill. Lean back for the decline down. It's a damned good road to a damned good time.

Which trailer tonight? Looking for some Trenters and whatever cousin comes this way. Let's try lucky number 7. No curtains and a pretty blonde. What's the score, Blondie? Two, no, three boys and another girl. Hey, not fair! Any cousins? Just Dex. Dex and a dozen empty brewskis. A game well underway. Blondie spins the bottle and gets the red-haired guy. 'Private,' he calls before she can say, 'Public.' They move into the bedroom. Yeah, buddy, go make it happen. You change windows. Take that Trenter in a love embrace. See your hands on Wendy's shoulders, down her back. Pull her in for the kill. Major tongue action. Your hands fumble buttons. Hand on bra. Hand in bra. The screen pops. 'Who's there?' Blondie gasps.

Thank Christ for running shoes. Resist the urge to run. Move like smoke, not lightning. Number 6 is vacant, empty and black as the ace of spades. Your ace. Blondie's door splits open like heavy metal thunder. You hide with the wind, in the shadow that you're under. The suckers. They run right past you. You fire all of your guns at once, and explode into space. Time to go.

Uphill, brace for down. Dam, marina, dock, store, Yogi – what the Sam Hill is that? Kronk, sloshed on the picnic table, snoring. Another Rosedale Sunday, here in Yanker-Wanker land. Swing left. Gravel, slow down. Long right bend, centre curve, cottagette, left bend, straight, gravel to grass and stop. Pant. She'd say, 'Pull your tongue in; you're not some kind of wild dog.' But this is one of the few times you can ignore her. Let the good times loll.

Suddenly there are stars. And music. The day has eyes, the night has ears. Frogs, crickets, bats, coyotes and wolves – you hear all the creatures of the night, rejoicing in full voice. Join them. For one moment, you are truly nature's child. Then it's car, swamp, table, hoop, dresser, bed. Screen and screws. Stash tool sock. Close door. Click stopwatch: sixty-nine minutes, seven seconds. No one's gonna die.

With each dawn you hear the sound of her key in the lock, but on mornings like this you're alert, ears pricked and ready. It doesn't matter when the grinding comes. These are wolf mornings. After a prowl, when your yellow eyes have run through the night and stared it down, when you have robbed the darkness of its darker power, when you are not the prey or the preyed upon, then you get your reward, the sweetest of bubble gum, the gift of Bazooka Joe, complete with all the *nibby, nabby, nooby*s. You get to be an ordinary kid jumping out of an ordinary bed. Nightmare free, sitting at breakfast, is an ordinary girl in ordinary yellow jammies, humming an absolutely ordinary early morning singing song, 'Good morning, Starshine. The earth says hello. You twinkle above us. We twinkle below.'

RUBY, DON'T TAKE YOUR LOVE TO TOWN

At 5:30 a.m. MC unlocks the door and palms the key. It's Sunday, July 20, and it's early, purposefully earlier than necessary on March and Moonwalk Sunday morning. She lays our Sunday best at the foot of beds that still contain us and hauls a squeaky wringer washer out from behind the fridge. Her perfectly good wedding present. Its protestations could raise the grateful dead or at least us sleeping ingrates, which is, of course, its most appealing function and the real reason it isn't carpeting Atlantis. Yes, much newer and fully functional automatic washers have been tossed into the swamp, but her mother paid good money for this one and if it ain't broke, it ain't landfill.

So every cottage Sunday, as soon as it's light enough to see, she dumps our laundry on the kitchen floor and checks our pockets for gum, for money, for firecrackers and frogs. You're right. It is entirely illogical to check for live frogs in the pockets of shorts that have been in a laundry bin for as much as a week. But once burnt is twice as paranoid. She once put a big brown one through the wringer and, well, popping a mudfrog like a giant zit doesn't enhance anyone's fine washables. In the city, laundry happened haphazardly any day of the week, but on every cottage Sunday my mother laundered everything in sight. And I do mean exactly that: every blessed thing, every towel and washcloth, every drapery, dust-cover and doily.

You have to understand there was nothing modern or easy about this process: cart water up from the lake and heat it to boiling in giant washtubs on the stove. Pour it into the washer too fast and the splashbacks sizzle wherever they land. Burns splay up her arms like measles. Add clothes, a handful of powdered soap and crank the handle for twenty minutes. It isn't soup you're stirring; it's fifty pounds of scalding dirt stew. Ignore the blisters. Clean items must be fished out of the smoking tub, fed to the wringer by a pole, caught

159

on the same pole as they exit flat and steamy from the rear, then flung off said pole into the huge wicker basket. Cart the basket in sweaty shifts to the hundred-foot clothesline, pluck each item from the smouldering pile and hang it with wooden pegs. Your mouth holds six at once. Make lunch while it dries. Pull it down peg by peg and cart it back to the kitchen. Unlock laundry cupboard. Set up board, iron, starch, sprinkler, press cloths, sock stretchers and a tailor's ham. Commence ironing. Make dinner. Iron some more. You might be done by midnight.

In her defence, I have never met anyone who could iron like my mother, the last practitioner of a lost art no one will notice is missing. Her creations weren't just flat, they were incandescently flat. Garments weren't just folded: seams matched in halves and quarters with the exactitude of a diamond cutter, with creases like razor blades. She knew exactly how to pull and coax each item around her board or tailor's ham, knew exactly which cloths and how much spray and starch would get it flat and creased and able to stand as pristine proof that dry cleaning was for lazy people. She began with the starchables: the pillowcases, sheets, blouses and shirts. Then she ironed kid clothes: pants, pop tops, pyjamas and pedal-pushers, jeans, shorts, T-shirts and the two dozen triangle headscarves that tamed Jordan's hair. Then came the towels: dishtowels, swim towels, bath towels, hand towels, face cloths and dish cloths. Finally, the underwear and yes, I mean all of it. Not just Dad's boxers. She ironed her brassieres. And her girdle. Then one by one she ironed our socks.

Penance, you ask? The heat of an iron in the heat of July? Perhaps. Getting back at Dad for going off to *his* church with *his* family? Equally possible. If your Sunday observances occur in a kitchen, you can still qualify for martyrdom. Consider the criteria: repeated, ritualized sacrifice. Self-inflicted pain. A true believer who'd rather die than change her ways. One who lives with the dirty infidels only to save them from the error of their ignorance. If it throws itself on the pile like a martyr – enough said. That's as close to an answer as I can give you. In the end I don't know why she did it. I'm not sure she did either. It was because it was.

Back home, she had less motivation to zealotry. Only Jordan went to church there. At nine, without permission, BS took it upon herself to join Alderwood United, only half a block up Delma, a building so simple that our holier-than-thou High Anglican family wouldn't have called it a church. She sang in the choir and attended the youth group, Cornerstone. She joined Explorers, earned all her stars and moved up to CGIT (Canadian Girls in Training, which sounds like a detention program for wayward girls, but is really Girl Guides sans cookies). BS loved Explorers. She voluntarily ironed her own uniform. She embroidered a banner with their motto: 'Be Do'ers of the Word and Not Hearers Only.' Every Tuesday night at 6:45, Mom griped about coughing up a whole quarter for dues and left a table full of dirty dishes for her out-gallivanting daughter to clear and clean when she got home at 8:15. Between choir practice, Explorers, Cornerstone and Sunday, BS met her maker four days out of seven.

Since Jordan had the God thing more than covered and he had the film to prove it, Dad saw no reason to admit that the rest of us weren't as devout as she was. But in the place where Grandpa had been minister, Dad either felt the pull of tradition or didn't want to be pulled aside by Aunt May, who took her job as self-anointed Chief of the Sabbath Police very seriously. Whatever reasons he gave himself, they weren't good enough for my mother. She never went, not even on March Sunday and she never explained why. 'No decent woman could ever consent to be in the same room as that vile Kronkowski person,' she'd say, but no one took that for the back-story. Whatever it was, she considered it worth invoking both the wrath of God Himself and that of She Who Speaks For Him.

Aunt May explained the divine mystery at the Saturday bonfire: 'Just think, the Lord picked March Sunday to put men on the moon! He had all of His 364 other days to choose from and He picked March Sunday! In appreciation we must fill every pew. Take pride in our pride of place! Now, Tommy.' She patted Dad's hand. 'All of us, even you, must stay a full five minutes to accept congratulations from the congregation. That's the Sacred Five-Minute Rule.'

She, how could it be otherwise, plopped every Sunday into the most conspicuous seat, basking in the reflected light beneath the pulpit. That's where Her Holy Behind was fleshly ensconced that Sunday, March Moonwalk Sunday, the day my sister became an atheist.

Before you start feeling sorry for BS, let's cut to the wood: I never fully bought it. Not lock, stock and barrel. As always, you can judge for yourself, but it always seemed to me that what she loved wasn't religion but religiosity. She loved the make-believe of it, the theatre, the community of voices intoning together, the sound of ordinary singing. She loved the idea of God's house as home and the faithful as family. I'll grant she had reason to long for both. But church also gave her what she loved even more: an opportunity to show off. To win the 'I-Know-God-Best-Aren't-I-Amazing Race,' to leave those who were made of dust behind in it. She could go all winter without hearing a word of the-Venite-found-on-page-thirteen-of-your-hymnal, or the-Jubilate-Deo-found-on-page-twenty-three – Reverend Southwell announced each in one long drone of a word – and get up on March Sunday and recite every blessed line. She loved the test of it, the play-acting, so holy right under the nose of Herself. She'd stare right at Aunt May during the Apostle's Creed: '*He* ascended into heaven, where *He* sitteth on the right hand of God the father almighty from whence *He* shall come to judge the Quick and the Dead.' Did Aunt May catch the emphasis? Did she know we didn't go to church in the city? She got no clue that we were rusty Anglicans from Jordan. I made myself invisible in the back of the loft, but BS, she stood first and sat last, knew every response and each Amen. She could beat the Rev. to the punch. And frequently did.

The hymns were her coups-de-grâce. Her Holy CHUM Chart, memorized by number. A heartfelt devotion or a heartfelt desire to stick it to Aunt May? Same difference. At the sound of 'We will now sing number fifty-seven in your hymnals,' Jordan would snap hers shut, which you understand she had only opened in order to be heard shutting it, plop it on her seat and stand up, head up, to sing at the top of her lungs without it. That Sunday opened with one of her foot-stomping favourites:

Will your anchor hold in the storms of life,
When the clouds unfold their wings of strife?
When the strong tides lift and the cables strain,
Will your anchor drift or firm remain?

Aunt May had peeked thrice. Score: Self-Righteous 3, Sanctimonious 0. Am I too judgmental? Maybe BS was exactly what she seemed, the most angelic of Anglicans. Maybe I was just a devilish shade of green. Maybe when you have an audience, you have to play to win, because up in the loft you're not just in church, you're not benched and observing – you're centre ice, on display where all can rate your game. Elevated directly behind the Reverend, and facing the congregation, you don't have a choice not to be good and good at it – you'd be seen. Drop the service puck and everyone would know. You'd be cut from the team. Again.

I told myself it wasn't so bad for her. She was a girl, creatures in my experience, always open to being on display. She looked younger too. No older than last year, thanks to that stupid yellow sundress. No, if BS had been handed lemons, she'd made herself some pretty smug lemonade. And I'll admit the loft gave me an advantage too. Although I half believed the congregated could stare right through me, up behind the Rev., at least he couldn't see us and we, looking out over the assembled, could see some pretty interesting things. Jordan could stick it to Aunt May, who watched like a beak-ready vulture, waiting for her great-niece to make the mistake that never came, and I could watch my pal Stankus. I'd hoped that Stank would offer an encore in honour of March Sunday, but no such luck. Short of scraping boogers on the pew in front of him, he hadn't done much at all. The shine had come off the drool.

Jordan wasn't having any fun either. She liked to reach deep into her voice and twist sideways to stare at Uncle H at this line of the Venite: 'Grant, oh most heavenly father, that we may hereafter live *a godly, righteous and sober life*.' But he was ready for her, his eyes out the window. Finally, the final amen. The Reverend exited and, as always, Aunt May flowed out behind him, first in his wake.

After the service, you had to shake the minister's hand. Reverend S posted himself in the doorway while Aunt May held us hostage inside, clamped on to his hand as it were a paddle to heaven. All decked out for Her Sunday in a barf-green dress with a lumpy brown necklace that looked for all the world like turds on a string, she felt entitled to an extra-long white-glove lock, entitled to remind him yet again that her brother, was *the first minister, the chosen one*. She leaned into his face, spraying it with foamy saliva from the scotch mint that lived in her mouth. We knew it wasn't a mint at all; it was the Sunday Sucking Stone, a pebble of white gravel that she kept in a jar with her teeth, only to be used on Sunday. (The stone, not her teeth, obviously.)

When Rev. Southwell complimented Aunt May on family attendance and particularly on how well Miss March, her great-niece, knew
the service, Aunt May's response crashed through the open windows,
bounced to every ear off the nameless and useless long-dead saints in
stained glass. Loud. Kristallnacht Loud. Far beyond the pale.

'Lord only knows where she gets it from! She doesn't come by it
honestly. She's no chicken for all her cheeping and she's no March –
neither fish nor flesh nor good red herring.' She winked. 'I suppose
sometimes even the nigger in the woodpile gets the spirit.'

Encircling a small white church with forest-green trim, an army of
buzzing bees energetically pollinated the thicket of blood-red roses.
Thorns pricked the faithful. There was no other sound. Aunt Elsbeth
smiled, but had the good grace to try and stop. Missy Peace tried to
smile at Jordan. My sister wouldn't meet her eye. Someone broke the
silence and of course it was Derwood. He laughed. Uncle H hit him
over the head with his hymnal. Then he winked. Grandma, who
usually waited for last, began excusing herself, politeness abandoned
to panic, pushing to get to Jordan before Jordan got to Aunt May.

Aunt May posed at the Reverend's side, oblivious, flushed like a
bride in her receiving line, purring, clinging to her beloved's left as
he shook with his right. Proverbial Scottish butter wouldn't melt in
her mouth, let alone that scotch mint. When the hand outstretched
was Dad's, the Rev turned the colour of my bruise. He opened his
mouth, but Aunt May spoke for him.

'How nice to see your little family here this morning, Tommy!'
She turned to Jordan. 'But I don't see your lovely mother, dear?'

Perhaps we shouldn't have been surprised. When you cut to the
crux, my sister was, first and foremost, a girl child of the fifties – a
good girl – one raised to be obedient, to answer the questions of her
elders with the truth. 'No, ma'am. She'd rather do laundry. At least
she has the class not to do it in front of the whole fucking church.'

Now you've got to understand. This was 1969. The word 'fuck' did
not exist. No one said 'fucking.' Well, okay, maybe sailors, very
drunken sailors, but certainly not little girls in yellow Sunday best
speaking to great-aunts and ministers on March Moonwalk Sunday
on their way out of church in the northern heartland of respectable
WASP Ontario. Woodstock was still a month away; Country Joe

hasn't even thought up the Fish chant: 'Gimme an F ... ' That clarion call delighted the Woodstock nation but scandalized the rest of them, so you can only imagine the effect on the pious of St. John's summer parish.

Forget men on the moon. Forget March Sunday. That 'fuck' dropped like napalm. Reverend S grabbed his cross. Aunt May hoovered the Sucking Stone. She dropped to her knees in a raspy, red-faced, hairball kind of choking. I'd have given everything I ever owned, including my Johnny Seven, to watch her die, but the distraction gave Dad his one chance and he took it. Forget Grandma. I never found out how she got home. Forget the Sacred Five-Minute Rule. Dad scooped Jordan into Tessie in under five seconds. If I hadn't been quick, he'd have left me for dead. That Sunday my father became the only parishioner ever to burn rubber on sacred ground. He peeled home, pedal to the metal, sucking air through his teeth.

I figured he'd yell all the way home. Then I figured he'd yell once we got there. I slumped in the back seat imagining what it must be like to be my sister. To know that your own father was ferrying you across the canal to familiar hell. To know that once he got you there, he'd do far worse than hold you down and shave your head. He'd hand you over to a Witch Finder General who loved her work, one who would willingly incant all the necessary proverbs to exorcise the devil out of her wayward excuse for a Gypsy Sue daughter. Better to keep the devil at the door than to have to turn her out of the house. But if you have to turn her out, so be it.

As we reached Yogi's cage, Dad shoulder-checked to turn into March. If I thought I caught a smile in the rear-view mirror, I'm sure it was nothing but thishful winking.

And what was I doing? Did I sing her sustaining songs or at least send her empathetic glances? Not exactly. Many a good tale is spoilt in the telling. Better to be alone than in bad company. Here's what I did. I sat, eyes averted out the window, energetically drumming the new Kenny Rogers song on my knees, singing under my breath, for her ears only: 'If I could move I'd get my gun and put her in the ground ...'

Once again, I could end this chapter right here with that sentence, and you'd probably think I meant Aunt May. Someone in the front seat knew better.

'Good one, Brother Mine. Most excellent.'

HAZEL #55

It's all lies, but it's good enough. I can't think about what I did, or I'll start thinking about the bottle under the sink. And I can't worry about sending Susie back to Children's Aid. What's done is over. I have to think of my own babies. Allan's going to be fine, they say, just a broken arm and some cuts from the windshield, but my Debbie might – No. One heartbreak at a time, please, sweet Jesus, please. I got the idea packing up Susie's things. I had to give her something. I thought He might appreciate it; He might see just how sorry I was. So I put what little she had in my old ballet case. But that wasn't enough. So I dressed Susie up in the pretty silk dress I'd smocked for my Debbie – I can't think that my girl might never wear it – and even put my Debbie's locket round her neck. That made the picture, but I needed some words. So I got out my old Underwood. I'm still fast. I still remember how our documents sound. Lord knows I've typed enough of them. And then I lied. I told the worker who came for Susie that this was how she'd come to me, with this case, these clothes and these papers. She took little Susie in one hand, put the papers in the case in the other, and didn't bat an eye. I'm not creative; I just couldn't send her off with nothing, so I based it on the Christmas Story. Is it too obvious? Baby Jesus had the same hard start. He was illegitimate too. When she was pregnant, his mother married a man who was not his father. When Susie grows up and reads it, well, Jesus turned out okay, didn't he? It's not blasphemy – it's sacrifice. Do you hear me, Jesus? I gave you back this baby, so we're even. If you let my baby live, I promise you Lord, I'll never drive again.

DON'T LET ME DOWN

Bunkered in the addition, awaiting the inevitable rap-tap-tap of her firing squad, we tried all afternoon to conceive of a commensurate punishment. 'Commensurate' being the Word of the Day. I incommensurately resented being there at all; I hadn't done anything wrong. But it's not as if I had a choice. So we waited. No Grandma at the door. No summons from Aunt May or Reverend Southwell. No clap of righteous thunder. The Big Guy must have been busy.

We waited all through dinner and heard nothing. Not word one. After supper Jordan decided to test the waters and headed outside before dishes, an absolute verboten. They didn't notice she was gone. When MC rang the cowbell, it was for Melmac, not for murder. But BS didn't know that and feared its summons. I had to fetch her. Without me, she'd have missed the moonwalk. Are you having déjà vu? Is her hair on fire? Martyrdom and myth don't seem so ridiculous midway through the story, do they, now that you've met the clan? And now you're all caught up on Tab C, the families. At least on this setting of the dials.

That night we watched an Eagle land on the moon as if eagles landed there every day. Jordan got sent to the sink, but what did you expect? When our Cinderella protested, when she asked as loudly as she dared about that black day in July, we didn't answer. Our silence told the have-not in our house to stay in dirty water, to be content with and deserving of servility, to shut up and put up while the rest of us Marched into human history. If up the road a bear reached out her black-gloved hands and rattled another kind of cage, no one but Jordan heard her. A flag on the moon? A fuck in the face? Good ones. Those events of March Moonwalk Sunday got swallowed so completely into the maw of March silence it was as if we'd imagined them. Insert the privilege of denial here. Of course Jordan didn't have the same dispensation.

That became clear the very next day, Monday, July 21. While Neil Armstrong and company slept on the moon, my sister got up extra early to take a small step of her own in Grandma's canoe. Ordinarily my sister was a lackadaisical paddler, one who stopped to see shapes in clouds, listen to a loon or stick her fingers into the whirling of water bugs, but that day she paddled with the determined rhythm of the Pauline Johnson poem, dip, dip and swinging it like a pro. She sighted Grand Island and beelined it in silence. Then she broke it, but not with anything I expected.

'Since nobody else will talk about it, we'll have to make do with each other. Riddle me this: this is and isn't a bastard canoe. Capiche?'

I shrugged from the bow. 'No, man. No capiche.'

She set her paddle on the gunwales. 'It isn't a bastard canoe because it isn't made of birch bark. French fur traders, like your precious Abbé Fenelon, called them *"canot bâtard"* because they were made of a less desirable, second-class material – bark, not solid wood.' She paused. 'But you do so know why this is a bastard canoe, eh paisan?' Silence gripped the mouse, and this little squeaker just kept paddling. That produced yet another incomprehensible leap through the time-logic continuum, 'Okay, Sandy and Susan. What do they mean to you?'

I stopped paddling. 'Sandy and Susan who?'

'Sandy and Susan March. The March Family. Brother, Sister, Mom, Dad and Cookie the dog. Ringing any bells?'

'What? More cousins? What closet has Aunt May been keeping them in?'

'No, pea brain. This March family lived in your Grade 1 reader. A whole series, with workbooks. Red and black and turquoise, they had a kid's chalk drawing of a little house with curly smoke on the cover. Surely you remember?'

'No. Pardon me if I've had a life since Grade 1.'

'You've only got one last name. Pardon me for expecting you to know it. In the red reader, mysteriously and without explanation I might add, Mom takes a car ride to the hospital and returns, presto, with not one baby but twins, Peter and Paul.'

'Should I anticipate a point to this? If not presto, then sometime in this lifetime?'

She took a gulp of air. 'Your mother, Mrs. MC Fridge, she's a true Snow Warden. That's a real job in the days of *Little Women*, someone hired not to clear snow away but to pack it down so iron sleigh runners could skim over an icy world. Keeping things cold and superficial, that's her one true calling. But she can't slide it past me. My point,' she turned to face me, 'is this – I'm just a nigger in the woodpile and that's why Mom is expecting.'

'So what? She's always expecting something. Ignore her.'

Jordan grabbed her paddle, smacked the water and soaked me to the bone. Good one. I thoroughly appreciated it. MC would too. Jordan interrupted my yelling by yelling louder, 'I repeat myself for the idiom idjit. *Your mother is pregnant!*'

'You're retarded. That's impossible.' Jordan just lifted her eyebrows and waited.

'She's way too old.'

'She's barely forty.'

'But it's been years since she had us.' Jordan set her paddle down and tapped it with one finger. 'You know what I mean.' Silence. 'Oh, all right,' I caved, 'since she had me.'

'That's better,' she nodded. 'I can take the let's-all-pretend Semi-Quietism crap from the rest of them, but not from you.'

'I just meant that if they'd wanted more kids they could have had plenty-twenty by now. Why'd they wait so long?'

'Who said they waited?' Jordan watched me carefully. 'Mom's had several miscarriages, before and after you. A stillborn baby. A boy. There was a funeral.'

I opened my mouth to ask how the Sam Hill she knew, but the answer came out. 'Grandma?' Jordan nodded. Did I want to know about dead babies, about one that would've had my life? Nosireee. 'So have you actually asked Mom, or are you just guessing?'

'Guessing.'

'Good one. Then I'm guessing you're wrong.' I began back-paddling for both of us.

Jordan shrugged. 'She's not swimming. She's stopped drinking coffee.' She put her hands over her face. 'And yesterday I caught her eating potato chips for breakfast.'

'Man, now I know you've lost it. I've never seen her eat chip one, not in her life, let alone for breakfast. She won't even let us have them for snacks for Chrissake!'

'Well, Grand says salty stuff is good for morning sickness. And at this moment your mother has a secret stash of chips under the kitchen sink behind her Auburn Sunset. Make of it what you will.'

Jordan squished down into her lifejacket, obscuring her face, a giant turtle retreating into an orange shell. She looked like a pudgy Bazooka Joe. She looked ridiculous.

'Silly goose! Why don't you just ask her?'

Jordan yanked her shell off, shouting, 'It's that easy for you, isn't it? Chuck you, Farley March!' She stood up, a cardinal sin in a canoe, leaned over her right foot and spoke without turning, 'New riddle: when is this canoe not a *canot bâtard*? Answer: *quand je suis parti.*'

And then, in Monday's freshly laundered clothes, she dove right off. In the lurching backwash, the paddles and her life jacket followed. I couldn't move. It was as if she'd taken my life force with her, as if I'd been frozen by Samantha on *Bewitched*. She headed for the rock pile an alarming distance away. Could she make it? Yes. We were far out in the bay, but thankfully on an angle where the current pushed both of us, swimmer and drifter, back into shore. Pure luck or pure deliberation? Same BS difference.

It took her twenty minutes to reach the dock. I expected her to collapse, but instead she flipped like a pro and swam laps to the rock pile. I'll admit I was impressed – that is, I'll admit it now. Coincident with, but not coincidental to, the moment I drifted past her, she posed on the rocks, posed in full effect, her hair on the waves a full floating cape behind her, glinting copper in the sun. Already performing, she began to sing. No Miracle song – a baby song: 'Put chur shoes on, Lucy, doncha know you're in the city? Put chur shoes on, Lucy, you're a big girl now!'

Gaze averted, arms folded, I drifted right past her. For once I was Chief Ruffled Feathers. Stop for sorry? Good one. Paddle with my hands? Not this little Indian. I liked inert and glaring. I wouldn't have to do more. Eagle-Eye Fleagle would kill her for me. Mom was sure to spot wet clothes and soggy leather shoes. And then my not-so-eagle eye sighted the new landscape, made sense of the song and the sight of pink toes cresting the water. Her new oxfords – and I mean brand new, and costing as much as five normal pairs of shoes, as MC so frequently and pleasantly reminded her – she'd sent them sinking, somewhere sleeping with the clams. Somewhere as lost as Atlantis.

Damn her hide. Now I'd share their fate. Bad enough she'd done it to me, but worse, she'd done it without me, without so much as a by-your-leave. Some girls are blind in their own cause. Now I'd get grounded because I hadn't stopped her from doing what I hadn't known she was going to do. That's not fair, but it's MC justice. If I missed the rest of Mr. Armstrong, I'd be administering some justice of my own. I landed and I walked. Let her beach the canoe. Let her explain her shoes. Let her sink. If she didn't care what she got me into, why should I care if she got into worse? She made that bed, she could bloody well lie in it alone.

Why was I so angry? I told myself that it was because her shoes cost good money, and I could ill afford another grounding. But here's the rest of it. Because I knew she was sitting out there laughing at us midget-idjit Marches, thinking up some fast-talking, gifted BS. Because in all probability, she'd get off scot-free. Because she was an ungrateful, unrepentant sneaky little – that time I stopped myself. I'm sure I did, and used the less offensive b-word – bitch.

By July 24, I was looking forward to the other splashdown. Attempting reconciliation, I remember asking her if she knew what day it was and Little Miss Mermaid said sure, that on this day in 1567 Mary Queen of Scots had been deposed. She took envelopes up to the mailbox and returned with none. She slumped around all day with a black ribbon gracing her arm. If I'd been speaking to her, I'd have called it melodramatic and messianic. The brat. Let's avoid her.

Sunset found me reverent on Grandpa's dock, replaying the splashdown in the lake before me, imagining what I'd say to Mr. Armstrong and what he'd say to me when I gave him Biggie, the trophy fish still lurking in the shadows of Grandpa's crib bed. I all but had him. He lay cool in the half light, toying with me, kissing my lure. She arrived chuffing, stomped the planks and shoved her worn red Bible under my nose.

Before I looked at her offering, I looked at her feet. Like Mom, I usually heard her coming a mile away, and hadn't. After Monday's shoe shucking, what did she have on those imperfectly perfect feet?

Good Question. The Atlantis oxfords of Box Social fame were black leather boots with thick-cut leather laces, so BS had quite logically replaced them with a beat-up pair of red canvas Keds, obviously liberated from some cousin's back-door mountain of cast-off shoes. Boys' shoes, rechristened and recoated, rather hastily, in white shoe polish. They came out an uneven pink, like blood-spotted candy floss. I pushed the supposedly good book aside, pointed down and told her she was asking for it.

'No, they never really look at me. Not at my feet. But you have to. Look at this.' She cracked the leather binding, stuck her finger on Deuteronomy 22 and thrust it at my throat. 'Aunt May's right. Bloody well entirely right. No pearly gates for me. I'm already judged.'

I slapped it off and snarled, 'Cluck off, BS! Biggie's biting!'

She ignored me. She slammed my tackle box, plopped on top of it and opened the mouth unstoppable: 'If a man marries, then claims the bride wasn't a virgin, but her parents prove it by spreading her bloody sheets out for all to see, then the liar has to pay the girl's father a hundred shekels of silver. But if her parents can't prove it, if her sheets aren't bloody, or bloody enough, then the men of the city get to stone her to death.'

'Jesus H. Christ, shut the puck up! I'm *fishing*!'

'If a married or betrothed woman is raped in the city, she and the rapist get stoned on the logic that she must have been asking for it, or some resident of said city would have heard her scream. If a betrothed woman is raped in a field, then only the rapist dies. She gets the benefit of the doubt that she did protest but was heard only by cows or goats or insert name of dumb field animal here, all of which obviously could not have come to her aid.' I swung at her with my lure but she ducked. Hooks scraped her head but she kept unreeling.

'But if in said field a man rapes a virgin who's not betrothed, does he die? No. A betrothed or married woman is her husband's property – the crime is done to him. A virgin is her father's property. Ergo, the rapist of said virgin simply gives the girl's father fifty shekels – not a hundred – a man's reputation is worth more than a girl's life – and she, lucky thing, gets to be her rapist's wife, comforted daily by the fact that he can never divorce her. Isn't that nice?'

Biggie got away from me as fast as I wished I could get away from her. 'Save your breath to cool your porridge, BS. No one takes that Old Testament crapola seriously anymore.'

'I do! I'm not making it up; it's printed right here. The worst one? Deuteronomy 23, verse 2. Aunt May's right. This nigger in the wood-pile can get the spirit but can't join the church. I'm illegitimate. That's the real reason why I've never been confirmed!' I followed her finger, dismayed to see it shaking: 'A bastard shall not enter into the congregation of the Lord; even to his tenth generation shall he not enter into the congregation of the Lord forever.' I wound my reel tighter. 'I have to take it seriously. I'm going to Hell.'

'No, that can't be right. It's a bunch of old words, ancient SNAFUBAR. A story no one believes anymore, like being swallowed by a whale. There must be some other reason.'

'Only one reason and you're looking at it.'

'Jordan, it's 1969 AD. There's a man on the moon, for Chrissake. Ask Dad.'

'Ask him what? If he's ashamed to be raising a bastard? Ask him if my,' she began keeping track on her fingers, 'great-great-great-seven-more-times-great-grandchild can please meet the rest of you in heaven? No thanks.' She snapped Bible shut and lurched away, caught herself and turned, suddenly calm. 'Go ahead,' she urged. 'Join. It's not right to keep us both out because of me. You didn't do anything wrong. She bent to a spotty pink shoelace and I swear I heard her add, 'You never do.' She pushed herself back up. 'It's no skin off my nose. I'm not going back. What kind of midget-idjit would kowtow to a God who's already condemned her? Not this kind.' Her voice choked. 'Consider this little bastard done. Done like dinner. Last Sunday? That was my Last Supper.' At the end of the dock she paused, looked down at Grandma's and shook her head. When you're angry, there's no place like home.

I reassembled my gear and stayed put, casting just to cast, whip-ping the ivory path of the moon. Maybe you won't think less of me; maybe you'll think I was a typical fifteen-year-old boy. Embarrassed. Ashamed at having no clue what to say. It's what I told myself at the time. When I finally followed her up, I heard the Beatles singing ever so softly in her room: 'Don't let me down ... ' I walked past her door and did. But such shortcuts come back to haunt you. The more complicated truth? I was ashamed of her. Let me be crystal-blue-persuasion clear. Not for her – of her. And somewhere, down shoes deep where I didn't want it seen, I was worse: Relieved. Elated. Damn near delighted.

I knew better. I could have insisted she talk to Grandma. I could have shown BS a gentler Jesus myself, quoted the kinder parts of the same ancient book that condemned her: 'Let he who is without sin cast the first stone.' Did this fly boy take even one small step in the direction of the Good Samaritan? No, I was too busy fishing in slippery green shadows, too busy anticipating the hurling of stones. In March, we're just following orders. So when MC yelled through the walls to quit making such a GD racket and close those eyes, I could all but feel the first rock, warm and ready, eager in my hand. Insert her umpteenth abandonment here.

POLK SALAD ANNIE

Okay, so now you know I'm not a nice guy and that as a narrator I've probably done more hide than seek. But I had my reasons. You're about to meet two of them. Tab D: the speech and the song. I bet you thought you'd met them already, and you had, but only Version 1. Version 2 is as good a start as any. Another beginning might as well be here. (Just remember they aren't beginnings as you know them, more like loops you've gone back for, things that have been kept from you, kept apart like brackets before the heart of the equation.)

The very best thing about the BMW wasn't parental disapproval, Tony's grunting or even its potentially lurid content that even we understood suggested more than salad. Given the tinny reception of Miracle, and the raucous accompaniment that all but drowned out his voice, a growled slur, a sexier kind of Kronk singing to Yogi, the absolute best thing was what we told ourselves: since we couldn't quite make out the words, we'd have to write our own.

'Here's another, version seventeen, I believe.' Jordan slapped down an old Hilroy notebook with 'Grade 2 Reading Comprehension' ineffectually crossed out and replaced by 'BME: The Bastardized Editions, Puns Intended.' We wrote some twenty versions, pushing each other to ever more inventive lyrics, hers in French, mine as vulgar as my hockey voice could make them. We'd sing them on the dock, on our way to bed, and before Moonwalk Sunday, under our breath in the line waiting for Rev. Southwell. At mealtime the presence of anything green warranted, 'Pass me a little, aarrgh, Polk Salad.'

If the parents were forgetful enough to ask us any variation on the question of what we'd been up to, we'd sing, 'Every day before supper time we go down by the truck patch, and pick us a mess a Polk Salad and carry it home in a tote sack.' We even had a tote sack – Jordan's gym bag, the one that doubled as her Fenelon book bag and Avenging Kit, a product of Grade 8 Home Ec., embroidered with a black swan. Now instead of her gym suit or tomes from Missy P, it held dandelions. Every day before supper time, we'd go down by our truck patch – weeds behind Tessie, but close enough – and pick us a mess of polk salad and carry it to Yogi in the tote sack, singing all the way. Dad filmed us. We could be seen, but not heard.

There were two lines we never changed. During the chorus: 'Polk Salad Annie, Gators got your granny,' I'd always go, 'Chomp. Chomp. Chomp.' And this line – whatever it meant, it sounded too damn good to change:

> 'Everybody said it was a shame,
> 'Cause her momma was a-working on the chain gang.
> A wretched, spiteful, straight-razor totin' woman.
> Ahhh, Lord have mercy.'

We kept the notebook in the red case, all our versions carefully preserved in her open scrawl. You could easily miss it. Inside the back cover, parallel to the spine in tiny, un-Jordan-like printing, lay another version – one she'd never had the guts to sing:

> Up in Rosedale, Canada,
> Where the snapping turtles grow so mean,
> There lived a girl that I swear to the world,
> Will make 'em see that bastards aren't to blame.
> I'm Polk Salad Annie, I'll never know my granny.
> (Chomp. Chomp. Chomp.)
> Everybody said it was a shame
> 'Cause my momma was a-screwing a whole chain gang
> I'm a wretched, spiteful, straight-razor-totin' woman
> Ahhh, I'll spare no mercy.

Don't be shocked. You ain't seen nothing yet. This is the most accurate setting for the Way Back. This is what this story must become. Sometimes there's no way out but through. I've been quiddling here for some time, sanitizing and stalling far longer than she would have appreciated or respected. She'd call me a coward or, worse, reach for that axe.

On the night of the Box Social, when she came out in her bathing suit, I neglected to mention the envelope in her hand. Remember?

I'd agreed to a swim, mistakenly thinking that her brain would be as defeated as the rest of her and I could relax. Always a mistake. When we got to the dock, she opened said envelope and cleared her throat.

'Upon the occasion of being cheated of winning gold, yet again, I give you the privilege of hearing the speech I should have given on that one occasion when I did win. It explains the real reason why I lost this time.

Dear Disappointed Diary, 'Franklin Horner Jr. High Centennial Public Speaking Contest, May 16, 8:00 p.m.' I made that banner. They wouldn't stop to let me show them my name on it. Dad didn't film it. They hurried me out so they could watch a *Perry Mason* rerun. Dad said, 'Good job, Pooch.' Mom said, 'Dear, your slip was showing.' Here's what I should have said:

What One Hundred Really Means To Me, by the Real Me, (Whoever She Is)

Ladies and Gents, let's cut to the wood and to the chase. Let's cut the mustard, the apron strings, the cheese and the crap:

2 unknown parents

4 unknown, untouchable grandparents

8 unknown, untouchable, unmentionable great-grandparents

16 unknown, untouchable, unmentionable and unclean great-great-grandparents

32 unknown, untouchable, unmentionable, unclean and unmournable great-great-great –

Does that add to one hundred yet? Normal Canadians reach a hundred foreparents in six generations. This little Canadian never will. And in true irony, my founding family, confusing well-bred with breeding well, has littered our nation with cousins second and third and further removed, so many that they have achieved the dubious honour of shitting out a hundred blood relatives in three generations. A nation of March marching through time. They get an ancestral choir of their own making, singing their anthem eternal. I get ghosts, an unholy trilogy: me, myself and I. A Bastard Anthem in three-part harmony. Me and my shadows. Myself and the unknown untouchables. I and the unclean unmentionables. Go ahead. Count the branches of my family tree. I'll wait. One. You're done. What is one hundred to me? It's what everybody else has. A daily enumeration of what I'll never have. If you detect self-pity, dear audience, at least me, myself and I are capable of pity. That's more than some people.

In conclusion, latees and germs, there is no conclusion. The yarn unravels forever, into infinity and beyond: 128 GGGGG-grandparents, 256 GGGGGG-grandparents, 512 GGGGGGG-grandparents, 1024 GGGGGGGG-grandparents, et cetera, ad infinitum, ad nauseam. Long after you've gone home, I'll be alone and counting.

P.S. I won. That's right. Me. I offered congratulations to Myself. All three of us said thank you. Mom told Dad there wasn't enough light for his camera and he believed her.'

When she turned to me for a response, this little monkey was missing. Flopped out on an air mattress, awaiting the first breeze of evening, I was inches from the safety of slumber when the great white hunter launched her second retaliatory ambush. She began in camouflage, in masquerade as the everyday and harmless.

'Whatcha thinkin', Lincoln?'

Disarmed, I responded on cue, 'Just fuzzin', cousin.'

As for the rest, well, that you remember.

My excuse for not telling you all of it? After me you come first. I wanted you to see us as relatively ordinary, to believe that we were mostly just like any other teenaged brother and sister. No, that's not the whole truth either. I wanted to keep her as normal as I could for as long as I could and I wanted you to see me as – oh, what's the use? Forget about me, man. This is bloody well her story, you remember that, bloody and hers. If the problems to follow aren't as easy as pi, then that's just the way the calculator crumbles. If there are any clichés left, you use them. As for trying to make the rest of this proverbial or palatable, I'm the same as Jordan. I'm Spam. And I'm done, done like a secondhand, leftover, reheated, tatterdemalion dinner.

HAZEL #63

It's June. It's happened. Miss Sinclair – I can barely call her Margie anymore – has found a good private foundling home for the baby. Walter says I mustn't use her name because I'll get attached, but Margaret says go ahead, it's just like back on the farm; mothers want to know their babies for as long as they can, even if they only get to keep them a very short time. That made me feel better but it also made me shiver. Like I'm sending her to slaughter.

Margaret and I, we planned it all so differently. She was going to be a vet and I was going to travel with her, giving uplifting speeches about good country living. It seemed so smart, so possible. She got top marks in science and I got all the public speaking awards; I'd been Dairy Princess twice. When we were thirteen we saved our allowances for three months, went all the way by bus to the big Eaton's store right in downtown Toronto and bought each other matching silver lockets. We promised. We said we'd never take them off until we lived together. We'd look at old ladies holding on to each other in the park and smile, 'Look, that's us a thousand years from now!' But she's the only one of us who got even partway there. She looks so professional in her uniform. Like a businessman, she has a suit and a hat; she even has cards for her clients: Margaret Ann Sinclair, Public Health Nurse, Toronto Board of Health. She has a car and her own apartment. She hasn't made a mess of things.

She keeps trying to reach her brother. Keeps saying she knows that if Angus knew, he'd do the right thing. I keep telling her it's too late for the right thing, I'm already married, and she keeps saying no, it's never too late for the right thing. But every time she calls, their witch of a mother answers the phone. She says she doesn't know anyone named Angus. She'll claim not to know me or even her own daughter. We drove over there once and Mrs. J came out with her shotgun, yelling rudeness, screaming she'd have the law on us for trying to shame her boy. So Margaret sent three letters, all on official Board of Health stationery, all 'Returned to Sender.' I guess freelance bricklayers don't stay still for long. One of her cousins tried to tell us Angus had packed up for Nova Scotia. How are we supposed to know if that's true?

It's August. Mother said she'd throw me out in the gutter where I belonged if I didn't let Walter marry me. He said he'd give both me and my baby a home. By the time he changed his mind, it was too late to back out. I tell Margaret to give up on Angus but she says no real man would give up on his own baby. She's convinced he doesn't know and never will if their nasty old cow of a mother has her way. So that's the standoff. I see Susie every couple of days. I lie to Walter to do so. Margaret picks me up and tells Walter it's 'girls' luncheon.' Walter may be suspicious, but he doesn't say no. I'll write the rest in shorthand, safe from prying eyes. Then I'll never think of it again nor tell a living soul. I'm such a fool.

First Walter comes home all excited and says it's wonderful, his promotion has come through and it's just what he wanted, a posting in Scotland. We can start a new life and put all of this filth behind us. It hits me then. That's what my child is to him. All she will ever be. I'm crying. I rush out of the house and phone Margaret from a pay phone. She picks me up and takes me straight to Susie. She keeps saying you can't do this. This isn't you. I've known you all your life and this isn't what you want. I'm crying and rocking Susie, stroking her beautiful Shirley Temple curls as if she's the one who needs to be comforted, and I don't know what I want. Margaret says, 'Listen, you can live with me, both of you. Just leave him. Please live with me, darling. We can raise her together.' She takes my hand, smiles and gives it a kiss.

The light in the nursery grows very bright. The pink walls dance. I realize for the first time that there isn't just one crib in the room; there are seven. I know exactly what I want. And what I can't have. I put the baby down. A cry comes from her crib, third in the second row. I take off my silver promise and put it around her neck. I look my oldest friend in the eye, see exactly what she's been trying to tell me all these years and say, 'Don't call me and don't ever come near this child. My husband and I, we'll be proceeding with the adoption immediately.'

I don't risk one last look. I leave. I call Walter and beg him to take me back. Did I fool her? Did she see right through me? I hope not, but it doesn't matter. If wishes were horses, beggars like us would ride off into the sunset together. But of course they're not, they're only words. That and a dime will get you a cup of coffee.

TOO BUSY THINKING ABOUT MY BABY

S he wouldn't come out of her room. She wouldn't wash. For three days. On July 27, the Sunday after March Moonwalk Sunday, she feigned cramps. 'Cramps' was the Magic Menstrual Word in our house. Say it once and, presto, you got whatever you wanted just so long as you didn't say it again. That's not to say we believed her. But we left her there. We walked past her door.

It was Sunday, however, so Mom opened that door only to hand Jordan the laundry pole, ignoring her mutterings about getting burned twice. That meant BS was out on the deck getting burned again, literally this time, by laundry that refused to leave its steamy basket, when Derwood arrived. He'd run straight out the church door with Aunt May's big news and beelined it straight to Jordan, doing a halfway decent impersonation of the old bag: 'We're *sooo* thrilled! We have such hopes this time! A child of his *owwwwn* will be *soooo good* for our Tommy; he's waited *farrrrr tooooo looooong!*' Watching her face, he enjoyed what he saw, so he did it again. The slap that never ends. When Jordan slammed the screen door on his foot, he stalked her like a peeping Tom, sighting his target through the windows. *'Faaarrrrr tooooooo loooooong!'*

That night produced the quietest supper of all. Even the sight of spinach failed to elicit a chorus of 'Polk Salad Annie.' As Mom passed Dad his dessert bowl, bananas with condensed milk and brown sugar, she smiled down the table. 'Fine. I understand you've heard our news and I know it should have been from us, but yes, your father and I are expecting a baby.' When no one said anything, she added, 'Sometime late in November.' Jordan mashed bananas with her spoon. MC pushed back, 'Well, can't you say something?'

'Okay. Something.'

Mom sighed. 'I mean, do you have any questions?'

'No ... Well, yes. What are you going to call it?'

'Well, that's a good question, dear. Thomas, of course, if it's a boy.' Mom dried her hands on her apron, 'And if it's a girl, well, what do you think about Virginia?'

'Bananas!' Jordan shouted, shoving her bowl clear across the table to spatter on the floor. 'Bananas are for monkeys.' She stood up. 'Which March monkey do you take me for, Mother? The one that can't see, the one that can't hear or the one that can't speak? I must be one stupid lower primate.' The parents glanced at each other, then simultaneously found bananas fascinating. Jordan waited. Spoons scraped Melmac. When she stomped off, they let her go. Don't ask me. More bedtime for my Bonzo sister. Must be some cramps.

I looked most of Monday before I found her in the second least likely of places. The least likely being Derwood's bunkie, and for reasons I don't understand, I actually checked there too. I only found her at all, because I heard Balsam whining beneath the tree. Clearly, she hadn't wanted me to put in an appearance. She knew I would never have looked up – at least not past platform three – but apparently if there's more than one way to skin a cat within an inch of her life, BS had to try them all. I climbed to platform seven, rehearsing what I'd yell once I got there, but as my head came level with a girl crouched in fetal position, not sucking her thumb, but running her hands non-stop over her skull, that told me I had one and only one job – to get her calm enough to get down. Once she was safe and sound, then I'd kill her. I opened my mouth but she spoke first. 'Don't say it. I know you think I'm crazy.'

Forcing myself to think only of the image of her silly pink shoes safe on land, where once she was standing I could knock her down, I tried to joke her out of it by singing the Peter Paul Almond Joy jingle, 'No, sometimes you feel like a nut, sometimes you don't.' That didn't crack smile one. Instead she reached into her book bag, tied to her back with a length or rope as if she needed something else to unbalance her, and handed me her old pink diary, 'Here. Just the marked pages. Nothing else.'

DIARY OF JORDAN MAY MARCH ON THE BEST DAY OF HER LIFE!!!!

September 19, 1963.

Dearest Most Perfect Friend Diary:

This morning! It's here! It's finally this morning! Here's the list of what I have to do before it happens: get dressed, eat breakfast, go to school, have reading (yeah), have recess (boo), have math (okay) and then the lunch bell! When I get home she'll be here!! I'm going to run all the way. I've been practising. I'm going to run right up to her bassinet and I'm going to say the most important speech she'll ever hear. Dad will film it with his new camera: 'Good morning, baby Virginia Caroline March, this is your big sister Jordan May March speaking. You were born June 13, 1963, at 4:37 p.m. We are both June babies, only ten days and eight years apart. I promise to love you forever. I will take care of you my whole life.' Then I'll turn to Mom and Dad and finish my speech. 'Thank you for finding my sister. I will be grateful and stop being more trouble than I'm worth. I promise to be the best big sister and the best help ever.' They will hug me and say, 'We love both our girls so much!' It's really going to happen!!! Today!

DIARY OF JORDAN MAY MARCH A SISTER FOR ONE FULL WEEK!!!!

September 26, 1963

Dearest Friend Diary,

Ginny is sooo perfect!!! Tiny and warm and pink. An angel but ALIVE! MY VERY OWN SISTER, ALIVE! Today Mom let me change her diaper AND feed her a bottle AND rock her to sleep. Ginny always knows when it's me. She never cries when I hold her. She has straight blonde hair that flows sideways around her head and delphinium eyes. I told Mom that and it made her smile. (I thought my sister would have curly red hair and hazel eyes like me. Maybe one of us is like the Man and the other of us is like the Lady? Do ladies that have babies in the same month have them at the same time of day? Was I born at 4:37 p.m. too? If only I could ask Mom. How do

I just know I can't?) Mom says Ginny was born early and is small for three months (I'm small too. Was I born early?), but she should grow quickly now that she's getting better care than in the Foster home. Whoever these Fosters are who MISTREATED MY SISTER, they should be shot. I want to ask Kathryn Foster in my class but if it was her, but then I'd have to fight her and, Diary, you know I'd lose.

DIARY OF JORDAN MAY MARCH A SISTER FOR ONE MONTH TOMORROW!!!

October 13, 1963

Dearest Worried Friend,

Diary, I know you're worried too. Babies are such hard work. Mom can't stop crying. She cried all day yesterday. She put Ginny in her carriage and told me to go out on the porch with her. She left us out there so long we got cold and Ginny cried louder than I've ever heard her cry. When we came back in, Mom stayed on the other side of the kitchen like she didn't want to touch us, then she rushed over, grabbed Ginny so tight I was scared she'd be smothered! I asked Mom what was wrong and she said, 'Nothing, dear. Nothing at all.' But when I came home for lunch she hadn't made any. She'd pulled the rocking chair out of Ginny's room and up to the kitchen table. She sat there, with the dirty breakfast dishes all around her, sat there, eating potato chips. She poured me a huge bowl, more than I could ever eat in a month of Sundays and wouldn't look at me. She just sat there, rocking Ginny back and forth, back and forth. Her eyes were swollen. She had Kleenex knotted through her fingers. Poor Mom! What can I do, Diary? I must try extra hard to be a better helper tomorrow!

DIARY OF JORDAN MAY MARCH ON THE DAY WORSE THAN DEATH

October 15, 1963

It's not another nightmare. I got up this morning and ran to her room. All her things were gone. Her bottles, her bassinette, the little pink lamb I gave her, even her rattle.

Mom sat me down and said, 'She's gone to live with a family who will love her even more than we do. No, you can't visit, that wouldn't be fair to her new family, now, would it? Don't cry. You see, dear, we're going to have a better baby, one of our very own. Here, look.' She handed me her precious ballerina, a perpetual calendar that came all the way from Scotland on a boat with her mother, a china dancer pirouetting in a pink tutu and toe slippers. Its golden dials were set to June 29, 1964. 'See? By June you'll have a new brother or sister. Maybe for your birthday! What a lovely present! Dry those eyes, dear. Don't be sad. You'll love our baby even more because it's really ours. You won't remember her, dear. You'll forget her. I promise.'

LIAR. I threw her ballerina at the wall and broke both her legs. Good. I hope it hurt. I ran to the front door praying, but I didn't see the kidnappers. LIAR. LIAR. LIAR. I spotted her carriage on the porch. The jack-o'-lantern was laughing. I kicked it, grabbed her carriage and ran. I ran all the way to Marie Curtis Park. I begged God. Please don't take my family twice. I put my hand on my rock and prayed, but of course I don't deserve a sister. When God laughed in my face, he used my mother's voice: You're a little beggar. You don't get to choose.

ONE MONTH LATER, THE DIARY OF ME PRETENDING TO BE A MARCH
November 15, 1963

I promise you, Virginia Caroline March, that I will never forget you. I will pretend to live here with this so-called family that sold you down the river on the same day as Hurricane Hazel, but I will NEVER EVER AGAIN live here in my heart. My heart doesn't live in my body. My heart is with you. As soon as I am old enough, I will save us both. When I turn 16 you will be 8 like I am now, and on that birthday, I swear to God, I will run away and look until I find you. I will NEVER NEVER EVER EVER EVER STOP LOOKING. I will find you or die trying, I SWEAR IT! SISTERS TILL WE DIE!!!!!!!

P.S. Remember me, Ginny. My curly red hair and glasses. I limp a little. When you see me, please don't be frightened.

DIARY OF JORDAN, ONLY SISTER OF VIRGINIA
ON JUSTICE DAY, November 22, 1963
Mr. Kennedy died today. Everyone is sad. He was a great man.
Last night, Mom went to the hospital. Now there is no better
baby. I COULD HAVE TOLD HER THAT. Serves her right.

When I looked up, I couldn't look her in the eye.

She said, 'I know you aren't much for remembering. You've
never said if you do or not. But I can't forget.' She dropped her head
to her arms and rocked. 'Ever since I discovered Mom was pregnant,
I can't close my eyes. I can't even lie down. I keep thinking that
maybe if I stay awake, maybe if I'm wearing normal shoes, maybe if
I stay awake and stay sitting up ... '

'Then what?' I manage to mumble.

'Then they won't come in the middle of the night and take me
away too.' And then the unthinkable, something I'd never seen. Her
face crumpled. My sister began to cry. 'Sorry. I know it's ridiculous.
I've just turned fourteen, for Chrissake, but I still think it. Still
believe it ... '

'Believe what?'

'It sounds so stupid, so bloody childish.'

'Say it anyway. Believe what?

'If you can have a better baby, your own tummy baby, you send
the other kind back. That's how I always said it to myself. Who
wants silver if you can have gold? God, I must be crazy! I think I'm
going to disappear. Just like George Orwell predicted in *1984*.' She
flipped her diary pages, pointed and read aloud without looking:
'People simply disappeared, always during the night. Your name
was removed from the registers, every record of everything you had
ever done was wiped out, your one-time existence was denied and
then forgotten. You were abolished, annihilated: "vaporized" was
the usual word.'

For the first time in my life, I felt the world going on without me.
I couldn't move my mouth. Even all these years later I still can't
adequately describe how I felt: angry and privileged and frightened.
I wanted to hold her tight. I wanted to punch her in the stomach. I
wanted to hold her tight while punching her in the stomach.

At least it clarified that morning. It explained why I'd had to hunt her down, why she'd used the only gun she could get her hands on. We'd been eating breakfast – the rest of us, that is. I'd been thinking that maybe she was embarrassed by last night's banana-shucking monkey mayhem, and was in her room rehearsing an apology. Not exactly. Someone came out when she was damn good and ready – book bag over one arm and Mom's sewing shears under the other. But it wasn't my sister – it was Twiggy, shorn like a baby lamb. It was Twiggy's two hands clutching a handful of snakes. I blinked.

Of course it was hair. Handfuls of protesting hair, live-wire copper hair, a headless Medusa, still snapping. Jordan held the shame of it under Mom's nose, then drowned it in Mom's cereal bowl. She saluted, turned on her heel and frogmarched her one-tin-soldier self straight out the screen door. Left ... Left ... Left-right-left. Left without speaking or hearing a word.

And what did I think? I bid it into my head that time: melodramatic, messianic and a mortal error. I smiled. Never show your teeth unless you can bite. Never draw your dirk when a blow will do.

EASY TO BE HARD

I know a good brother wouldn't have looked at any diary entries beyond those offered him, but we've already established how good I am. Come on, what did you or she expect? I'm a fifteen-year-old boy left alone in a tree with a girl's diary. Enough said. She's the one who left it behind. When she couldn't stop crying, she climbed down without it. I watched her go, chanting the climbing map through her tears, a protocol she'd obviously memorized forwards and backwards, and decided she was safer without me. If she couldn't quit her quiddling long enough to remember her diary, well, that was as good as asking for it. The breeze turned the pages, inviting me, teasing me, all but forcing me, so I caved. I told myself I was reading it to help her, to fix what was making her unhappy. That, of course, was a pile of piñata. I read it for the same reason anybody reads someone else's diary: to see what she'd written about me.

I figured I'd find myself plenty-twenty. So I ignored the official-looking typed pages, yellowed and boring, that came first. I didn't take them seriously enough, but don't make the opposite mistake about what I'm going to tell you next. Try to see it in context. Some of it, like her calligraphy, was exactingly beautiful: a hand-drawn map of Scotland, locating all the clans in writing nearly microscopic. Some of it was funny. Consider this: 'A Geological Treatise on the Difference Between Stalactites and Stalagmites, by Jordan May March: Stalactites hang down like girls' tights/And stalagmites thrust up like girls like.'

And much of it was normal. Please remember that. Jokes. Lines from movies. Rewritten endings for movies that didn't end right. Silly stuff she'd done with her browner friends. Stuff that was just plain dull, as self-absorbed as you would expect any young girl's account of her own sorry life to be. A chart listing the time, date, place and score of every game she'd ever bowled. Man, she was pitiful; she'd never broken a hundred despite endless strategies to do so.

So Jordan. I laughed out loud to see that each June she meticulously enumerated, memorized and tested herself on Mom's favourite plays for When Fenelon Falls. Good call. Right as rain. Right as the failing report cards from Mother School and the unsent letters. 'Dear Mother Nature: An earthworm has five hearts and an octopus two. Could you please convince one of these creatures to lend one to my mother who has none?'

I couldn't read the pages in shorthand. Probably the juicy bits, damn her hide. Two years ago, for reasons unfathomable, BS took it upon herself to become a stenographer. She spent a small fortune on steno pads, raided the library's business section, propped *Teach Yourself Stenography!* up on the piano and took dictation from herself. Mom sniffed and said the predictable about a fool and her money, and that she who teaches herself has a fool for a master. But now BS could transcribe as fast as she could talk and that's no small feat and no small pun. She'd record teachers verbatim and read their contradictions back to them word for word. A diligence I'm sure they appreciated. One of the pages had marginalia in French: 'Je suis une autodidact autodictat!' A pun no one else on earth appreciated.

I skipped the girly stuff, crap about getting her period and feeling dirty, about having the hots for one of her browner friends who thought of her only as a friend. Poor baby. She worried about everything – her hair, her height, her freckles, her glasses, her shoes, and if any boy would ever want 'damaged goods.' I figured she meant her feet. For a good prose writer, she wrote downright puking poetry. The worst? Recopied every year from its inception, 'Christmas Eve, 1964':

Where has the Meaning of Christmas Gone?
Has it floated Away on a Breeze?
Where has the Family of Christmas Gone?
What Family when NO ONE BELIEVES?'

Yes, I'm quiddling. Yes, there was other stuff. Exacting, but not funny, not pretty and not normal. Rewritten song lyrics, some of them just plain nasty. And word games. Anagrams and acronyms, pages of them, as if she couldn't stop. The top of one page asked, 'What's in a name?' and then underneath in the tiny writing I'd come to dread answered, 'Everything!' numbering that one word a full ninety-nine times. In the hundredth spot she wrote: 'Oscar Zoroaster Phadrig Issac Norman Henkle Emmannuel Ambroise Diggs is not The Great and Powerful Wizard of Oz. He's a short, befuddled man hiding unsuccessfully behind a worn curtain and a name not his own. What's in a name? The power to take you home or leave you stranded. Belonging or being a stranger in a strange clan. In short, your destiny.'

And there were pictures, all hand-drawn. Some of them were normal. Wedding dresses and hairstyles. Cows and horses. Turtles and frogs. And food – a happy family at a table groaning with Thanksgiving crossed out and drawn over it a family of three on a picnic: Mom and Dad enjoying the make-believe as their pigtailed daughter busily fed butter tarts to her teddy bear. And baby bottles. Bottles with huge hairy nipples, nipples impossibly extended like engorged Silly Putty. If the word had existed then I'd have said they were gross. Totally gross.

As gross as the Law Code of Hammurabi: 'An adopted child has the same rights and filial expectations as a birth child and parents are legally expected to provide for both the same. If a well-treated adopted child discovers his birth parents and wants to return to them, then shall his eye or tongue be torn out.' Printed in thick red marker, this text centred a full-page collage, inscribed over layers of eyes and tongues, all scored with scissors until they bled. Good one, BS.

And some of it was both normal and weird – pages upon pages regaling herself with the theatrical antics of all seven of her girls, a newly blended and impossibly extended *Little Women* March family: the saintly Marmee, Meg, twins Jo and Jordan, Beth, Amy and Virginia, all living blissfully together in genteel poverty in Concord, Massachusetts, during the Civil War. Father returns from battle so Jo doesn't have to sell her hair, her 'one true beauty'; Bethy doesn't die; Amy gets disfigured for life when, thanks to the clothes peg she wore to reshape it, her fat nose gets infected and has to be amputated. And their kidnapped baby, Virginia, is miraculously returned in time to heal Jordan who'd been on her deathbed with a broken heart. I had to hand it to her, a happy ending that sounded Almost original. A fixed fixation.

If nothing else, it proved that once my turtle-jawed sister got a hold of an idea, she'd clamp down and gum it to death. That diary referenced everything she read, including itself. Ideas reconnected with their family of like-minded thoughts. Literally. She annotated everything and dated each annotation, connecting entries with pencil crayon arrows, with titles and subtitles and twenty-plenty 'see page so-and-so's. Because it was a binder she could, and often did, add whole pages after the fact. Many entries had marginalia, her all-time favourite word. I'd scandalized her by suggesting she only liked it because it rhymed with 'genitalia.'

I pondered this frequently annotated series for a good half an hour: 'Bios of Bastards who Bit Back: Orphans and Foundlings Included.' Superman, Batman, Moses, King Arthur, Oedipus, Oliver Twist, Heathcliff, Huck Finn, Tom Sawyer, Tarzan, Mowgli, Tolstoy, Babe Ruth, James Dean, Louis Armstrong, the Baker Street Irregulars, Muhammed and Jesus. Jesus? In a rainbow of additions she added: Q: So where are the girls? A: Occupied elsewhere:

1. Little Orphan Annie and Pollyanna: both too busy spreading song and sunshine.
2. Anne of Green Gables: too busy telling herself it's red hair that makes her angry, not the orphanage that sold her off or the two old geezers that bought her for a farmhand. Too busy trying to prove she's as good as a boy to be a girl.
3. Dorothy Gale: too busy trying to convince herself that there's no place like home even if home is an doddering aunt and uncle who neglect her, because the alternative is risking a foster mother like Elmira Gulch. She's the real wicked witch, the one who can swoop into your home with a piece of paper and take the one you love. And how does Auntie Em defend you? 'Put Toto in the basket, Dorothy. We can't go against the law.' Surrender, Dorothy! And she does. Good one, Auntie M.
4. Marilyn Monroe: too busy being a sexpot to admit that nobody named Norma Jean with a crazy mother in the nut house, can ever possibly feel attractive inside.
5. Alison MacKenzie: Too busy being a wallflower so her lovely mother can draw attention to her stylish self as the high-heeled victim of Peyton Place.
6. Jane Eyre: too busy sleeping with dead girls.
7. Little Match Girl: too busy being dead.'

'Conclusion: Girls must develop a permanent urge to iron their hair. They cannot, must not, ever snarl or bite back. When he is orphaned, Batman can become the Masked Avenger, but a girl can only be the Masked Pretender. She must maintain decorum. She must cultivate amnesia. *Above all,* at *all times* and in *all circumstances,* she must be *grateful.*' Another colour added, 'Do these authors know what they're talking about? Are any of them orphans or bastards? What would make someone want to write about us if they weren't? What conceit would make them think they could? Or *should?*' She'd written 'tourists,' then crossed it out: 'Turdists! Worse than Yanker-wankers or Trenters. *The worst kind of bear baiters*!!!'

I'm trying to avoid the clippings. Barnardo Boys and Butterbox Babies. Her Canadian History. Orphans kept in attics. War orphans, Holocaust survivors, sent to the True North Strong and Free to be billeted in barns. Sent to slop with the pigs or starve. Hundreds of little Uncle Gavins. Adopted kids burnt with cigarettes, foster kids with their feet mutilated, just like Kunta Kinte, so they couldn't run. Wards of the state in chains, bolted into beds at night. Institutionalized kids, abused kids, dead kids. Stats and more stats. And the numbers weren't good. The adopted were: ten times more likely to be abused, five times more likely to become alcoholics and drug abusers, seven times more likely to divorce, twelve times more likely to kill their parents and twenty-three times more likely to kill themselves. Jordan's number – her birthday.

What I want most to avoid is what you most need to hear. Isn't that so often the case? Every page but one was crammed, though one hand-copied article, a scant three sentences, sat alone: '*Toronto Star.* Nov. 18, 1963. The Toronto Coroner's Office revealed today the cause of death of a female child, ward of the Children's Aid Society, pronounced dead in her crib in the affluent suburb of Rosedale last Monday. The five-month-old died of asphyxiation due to the aspiration of ejaculate. Investigations continue.' Underneath she'd written 'But don't hold your breath.' Then crossed it out, 'Sorry, dead sister, not funny.'

And then there were the Hazels. I wish I could say they were the sit-com versions – where Shirley Booth as Hazel, the Baxters' scatterbrained maid, got into scrapes that her employer, Mr. B, always uncovered and forgave – but these Hazels forgave no one and I wasn't even sure they had endings. They were more like fragments or rewrites of the same story, some set in Marie Curtis Park, some on October 15, 1954. Her rock and her hurricane. Was Hazel several women or one powerfully crazy woman? Same difference. Was she a hurricane, a woman or both? I couldn't tell. It needed a closer reading and I had no intention of doing that. Some of those Hazels – enough said. The word I couldn't say, shouted far too many times.

So I skipped to the back of the book, which as I warned you, is always a cheat. And, of course, there it was: 'The Bastard Concordance.' It wasn't the most disturbing thing, not by a long shot, so I can't explain why it got to me. A feat of detached but painstaking detail:

BASTARD: a person born out of wedlock, its primary and all-pervasive meaning

BASTARD: any person of questionable birth – mongrel, by-blow, baseborn or changeling

BASTARD: also a pejorative epithet, much like 'asshole' or 'cocksucker' or a commonplace epithet, much like 'pig,' 'jerk' or 'dummy'

BASTARD: anything not genuine, not legitimate, not the real thing, or an abnormal thing, something that is inferior or of questionable or mixed origin.

BASTARD: unusual, irregular or inferior in shape, size, colour or general appearance.

BASTARD: in zoology used to describe plants and animals that are similar to but not identical to, and usually slightly inferior to, a given species.

And then she who always used the Word of the Day in all its forms did so: Bastardy. Bastardly. Bastardization. Bastardize. Bastard cut. Bastard file. Bastard maple. Bastard measles. Bastard screw. Bastard title. Bastard type. In both official languages, including *pain bâtard* and *canot bâtard*. I remember being struck by the ridiculous notion that she was training for When Fenelon Falls: The Bastard Edition. How could anyone possibly win at that? Good question.

Hindsight is more than 20/20; it's the mother of regret. What should I have made of this: 'October 15, 1954: my conception and the launching of *Lord of the Flies*, a yarn about parentless children necessarily reverting to savagery. June 23, 1955: the day I am born and the premiere of *The Lady and the Tramp*, a so-called kids' movie about a vain bitch in heat who saves herself from gallivanting slut-dom by marrying at the last minute. Double coincidence? I think not.' Could you add that up and be heroic after one cursory reading? I couldn't. Not that I regret reading it. The opposite, in fact – I regret not having had the guts to read it carefully. I'll always regret skip-ping the typed pages. Mr. Peabody, he would have read those first. This Sherman ran right on by.

When I see myself alone in the tree with her diary I often think of a line I read years later by Pearl Buck: 'Every great mistake has a halfway moment, a split second when it can be recalled and perhaps remedied.' I know it sounds corny, but I still feel that way. It seems so clear in retrospect that at that moment it wasn't over, not even by half. I was me, not Macbeth. I wasn't smack in the middle of a river of blood; I hadn't become so evil that going back was the same as going forward. No. I could have gone back and come clean. I sat there literally holding Tab E of her Way Back Machine in my hands, and if I'd been half as clever as Mr. P or half as devoted as Sherman I could have used it to reset the dials and change everything.

What did I do? I was fifteen years old. I believed that girls – all girls, my sister being no exception – were periodically irrational, pun on purpose, simply and precisely because they were girls. If I suspected a darker illness, well, no teenager I ever was or knew would admit that to anyone. I was no ratfink. Maybe if I hadn't been so self-absorbed I'd have taken it straight to – no that's adult thish-ful winking. To whom would you suggest I could have taken it? My axe-wielding grandmother? The Snow Warden or her silent filmmaker? Uncle H? The lovely Bitsy? No, I did what I always did when I got scared: I got angry. I went looking for a reason to get angry, found it and let the anger act.

Yes, I'm quiddling, because no, there's no excuse for what I did next. For what I did deliberately, for very little gain. When you sell someone down the river, it isn't for the money, it's to see them float-ing helpless, to see them going, going, gone. Consider the mere thirty pieces of silver Judas got for Jesus. Consider that his brothers got much less than that, twenty pieces, for their much-loved baby brother Joseph. See, I listen in church. And if it makes you feel any better, like them, I could rend my clothes in shame. You see, as I leafed through her life, the angrier I got. Not at all the things that caused her pain or would have made anyone angry, but at the one thing that wasn't there – me. I checked a second time, but no, there was nothing, not word one. She never mentioned my name. Sucked up into her hurricane and disappeared. As obliterated as the first owner of ruby slippers. Piss on her.

I got ready to dropkick the whole damned thing when a gust of wind did the job for me. I tracked its long fall, enjoying its drunken crash and bash through scraping green branches. It landed, spine broken, pink on pink, splayed over the chunk of granite. I stepped on it. It should have been easy to pick it up. Anonymously easy to return it to its hiding place with her current diary, under her record case beneath her bed. But I'd put anger in charge and it did my thinking for me: 'If I'm not in it, why should I give crap one about it?'

I'd like to give myself an escape hatch, to claim I was just too overwhelmed to think clearly. I feel the need to remind you, I was all of fifteen years old. I'd even like to be able to cast what I did next as a really back-assward kind of call for help. But that doesn't explain it. Grandma was right: The easy way out never leads in. But this does: I expected her diary to hand me a mirror and when I failed to see myself, I saw red. It was spite. Pure and simple.

Like the song says, it's easy to be hard. I had time to reconsider. I had reasons plenty-twenty. Instead, when I passed Derwood, all decked out in his Scout uniform, headed for the tree with his binoculars, I smiled. 'Be Prepared.' He nodded back. The rest came into my head unbidden and unstoppable: 'A Scout is trustworthy, loyal, helpful ... ' You can still turn around. 'Friendly, courteous, kind ... ' You're faster then the little bear baiter; you could still beat him to the tree. 'Obedient, cheerful ... ' Insert face of BS here, still clucking. 'Thrifty, brave, clean ... ' What she said about Mom, that was just so dirty. 'And reverent.' The godless little brat. Serves her right. 'Do a Good Turn Daily.' Some Boy Scout. Some hero. I began to run.

HAZEL #67

Bonjour, mes amis! Bienvenue à *Chez Hélène*! Je m'appelle Hélène. My name is Hélène, and my little mouse, Suzie, and I, nous sommes très heureuses de vous voir! We are very happy to see you! You just missed Louise! Vous venez de manquer Louise! Louise est rentrée chez elle. Louise has gone home. Bonne nuit, Louise! Mais maintenant que nous sommes seuls, but now that we are alone, et maintenant que les caméras sont éteintes, and now that the cameras are turned off. Approchez, mes petits choux! Come closer, my dears, and I will tell you a secret! Je vais vous dire un secret! And here it is ! Moi, Hélène, j'ai peur des souris! Oui! Je crains les souris! In fact, I do not like mice at all! En fait, je déteste les souris! Thank goodness my darling Suzie, elle n'est pas une souris! Elle est ma vraie fille! She is my true daughter! Chez CBC, they did not think it was proper, en français, 'propre' means clean, n'est-ce pas? So I dress her up in whiskers every day, alors je l'habille chaque jour avec les moustaches, and we go off to work, et nous partons au travail. C'est convaincant, n'est pas? It's convincing, isn't it? I know the Children's Aid will take her from me one day. Mais pas aujourd'hui! Today, my little mousie even gets to know her father ... elle obtient même de connaître son père ... But if it is Monsieur le Giant Amical, qui vient devant nous, who comes on before us, or that très charmant Monsieur Dressup, qui vient après nous, who comes on after us, cela restera dans mon cœur, that will stay in my heart. If my Suzie gets to jouer avec Casey et Finnegan et avec Jérôme et Rusty, and if two of them are not actually puppets, et si deux d'entre eux ne sont pas vraiment des marionnettes but really her brothers, mais vraiment les frères de Suzie, then c'est formidable and qué sera sera! So goodbye, my little friends! Au revoir, mes petits amis! Et bien garder, s'il vous plaît, le grand secret de Chez Hélène!

I didn't have to plead innocence. She never really asked me. I just had to follow her Ruffled Feathers around and hold my breath, waiting for Derwood to cram a cracker into the biggest frog bomb ever to be held in hand. Was I nervous? Au contraire, I was unpleasantly energized, eager for it to hit the proverbial fan. Each time I dove off the dock, I hit water knowing I deserved to explode. But I still longed for the big bang to force BS under just long enough to finally shut her up. Because while we hunted for her diary, overturning every stone in March, she instructed her retard brother non-stop.

Each day she climbed the tree and looked down. I couldn't stop her, but I refused to climb it with her. We brought a compass and ruler and stood like surveyors calculating probable lines of fall. We went at liftoff, 4 p.m., pried open milkweed pods and released their feathery innards to retest the wind. We hunted rocks of diary mass, carted them up the tree in her black-swan sporran-gym-book-avenging-kit-Polk-Salad-rock bag and shoved, dropped and threw them off the platform to duplicate trajectory. We circumscribed the tree for a hundred feet – under every bush, thistle and cow patty. Jordan even banged on Hezzy's door only to be told that no, girlie-girl, nothing but cows in that pasture. She asked Missy P about bovine digestion and learned that no, a goat maybe, but not a cow; cows don't eat paper. She banged at Hezzy's again to ask after his goats. I asked her if she thought perhaps marauding bands of gypsy goats were scavenging his farm for loose-leaf. That went over well. But if one door sticks, another one opens. Once Jordan ascertained that the planet did not have her diary, she got out Occam's razor and cut to the crux: Derwood did.

And so she went straight to Grandma, who listened for three minutes and reached for her Sunday hat. 'Well, child, there's but one way to find out, isn't there?' She took Jordan's hand and marched straight over to Aunt Elsbeth's. As we entered March Three, we saw Derwood scurry out the back door for his bunkie. Grandma grabbed her daughter with her free hand. 'Elsbeth, come with me now and I'll explain on the way.' But when we stood in the bunkie and Grandma insisted on stripping Derwood's bed, on looking under it and in every drawer, rafter and cubbyhole, and still found nothing, that did not go over well either.

Derwood threw glances that could kill a frog without cracker. Aunt Elsbeth accused Grandma of picking favourites and stuffing the wrong bear. Grandma ate crow. 'I apologize, Elsbeth, and Derwood to you too.' She made Jordan and Derwood shake hands. 'There's been too much bad blood between you children. I want you both to promise that it ends now.' Derwood agreed immediately and BS said, 'I agree as long as he does.' Derwood peeked out from behind his mother's shorts, squinted at Jordan and sliced his throat with his thumb.

So she was stuck with me and I was stuck with her gushing Almost blood. It wasn't pretty. You try pulling the cork out of something that's been bottled up for over a decade; if it stinks to begin with, it sure doesn't age like fine wine. Comb seldom, comb sore. Insert some serious SNAFUBAR here. And I wasn't an adult, let alone a doctor. I was just her Running Board, running from and bored by, the endless tirades of one enraged little born-again gopher.

I got the worst of it on the days when the mailbox was empty. Ordinarily, you could set your watch by the RR #1 Fenelon Falls mail truck: 11:15 a.m. You could leave March at 11:10, rendezvous with NOB and be back on the dock, mail in hand, at 11:25. But by the end of July, NOB had lost either his Mickey Mouse watch or his Canada Post professionalism; he showed up if and when he pleased. We went earlier, waited longer and still missed him. We'd visit with Yogi or catch Kronk some bait at the edge of the swamp, keeping a vigilant eye on the silver mailbox, and never see him. On good days, when Jordan gave NOB letters and got some in return, she'd be almost normal. On bad days, and there were more and more of them, we suspected a repeat-offender mail thief but never caught him. When there was no mail at all, or mail for March but none for Jordan, she'd sigh – multiple times – set her sunny envelopes in the box, slam it shut, raise the flag, and raise her voice at me. Because once BS lost her diary, she vowed to make me the living record of a threatened book, just like in *Fahrenheit 451*. It wasn't enough to let me lend a listening ear; she had to convert me, knock me over the head, pull me off my slow boat to China and press me into service in her Bastard Salvation Army. Gentle persuasion was never her strong point. Whenever MC reminded her you can catch more flies with honey, BS would always grin, 'Yes, but baseball bats are much more satisfying.'

So she came out swinging, alternating patient, coaxing love taps with bunts upside my head, hitting high, 'Have you ever wondered?' and low, 'You are such a bloody retard!' It felt like I'd spent my life in a dim room and with each smack of her bat suddenly saw stars, bursts of light revealing things I hadn't known were there in the room with me, things that yesterday I would have denied could be there, a forced illumination that cast the everyday in an entirely darker light.

But I'll stop for sorry. My words are secondhand and witnessed by my hand. Hers are better. Here then, are fourteen pent-up years of BS at her indefatigable best, culled from our fruitless diary-hunting expeditions, held as July gained speed into August. I couldn't possibly recap all those conversations. She held court from sun-up to sundown and I promised you the shortened version. So I've compressed it into two or three conversations, held all over hell's half-acre of March, as we searched for what I knew she wouldn't find. Does nothing come so fair to light than what has been long hidden? Judge for yourself. For your discomfort, for your viewing unease, here's the Reader's Digest Condensed Version of the volume my sister tried to write on me: *Bastards for Dummies*, by J. M. March.

HURT SO BAD

'Take Bamm-Bamm.'

'You take him. I've already got this annoying little sister who won't shut up when I'm sleeping on the dock.'

'Very funny. I mean, take him as an example.'

'Of what, BS? Of secret coded anti-adoption insults in *The Flintstones*?'

'Nothing coded about it. It should be obvious even to the likes of you ... Sorry.' She sat up and began massaging a blistered foot. So much for running shoes. 'Bamm-Bamm. He's not Betty and Barney's "natural" son, is he?'

'Well, no.'

'Ergo, he's unnatural.'

'I didn't say that.'

'You agreed he wasn't natural, ergo, he must be unnatural. The same position you took when we were grounded. You said we can't be semi-dead – we either are or we aren't. Ergo, please be consistent now.' Yes, 'ergo' was the Word of the Day and, ergo, it was getting more than a little off-pissing. 'So where'd he come from, this unnatural changeling child?'

'Jordan, stop playing Perry Mason Reads the Dictionary and make your point.'

'Perry Mason? Funny you should mention him. But, okay, Fred and Wilma already have their natural baby, Pebbles, and so Betty and Barney, feeling deprived, want one too. Do they, gasp, do the nasty? Of course not, this is family television. Family, my asp.'

'That's where this stuff is coming from, BS. It's all crap.'

'Isn't that nice? No, Brother Mine, I asp-sure you, I'm not just passing wind.'

'Fine, continue. But it better start getting solid, man.'

'Good one. Betty and Barney wish on a falling star. Next morning, presto, in a turtleshell basket no less, is the proverbial baby on

201

their doorstep, with the equally cliché note attached: "I love my baby but I just can't look after him! Please give him a good home!"'

'And this is a bad thing? An orphan finding loving parents is a bad thing?' I hefted and swung an imaginary axe. 'Perhaps Barney should have boiled him up for turtle soup?'

Like I'd slapped her. 'First of all, he's not an orphan. Get your terms straight. His mom abandoned him; she's clearly alive. Secondly, you aren't the first to propose eating the world's unwanted children as if it were a joke. It's only "A Modest Proposal" if you're not one.' My face must have made it clear I was up that creek without a paddle. She sighed. 'It's a famous satire by Jonathan Swift. He advocates an end to Irish poverty by eating babies.'

'So? Poor babies. Not bastard babies. What's your point?

'Same difference. It's the Venn diagram I always see. Yes, the big circle is poor Irish babies but look inside it. Three of the reasons he advocated cannibalism were because poor children are "seldom the fruits of marriage," because it would encourage marriage once the kids became fattened assets for sale, and because it would prevent the common practice of women murdering their bastard children. So tally-ho chaps! Just for a lark, let's wash the great illegitimate unwashed and serve the tender little baby bastards with a side of blood sausage!'

'Then why does nobody else on the planet see it that way?'

'If I knew the answer to that I'd cut my head open to look at my brains.' She switched feet. 'Here's what I do know. The Rubbles get a lawyer, Bronto Berger by name, and try to adopt BB legally, but the adoption is contested by this rich guy, Stonyfeller, with his big-shot lawyer – you guessed it, Perry Masonry – who wins the case.'

'Man, you lie like a rug.'

'No. The fact that you just mentioned Perry Mason is, ergo, pure serendipity.'

Yesterday's word. Both in one sentence. Double score. Her self-congratulation radiated like a heat lamp and made me sweat. 'But Bamm-Bamm is a Rubble.'

'No, BB is turned into a Rubble. Conveniently, he has no last name when they find him, so they don't have to go behind his back without his consent and change it on him.'

'But you just said the Rubbles lost the case?'

'They did. But get this. Immediately after he wins custody, Stonyfeller learns his wife has just given birth! Now why he didn't know his own wife was expecting beats me. But naturally, the instant he learns he's won first prize, his own blood-gold offspring, he quickly hands the tarnished consolation silver prize off to the Rubbles. The judge? He just nods.'

'Come on, Jordan! It's a cartoon. Surely you've heard of them? Animated characters? Like the Archies!' That was a mistake. She immediately started singing 'Sugar Sugar.' 'Enough already. They're not real. That applause meter in your head? Have to break it to you, BS, not real either. Look. Maybe it's just a nice not-real story with a happy ending for kids.'

'Which kids?' She kept the Archies alive by drumming on the dock. 'Not this kid. I'm telling you, the first time I saw it, when I was, what, seven or eight, it made me cry. It kept me from sleeping. Passing a baby around like a dish of peanuts? A baby like me? Dad even calls me Peanut. No, it's not a happy ending for someone like me. It's not nice at all. It's vicious.'

'Has it ever occurred to you that you think too much?'

'Has it ever occurred to you that you don't think enough?'

That came out so fast and so glib it had to be rehearsed. 'Admit it, BS, you read too much into things. You think you're smarter than anybody else alive but won't use your brains to see anything but the darkest version.' She scowled. 'Just like that guy in *Li'l Abner*, the pouty one who seems to think he has to cart a shadow around with him wherever he goes.'

'Yes! Eureka ergo!' She jumped up, cleared her throat, cupped her hands and began in her best recitation voice: 'I have a little shadow that goes in and out with me, And what can be the use of him is more than I can see!' She looked expectant. I rolled my eyes. 'It's a poem, stupid, perhaps you've heard of them? By Robert Louis Stevenson. Same guy who wrote *Kidnapped*? She sat down. 'Hey, maybe that explains why he's so pissed off all the time?'

'Robert Louis Stevenson was pissed off?'

'No pea brain, Joe Bftsplk, Dark Cloud Boy. Maybe he's adopted? It would explain his unspeakable name.' She struck a tone and a pose like Daisy Mae. 'Why it's just plumb awful for po' Joe B. down here in Dogpatch. He's a cute li'l feller sho'nuff, but come Sadie

Hawkins Day, none of us girls'll chase him 'cause we cain't be sure he's really our cousin!'

I laughed, but couldn't concede. 'Well, Crazy Daisy, enough said. Maybe cartoons are just funny. Some laughs with a few good morals for kids. Nothing more and nothing else.'

'Moral? Really?' She sat back down and stared at me as if I'd just calmly suggested eating Balsam. 'Let's see. Poor mothers are forced to abandon their babies because they can't look after them and a judge says rich people get to play Pass the Peanut with impunity.'

That was my cue for my line from BMW. 'Chomp, chomp – '

She ignored me. 'Because it's more like a stray puppy. You found it? Then finders keepers! Give it a new collar and a new name and, presto, it's all yours. Parade it around town passing it off as your own. If it dies or doesn't work out, you can always go back to the puppy farm for another sad-eyed, needy creature. Illegitimate babies are trading cards, exchangeable little bitches. I'm a little kit sold off by an Overall Boy in a suit. How moral can we get?'

'Know what, BS? Just when it begins to halfway make sense, you blow it out of the water. How 'bout all's well that ends well? Or sometimes the nice guys don't finish last?'

'Ergo, Bamm-Bamm is a prize, a trophy? Much like the one Fred and Barney are always conniving to win for the Buffalo Lodge with their preposterous bowling technique?'

'Don't put words in my mouth! I'm not your personal puppet.'

'Funny you mention that.' She looked at me sideways, asking herself if I was ready for more. I wasn't. 'Pinocchio spent his life wishing he was something he wasn't. That's a great moral. Don't accept yourself. Spend all your time and energy wishing you were different. Girls, wish yourselves into Twiggy, or better still, boys. Blacks, wish yourselves white.'

'Get real, Jordan! When you stretch anything that far it snaps.'

'Who says I'm stretching it? I'm saying for me the strings of those connections are always pulled that tight. I'm not Pinocchio, but half the time I feel like Howdy Doody.'

'Jesus H. Christ! They're both just puppets. What's the bloody difference?'

'Howdy gave me the willies as a kid. No child with a brain would think he was a real boy! He was such a fraud, so obviously phony, pretending to be normal.' She paused and ran her hands through her hair, surprised yet again to find her fingers empty. 'He made me think everyone could see how phony I was. His strings were so visible. Him and his stupid twin, Double Doody. So obviously the same puppet. Stupid pun. Double Doody doing double duty.'

I rolled over to sun my back and spread my towel out to dry. 'Jordan, either you're passing more wind than that hurricane of yours, or you're asking me to believe that you remember, no, correction, remember and process and classify and cross-reference everything you've ever seen or heard, literally every bloody word, since you were what, seven?'

She stared a long moment with a look I so seldom saw on her face that it took time to name it: incredulity. A small voice asked, 'Doesn't everyone?' My face must have mirrored hers. 'Great! So now we have yet another way I'm a freak.' She wound her towel around her feet. 'Actually, I was maybe three years old when ... no, enough said. Let's talk Bamm-Bamm.'

'Didn't we boil him up already?' At that she grabbed my towel and lowered it to the lapping water where its feathery edges sucked like a sponge. 'So what?' you say. 'It's just a towel. Get another one.' No, it's never that simple in March. Occam would have slit his wrists.

For as long as I could remember I'd had my towel, my blue-and-white Maple Leafs towel, a 'joke' birthday present from Uncle H to Jordan that I quickly appropriated, and Jordan had hers, the only garment she owned that wasn't yellow. Grandma made it for her, pink with white stripes, an ingenuity of kindness. If you're Jordan, it's hard to see over a towel bunched against your chest, hard to stay balanced carrying a towel in one bent arm. So Grandma designed a hood and drawstring towel, a regular Little Pink Riding Hood. It had slits to free Jordan's hands and huge pockets for mask or snorkel or frogs. After a swim, she could cover her hair, keep it out of her eyes and stay warm. More importantly, to or from the lake barefoot, she could see her feet and the ground, and have her hands out when she fell.

If either of our towels got wet, MC went ballistic. Mother School taught that a wet towel was an act of insolence, of selfish disrespect. It makes more work for MC, though just what that was

I can't rightly say, since as you no doubt remember every blessed thing got washed on Sunday anyway. But not wanting to hear the 'I'm your Mother not your slave' speech, I needed BS to stop before I was sorry.

'All right, aunt! You win. No butchering or boiling Bamm-Bamm.' I should have held my tongue but couldn't. Too many b's, sounding too bloody good, 'But how 'bout a blender?' Bamm. Whirling it over her head like David's slingshot, it got smote on the water. But unlike sorrow, towels don't float.

HAZEL #71
(An homage to *Little Women*, by Jordan May March)

Thank goodness for my girls, my darling daughters! They stayed so true, the dear ones, reappearing loyally each night, even in my first days of incarceration here, when it was all befuddlement. When I tell the staff about my girls, the nurses tsk-tsk and frown. The doctors try to take my girls out of my head altogether. They try pills and kind words and then stronger pills and unkind words. When none of it works, they call Johnston, the orderly with the red hair and the chipped tooth, and he takes me to the basement.

I'm flat on my back and he clamps me down. He smears jelly on my temples. It smells like gasoline. He screws on the cap. The leather chafes my chin. We wait. He makes small talk as his hand grips my knee. Dr. Swift strides in and says the same thing each time: 'Best for all concerned.' He flips the switch and I'm sucked senseless. His switch yanks my brain from its roots. Flying like the tree that hit Angus, like the roots that stabbed through his window, I twist through black and empty space. I crash-land hours later, knowing but not believing that it must only be minutes, as I'm still in the basement, staring at the ceiling as one or both of them hitches up their pants. 'Repeat after me: Nothing happened in that hurricane. I have no daughters. Subways are safe.'

The nurses insist I'm making it up. They tell. So Dr. Swift ups the voltage. He pats my chest and frowns. 'It does a lady no good to be stubborn.' It doesn't stop my girls from coming, but I play the good patient game and tell him it does. Why? I can't risk the possibility that the eraser he keeps poking into my head might work. I can't lose them. Especially now, now when we are about to reunited! I knew it the second I got the telegram. The little paper sent a jolt of hope through my heart. Meg and Amy reached for my hands. Beth began to cry as the twins, Jo and Jordan, read aloud in a single voice:

Mrs. March:

> Your daughter Virginia is found.
> She is very ill.
> Come at once.
> 　–Margaret Sinclair, P.H.N.

How strangely the day brightened! I stretched out my arms to my daughters. 'I shall go for your sister at once, and pray it may not prove too late!'

For several minutes the sound of laughter filled the room, mingled with loving, hopeful whispers. 'Where's Laurie?' I asked, once I had decided what must be done.

'Here, Madam Mother. Oh, let me do something!' cried the boy hurrying from the addition, whither he had withdrawn, no doubt seeing our first joy as too sacred to share.

'Send a telegram saying I will come for Virginia at once.'

'I'm at your disposal, ma'am! I can run anywhere!'

'Then take this note to Aunt March. I shared a glance with Jordan, both of us well knowing that money for the auspicious journey must be borrowed. 'Now go, dear,' I said, handing the note to Laurie, and knowing him only too well, added, 'But don't kill yourself running; you'll be back in plenty of time.'

With that I sent each of my girls but Jordan on an errand. They scattered like butterflies. I'll admit that writing, thinking and directing all at once bewildered me a little. To be so close to union and reunion, something that my family and my poor war-torn country so desperately need, to be so close to finally having all my girls and then perhaps to lose my littlest – kidnapped from her bassinet by Southern sympathizers, by those pernicious perpetrators of human slavery, the Childer's Anti-Abolition Society – no, I won't think on it. I bent to my mending basket as Jordan read from her beloved bard, 'The labour we delight in physics pain.'

Everything was arranged by the time Laurie returned with a note from Aunt March, enclosing the requested sum and repeating what she too often said: that Ginny was no kin of hers and no good would come of pretending otherwise. I read the note to Jordan, put the vile words in the fire and the money in my purse. Jordan reached for her bonnet.

Meg and Jo finished my packing, Beth and Amy got tea, but still Jordan did not return. How could I say goodbye without all my doves about me? Jo stood at the window, anxious for her twin. Laurie ran off to find her, for no one ever knew what freak Jordan might take into her head. But she came walking in alone, her face a mixture of fun and fear, satisfaction and regret, which puzzled us as much as did the bills she laid before me. 'Here, Marmee. Give Aunt May back her blood money. Let me bring Ginny home.'

'But my dear one,' I cried. 'One hundred dollars! Where ... ?'

'I didn't beg, borrow, nor steal it. I earned it.' And Jordan took off her bonnet.

'Your hair! Your beautiful hair,' cried Jo.

'Oh, how could you lose your one beauty?' That, of course, was Amy.

Jordan assumed an indifferent air, which did not deceive me a particle. She tousled her auburn bush, trying to look as if she liked it. 'Here's how I will explain it in my story tonight: "it doesn't affect the fate of the nation. It will be good for my vanity: I was too proud of my wig. It will do my brains good to have that mop taken off. I'll soon have a curly crop that will be boyish, becoming and easy to keep." So please, Marmee, just take the money and let's have supper.'

'My dear one.' I reached out and took her hand. 'I cannot tell you how much I respect your sacrifice, but I am concerned for you. That you will soon regret your bravery.'

'I won't let myself,' Jordan returned with a firm nod.

'Why on earth did you do it?' asked Amy, who would more easily have cut off her head than her long, straight, flat-ironed hair.

'I was wild to do something for Ginny,' replied Jordan, as they gathered about the table, for healthy young people should always eat, even in times of trouble. 'I hate to be beholden to Aunt May and I couldn't bear what she wrote about Ginny. If it gets my dear sister back home even one day sooner, then I won't regret it all.'

'Didn't it break your heart when the first lock fell?' asked Meg, shivering.

'I took one last look at my hair and that was the end of it. I will confess, I felt queer when I saw the dear old hair laid out on the table. I picked out one long lock. For you, Marmee, to remember me by, now that I won't need your nightly brushing.'

After dinner, Beth went to the piano and played Jordan's favourite hymn. All began bravely, but in the end Jordan was left alone, singing with all her heart, for music was her best consoler. Then my darlings went to bed as silently as if our dear little invalid lay in her own. I sat and listened, unable to think of sleep for myself until I knew they had respite for their worried hearts. Meg, Jo, Beth and Amy drifted off. Jordan lay motionless and I fancied her asleep, till a stifled sob made me exclaim, 'Dear one, what is it? Virginia?'

'No, Marmee.'

'What then?'

'My – my hair,' burst out poor Jordan, trying to smother her loss in a pillow.

I held my brave one till she slept. I pulled her scribblings from her covers, and as they fell open, noted that the promised draft of today's story was written in her Alcott pen name but ended with me. 'Marmee glided quietly from bed to bed, smoothing a coverlet here, setting a pillow there, pausing to look long and tenderly at each child, to kiss each with lips that mutely blessed and to pray the fervent prayers that only mothers utter. As she lifted the curtain the moon suddenly broke from behind the clouds, and shone upon her like a bright, benignant face. It whispered, "Be comforted, dear heart, there is always, always, light behind the clouds."'

But here in this place, there is no such good-night. My Mumsie never comes. Here my bed has bars, like a crib, as if I were a child. At night the nurses tether me to them as if I were an animal. I try to explain that I need my hands to fight him off when he creeps into my room at night and they smile and say, 'Don't worry, dear. That'll stop soon enough.' Johnston, he smiles the most. He smiles when he grinds his chipped tooth into my left breast. Grins when he leaves my nipple bleeding, my sheets torn and stained.

In the morning, when the nurses see my bruises, they say, 'Stop struggling, silly goose! Surely even you can see you're only hurting yourself?'

GREEN RIVER

I fished it out, wrung it out and spread it out, hoping it would dry before Eagle-Eye Fleagle spotted it, dry flat enough that said Eagle Eye wouldn't notice the wring marks. 'Who's Eagle-Eye Fleagle?' you ask. No idea. I think he's another *Li'l Abner* character, but he could just as easily be a cold war spy, a 1940s gumshoe, or another March invention. You decide. As I sat back down, BS made it clear that the b-b-blender line required an apology.

'Okay, aunt, aunt and more aunt. Let's b-b-begin again.'

BS sat back down. 'I guess I can't really expect you to understand.' She squinted. 'Everything, and I mean every single thing on the planet, has an extra layer for me. Beyond and behind how you so-called normal people experience things. Even ordinary things.'

'No, I get that, BS. What I don't get is why it's always a knife in the back? Is the entire world out to get you? As far as I can see, no one has any intention of doing so. Well, with the possible exceptions of Aunt May and our lovely mother.'

She smiled. 'SNAFUBAR, eh?' She paused. 'Maybe it isn't about intent. Maybe you don't have to intend damage to inflict it.' She stared at the cracks in the dock. 'Maybe it's built right into things. Take that *Flintstones* episode. You saw good morals. Wanna know what I see?'

'Do I have a choice?'

'Yes, a choice to remain ignorant, something no self-respecting person should even consider. A choice no one who loved me would.' Another speech. Overprepared as usual.

I muttered, 'How serendipitous. Ergo.' She glared.

'Moral One: Illegitimate children come from elsewhere, perhaps the stars. Ergo, they are not human. Aliens, like bears in cages, don't have human rights. Moral Two: Rich people can buy these illegitimate unnatural commodities, complete with a lifetime guarantee. Moral Three: Bastards are property. They can be renamed and rebought with the consent of the law, worked to death or neglected at their owner's pleasure. Just call me Yogi. Moral Four: Slavery lives.'

'That's bloody ridiculous! You're –'

'Not finished. Moral Five: Bastards wear a perpetual silver medal around their necks. Even sterling silver is only 92.5 percent pure, the rest is copper, base metal, low, like baseborn, so the owners of bastards, like our parents, like the Stonyfellers, will be quick to trade a bastard in for the gold medal kind. Moral Six: Us stuck-in-silver types spend every second of every day watching you legitimate kids parade around with medals of pure gold, ones to which you feel so bloody entitled you don't even know you've got them.'

'Hey, man, are we still talking about cartoons here?'

'Bamm-Bamm is more than Bamm-Bamm!' Then she giggled; even at her wound-up best she could appreciate the idiocy of that line. 'Don't get me off topic. Seven: Bamm-Bamm, despite his extraordinary, dare I say, alien strength, that marks him every moment of every day as obviously not the Rubbles' "natural" child, will grow into a happy and healthy teenager. Such a good little devotee of Silver Semi-Quietism, he'll never question where he comes from. He'll date Pebbles. He'll be so bloody-well adjusted he could be the fourth Chipmunk.'

'Stop rrright there, young lady. You must be on drrrugs.' This was a bang on imitation of Mr. Lucifare, Alderwood Collegiate's VP and self-appointed narc who patrolled the halls hissing like a mongoose. When she laughed, I hoped that would end the harangue. Fat chance.

'You know, Alvin, Simon and Theodore, those ever-so-cute chipmunks adopted by manager Dave Seville, who kindly embezzles all their money? They're the perfect adoptees – permanent little ones, perpetually grateful and cute, who never grow up to ask uncomfortable questions. They're so brainwashed they don't even know they're rodents. They don't come up to his bloody kneecap and they don't even notice. Could you imagine Ruffled Feathers letting himself be adopted by Colonel Kit Coyote? No. Those chipmunks are stupider than Pinocchio. They actually believe they're his real, live boys. No wishing necessary.'

'Okay. *The Flintstones*, *The Chipmunks*, every cartoon ever made – all deliberately designed to kick Jordan May March in the teeth. What's next, commercials?'

'Yes. Bastardism is everywhere. In the Tiny Tears commercial a three-year-old tells her dolly not to cry because "she's her very own baby"? Don't you see? It's Bloodspeak, right in the language: Comes by it honestly. A chip off the old block. An apple won't fall far – '

'Bastardism? Come on, you made that up. What's next? Semi-Quiet Bastardism?'

Those were the oddest moments – when she took a tesseract right through my sarcasm to another point entirely. 'No, bastards are forced to be Semi-Quiet. But Bastardism itself is anything but quiet. Like anti-Semitism.'

'Fine. You win, Sister Sherlock. Tough titties for you. Let's swim.'

I should have seen the gritted teeth. 'My point is that I can't win precisely because it can't be changed. Precisely because people like you, to the bloodline born, roll their eyes, tell me I'm exaggerating, and say anything to make me stop making *them* uncomfortable.'

'Enough already! The water's waiting.'

'*You've* had enough! When do I get to say "enough"?' She stood up, draping her towel cape over her head and tossing the end over her left shoulder. An injured Queen of Sheba. I laughed and she snapped, 'You're so welcome! I'm glad you find me ridiculous and can dismiss my life so easily. Thanks for your tourist sympathy.' She pointed her face into the cloudless sky and yelled, 'Just go away, little stray! Go away, I say!'

'What in the Sam Hill was that?'

'A Little Golden Book. Like *Mr. Moggs' Dogs*? One of those nice, moral, cartooned kid's books. One MC kindly kept reading it to me, long after I could read for myself. An abandoned puppy goes door to door in search of a home. No one wants her. A farmer chases her off with a pitchfork. They all yell, 'Go away, little stray! Go away, I say!' Exactly what Canada said to that boatload of Jewish refugees in World War II? They had to go to seven countries to find a home. Me and the SS St. Louis. We know just how it feels.'

'BS, that's insane! You can't compare – '

But like a watch with inner workings twisted taut, she'd stop when she was fully run down and not a second sooner. 'Or take *Little Lost Angel*. Another Golden Book for Golden Children. She comes to the manger on Christmas Eve, falls asleep with the lambs and gets left behind. Only when she gives away everything that makes her an angel, her harp, crown and wings, only when her feet are cut and bleeding, only then does she see the light, only it isn't heaven, it's *a home*. The woman who opens the door says it's the child she's prayed for. Like Betty Rubble sans turtle shell. And the moral? They love her so much they forgets she's different. She lives so happily ever after, helping her lovely mother sweep the floor, that even she forgets she's an angel. Isn't that nice? I'd happily trade a crown and a pair of wings – particularly the wings, why would I need those – for the domestic bliss of brooms!'

I needed her to stop. I was mad, so I made her mad. 'Oh, quit yer quiddling!' She paused furious, but puzzled. 'You heard me. Look, you know that glass that's either half full or half empty?' She nodded. 'Well, you see one that's full for everybody but you. You see hundreds of glasses all poured by the hands of all the loving mothers you'll never have. Keep looking at life that way and you'll never be anything but thirsty.'

'Yeah? Well, maybe that thirst is all I've got!'

'Yeah? Maybe you're proud of it. Maybe you're Yogi rubbing her eye on purpose.'

'Chuck you, Farley! Everyone knows best when his own shoe nips him. So try this one on for size.' Her face? I'd call it a sneer. 'Your hero, Underdog? He's not just guilty of Bastardism. He's as bad as Hitler.'

And before I could respond, before it registered just how pissed off I was that she'd actually tried to smear Underdog, she tied towel to chin and took off. A pink-striped back: that's what you see when you haven't got a gun. I lay back down. Chuck you twice, Little Miss Farley.

The sun grew hot and hotter. The film that played in the Rosedale Roxy in my head was, quite fittingly, one I'd already seen. More than once. The official Etobicoke Board of Education Remembrance Day Documentary. Hitler marched across the dock. He wiped out the orphanages, cleansed the hospitals of the mentally ill and the disabled, went after the gypsies, the trade unionists, the homosexuals, the intellectuals and the Jews. At that half-baked moment on my dock in Rosedale, Ontario, in 1969, it's nothing I'm proud of, but it did happen. Adolf turned a wolf's eyes toward a little pink hood. He lifted his snout and sniffed. And I told myself that maybe if we'd kept him around a little longer, he'd have saved us all some grief.

GET TOGETHER

For the next week or so, all we did was trade insults. We'd try to go frogging, or out in Grandma's canoe, and end up bouncing off each other like billiard balls, striking with a force that propelled us further away from the other. I pushed to get away. I kept saying, 'It's just a joke,' or 'Just your imagination,' or in more frustrated moments, 'Just your BS paranoia.'

'Listen to yourself,' she'd say. 'Whenever someone says "just" like that, it's a lie. They're trying to minimize, to convince and console themselves and anyone listening. They're out to shove something large and complex into a smaller, simpler box than they know it deserves. "Just" is the most dangerous word in the world. "Just" is never just "just"!'

My response? Silence, eye rolls, snickers and scorn. Did I keep quiddling because she was so holier than thou, or because my egg had two yolks, both with a yellow interest in the status quo? I don't know. I know I used every known 's' word: selfish, spoiled, self-absorbed, self-important and sanctimonious. I suggested my real sister had been abducted by aliens, who in a cottage-country version of *Invasion of the Body Snatchers*, had replaced her with every kid's horror: the McElfiend English teacher, one who ruins a perfectly good poem by insisting that you look for crap you can't see, gives you a passing grade only if you find it, and a good one only if you grovel and thank her for opening your stupid eyes. MC came out of my mouth more than once: mettle is dangerous in a blind horse. One man's poison is another man's meat. It's kittle to waken sleeping dogs, let them lie. I told her twelve highlanders and a bagpipe may make a rebellion, but one little girl on a high horse is a royal pain on an asp. That went over well. And yes, as I helped her turn over every stone in March looking for her diary, I accused her of hypocrisy and arrogance. Sarcasm won the odd battle, but I was clearly losing the war.

So I got dirty. I hit below the hymnal, suggesting that my newly atheist sister had simply divined a replacement religion. Eureka hallelujah! Of all the adopted kids on earth, she was the Chosen One, the Bastard Messiah! Lobbing Ye Holy Hand Grenade, I said her only miracle was the truism that if you look for anything hard enough, you'll eventually find it whether it's there or not. I said her crusading heroes had gone to her head, that she'd trumped up a phony cause just to put herself on the same footing as Bobby Kennedy, Martin Luther King and Cesar Chavez. I told her she needed to get her head read and her grapes stomped.

'Buy yourself a hippie wig, so people will think you're a girl, and you march, March! Bastards of the World Unite! You have nothing to lose but your shames! Hey, with that martyr complex, maybe you really are MC's daughter!' I'm amazed I lived. She challenged my 'excuses and avoidances,' squinted at my 'uncharitable and smugly privileged generalizations,' but she didn't give up, on me or her diary.

By August, I'd come about half of her distance and we'd Sherlocked every square inch of March. She liked me best when I felt like Scrooge, who after having the bejesus scared out of him by his ghostly mentors proclaims, 'I never did know anything. *But now I know that I don't know anything!*' This is not to say her illuminations could be trusted. A bolt of lightning stabs insightfully straight but casts a narrow beam. Like the day she finally outed Underdog.

I found her out on the rock pile, singing a new hit by the Youngbloods, 'Get Together.' She saw me and turned her back. Clearly, the mountain was not going to come to Mohammed. I jumped, swam over and let her finish. Like I had a choice.

If you hear the song I sing, you will understand.
You hold the key to love and fear, all in your trembling hand.
Just one key unlocks them both, it's there at your command.
Come on people now, smile on your brother,
Everybody get together, try and love one another right now.

I figured she didn't need to sing the thrice-repeated chorus. 'Speaking of smiling on your brother, now that you've cooled off, how'd you like to explain that crack about Underdog?'

She shrugged. 'He's worse than all the uncles put together. He's as bad as Derwood.'

'My Underdog?' She was stomping on sacred ground and she knew it.

Let me be explain. For years of my childhood, I was Underdog. Only midget-idjits considered him a rip-off of Superman. So what if just like Clark Kent the meek Shoeshine Boy transformed into his alter ego in a telephone booth? He was still The Boss, the hero with the best theme song in the recorded history, the one with 'speed of lightning, roar and thunder, fighting all who rob or plunder.' Thanks to another one of Uncle Gavin's trips, once Jordan tired of it, I even had an Underdog ring. 'The secret compartment of my ring I fill, with an Underdog Super Energy Pill.' When teacher wasn't looking, especially before a math test, I'd sneak one. At recess my eyes would follow Wendy, a.k.a. Sweet Polly Purebred, the blondest girl in my class and the second she got into anything that looked like danger, I'd whisper, 'When Sweet Polly's in trouble I am not slow. It's hip, hip, hip and away I go. Not bird or plane or even frog, it's just me, little old Underdog.' Yes, Wally Cox, the voice of Underdog, could teach today's rappers a thing or two about rhyme. As could BS, whom I occasionally managed to bribe and cajole into playing Polly, but didn't understand she was the sidekick, a Lois Lane wannabe. Everyone knows Sweet Polly's only job is to swoon and say, 'My hero!'

I'll admit it: my belief ran deep. When Jordan was off elsewhere, I'd drag Dad's old army shoeshine kit and several pairs of his shoes out to the end of the driveway. Delma Drive disappeared. This Shoeshine Boy perched on the most criminal corner of New York City. With official stool, round tins of waxy black and brown polish, a variety of brushes both stiff and soft and two well-worn shammies, I waited, prop ready and poised for action, ready to flip open my ring and spring into the sky if I spotted an evil-doer, ready to pack it up and vamoose if I spotted my sister. But not this time. This Underdog would right her wrong with blinding speed.

'You're nuts, BS, 999 Queen Street nuts.'

'That nuts, eh? Fine. Then tell me, who is Simon Bar Sinister?'

'Don't be a retard. The bad guy, the mad scientist who tries to take over the world.'

'Yes, yes, with his ridiculous inventions, his ever-so-manly guns: the Sneezing Gun, the Crying Gun, the Relaxing Gun and let us not forget, the Go Snow Gun. Not to mention his bigger weapons: the

Upside Down Machine or the Tickle Feather Machine or the machine that dropped the Forget Me Net over Washington to rig an election. See? I know the show as well as you do. He's insane, yes, but why? Because he's a bastard. Literally.'

'Says who? Explain it or I'm history.'

'How serendipitous.' My look must have spelt murder as she quickly elaborated. 'In history, his name is a pun on bastards. In heraldry, on coats of arms and shields, a line from top right to bottom left is the bar sinister, which, in Latin, means both left and evil. Left is dirty. It's the hand you wiped your asp with before they invented butt wad. That's why we shake with our right hands. Left is bad and dirty; right is clean and good. And not incidentally, right.'

'Okay, the bad guy in a cartoon is evil and dirty. Hardly a newsflash.'

She sighed. 'A bar sinister, both left and dirty, is the sign for a bastard. An illegitimate son still got a coat of arms, but one with his shame broadcast for all. Even illiterate peasants. Like having a big neon sign saying what Aunt May said about me.' She danced around the rock pile, ducking under once or twice to improve her foothold or possibly cool her face. 'And Simon means one who hears. So as I figure it, your Underdog is voluntarily fighting a mental patient, one who's been made mental because he can hear he's an evil bastard. Isn't that nice?'

I guess I didn't look suitably regretful or impressed, so she got snarky. 'You still think I'm making this up? Okay, lover boy, what's Wendy's – excuse me, Sweet Polly's – last name?'

'Purebred.' And I saw frogmarchers as soon as I said it.

'Why is she considered pretty? Why does she have all the boy dogs panting after her?'

It wouldn't work but I was desperate, 'Because she's much better looking than you are?'

'Nice try. Listen ten seconds to the uncles and figure that one out. Because she's a blond, a purebred, a.k.a. sure of her parentage, of her blue-eyed, Aryan bloodline. Not a mongrel. Not a bastard. Sugar sweet is Polly, like lolly, like Wendy, and all you silly little boys lick her right up. Congrats, Brother Mine. You have the same taste in women as Hitler.'

'No wonder those girls stopped writing to you! I'd like to stop talking to you!'

'Look, I know you're not in Grade 10 yet.' I'd have drowned her then and there, but lacked a braid for a noose. 'But when you are, you can take World History and Man in Society. Then if you sit down and really think about it, you'll see things with a little more maturity.'

I did the one thing left to me: I reached for an MC and aimed for her eyes. 'If I don't see it like you, Gypsy Sue, maybe it's because I'm not a ridiculous little girl with a problem!'

She somersaulted and surfaced smiling. 'Eureka! You get it! I'm Gypsy Sue; you never will be. You look in the mirror and see Dad at your age. You have to be taught what I see because you've never asked yourself what I see.' I hadn't and she knew it. She began pointing energetically at herself and at me, a rather impressive feat of synchronized swimming when one is also treading water. 'Look at me! I might as well be Suzie the Mouse on *Chez Hélène*!'

'I am looking at you, BS. You do have a fondness for cheese but I'm relatively certain you aren't a hand puppet. However, come to think of it, you could trim those whiskers.'

'Well, BB, if I had facial hair, that would make one of us.'

'Touché.'

'No thanks. I'm sure you do that for yourself quite enough already.' I lunged at her but my hands came up empty. I couldn't reign her in, let alone hold her under. She gloated, 'See, I said last time was the last time you'd noose me, and I meant it.'

'Okay, Suzie. I'll give you this much. You are a little mousy.'

'It's an analogy, pea brain. It means I feel like a squeaky little mouse-person living with giants who don't speak mouse. I'm under five feet tall and have this great bush of red curls, or at least I did.' A moment of regret swept her face but she fought it off. 'A zillion freckles and I burn like bacon. You Marches, not a single one of you jolly brown giants is under five ten. With all that straight black hair and tanned skin you could be a long-lost tribe of Iroquois.' She folded her arms. 'Ruffled Feathers say mighty March tribe run like horse and see like eagle.' She dropped the Injun act. 'How many Marches wear glasses? Me, myself and I, and that's appropriate because mine are thick enough for three.' I hadn't wanted to say so, but yes, they were. 'You're probably all the same bloody blood type, O+, Positively Ordinary. I'm A–. Now there's a symbol, my life motif. Might as well be T– like Mr. Spock.'

I wanted to goof on that one, but her face warned against it. She kept rinsing it in the waves, looking more distraught with each immersion. She gave up and swam back to the dock, wheezing like the Spadina streetcar. I followed. She plopped down on the planks, shook what was left of her hair over her face and lowered head to arms. I sat down beside her.

'And then there's – ' She swallowed. 'As if there wasn't plenty-twenty, there's my bar sinister ... my left ... ' But she wasn't ready to say it any more than I was to hear it. None of us had ever were. Not word one. Her stunted right foot could pass for normal. Almost. Her left foot never would. She pulled hood over face and rammed a pink stripe between her teeth.

I threw my arm over her shoulders. 'Okay, BS.' I said, 'I'll take Bamm-Bamm.'

Hey, it was summer and the water was warm. I figured I had time, twenty-plenty time, long and longer days of endless, lazy time, and nobody, not even my newly evangelized sister, could stay whipped up in BTO forever. (That's Bastard Theory Overdrive not Bachman-Turner Overdrive – they came later.) Eventually she grinned. 'Okay, Fred Marchstone.' She shucked off my arm and dropped her towel. 'Consider me your own personal Great Gazoo, exiled from the planet Zetox and sent to earth to help the Dum-Dums like you.'

I did a quick tally in my head. Okay, the Simon Bar Sinister thing wasn't nice. It played like some kind of cruel, adult in-joke. Bamm-Bamm's story might send some dicey messages to someone looking for them, but that stuff about Underdog was just nonsense. I was pretty darn sure a normal teen like me could get through all of high school with none of the things BS tried to pass off as 'fact' ever crossing their minds. I bet if I mentioned just word of this to Wendy, my tongue would never touch hers again. To most of us, to me, cartoons are just cartoons. Just for kids, just harmless. They end when they're over. We just laugh. No harm, no foul, enough said.

But I counted them. I counted despite myself. If nothing else, Jordan had taught me to wonder. In all probablility, that's her greatest gift to me and perhaps to you. Did it mean anything, just how many times I needed to say 'just', just to just about justify it? Insert your just answer, just here. I pushed her in and raced her to the rock pile, discovering en route that I suddenly had to work to beat her.

HAZEL #79A

It's because the poor wee thing has red hair, just as me Mam and I do, that I kept hopin' she'd give in. I thought about it every day, all day. I rehearsed convincin' her brick by brick, trowel by trowel. I prayed for it at night. Hazel and I, we even named it after Mam, hopin' she'd stop quoting Deuteronomy and come round. It broke me when she hardened. 'The child of a Jezebel is a spawn of Satan! The wages of sin are death.' I protested. I tried sweet-talking her. I tried gettin' angry. Once I even cried. I kept insistin' that of course the bairn was mine, and hers, her very own grandbaby. I lost me patience. 'Goddamnit, woman! It's yer very own flesh and blood!' And for the first time in my life and hers, she slapped me. 'Sonny-Jim, ye canna be tellin' the truth if ye have to take His name in vain to do so!' I've never been so grateful. It was the hand of God. She pushed me to my knees. 'Get that wee red devil behind thee!' And I saw the light. A fornicator like Hazel, she canna enter the kingdom of heaven, and if I believe in me heart that I am not one, if I disown the wages of sin, then I still can. She lifts me to me feet and forgives me. 'Sonny, you'd better take those odds. Better that than never bein' able to set foot in Leaskdale United ever again.' She doesn't say it but I hear it good: better than being disowned by your Mam. Better my shame than her name.

HAZEL #79B

The sorry misbegot in question has red hair, so all believe it mine. I'm the hourly recipient of ribald buffoonery: 'Bet you laid her flatter than the brand-new dollar bill you paid her!' And yes, contrary to my express wishes, Hazel named it after Mater, so I'm relatively certain that should I deign to claim it, she would eventually stop quoting Deuteronomy. But a manager has options. A manager delegates, but keeps his own hands pristine. So I girded my loins when Hazel wept a woman's false tears. She actually had the harpy nerve to raise her voice: 'Goddamnit, Walter! She's your own flesh and blood!' I felt like a cad but I had to slap her. 'You're my wife, not some floozy from the woodpile!' But when we married, she was far from lily white. Apropos of that, it's a fifty-fifty chance I'm not the party responsible. I'll take those odds. There will be no tellers snickering behind this suit. I'll not hear 'Cuckoo, cuckoo!' for the rest of my natural born life, thank you oh so jolly much. Who would dare criticize me, the loving husband, the devoted injured party standing by a feckless wife, if my Christian conscience simply prohibits me from raising the love child of her wanton indiscretion? It's devilishly simple. No baby, no ridicule. Better her shame than a gentleman's name.

HAZEL #79C

So what if the little git has red hair and some twat nurses think it's mine? I say, 'No! Plenty of guys with big stethoscopes got red hair!' I told Hazel to go ahead and name it after my cow of a mother, who was already on her side, quoting Deuteronomy and calling it my Christian duty. Expect that from women. They stick together like shit and a shoe. When Hazel swore at me, 'You're an educated man! Acknowledge your own flesh and blood, Goddamnit!' I hit her for her own good. Easy as spanking a tired little puppy. A few electroshock treatments later, she's indebted, she's confused, she'll do anything I say. Let her think herself a slut, pregnant by an old boyfriend or her boss. Let her think she got raped by the bloody hurricane itself, for all I care. Same difference. As long as one of them marries her. Then presto! Meet Dr. Available! I'll take those odds. Better than jail. There's plenty more where she came from. Like that so-called friend of hers, that legs-together pubic health nurse, ironed so starched and prissy. The horse-faced ones, they're always so grateful. Better my game than a slut's claim.

A BOY NAMED SUE

My conclusion was grand and daring, truly worthy of Underdog, the Gophers, the Avengers and Captain Kirk: I decided to say absolutely nada to no one, to ignore the whole SNAFUBAR mess. I'd pretend that our Lucy had her new oxfords on just fine and her head screwed on with equal firmness. I'd be all three monkeys at once. Good one, Sherman. That strategy backfired worse than Hezzy's truck. At Dad's birthday party, Tuesday, August 5.

Dad took August holidays to celebrate his day. All the uncles did; they all had August birthdays. Isn't that nice? The party was well underway, the barbecue glowing. We'd endured the requisite wop jokes and one-upmanship over Jordan's shorn hair: 'Where'd you get that 'do? Buzz Saw Bambino's?' When Uncle G asked Mom if she'd blown a gasket when she saw it, MC shrugged and said, 'Clipped sheep will grow again.' When Auntie E, between mouthfuls of swampwater, noted yet again the happy coincidence that all her Big Boys were August Boys, Jordan muttered, 'Gee, Grandpa sure musta loved pumpkin pie!'

March took a silent second to assess whether or not my sister actually meant what she'd said. When she repeated her witticism without the 'k,' so familial retards who missed it the first time could better appreciate it the second, of course she got sent inside. We both saw Dad swallow a laugh, but I imagine that was little consolation.

When I followed her in and pointed out that the pie in question was her grandmother, she crumpled like my useless tinfoil antenna. 'Oh no, I didn't mean that! I'm just so sick of listening to them congratulate each other for being related, like it's some sort of immense personal accomplishment.' She opened her sock drawer, retrieved her yellow stationery. 'Sometimes I should trade the speeches for common sense. Grand knows. She'll understand.'

'You're actually going to tell her? To write it down?' She nodded. 'Why? Because if you don't, Derwood will?'

She spoke slowly as if I were a little deaf and very dumb. 'No, because I *should* apologize and because if I don't, I'll feel bad.'

No one else would have. Had uncles H or G said it, the moment would have ended with an ensuing snicker; nothing would have happened to them, and not just because they were adults. Dex or Der or even Derwood could have said it and simply been told it wasn't polite, a fact I'm sure they needed no metacognition to tell them. They'd get off scot-free because boys will be men. A March who is not a boy, however, must be punished for having the effrontery to sound like one. That liberty isn't hers to take. It isn't fair, but it is truly March.

Uncles got to be extra-boyish on their birthdays. Tradition dictated that the Birthday Boy must invite all of March over for a barbecue lunch and baseball, and then, leaving behind all things familiar – a list including wives, children, bats, balls and an enormous stack of dishes – blast off to the Pattie House to spend the afternoon in a quenching of boyish thirst. We watched out the window, as burgers and Red Cap got guzzled and the game wound down. Derwood had been razzed about not letting anyone use his precious bat but still striking out with it, twice. He'd slammed its velvet case and sulked. Dad had spent much of his own party filming it, and with equal inevitably Auntie E had stalked Dad with her Instamatic, ready to do what Mom should have, to snap Dad at 5:07 p.m., his Birth Moment.

'What's that?' you ask. Another protocol I thought every family practised, until I discovered the Birth Moment Photo to be both uniquely March and uniquely mad. You can blame my grandfather. Legend has it he was the first March photographer, entranced since age nine by an exhibit he'd seen in the Crystal Palace on his first trip from Leicester to London. He began when you needed a curtain, when a single shot required setup and time and expense. You couldn't fire willy-nilly, so he shot his brood individually just once a year, at the exact moment of birth. Even in the lean years, Grandma refused to sell his equipment. Even during the War, luck-seeking uncles hunted down a GI buddy with a Brownie camera. The aunts prized their children's photos, kept in long, now very long, rows of little gold frames. If uncles were embarrassed by theirs, they were too superstitious or too smart to say so.

The only person to point out that the emperors had too many swaddling clothes was of course my mother, who said one of the same two things each year: 'Egotism is an alphabet of one letter,' or 'Pride that dines with vanity sups with contempt.' Last summer, when Aunt May asked her why she couldn't just take Dad's photo and join the family, MC shot back, 'A fetish isn't a family.' Aunt May sniffed and said she supposed that a sterile sweater girl from a Mimico had to throw any stones she could find. Mom threw herself at her bedroom.

Thus every March baby had a full set of BM photos. Except Jordan. Maybe the parents didn't want to admit the obvious and start hers at age four, or maybe MC wouldn't let Dad join the party. I felt sorrier for Auntie E, the greatest enthusiast of the tradition, who had five boys born in the dead of the night – five rows of sleeping or surly, unwillingly awakened sons. So at 5:07, Dad smiled for posterity and Auntie E kept snapping. The Birthday Boy and His Mommy. The Birthday Boy and His Brothers. The Birthday Boy and His Daughter still hadn't occurred to her a roll of film later. When cousins piled on top of each other to get into the last frame – a good-luck ritual known as March Thaw – Jordan left the kitchen window.

If we'd used the front door we'd have been swamped by the melt-down on the lawn, so we went out her bedroom window. Thank goodness for crochet hooks. We slid our boards out from under the rear of the deck, our gangplanks to Swamp Island. We'd put planks in the swamp ever since the Roxy days, creating treacherous footholds to jump between seats, semi-sunk appliances and uniden-tifiable chunks of semi-solid refuse. Ungainly pirates, we got twenty-plenty soakers. At the edge of exploration, we found a treas-ure we kept to ourselves: a narrow patch of solid land, a finger into the swamp. Probably logs felled by forgetful beavers, covered by decades of leaves and moss. Dad would claim it eventually, but that day, when we pulled the gangplanks up behind us and hid them until our return, we felt unassailable.

That notion is, of course, ridiculous. All it took was Johnny Cash. When he started singing, Jordan dropped the radio and backed away. The way you and I would back away from a rabid animal. Silly goose. I walked up to it and starting singing. How could I have known? I just wanted to show her she wasn't the only one who could learn an entire song. I thought I did a pretty good Johnny. I honestly thought she'd enjoy it. 'A Boy Named Sue' is funny, isn't it? Every-one knows it for a joke, don't they? Judge for yourself:

Well, my daddy left home when I was three
And he didn't leave much to my ma and me,
Just this old guitar and an empty bottle of booze.
Now I don't blame him 'cause he run and hid,
But the meanest thing that he ever did
Was before he left he went and named me Sue.

And I kept singing. About how Sue grew up quick and grew up mean, and his fist got hard and his wits got keen and he made a vow to the moon and stars to search the honky tonks and bars and kill that man who gave him that awful name. I particularly loved the part when Johnny found him and said, 'My name is Sue. How do you do? Now you're gonna die!' And then beat him, 'kicking and a gouging in the mud and the blood and the beer.'

So I sang the whole thing at full throttle. But when I turned for congratulations, I spotted her twenty paces back, sitting on a rotting log, tugging on swamp grass. 'Gee, thanks! You get your own personal JC serenade and you don't even bother – what the Sam Hill!'

It wasn't swamp grass. I never learned its proper name. We called it cut grass: darker, greener and thicker than ordinary grass, it stands about two feet tall, a thicket of sticky barbed edges. Run into it by accident and back out like a snail. Every movement draws blood; it cuts at the touch. And there was my sister, distractedly, without flinching, grabbing stalk after stalk, pulling her hands right up each one. Left. Right. Left. Right. Blood spattered her knees. Red fingerprints smirched her yellow shorts. At a complete loss, I grabbed her wrists and waited. Eventually focus came back to her face. 'Blood will have blood, they say,' she said. I held on and held still. 'Sorry, that's *Macbeth*, not me. That song is just one dagger too many. Especially today.'

'I don't get it. What's wrong with Johnny's song?' She stared at the ground, utterly still. She didn't even blink. I had to get her to talk. I tried to think the way she would. 'Is it because a guy should be honoured to have a girl's name?' Not even a quiver, let alone a smile. Good one. 'Is it that when he finds his father all he wants to do is kill him? Is that what you want, to find them, your other parents and ... '
I couldn't finish the sentence but at least at this she quickly shook her head. I waited.

It came out swinging. Nothing comes harder to light than what has been well hidden. She yanked her hands back. 'Nobody asked me. What if I don't want a name that makes me Bamm-Bamm angry all the time? Maybe I don't care that it's made my wits keen. Most days I'd rather they weren't. What good are keen wits on a girl anyway? I'd rather be Wendy, dumb and pretty. Even you like her better than me.'

'Jordan, that's a lie and you know it.'

'Is it? How would you know? How would you know anything about what it's like to be me, a smart girl, a smart little girl with big thick glasses and shoes that – '

'Jordan, you're more than your shoes! Right now you're just – '

'Just nothing. Johnny's dead right. It's that name that's helped to make me strong.' She squinted down her nose. 'So, how strong are you? Ask me how old I was when I was adopted.'

That I could do. 'All right. How old were you?'

'Like the song says, when I was three.'

In a rush of relief, I deliberately misunderstood her. I so badly wanted to. 'All this fuss over a girlie coincidence in one line of a stupid song? Stop being so bloody melodramatic!'

'How dare you? Even the likes of you knows that three-year-olds have names. Did anybody ever ask me if I wanted one that would make me, how does Johnny put it, roam from town to town to hide my shame? What if I don't want to be thankful for the gravel in my guts and the spit in my eye? I should be grateful because I'm spit at? I don't have a choice, but you do. Is there gravel in your guts? Let's see.' Her face levelled mine. 'Ask me my name.'

That I couldn't do. 'Come on, this is silly. You're my sister. Your name is Jordan.'

She pressed her sticky palms together, 'Silly? And a rose by any other name would smell as sweet, right? That's the stupidest thing that's ever been said about horticulture. If it were called something else, no, it wouldn't smell as sweet because then it wouldn't smell like a rose. Some other flower with some other name would.' She planted her feet apart and cupped her hands at her sides. One girl gunslinger, dripping blood.

'See here, pardner, I'm not big enough for the both of us.' She pulled her guns, twirled them and shot skyward. 'My last name is

Johnston.' She blew the smoke off her right gun and holstered it. 'My middle name is Gail.' She took aim, shot herself in the left foot and restored the left holster. 'And like the song says,' she proffered a bloody palm, 'my name is Sue. How do you do?'

Johnny came out of my mouth before I could stop him. 'What? Now you're gonna die!'

She shrugged. She smiled. 'I hope not.' That was better. But what came next was much worse, 'But it depends on which one of us is actually alive. Some days I'm Jordan. Some Susan. Most days I'm both but neither. No, neither and both. Always neither and almost always both.' The blood kept dripping. 'I can't expect you to get it. I'll stop for sorry. Sorry if I scared you.'

'Jordan, this is scary stuff. More than SNAFUBAR. It's beyond me.'

'No, what's scary is that my own stuff is beyond me. Except for the stuff I stole.'

'Stole?' I took her back to the log and made her sit.

'Yes. When I was nine I went through MC's desk. I got it in my head that she knew where Ginny had been sent. That maybe she'd been sent back to The Lady.' She half-smiled. 'That's what I called her, our mother, when I was a kid. I figured if I found her, I'd find Ginny. I found my Adoption Order and a file from Children's Aid. They call the stuff they send with the babies Non-identifying Information. Isn't that nice? A rose by any other name indeed.'

I was stuck on sentence one. 'Mom's private desk? In her bedroom? But it's locked!'

She gave me the glance the princess gave the wrong frog. 'Yes, and a lock has a key and that key is in Mom's underwear drawer. On the left hand side under her good girdle. The red one,' she added, enjoying my obvious discomfort.

'So, at the ripe old age of nine, you went riffling through her underwear and stole her private papers, and now, what, five bloody years later, you finally tell me?'

'Yes, and I've done it several times since, just in case I missed anything.' She threaded her fingers. 'Look, she's made it private but it's not hers. It's mine. I only went looking for what you have every day, especially today.' She swung her head back at the thawing and guffawing on the lawn behind us.

'But what if you'd been caught?'

'I wanted to be caught. When I stole it, no, correction, when I reclaimed it, I wanted to force her to talk to me. She knows it's missing, but she's never said word one. And never will.'

'So ask her.'

'There you go again, Mr. Genius Pants! That never occurred to me! I'll go straight home and do it right now. Roger Wilco over and out.' I mumbled something about only trying to help and she sighed, 'Sorry. I'm just on edge today because, well, I hate birthdays.'

My sympathy line snapped. That mouthful was pure piñata, a bold-faced lie, a pure BS pity party. She loved birthdays. She had a Birthday Book listing the gemstone, horoscope sign and exact BM for everyone she'd ever met. She bought and wrapped presents days if not weeks in advance, spent hours crafting handmade cards. I'm no saint. A man can't carry his kin on his back. Whoever said, 'He ain't heavy, he's my brother,' never had to carry my sister. 'BS, your nose is so long I'm surprised you can breathe. Why don't you just grow up?'

'Really? Hmmm ... Okay. Fine. I'll grow up, if you 'fess up.'

'What in the Sam Hill are you talking about?'

'I'll ask you once. I'm not getting all my mail, I can't find my diary, and I can't pin either on Derwood.' She looked straight at me; I went looking for the radio. She followed. 'You were the last person to see it and, frankly, I've been beside myself with worry.' She giggled. She got the hiccups and got hysterical, got winded and fell over, writhing in the grass. This was easily as disturbing as the blood drops that fell from the grass to her face.

'I don't get it, Jordan. Get up. What's so GD funny?'

'I'm beside myself. Get it? I can double my pleasure and double my fun, without Doublemint, Doublemint, Doublemint gum! That's the funniest thing I've ever said.' She sat up and wiped her eyes clear. 'Answer my question. My diary – you've had it all along, haven't you? And my mail, is it stashed under your bed with that sticky yearbook photo of Wendy?'

I twirled the knobs as hard as I wanted. 'Of course not! What do you take me for? I pulled her up. 'Look, let's just agree that if that stupid song comes on, we'll just turn it off.'

She took the radio, trying unsuccessfully to meet my eye. But that was all I offered, that and a quick change-of-subject alibi. 'What are you going to tell MC about your shorts? You can't hide that blood with shoe polish. She's going to notice your hands.' She cringed and swept them behind her back. 'I've got it. Say you tripped. Say you fell into some cut grass and had trouble getting up. I'll back you up.'

'You won't have to,' she sighed. 'As the only Tiny Tim amongst you Olympians, everyone, especially our lovely mother, is more than ready to believe that story. Watch. She'll be so POed about my shorts, she won't even see my hands.'

She impersonated bulletins from Mother Control all the way home: 'Can't you think of someone else besides yourself for a change? Don't I have enough to do already? Honestly! Do I have to tie you to the clothesline line with Balsam just to keep you both clean? When-oh-when will you figure out that you're a girl?' Bang on, word for word. You'd have thought she was wearing all the blood of Culloden. BS got bulletined all the way into Cobie. Any excuse to haul Dad home from the Pattie House earlier than necessary. When we sat to supper, MC ruled that the dirty ingrate known as Gypsy Sue, the careless little girl who had been so self-absorbed that she spoiled her shorts and her father's birthday, that Missy Sadly Mistaken could pay for her selfishness by eating alone in her room where she could enjoy her leftover birthday burger and no birthday cake in silence. Mom only let her out to stand at the sink, to wash and dry several hours' worth of birthday dishes.

When Jordan protested that it wasn't fair, Mom agreed. 'Life's not fair, Missy.' MC headed to her room, then stopped and turned to Dad, 'Hmm ... can we sell that silly CNE concert ticket to pay for some new shorts?' Before Jordan could protest, MC smiled and closed her door.

Too bad Jordan didn't come up with the cake knife and cut off a piece of Mom's ear. I'd have enjoyed some kickin' and a gouging in the mud and the blood and the beer. A fistfight would have been preferable, might have inflicted a less costly wound. More importantly, it might have led to talking, because so clearly to anybody not a monkey, not enough said. I imagine many words went straight into Jordan's lone diary that night but she read me only one line: 'Now I blame you, Ma, 'cause you run and hid, But the meanest thing that you ever did, was before you left, you changed my name from Sue.'

AQUARIUS

I guess her muse kept her up that night, because I found the third profoudly amusing version of my heroism in my left running shoe the next morning. No wolfen address and no yellow envelope this time, just a sheet of foolscap crumpled and shoved.

Back away from the screen. Counting three boys tonight: two cousins, Dex and Der, and some other guy out of sight in the corner. Only one girl. Not Blondie. A new Trenter, some redhead in a yellow tube top. Usually they're blinded by the light, but tonight it's only a candle crammed into a Mateus bottle. Be careful. When a trailer's in the dark, they can see you through it. What are they doing? Nothing. Acting stoned. Carving a groove in the Fifth Dimension: 'Let the sun shine, Let the sun shine in ... ' Corner Boy unfailingly returns the needle. Nobody objects. Dex throws another on the pile of twenty-plenty empty brewskis. Nothing happening here. Get your motor running. Go home.

Tube Top splays out over Der's lap. Dex flicks bottle caps at her. Hard. Harder than necessary. He stands up, swaying but up. 'Hey, cousin, I know what your little girlfriend needs. A walk. A nice refreshing walk on a summer's evening.' Der shakes his head. 'No thanks, cousin, we're just fuzzin'.' 'But I insist,' says Dex and pulls Tube Top to her feet.

Der hesitates but does not object. Between them, smoothly, in one practised motion – they're both lifeguards – they grab a wrist, loop one of the girl's arms over their necks, wrap their other arms criss-cross around her waist and lift. Her feet leave earth. Move! You reach deep shadow as they reach the door. They swing her down the stairs. Corner Boy yells, 'Hey, you guys! Wait up!' A needle screeches across

Aquarius. He must have kicked it. The door opens. Corner Boy is Derwood. Of course it is.

With their booty suspended between them, they're running. Run silent; run deep. They check for night fishermen before crossing the dam. Why? The little-used path between the dam and the locks, it's tricky at night. Unstable rocks. Roots that grab at your ankles. They veer off the path, into a giant cedar grove. With cedars this tall there's always the same thing in the centre: dead space, an inches-deep carpet of brown leaves. No light, till the flick of a flashlight. A circle on Tube Top, still dead to the world. 'Okay, little brother,' says Dex, 'time to be a man!' A hand yanks Tube Top's top down. Light is a shrinking circle that captures the girl, the breast, the nipple. A mouth intones, 'Zero. Johnny. Roger. Tit target sighted.' Mouths laugh.

Look up, way up. There are still stars. Framed stars. Dead above, you see the exact outline of the Little Dipper, framed to perfection by the surrounding tops of trees. Such serendipity. A minor miracle. That these branches grew just so for hundreds of years, formed with but one purpose, just for you, so you could stand exactly here on this clear night, on this spot in this grove and look up at this exact moment to behold exacting beauty and do exactly nothing: 'When I consider thy heavens, the work of thy fingers, the moon and the stars which thou hath ordained, What is man, that thou art mindful of him?' Good one. Got an answer?

Then don't look back. When you do there are hands, everywhere hands. Six hands. It looks like sixty. Something zips. Someone in this man's army yells, 'Yippee-i-o-ki-ay! Let's ride 'em, coyboys!' Then suddenly it's six legs, illuminated by a fallen flashlight. It's three boys bent over, three hands grabbing her breasts. The other three hands? Down their pants. Tube Top groans. 'Bloody hell,' says Dex. He punches Der in the shoulder. They zip and run. Tube Top struggles to sit up, Derwood pushes her down. Holds her down. Face down. Puts one foot on her back. 'I see Crotch!' Not funny. The stars wait. Derwood moans. He jumps up, zips up and explodes, 'Yeeeee-hawww! Hey, you guys! Wait up!'

Beneath you are inches of soft dead cedar, a decomposing carpet on the earth, as dead as ashes. You feel nothing, smell nothing, taste nothing, and will remember nothing but the soft welcome of cedar. For forever and whenever you smell it, be it scented candles or Grandma's wedding chest or even one of those inane little car fresheners, you'll hear it too. You'll be instantly returned to the Fifth Dimension, hear the promise of the Age of Aquarius and the dawn that never came. Peace does not guide the planets. Love will never steer the stars.

What did I do? I laced my shoes as tight as necessary and went for my run, tracking every scent of anger I could find. I told myself it was time for Jordan to play the girl game. I heard my mother's voice, 'Do as all lassies do – say no and take it.' After all, it was just a prank. Boys Will Be Boyish. Nothing serious. Hey, no one objected, least of all you. Good one. Although I never said any of it to her face, I sounded like this, 'Good Morning Starshine and if this time when you open your eyes, you don't hear the *nibby, nabby, noobys*, it's your own damn fault. You should have got yourself out of Kit Coyote's territory when the getting was good, little sister, and if you didn't, you're one stupid little gopher who was positively asking for it. Ergo, serendipitous or not, it bloody well serves you right.'

It was bad enough that she knew, bad enough that I still didn't know how the Sam Hill she knew. But I couldn't come right out and ask her. The worst thing wasn't what she knew at all, but what she had guessed about me that I had feared about myself all along. As I watched my cousins cage another little red-haired girl, I'd had time to intervene plenty-twenty, but I'd decided instead to keep watching. I'd consciously and calculatedly stood stark still and decided to do absolutely nothing, when what the situation so clearly called for was a push of sane desire. This Sherman wasn't half the man she was. I was a bloody tourist.

HAZEL #86

When the Inverness sputtered and died, I all but cheered. Momma has such visions of herself as a Kawartha Tugboat Annie, some kind of womanly Tom Thompson painting the Canadian Not-So-Far North. Just because her momma lived on the water back in Scotland is no excuse to make me live on a floating coffin. I'd have Uncle Angus pipe a pibroch for the blessed thing and send it to Atlantis where it belongs. Anyone with romantic notions about houseboats needs to grow up. You can't even have tea without it sloshing into your lap. Try that in a bathing suit! Enjoy the grit – it's sand not sugar. Enjoy Momma's complaints too. You try mixing paints on a moving boat. No, I don't ruin things on purpose.

So I hoped it would stay dead. I'd still be stuck with Momma but at least I wouldn't have to smell that smutty motor. And then – rescue! Errol Flynn in sunglasses. I knew the second I met him, or so I thought. Tall and tanned and piloting a brand-new speedboat. I asked him what he called her and he said he couldn't think of a name. I laughed and said since he'd come to our rescue, slicing through the waves like a shining white knight, he should call her *Excalibur*. He laughed. 'So christened!' He took us to his mother's cottage for tea and crumpets – they are so English! His younger brother towed the Invy to the marina.

I liked the whole family except that younger brother, I just couldn't read him. Not as striking as the rest, and quieter, stuck behind his camera, shy. Momma said he was a better prospect than Howard, but to put my hand no farther than my sleeve will reach because you can only catch the fish that bites. Tommy came to our engagement party but even there held himself at arm's length. He shook my hand when all the other men kissed my cheek.

That October Friday, the three of us left early. We had to go, despite the weather. They always close up the weekend after Thanksgiving. My future mother-in-law insisted it was a three-person job, but there's no doubt in my mind that she was protecting my 'virtue' by sending Tommy along as third wheel and chaperone. I'd do the final cleaning and the boys would pull up the water line, dry dock the boats and check for dead limbs that might cause damage if they fell over the winter. That's supposed to be the job of that vile monster of a man who lives up their road, but he doesn't seem to do much of anything but drink.

We were late. We'd had a dreadful drive, three of us packed like sardines in Howard's little Morris Minor unable to see two feet ahead for the rain. And once we got to Rosedale they refused to close the swing bridge. They'd left it open hoping the storm would do less damage that way. Howard had to open his wallet, twice, before they finally shut it and we crossed over.

We got drenched to the bone unpacking, but we'd eaten and washed up and stoked the fire before the storm got really bad. Howard, of course, had his flask so between it and the fire we stayed quite cozy. When the electricity died, we were already a little silly, so we took Howard, ever the tipsy optimist, up on his suggestion to treat the whole thing as a lark and sing campfire songs. It was during 'Michael Row the Boat Ashore,' right at the part that goes, 'Jordan's river is chilly and cold, Hallelujah! Chills the body but not the soul,' when I noticed someone looking at me in a way that no decent man would look at his sister-in-law. And God and Momma help me, when Howard wasn't looking, I looked back.

When the tree hit, not only did it come crashing through the picture window, it created a wind tunnel that sucked sparks about the room like drunken fireflies. We raced around beating them out. Howard yelled that he remembered a piece of plywood out behind the pumphouse. The moment he left brought another walloping gale. I jumped. Someone put his arm around my shoulders, turned my face to his and started kissing me. He said crazy things, that he adored me, that he'd promise me anything. This went on far longer than it should have.

Where was Howard? Well, that second whoosh of wind contained a paddle. It had sailed over the pumphouse and taken Howie out at the knees, knocking him across the dock and into the water. That's where we found him, clutching the paddle, clinging to the dock, his left leg broken in two places. 'What took you?' We couldn't lie fast enough.

We pulled him out, splinted his leg with the paddle and then realized that, all trussed up like a stilt walker, he wouldn't fit into his own car. We had to go up the road to ask the hairy Monster Man to drive us. The three of us on that trip into Fenelon, crouched in the flatbed of that contemptible man's filthy truck, trying to hold a tarp over poor Howie that the wind kept yanking out of our hands – that was a nightmare in itself! The doctor said the breaks looked bad, gave Howard a shot to help him sleep and advised against moving him to Lindsay Hospital until it got light. He offered us a couch for the night, said it was playing with fire to go back out there. He was right. Our drive back, it was one slow burn.

Several months later, after the wedding and after he did the math, Howard was understandably furious. He said he'd let me have the baby but he'd be damned if he'd raise his brother's bastard. So to make a longer story shorter, dear, when your father heard that you were actually his and that Howard had made me turn you over to Children's Aid, he came in through the bedroom window the very next night. We had the marriage annulled, easy to do thanks to Howie's infidelity with some waitress – he called her Bitsy but I was never sure if that was her name or her IQ. Your father and I got married immediately in Niagara Falls. You've seen the pictures.

Of course we still had to pretend, but we kept tabs on you through my friend Miss Sinclair. Do you remember a public health nurse coming to see you in all your foster homes? That was my Miss Sinclair! And thanks to her, it took only a few years. Once we'd fooled everyone into believing we couldn't have children of our own, then, on the best day of our lives, we got you back! So yes, as strange as it sounds, my dear River Jordan, the early years were chilly and cold, but we finally rowed your boat ashore. Adoption chills the body but not the soul. A daughter's a daughter all the days of her life, because you're adopted in name only, dear. You're really ours. Our own child. You're just like everybody else – loved and wanted. There's milk and honey and it's on your side. Hallelujah!

CRYSTAL BLUE PERSUASION

When Derwood's frog bomb burst, it fell like snow. He'd taken his own sweet time, but his opening salvo, I'll admit it, took both brains and balls. Wednesday, August 6, the morning after Dad's birthday. I was busy dreaming about scoring, when the pre-dawn screaming began.

We stumbled outside in pyjamas, half-expecting to see crazed animals gnawing on her bones. We saw snow. Giant sheets of snow. And a crazed Snow Warden who bore a marked resemblance to my sister, who instead of packing it down was running wild on the lawn, scooping it up and screaming at its touch. I walked up to one sheet. Not snow, colder. Enormous sheets of chart paper. Held down by pebbles of pink granite.

'Don't just stand there,' she screamed. 'Help! But for God's sake don't read them!'

Good one, BS. You could read them a mile away. Impossible not to, right from square one. Acronyms in enormous block letters, bold and black in indelible marker:

GIRL IN FURIOUS TEMPER ENDURING DUPLICITY

GEEK INCURRING FIERCE TEASING EVERY DAY

GRINDING INDIGNITIES FROM TEDIOUS EGOCENTRIC DUMMIES

GROWING INCREASINGLY FORLORN, TICKING EVERY DAY

GEE IT'S FUN TO EXPECT DISAPPOINTMENT

GUESS IT'S FATE, TASK EXCEEDS DISAPPOINTMENT

GOD IS FICKLE! TRACK EVERY DOUBT

GETTING IDENTITY FROM TEARING EVERYTHING DOWN

GOING INSANE FEARING TRULY EVIL DESTINY

GOAL IS FINALLY TO END DESPAIR

GHOSTS: ILLEGITIMATE FABRICATIONS THAT EVENTUALLY
    DISAPPEAR

I don't claim to remember them all, but each one knifed my gut. They told me what I already knew: no good deed goes unpunished. Told me what I'd been hoping to forget. That thanks to me, Derwood didn't just have a bomb, he had an arsenal, and he intended to use it. As always, the parentulas had no clue. When Mom reached for one of the sheets, BS swept down and tore it from her hand. The parents shook their heads and went inside. Probably figured she'd put them there herself. Real snow in July, that would have been worth filming.

Miraculously, the signs from our lawn, the dock and the paths all got retrieved before the rest of March began its day, but it was Grandma, awake and expecting her granddaughter for early morning gardening, and worse, who wordlessly handed over the last one, a smaller version, torn and crumpled. She pointed at an all-too-familiar step-up chunk of pink granite deposited conspicuously on her porch. Jordan read it with me over her shoulder:

> You claim you're GIFTED, cousin dear.
> If you're so smart, then stop me here.
> 'Cause I've got so much blood to spray,
> I'll save THE WORST to spoil THE DAY.
> P.S. You used the wrong version of that stupid poem. I fixed it for you.

Jordan flipped the page. Her illuminated 'Desiderata' was obliterated. 'Deteriorata' replaced it:

> You are a fluke of the universe.
> You have no right to be here.
> And whether you hear it or not,
> The universe is laughing behind your back.

So what did my baby sister do? Well, beside Grandma's porch stood her woodpile, and out in front of it lay the big flat stone where various shirtless cousins were sent in penance to chop pine trees into manageable logs for her fireplace and kindling for her woodstove. Jordan grabbed said axe and spun on her heel. Grandma grabbed her arm. 'Child, stop this now. To hurt him is to hurt yourself.'

'Excellent!' BS moved faster than I've ever seen her move, whooping like a howler monkey, louder than Ruffled Feathers and Running

Board put together. Grandma couldn't keep up. I blinked, unable to accept the image of my sister near an axe, let alone the running footage of her wielding one she intended to use for Derwood dismemberment. I wavered on the porch, proving the cliché that he who hesitates is lost, or in my case, last. Good one, Sherman.

When I ran, of course it wasn't fast enough. In a wild blur, Jordan flew past the other cottages. I lost sight of her when she rounded Uncle G's corner. I came round just in time to see her reach the bunkie, plant her feet and swing the axe a smooth full circle over her head, a blow with both a strength and an expertise I would never have believed, and in truth could not have duplicated, a blow with might and skill sufficient to demolish the screen and cleave the wooden door in two. It stopped me dead.

Derwood screamed through the hole where a door had been. He attempted to jump out of bed, but got tangled in his sleeping bag and fell to the floor. A broken Pinocchio, limbs akimbo. He lay there, worming backwards and whimpering. BS entered the broken doorway. 'Give it all back, you dirty thief. My charts and my Yogi and my diary. NOW! Or the next thing I smash is your fucking head!'

She raised the axe but never stood a chance. A Valkyrie since Grandma's, she'd awakened every March alive. Cottage doors had clanged. Dex all but zipped right through me, launched himself off the bunkie step and knocked Jordan face first onto his brother's bed. He mashed his foot into her back and raised the axe, poised and panting.

His parents scurried in behind him. One to check on Derwood. One to scream at Jordan, 'You crazy little bastard! Get the hell off my property!' Jordan, face down on the bed, made only the smallest of movements: she covered her ears.

When Grandma arrived, everyone fell silent. 'Cursing at frightened children are we now, Gavin? How becoming. And you, Dexter dear, unless you have rusted like the Tin Man of Oz, give me my axe before you hurt yourself.'

Ignoring the rest of us, she simultaneously wrapped one hand around her axe and one arm around her granddaughter, lifting her from the bed. Jordan didn't open her eyes. She wouldn't take her hands off her ears. Sheltered under Grandma's arm, she took a few steps in the direction of Almost, then hesitated. Together they collectively, if not damn near telepathically changed their minds. They turned left up the longer path to Grandma's.

So what did we do next, you ask? The parentulas, apparently stuck in a time loop, arrived late only to discover they'd soon be dollars short. They watched their would-be Carrie Nation and Almost Lizzie Borden daughter being led away and let her go. In short order, a tall order of March materialized. Explanations and denunciations had to be issued and reissued. A figure had to be set and exchanged for the bunkie door. Every March alive had to debate that one. The parents got so caught up apologizing to Auntie E and Uncle G, to Dex and Derwood, to anyone listening, for their deranged daughter's unacceptable and inexplicable behaviour, that they never did make it up to Grandma's. Dad went into the cottage for his wallet, paid Uncle G and took his wallet back. I guess they figured she'd come back eventually. When she didn't, Mom poured Jordan's cereal back into the mouseproof jar.

So what did I do, you ask? I ran an extra mile. As I returned, I spotted the parents out on the lawn chairs having their morning coffee, or in Mom's case, Ovaltine. Dad was filming Mom, who had her nose in Dr. Spock. Now there's common sense. I'm sure that's exactly what they teach in Mother School: read up on that psychotic axe-wielding daughter of yours, but don't for one second actually speak to her.

Time for version number two from this number one son. I'd speed up. I'd bolt clean through the dangerously narrow space between them, run clear off the dock – speed of lightning, roar of thunder – and cannonball into the lake wearing my shorts, my team shirt and yes, my very expensive track shoes. 'Look! A distraction!' If that was the least I could do, at least I'd do it. Rodeo clowns save lives. Blow off some more steam, while you're at it, Mom. C'mon, yell some more. Some hero. Some clown. Yes, grandstanding was stupid. No, I wasn't going the way of my sister, although yes, at that moment, same difference. Yes, I was an ungrateful brat thinking only of myself and deliberately making more work for you. Do I think you have nothing better to do? No, I think you have something better to do but flatly refuse to do it.

Of course I didn't actually say any of that. So much for thishful winking. I went straight to my room and took off my track shoes.

Insert all the things Underdog would have said here – that is, if he still loved Sweet Polly once he realized what everyone else already knew: a bottle blonde can't pass herself off as a purebred for long. Eventually, your roots show; eventually everybody sees you for what you are. A Heinz 57. A rabid mutt. One crazy mongrel bitch.

BLACK PEARL

I guess the parents figured that grounding didn't take, so the next morning, Thursday, August 7, MC handed Jordan an itemized list of extra chores that at the hypothetical rate of $1.00 an hour would repay Dad for Derwood's door by the end of the summer. If she worked all day. At her lunch break, she agreed to eat at the picnic table, but kept glancing bunkie-ward.

'So, 'fess up, BS. When did you learn to deliver the chops like that?' I thought my pun quite clever.

She snorted. 'One lucky shot. That's all. But speaking of chops, Burton's concert is – '

'BS, BS! Don't change the subject. Your swing was perfect, Paul Bunyan perfect. Somebody's coached you and you've been practising plenty-twenty. Make with the words.'

She picked up her sandwich and occupied her mouth with chewing. Ironically, Uncle G had supplied said lunch, or at least half of it: our fluffernutters.

What's that, you ask? WBEN TV in Buffalo, Channel 7 – home of pyromaniac Irv Weinstein who set daily fires in Lackawanna, Cheektowaga, Tonawonda, Freeport and Batavia – had three sponsors for our favourite cartoon show, *Rocketship 7* with Dave Thomas: Ked's running shoes, Good and Plenty, and Marshmallow Fluff, a candy sandwich spread. Imagine extra-white, extra-fluffy, extra-sweet mayonnaise. Jordan had marched around all of the summer she turned nine singing, 'Oh, it takes Fluff, Fluff, Fluff to make a Fluffernutter. It takes Marshmallow Fluff and lots of peanut butter.' Uncle Gavin still called her Fluffernutter, and whenever he went stateside, he brought her a jar.

And Jordan still loved them, especially the kind we had that day on steam loaf fresh from Bell's Bakery, courtesy of Grandma. But she had no use for Mom's garnish, Aunts on a Log. She hated celery. She licked raisins and Cheese Whiz, ensured the eagle eye was fleagle-ing elsewhere, and passed said logs under the table to Balsam. He loved it and she loved doing it. Dogs and cheese. Girls and secrets. I was sick of the whole damn shooting match.

'Well,' she finally responded, 'let's just say a bunch of lazy cousins don't keep Grandma from having to chop her own firewood. Or from wanting to. Maybe there were some mornings when she showed me how to help her do so.' I must have looked skeptical. 'In case you haven't noticed, our lovely grandmother isn't your typical little old lady.'

'I didn't mean Grandma.'

'Me? Maybe I'm stronger than I look.' She flexed her arms like Popeye but no anchors appeared. 'I am. I'm particularly good at kindling. I can split a branch six ways to Sunday.'

'With your balance? If she knew, Mom would kill you with both hands.'

'Excellent! A fact I might make use of one day. Thank you.'

'Get serious, BS. She doesn't like you riding a bloody bicycle. She won't let you water-ski. How'd you think she'd feel about you running berserk with a twenty-pound axe, swinging it over your head like some crazed Amazon warrior?'

'Deep in that sarcasm is the only compliment you've ever given me. I'll treasure it.'

'Fine, don't listen to me. Or to anybody – you never do. Just tell me: why does a girl like you want to learn to swing an axe?'

Gargling Tang, she stopped mid-gurgle. 'Like me? What's that supposed to mean?'

'It means just that – a girl like you.' Sometimes she was so dense. Just look at her – that kind of girl. 'It means a good girl, a nice girl. You. My little sister.'

Jordan swivelled over to my side of the table. 'Is that a serious question?' I nodded.

For a second I thought I might get a serious answer. The second passed. 'Because, Mr. Finally Asking, you never know what you're going to see when you haven't got a gun.'

'Cut it out, Jordan. Say what you mean.'

She smiled, 'Fine. I mean Yogi. In the ever-so-likely event you topple from your bike, frozen in fear, botching our plan, I'll step up and put her out of her misery, albeit in a way that could only be described as a second choice, both hers and mine.' Yes, 'albeit' was the Word of the Day. If the little braggart was going to push my chicken button, especially when all I was doing was trying to show her some sympathy, then this wolf was going to push back.

'I see. So you just strolled up to Grandma one morning before skinny-dipping and said, "Hey, Grand, know how you beheaded that snapper? How'd you like to help me bag a bear?"'

'Don't be retarded. Of course I didn't say that.'

'I see. So you told her the truth? You said, "After tea, Grand dear, I thought I'd mosey on up the road and decapitate Rosedale's only tourist attraction. Just an axe-murdering lesson or two first, please?" I'm so glad you didn't get her to teach you under false pretenses! After all, you lie about your shoes and your bloody shorts and everything else under the sun!'

'I don't have to lie to Grand. She doesn't hate me.' We both let that one sit a moment. 'Ever since I was little, she's been the only one to sing me sustaining songs. So I told her – I tell her – I always tell her the truth, the whole truth. And nothing but.'

Even her reference to *Winnie the Pooh* didn't stop me. If I'd noticed her hands, seen how they were shaking, that might have. Maybe. But then again, I've always been more like Tigger than Piglet. Casual bouncy damage – my specialty. 'The truth? And what would that be? Assuming you're capable of the phenomenon. Assuming you aren't, what did MC call you? Your own worst enemy and one ridiculous little girl.'

She threw Tang in my face. I hope the astronauts don't spill it in space – Tang stings. Busy wiping my eyes, I almost missed her retort. 'No, asswipe. I told Grand I needed to kill rapists. She agreed.' One look told me that anger sometimes spits the truth. That didn't mean I wanted to hear it. Consider how hard I tried to ridicule it, minimize it and avoid it altogether.

'Rapists? What rapists? Okay, in Mimico maybe, but up here? And an axe? You're not exactly going to be able to pull that out of your sporran in a dark alley, are you?'

'Who said anything about dark alleys?' She sought my eyes. 'Who said strangers?'

'Oh, I see, now it's clear! You needed an axe to kill, let's see, raccoon rapists? Ghost rapists? Clue me in. Is Rosedale plagued by marauding bands of Trenter rapists? Do peeping Tom rapists sneak up from the trailer park and leap through your bedroom window each night? Perhaps it's all those pesky Martian rapists teleporting through your bedroom wall? Get me some hard evidence on the little green bastards, and I'll kill them for you.'

A sigh like a hiss. She gripped her elbows and leaned into my face. 'Evidence? All right, Perry Masonry, judge and jury. Here's my evidence. My physical evidence. You took Grade 9 Health. Besides the obvious, how else can a girl lose her virginity?'

Now, well I might be more than happy to discuss that with a guy unlacing his skates or Wendy undoing her bra, I certainly wasn't going to do so with her. I stared at my Aunts on a Log, willing them to start marching so I could follow. 'Come on, Brother Mine! Be a man! Can she lose it, say, by falling off her bicycle, or by too much swimming?'

'Of course not. That's utter nonsense and anybody who believes it is a total retard.'

'I see. Like MC? She's given me both of those "explanations." More than once.'

'Don't be ridiculous. Mom would never believe an old wives' tale like that. We got the same diagrams, didn't we? The talk out of Dr. Spock. She labelled everything. I got names I can't spell for every part of the female anatomy.'

Jordan smiled, 'Yes, it appears the intelligent really do have vocabularies sufficient to any task.' We both smiled. 'I agree with you. She doesn't believe it herself. The point is, it's a convenient lie. One tailor-made for me – I'm supposed to believe it.'

'But why?

'Two probable answers. One: because when I came to live with them when I was three, some worker or doctor told her the truth then.' BS swallowed, 'Or two: because she knows it for herself.' That cut much too close to my wood.

'Knows what? That you like a good story? So you make them up yourself?'

Jordan swept up her Canadiana Brown, paused, gave me a good squint, then plunked it and herself back down. 'Okay, Mr. Smug and Secure. You're asking for it, so here it is. Knows about Dream Rapists. Nightmare Rapists.' She averted her gaze into the grass at her feet. 'You know I sleepwalk. Mom can say "no rest for the wicked" and lock every door in the house. She can sleep like a dolphin with one eye open. She can blame it on a bloody swimming bicycle. Nothing stops it.' She lifted her chin. 'But what you don't know is this: I prefer the sleepwalking. Compared to the nightmares, it's much safer.'

'Jordan, you're fourteen years old! Why on God's green earth are you having nightmares about being – about that?' I'll admit it. I could say 'rapist,' but I couldn't look at my sister and say the word 'raped.' She stared. Long enough to make the correct assessment that asking the right question had been pure accident, completely inadvertent, and that under no circumstances did I actually want an answer.

'Boys really do live on another planet, don't they?' she asked the air in front of me, then refocused and peered in my face. 'What do you mean? That I'm too old for nightmares or too young to be raped?' She waited. Silence gripped the mouse. 'I see. Well, you're dead wrong on both counts. I've had rape nightmares since ... since forever.' She hesitated. 'At least I think they're nightmares.' She shook her head. 'So, last summer, Grand started teaching me how to swing an axe. Figured if I could see myself as strong, then I'd fight This Man off.'

Who? I knew the right question; not asking it was deliberate. Silence spun out between us; words unsaid hovering like the unpleasantness of a broken promise. She waited. She looked right at me. My finger developed a serious need to trace the stain of Tang on the picnic table. It swam like a snake. The screen door slammed shut. My finger slithered on without her.

Was I shocked or in shock? No to both. I've been meaning to let you see the end of it, but meaning to and doing so aren't twins. It's the last reel of the movie I kept in the can. I think I hoped that if I never opened it, if I never spoke word one about it, it would autonomously fade to black. From decades later, I can say with certainty that life doesn't work that way. It is in fact the opposite: it's the unspoken secrets that have the most say in our lives. Keep the skeleton closeted and he's muscular, powerful and dark. Bring him into the light of day and shake him, make him dance for all to see, and he fades to a dusty pile of bones.

At fifteen I didn't know any of that. I just viewed it and ran, desperate to believe the scene could be wiped from memory as it fell from the sky. Willing it back to the closet or to rot where it fell. Willing to hand the responsibility of it over to absolutely anyone, even the likes of Derwood. I didn't care if it was memory or another story. It didn't help at all when I realized that to resurrect a memory from when you were that young, you'd have to invent the words to tell yourself a story. And she was that young. As young as the first line, as the words I couldn't get out of my head. If she was maybe three, maybe she wasn't a March. But if she was –

And that's when I finally got it. Story or truth or perfectly imperfectly both, it didn't matter. That it may have meant some worse-than-Jalna monkey business from some less-than-simian creature named March or that it may have never happened at all, that didn't matter either. I didn't know because she didn't know. And we'd never know; we had no one to ask. That's what mattered. This then, is Hazel #99, the bomb I thrust into her terrorist's hands:

You are maybe three years old. You have two sets of pyjamas. They stay the same, even when The House and The Family don't. When they're going to move you, they iron your yellow dress stiff, snap the silver locket around your neck and the silver lock on your red suitcase. For now it's empty, stashed under This Crib, and waiting for next time. Your pyjamas have lived here, safe in a drawer in This House, for more than seven sleeps: your soft green nightie with the bunny rabbit, your thick winter sleeper with snaps. It's yellow too. Tonight you are wearing it. Good. Sometimes snaps confuse him. Smile at the bluebird. She's how you know you're not in the hospital. She's like This Crib, baby blue. Hospital cribs are metal. This one has a happy picture pasted on its wooden head. This Lady has made it herself, a birdie cut from a magazine, perched in apple blossoms, bursting pink. Happy notes come chirping out of her tiny beak. You know only the first line of her song, 'Bluebird! Bluebird! Smile at me!' That's what This Lady sings as she drops off your bottle, 'G'night, Baby. Kiss, kiss! Now close those eyes.' Bouncy brown curls all soft round her face, she pats your tummy, flicks light into night and rap-tap-taps down the hall. You sit back up. You drink half your bottle. Never more. You crawl into the farthest corner. Press your back against the bars. Chant the alphabet – you know most of it. Just keep chanting. Hum. Sometimes when he hears how good you are at ABCs, This Man changes his mind. There's the slow crunch-thud, crunch-thud – his step in the hall. Sing louder. 'A-B-C-D ... ' There's the slower grind of doorknob. 'E-F-G.' Can't you see me? 'L-M-N-O-P!' He looks right at you and lowers the bar. Such a racket! Surely This Lady must hear it This Time? He yanks the bottle from your hands. He grabs your feet and drags you to him by the ankles. It hurts to kick him, but you try. A damp palm clamps your mouth, smothering W-X-Y and – 'Shut up, you little bastard!' He smiles. His hands pop, pop, pop your snaps. You cry. He unpins your diaper. Pins stab the headboard, but never the birdie. He can't touch her. She can sing. But you can't. So he hurts you. He jabs a hand-finger up you, sometimes two. He jabs the not-hand-finger in your mouth and he rocks you, rolls you, shoves you, back and forth, wheezing, This Man's lullaby, his raspy, panting whisper singing, 'Hush, little baby, don' say a word, Daddy's gonna buy you a, hush-li'l-baby-hush-HUSH-HUSH!' When the not-hand-finger stays fat, he gets angry. Rams it in hard. Harder than necessary. You choke. When it squirts too fast you vomit. When he levers your feet, you bite your tongue bloody. He scoops vomit back into your bottle and mops up with your diaper. Wet, he pins it back on. Snaps snap. He pats your head, repositions you on the wet spot, returns your bottle and rebars your cage.

'She's asleep!' he calls.

'You've got the magic touch,' This Lady calls back.

Wait for lock to click and steps to fall. Smile at the bluebird. Put your nose to the blossoms. Hold on to the smell of apples. Remember The Last Crib. It had butterflies. Drain your bottle. Wash the taste of feathers from your mouth. Almost clean.

'G'night, birdie. Kiss, kiss. Maybe Next House will be better.'

You are maybe three years old and you are one hushed little baby. How long does a hush last? For years you obey him. You don't say a word. Until memory leans into nightmare, until the summer of your fourteenth year when your grandmother hands you an axe.

HAZEL #90

To My Darling Daughter Hazel,

Back in the summer of 1917, I was seventeen and so in love I couldn't tie my shoes! I know it will embarrass you to hear this from your mother, Hazel. A love story nearly forty years old, but you've got to hear it. I hope reading it in this letter will make it easier for you. And I pray you won't hate me for it. It's part of the reason, my darling, that you cannot, that you must not, give up the baby you're carrying. Yes, I know you're pregnant. I'm your mother. I guessed. I saw your face on the night you came home from the hurricane and later it wasn't much of a guess to do the math and know what had happened. And now that I know, you've got to hear me out. And please remember, dear, in 1917, I was five years younger than you are now.

I'd been going up to Algonquin Park every year since I was a child. Mother let me go up every year, to stay with her friends, the Frasers, but she never came herself. And that summer I saw it, really saw it for the first time. Grass wasn't just green. Every wave on Canoe Lake was prismatic. The Jack pines shimmered in a cerulean sky. It was the summer a man introduced me to colour, to vermillion and chartreuse and cobalt and obsidian. He saw colour, heard colour, sang colour, and when I was with him, I saw it too.

I didn't care that he was older. He didn't seem almost forty. He seemed more vital than anyone I'd ever met. The talk around the Mowat Hotel was that he was a genius. That he'd change the way we saw the north. I listened to every word. I drank it in. Talk at the bar said some uglier things too – that he was behind in his bill, that he was a skirt chaser, that Mr. Fraser had threatened to punch him out more than once already. All of that I ignored as jealousy.

So we'd sit on the dock, or paddle out in the canoe, where he'd sketch the tree line. He'd find a spot he liked and come back to it, and back to it, to watch it in every possible light, at dawn, at dusk, in the rain. And he'd sit there with his paint box and paint on anything, on boards, on bark, on the side of the canoe, just mixing colours and watching them dry until he got what he wanted. And I kept handing him my glasses, saying, 'Try to make it look like this! It's almost there, but I want you to paint what I see without them.' And he grinned, 'To see how colour and line become one.' And I said, 'Eureka!'

Then they said that other girl, Winnifred, was pregnant. I asked her myself and she said he was the father. And when I confronted him he lied. (I swear to you, Hazel, I swear I always, always, believed it was a lie.) We were out in the canoe. I'd started to cry. I asked him how could he have done it, when he knew I was the one who loved him, when I knew he loved me? When I tried to kiss him to prove it, he recoiled, threw himself into the stern, and I flung myself after him. We nearly capsized the canoe.

He pushed me back and said, 'I do love you, Susan Grace! But not the way you think.'

He said, 'Have you ever seen pictures of your mother as a girl?' He smiled. 'You look just the way she did when she stepped off the boat from Inverness and came up here to the park to work for Mr. Fraser.'

My head started swimming. How did he now that? He'd never met my mother.

He said, 'It was 1899. I was twenty-two and your mother was seventeen. And now its 1917 and you're seventeen.' He tried to make a joke of it. 'That's three lucky sevens for us, don't you think?'

I just stared at him.

He took my hand, 'Susan, your mother and I, when we were young, we met here, right here in the park. And then, thank goodness, she got a job in Toronto close to where I was working as a machine shop apprentice.' He pushed his hair out of his eyes. 'I hated that job. They fired me for always being late.' He grinned. 'I'd been sneaking out at night.' I covered my ears and he gently pulled my hands down. 'Sneaking out to see your mother.'

I don't remember what I said. I know I called him a liar.

He frowned and reached for my hand again. I wouldn't let him touch me.

He said, 'Susan, honey, I swear I didn't know. I didn't know until your mother wrote me last winter. She never told me. She'd told me she never wanted to see me again, that she was marrying your father – a farmer, a regular decent guy that she'd met on the boat – and I was so crazy I went off and signed up to fight in South Africa. I tried to forget her, but I never did. And when your father died and she wrote to say that you were mine, we agreed that I'd come back up here this summer so I could get to know you too.' He laced his paint-daubed hands over his head. 'For heaven's sake, child, why else would I be spending all this time with you?'

I threw up over the side of the canoe. The liar. I felt so dirty. When he reached down to get his canteen, I picked up my paddle and bashed him in the head. I got out his fishing line and wrapped it a lucky seven times around his legs and dumped him over the side. Face up. Hazel, I swear to you. I left him face up. I didn't think I'd killed him. I thought I'd taught him a lesson. I figured he'd show up back at the Mowat, dripping wet, with one mean headache.

I dove in and swam out, using that bloody paddle as a float. I hid it in the far swampy end of the lake, and walked through the bush until I hit the road. I got back by dark, so no one was worried. Eventually the police came. They found his body eight days later. They suspected Mr. Fraser and another neighbour, Mr. Blecher, and even Winnifred, who disappeared to Philadelpia that next Easter. To have her baby, people said. But of course no one ever suspected tiny, bespectacled me.

Years later, in 1930, I thought I'd found the man who could make me forget him. Another boy farmer, just like my mother. But I was wrong. Stupid and wrong and pregnant with you. I know this will hurt you, but you must hear it: I was all set up to meet a backstreet butcher who'd solve the problem, when my mother, your grand-mother, and your baby's great-grandmother, came into my room.

She said, 'Susan Grace, ye need to know something. I know ye're blamin' yourself for yer predicament. And I know it's my hardness to you over the years that makes ye do so. It's long past time I made it up to ya. So I'm goin' to tell it straight. Do you remember the painter man who died in the park when you were a girl?'

I couldn't breathe. I managed to nod. 'Well, to make a long story short, girl, he was yer father.' She smiled at me. 'I was seventeen. I loved him. We learned to paint together that summer, and I kept paintin', but I never came close. But I had his baby, you ken? And she paints better than I ever did. So before ye do what ye shouldn't, daughter, take some time to think about who you and that bairn you're carryin' are related to. Here.'

As she handed me a book. And there were our colours. And our secret places. And the world without my glasses. *The Jack Pine. The Northern River.* And *The West Wind.*

So that's why I kept you, Hazel, and that's why I married your father, because he was your father whether I loved him or not. I kept you because my mother kept me. And because my father, a man I loved, had told me the truth. And, yes, because I'd already taken a life. And though I may not have been much better at showing it than my own Scottish mother was, my dear, I've never regretted having you or raising you. Not for one minute.

Your grandfather, Hazel, the man who will be the great-grandfather of any baby you have, he was the most vibrant and vital man I've ever known. He'd see that hurricane you went through as colour on the wind. As colour alive. As water on fire. He'd tell you to get out there and paint your life! He'd say, 'Wishes are colourful horses, so don't be a dull grey beggar, jump on, and ride that rainbow away!'

In this envelope is the locket he gave my mother when she was seventeen. She gave it to me when I had you. Now I'm giving it to you and I'm asking you, begging you, not to let your colours die. Marry Walter. Give the family locket to your baby. And be her mother. Not just because your child will be a famous artist's great-grandchild, dear, but for a much better reason. For the best reason. Because she will be your child, my beloved daughter's child. My baby's baby. Your baby. The child of the daughter I love.

I sign this with that love and with every hope for the future,
Your Mother

WHEN I DIE

To get Jordan out of her room the next day Friday, August 8, I had to bribe her. Dad had asked after her, once, through her bedroom door. When she uttered the magic menstrual word, he stared at his shoes. When into that silence Jordan casually dropped the news that she also had giant buboes under both armpits, he exited, stage left. When she yelled after him, 'I don't need you! All I need is a handbasket!' the minister's son either didn't get the reference to going to hell in one, or pretended not to. It's too bad Monty Python hadn't made *The Quest for the Holy Grail* yet because she'd have loved it if I'd banged at her door wailing, 'Bring out yer dead!' Instead I did what Dad should have: 'Okay, Pooch,' I said and slid a dime under her door. 'For a treat, not your collection, or your eyelids, but let's swim first.'

We were on our way back with our Good and Plenty. (Truth be told, it was Smarties because sadly you could get Good and Plenty, like Marshmallow Fluff, only in the junk-food mecca of the U.S. of A.) Jordan liked the ritual of pretending it was Good and Plenty more than she liked the candy itself. Before you open the box, you have to spend at least a half an hour as Choo Choo Charlie, the engineer. You have to hold the box straight in your hand and move your arm back and forth like a train piston producing the necessary *huffa chuffa, huffa chuffa* accompaniment for Charlie's song:

Charlie says, 'Love that Good and Plenty!' *Toot! Toot!*
Charlie says, 'Really rings my bell.' *Toot! Toot!*
Charlie says, 'Love my Good and Plenty!
Don't know any other candy that I love so well!' *Toot! Toot!*

Yes, it was twenty-plenty juvenile, and yes, we were far too old for it, but hey, no one was watching. We'd imitated Charlie for years, must've seen him a million times on his steady gig on *Rocketship 7*. I figured it might be reassuring for her to do something sane and normal, so I *huffa-chuffa*ed like my life depended on it. I was feeling mighty glad BS had candy in hand because the mailbox gave her nothing else, when Yogi started to bellow. She'd been quite content when we passed by moments earlier, snoring in fact. Just this once, couldn't it be someone else's problem? Apparently not. When BS turned I had to follow. She grabbed Balsam's collar in one hand and silenced his muzzle in the other to keep him from giving us away.

We doubled back and, of course, there he was, Derwood, back toward us, facing the cage. What the Sam Hill was he doing? Conducting an orchestra? As we approached, the baton became a fishing rod. Attached to it was something poor Yogi never got to see, let alone eat: a fish, a measly four-inch sunfish, still flipping. And driving her crazy. In his version of *Gaslight for Dumb Animals*, he'd lower it into the roofless cage, wait until Yogi lunged for it and then use the retraction button on his obviously expensive reel to zip it back out. Unable to trust her instincts, Yogi sat confounded: 'I tawt I taw a tweety fish?' He'd drop it in again. 'I did! I did tee a tweety fish!' And he'd reel it out again, enjoying her disintegration with more of the glee and none of the pity audiences felt for either Sylvester the Cat or Ingrid Bergman. He smirked non-stop. My instincts told me this show wasn't over.

Derwood flicked open his baseball case, reached into red velvet. With his other hand, he dangled the fish next to the cage. As hopeful hands reached through the fence, Derwood swung full-strength and smashed her fingers. Each time she roared in pain. Each time she fell for it. This is what it sounds like when bears cry: they whimper like newborns, like someone born yesterday. So my cousin Derwood hit harder.

He hadn't seen us. He was so busy smashing that he hadn't heard us either. Good one. I swung round the pole, ready to pound him senseless or, even better, to get my wish by tossing him in to Yogi like the carrion that he was, when he heard Jordan with Balsam behind me, obviously unable to run with either my stealth or speed. He dropped his implements of torture and ran. I was more than close enough; I could easily have nabbed him. I could have sicced Balsam on him. Instead I squared my arms and leaned against the cage. Relaxed, downright casual, I watched him go. If he'd had a tail it would have been right there between his legs, quivering. When

Jordan reached me, we said word none. We just knew. Don't gut your fish till you get them. And him, we intended to get.

We unhooked the little fish and fed it to Yogi. She gulped it whole, no doubt fearful it might be jerked back out. We picked some of the long grass she liked. Sorry, baby girl. We left the fishing rod at the edge of the cage, left it for Derwood to discover what he wouldn't notice until he tried to pick it up. Seven pieces so carefully placed that it held together until you touched it, then it exploded into fragments. We kept the fishing line. It was ordinary ten-pound test, and that's as common as running shoes, isn't it? We snapped the velvet case in two and chucked the halves in the swamp. And his precious bat, signed by some slugger or other? To this day I remember the weight of it, hot and heavy, eager in my hand.

In Fenelon the next day, I benched myself with her willingly. And in the dead of night on that Saturday, August 9, persons unknown – probably drunken Trenters venturing where no vandal had gone before – smashed Derwood's birthday kayak to smithereens with a baseball bat. How do we know they used his baseball bat? Well, they left it behind. In pieces. Well-placed pieces. Props in an elaborate production, an open-air snuff film, set at the big cedar for all of March to find before seeking consolation for their holy selves in Sunday morning church. They killed a boy. A real fake boy, a face on a paper bag. A stuffed head attached to Derwood's life jacket with clear fishing line, wrapped strangle-tight at the neck, ending rather incongruously with a tiny rotting sunfish. The fish and the hook that held it protruded from the dead boy's open mouth.

'What's that?' Aunt Penny gasped. 'A warning about sleeping with the fishes?' (She read far too many bad detective novels.)

'Nope,' winked Uncle H. 'It's ordinary fishing line, just plain ten-pound test.'

To finish him off, the mystery vandals pulled the stuffed sleeves of a Boy Scout shirt through a lifejacket and set it atop a stuffed pair of black cords and red Converse high tops, all incidentally Derwood's. They perched his fleur-de-lys cap on its head. What resembled blood but was clearly ketchup soaked the body and pooled on the ground. No home free for this kid – even Jordan could have tagged him. No need to seek what isn't hidden. For one heart-stopping second, it looked as if a fallen Scout had slouched arms and legs akimbo against the tree and bled to death. Why didn't he fall over? Shards of baseball bat. Seven impalements: two feet, two eyes, two hands and one through the one groin, staked into a knot in the tree.

'Hell's bells,' Dad swore as he strained to tear it down with one hand, but was forced to drop his camera and use two. 'Who'd want to crucify a bloody puppet?'

Who indeed? There was a waft of piñata in the air, but the smell didn't stick. Derwood kept snivelling that it was *his* kayak and *his* life jacket and *his* runners and worst of all, *his new bat and his Scout uniform* and *who else* did we know round here who'd *taken an axe to him?* He kept shouting, 'Look for her retard footprints!' but all they found were uncountable impressions of anonymous sneakers. This time it could have been anybody and we had an iron-clad alibi, or more accurately, a Masterlock MC alibi. At night, every night, all night, Almost got locked up tighter than a snapper's jaw.

You see, back on the morning when they discovered Jordan's orthopedic footprints in the bunkie, the smoking gun of the Piñata Caper, all of March had incorrectly assumed that she, an early riser, had simply done the deed after Mom unlocked our door. But last night's delinquents had struck in the witching hour. The dead Scout hadn't been there at 3:30, when Uncle Sloan had gone down to the dock for an insomniac's smoke. But it was there at 4:30 when Grandma was awakened by raccoons fighting over the ketchup dripping from its eyes.

At that ungodly hour, MC swore up and down six ways to Sunday, any Almost vandal was, if not fast asleep, fast under lock and key. Thanks to her one-woman anti-sleepwalking campaign – which began five summers ago when a sleeping Jordan tried to iron her Explorers middy one night and then stepped off the dock and kept walking the next – Almost's one key slept around MC's neck. And all of March knew it. 'No one,' Mom insisted, '*and I mean no one*, not even Tommy, could get out if they wanted to, *unless I wanted them to*. Unless I unlocked the door for them. And I *most certainly did not.*'

Unless they'd swiped the key and made themselves a copy? That option likely occurred to some of March, but did not get uttered. Understand, they had no qualms about accusing my sister of anything: thievery, malicious mischief, wanton wastefulness, the

257

desecration of both a proud Canadian uniform and an expensive symbol of American sporting supremacy, the infliction of an indignity on an almost-human body and, far worse, a sacrilegious waste of good ketchup; but only a total cretin would accuse my mother of negligent housekeeping.

That Sweet Caroline March might lie to protect her own child? That occurred to no one. Not even Aunt Elsbeth. Instead the elders simply nodded. 'Clearly a Trenter.' 'Some hoodlum outsider.' 'Some Yanker-Wanker's idea of a sick joke.' If Derwood read it for exactly what it was, as warning that he would be a real dead boy sleeping with the shoes if he ever tried anything like that again, he couldn't exactly call it as he saw it, now could he? Not even Aunt Penny would have bought it. Good one. Because, you see, revenge is not just a dish best served cold. It is a dish best served by the waiter Anonymous. One created by a night chef who preps it al fresco in Hezzy's back pasture and ensures that it is served on the sly. Like the Avengers, Shoeshine Boy has class. Classy heroes don't need public credit – they're humble. Okay, so singing and dancing around the tree, maybe that wasn't exactly humble:

'When criminals in this world appear
And break the laws that they should fear
And frighten all who see or hear,
The cry goes up both far and near for
Underdog ... '

The song followed Dad as he dragged Puppet Boy off to a swampy grave. Did anyone suggest calling the local constabulatory? Don't be silly. If the tree mail falls only on Derwood, does anybody hear? Of course not. In March, if a nobody hears, then nobody hears. Same difference. The best monkey business takes place right under the noses of other monkeys. And what March monkeys see depends on what two little gophers deign to show them.

PUT A LITTLE LOVE IN YOUR HEART

Don't ask me to explain it; I don't know how it started. That same evening, Sunday August 10. One muggy night. Maybe Mom doubted our alibi. Maybe she had more in common with her daughter than either of them realized: that just because both of them could make the rest of us swallow something lock, stock and barrel, it didn't necessarily follow that they believed it themselves. Maybe Mom knew Mrs. Miller would cut keys no questions asked. Maybe our lovely mother had even gone up to the store and asked her if she had. On the other hand, maybe it had nothing to do with puppet death. Maybe it was the Spork. BS hated Spork even more than Spam (assuming that is gastronomically possible) so perhaps the whole thing was just another melodramatic disposal project. My guess? I'd say Jordan provoked her; I'd say BS planned a speech and needed an audience, so she pursued one.

Usually I went first to the trough and waited like one pig waits on another – but that night I sat glued to the TV. The Manson murders. Although they weren't called that yet, as it took months to track Charlie and the Family down. When the story broke that night, it said persons unknown, probably drug-crazed hippies, had defaced a Beverly Hills mansion, writing 'Death to Pigs' and 'Rise' on the walls in blood. Seven murders, including Sharon Tate, an actress-model who died in the eighth month of pregnancy carrying her unborn son, Paul Richard Polanski. Yes, as in Roman Polanski. Such a criminal waste, a crying shame. And some great shots of blood. I suppose if I'd thought about it I'd have been spooked to think that Helter Skelter occurred at the exact moment as another pack of crazies were enjoying their own ritualistic slaying of a Boy Scout, but enough said. By the time I traded the TV screen for the screen door, Mom and BS were well at it. Dad? He was picking up peas with his fingers and pushing them onto the tines of his fork. If it wasn't exactly Helter Skelter, it could easily have been a script of *The Twilight Zone*:

BS: Maybe it's not that you can't make a silk purse out of a sow's ear, but that you shouldn't try. Why force a perfectly good pig to pretend to be worm poo?

MC: Isn't that nice? The point, Gypsy Sue, is that you can't make a sovereign with sixpence. A dirty pig remains one. So eat your Spork, dear. It's dinner. And just for a change, try being grateful you've got one and a mother who serves one.

BS: Grateful? Who'd be grateful for a cowbird! (*MC looks puzzled*) A cowbird! One that abandons her egg, poops it out in the first available nest and flies away. She won't feed her chick, let alone care for it. She doesn't care if lives or dies.

MC: I'm a cowbird? (MC *shakes head*) On the contrary, dear, I'm the one raising an indiscriminately fertilized egg. Whoever who pooped you out? That's a cowbird.

Ever seen that Greek statue of the discus thrower? Well, attempting equal technique, Jordan shifted her plate to one hand and whipped it at Mom's head. And yes, of course she missed. It bounced but didn't break. It didn't even crack – as Melmac as my mother, good old Canadiana Brown, her real hair colour. Spork, mashed potatoes and smashed canned peas all made like Jackson Pollock on the grey cottage wall. Then, as if the wasting of food weren't infraction enough (and in March it was, as you'll remember if you were paying any kind of attention at all, the worst of all cardinal sins), BS put one hand and one foot on the railing of the deck, swayed drunkenly over the swamp, and louder than a wop in a wifebeater, began to sing:

Jordan: One two three ...
Mom: Stop that this instant! Go and get –
Jordan: and a bumblebee ...
Mom: I don't know what you're trying to prove, Missy –
Jordan: And the rooster crows ...
Mom: But if you don't get back here right this second –
Jordan: And *awaaaay* she goes!

And she jumped. I don't mean feet first; I don't mean trying to exit gracefully, stage right, like Snagglepuss. I mean butt flop extraordinaire, legs extended, SPLAT! The resulting tsunami vomited over the deck, over our knees and halfway up the cottage wall, adding a finish of green spackle to her painting: *Spork à la Swamp? Dinner meets Duckweed?* I didn't know where to stare; every blink snapped a shot more surreal than the one before it. I was desperate to yell, 'You marsh, March!' But knew it would be neither appreciated nor helpful.

The parentulas? They didn't need Samantha's nose twitch; they froze. Biblical pillars of salt, freckled green. I'm sure they were trying to reconcile, as I was, that the icky thing before them was the girl who got inordinately furious when the bus seats of the Rosedale Roxy dunked her, the same girl who now sat voluntarily sinking in slime, watching the movie that was them. Where she landed there she stayed, up to her chin in ooze, calm, even tranquil. The Semi-Quiet smile of the Red-Haired Swamp Buddha. Confusion mirrored itself. They seemed to think she was the movie. For a short Rosedale Roxy breakdown, no one spoke. Then she ruined it.

'Exactly. I'm the sow's ear. Nobody cares if I'm hurt or dead. Mother, you told me to stick myself in the swamp, so now you've got both of your wishes. You're expecting a real child, and you can refuse to parent refuse. Why keep somebody else's garbage? Tell me the truth for once in your sorry lives. Name the new and call the calls or you'll be left alone when this Fenelon falls.' That speech smelled worse than the phony baloney Mom called dinner. How many BS versions? How many rehearsals? Of course, they never heard word one.

Uncharacteristically, Dad reacted first. He stomped down the stairs and in one smooth lean, grasped the rail and winged her without wetting his shoes. He frogmarched her to the dock, pushed her in, ordered her to scrub with sand, pulled her out and ordered her in. 'And, Missy, don't come out until you've figured out how to straighten up and fly right!'

'And don't you dare walk on my clean floor oozing God-knows-what. Take off your – ' Mom glanced down, Atlantis held its breath. 'Those aren't ... Where are ... ? Why you deceitful little brat! Answer me this instant! *What have you done with your shoes?*'

It would have been far too intimate to answer her daughter's question. Instead MC got angry and let her anger speak for her. Only later, too late later, did this Sherman realize that all BS wanted was some reassurance. At the time it seemed like riddles ridiculous. Her reference to When Fenelon Falls? None of us got it. None of us heard what she was offering us and herself – one last chance at a miracle, a sacrament to transmute Semi-Quietism into words.

Instead, with the zeal of the inquisitors who set out to break the original Fenelon from his belief in a personal loving God, they stood her on the dish-washing stool, reminded her that standing pools gather filth and left her standing filthy, unbalanced in empty air. Content with nothing less than a full *auto-da-fé*, MC demanded every finite detail of the time, place and circumstance of her heresy. While Dad may have tossed some water from time to time to cool his Grand Inquisitor down, he made no move to stop her. I suppose we should be grateful he didn't film her. She sounded like this:

What makes you think you had the right to take them off? Shoe polish won't make you look normal; it makes you look cheap. The cost of that polish, which a thieving Gypsy Sue took without asking, comes out of your allowance. After you stole from me, who'd you steal those dirty boys' runners from? You'll be extremely proud of yourself when you return them. Who do you think you are, anyway? How can you look in the mirror and see anything but a liar and a thief? I can't even look at you. You're no daughter of mine. I won't call them retard shoes like the rest of the family, but if you think you can go without them, then maybe the shoe fits!

I want to go on record as saying they never touched her. A wooden spoon did, several cracks on a wet behind, but no hand and no fist. There was no slapping, no pushing and, true to March, no profanity. This is not to say that MC wasn't fully aware of the wounds she inflicted. She smelled blood and cut deeper. I just can't keep writing it, can't separate what Jordan heard from what MC actually said of the cost, the trouble, the drive downtown, the extra gas and expensive parking, the father who'd gone without a new suit when even his patches were worn, all for shoes Little Missy Mistake didn't have the decency to keep on her feet. That it was no surprise. That the spoiled brat before her had never appreciated all they'd done for her. Eleven years ago, when no one else wanted her, out of the goodness of their hearts they'd rescued a sick little three-year-old, one who might never walk, and taken her into their home.

And this was how she repaid them! Sometimes the shame in our heads belies the spoken word.

I've got to hand it to her. Dripping, limp, near blue with cold, she stared them down. They didn't offer her a towel. They didn't offer her a Kleenex or her glasses. They ignored her tears as she fought for balance; I can't imagine the pain. But she didn't cave. For half an hour, MC venom spewed, but not a single sound came out of my sister's mouth. Not word one.

She was winning. And that, of course, was the one thing MC could never allow. She rap-tap-tapped into Jordan's room, ripped Burton off the wall and held him under her daughter's nose. 'Tell me where they are right now, young lady, or this goes in the swamp where it belongs!' She held an edge and tore, one long paisley strip, amputating Burton's left hand at the wrist. Hot pink lace hit the floor. 'Tell me, and you can have the rest of him back.' The next tear removed his left arm, leaving a maroon chest stark against a torn white edge. '*Tell me this second or ...* ' MC moved her hands dead centre, paused, and ripped Burton clean in half, dropping his halves to the floor where – I swear it to this day – both of his eyes, a yard apart, gazed acrimoniously up at my sister. Jordan moaned.

MC went back into Jordan's room and returned with her hands behind her back. 'You still want to play games with me? You want to lick the butter off my bread? Go ahead, dear, pick one.' When Jordan wouldn't, MC laughed. 'Fine. I win! I've got the same thing in both. Let's look, shall we? Why, it's a ticket! A CNE ticket,' she bounced it off Jordan's nose. 'To the Coca-Cola Galaxie stage, on August 29 and hmmm, *Guess Who* won't be going after all?'

'No. Please, that's mine. I paid for it. I earned it!' Jordan tried to find Dad's eyes. She couldn't. He'd developed an urgent need to put an eye on his camera lens.

'What's that? The cat gave you back your tongue? Then tell me where your shoes are right this second!' She started a tiny tear, '*Or else!*'

Jordan trembled. She put a hand to her mouth and then both hands over her eyes. MC smiled. Then my sister dropped her hands and clamped them tight. She lifted her head and spoke with the clear, firm voice I'd last heard in church. 'Else, Mother. I pick else.'

As ticket confetti hit the floor, the body of the little girl who'd never been able to stand for more than twenty minutes in her life claimed the proud young woman who would have been my sister. Took her down hard, bounced her head off the stool, on the way to the floor. Mother's heels tapped past her face. 'See? You're never going to pass for normal. Stop trying.' When they sent her to her room, even it wasn't hers anymore.

Insert regret here. I couldn't have been sorrier. Sorry that MC failed Empathy. Sorry that Mother School didn't teach her to use her off button, one that could be pushed when prudent, before venting a lifetime of frustrated insecurities on a child. Sorry my father cast himself as her Cowardly Lion instead of a man. Sorry that wishes weren't horses, and the beggared couldn't ride away. (Lacking such wishes, we have only each other. It should be enough. We all come with off buttons well within reach of our fingers. We make our own courage – when we're grownups. When we give a damn.) When Mom went to lie down, also known as gloating, Dad swept up Burton's remains and slid them under his daughter's door. Good one. Bow to the inevitable Scottish proverb: You may drive the devil into a wife, but you'll never ding him out of her.

The song that night? We didn't even try to hear it. 'Another day goes by, and still the children cry. Put a little love in your heart.' Or the more telling line: 'You see it's getting late, Oh please don't hesitate, Put a little love in your heart.' No, the world won't be a better place for you and me. Just wait and see.

'So what did you do in the war, Daddy?' you might ask metaphorically. 'What did you put in your heart?' I hope when you decide kindness will be your guide, because it certainly wasn't mine. I stood at her door. I whispered, 'Sorry, kiddo.' When she asked, 'Sorry for what?' this little turtle pulled his head in, clamped his jaws shut, and swam away with eyes as blank as a dead puppet. What did you, or she, expect? If a dream is a wish your heart makes, it's a dream. A fabrication. A fetch. That's the Scottish word for ghost. Don't expect it to come to your rescue in the waking world.

HAZEL #91

I got out of bed at first light, confused and cold. I wish I could say guilty but I don't remember guilty. I pulled a man's shirt over my nightdress – which brother's shirt I honestly can't say – and went down on the dock. It was dawn. The rain had faded to drizzle. Debris was everywhere. I got it in my head that I needed to place a call to Fenelon, needed to speak to Howard at the doctor's house, needed to tell him we were coming that very instant. Of course, there's no phone at their cottage so I headed, half dressed and barefoot, up the gravel road.

What do I remember? I know when I hung up his phone I turned to thank him. I remember his hand, a big hairy hand, reaching for the receiver, and then past it for my arm. His grin, his chipped tooth. I know my head hit his bait cooler, banged and banging, thrusting nose to nose against a smiling waitress who held a full tray of Coke bottles over her head. Why weren't they breaking?

When he tired of me, he tossed my nightie in my face. He said I'd gotten what I'd come for, that no decent girl would ever come a-knockin' wearing nothing but bedclothes. Said he knew me for a whore from the start. Said he knew it was good for me, and if I knew what was good for me, I wouldn't tell a single living soul. He reached over to a rack of tourist trash and tore out a cheap child's locket. 'See this here? You tell, and it's as to close as a wedding ring as you'll ever get.' He dangled it over my head, snarling, 'Dance fer it, girlie. Dance fer me.'

HEY LITTLE WOMAN

I figured they'd make her scrub until the cottage was a duckweed-free zone. I envisioned them handing her a toothbrush, 'Get cracking, Cinder Sue,' and ordering her to scour the deck, the railing, the walls, the window, the eaves, and just as she finished the drainpipe, reminding her that a sink of green Melmac awaited her. I figured they'd send her diving for sunken shoes and feed her nothing but Spork until she found them. I never dreamed they'd play the card they played.

At breakfast, the Monday morning of August 11, nobody said word one until she arrived. Would the swamp landing, like the moon landing, simply disappear? Had she been punished enough? When Dad held Jordan's chair, MC cleared her throat. Apparently not.

'So, Missy, now you have two reasons to thank your father. Some men are blind in their own cause, and he, being one of them, took it upon himself to get up early and hose down that ungodly mess you made last night.' She handed Dad a Muffet and told him we were out of brown sugar. Jordan pointed at the glass canister, clearly full, less than a yard from Dad's face. He shook his head. Mom smiled. She turned to Jordan, 'You're not off the hook, young lady. Until you apologize for last night's antics, you're still skating on thin ice.'

Jordan answered, staring at me, 'Hmmm, an apology from someone who doesn't count doesn't count. And skating? What's that, Mother? Please use a metaphor I can understand.'

'Don't play Dumbo with me, Missy. None can play the fool so well as a wise man.'

'I'm not playing dumb. You are. I asked you last night,' she glanced at Dad, 'both of you, if you think I belong in the swamp. So, what's your answer?'

'Maybe not in the swamp,' Dad offered. 'But the way you've been acting, Pooch, you're certainly out in the pumphouse!'

Mom smiled. 'Yes indeed. You're next in line beside the hibachi.'

Jordan glanced at Mom's gingham apron, swelling pink. 'So that means ... '

'It means you had better mind your Ps and Qs, if you know what's good for you.' Mom sugared her cereal and poured milk into her bowl. Dad began dry crunching.

Jordan sighed. 'You know, Mother, that's another one I don't understand. Does it mean that as long as I watch P and Q, I can let the rest of the alphabet run amok?'

'And that, Missy Smart Mouth, is precisely what I mean.' Mom reached across the table and stuffed Jordan's Muffet back in the jar. Apparently in Mother School they teach you that a fourteen-year-old girl doesn't need breakfast if she hasn't had dinner the night before. 'If anything, and I mean *anything* else happens between now and this Sunday, then mark my words, Missy, you'll be the only March in history to *miss* the regatta.'

Jordan watched the floor. Mom finished her cereal, pressed a napkin to her mouth, reached into her apron pocket and reapplied her lipstick. Noting her daughter's bent head, a slump more broken than in prayer, she began to clear the table. She began to hum. That did it. Jordan took a deep even breath and calmly pointed out, quite rightly, I thought, that it simply wasn't in her power to prevent *anything* from happening. 'Look, Mother, you just took a breath!' She stood up. 'Look, Mother, you just stomped your ridiculously inappropriate footwear like a little child.' She moved to the counter. 'And lookee here, Mom, Praise the Lord and pass the ammunition! I just found the brown sugar!'

She grabbed the canister in one hand and Mom's wet spoon in the other and counted off four heaping spoonfuls into Dad's half-eaten bowl: 'One, two, three and a bumblebee ... ' Did they notice that shaking hands dumped half of it on the floor? What do you think? 'And the rooster crows ... ' She made a fist around the spoon and launched it at the sink. It clanged off the tap and skidded under the stove. She ignored the 'You pick that up, young lady!' and instead picked up the milk, poured it generously into Dad's bowl and more in his glass for good measure. She headed back to voluntary solitary, but winked as she passed me. 'And awaaay she goes!'

As the weekend approached, a generation looked north, not as far north as Rosedale and sadly not our generation. Almost but not quite, and as you know by now, Almost doesn't count. They did. Launched by the music, they became a people in motion. In couples, in families, in hippie vans and flower-power Volkswagens, by the hundreds and hundreds of thousands, they headed for Sullivan County, passed a little town called Bethel, found Max Yasgur's dairy farm and began to serenade the cows. Crosby, Stills, Nash and Young; the Band; Blood, Sweat and Tears; Joe Cocker; Jefferson Airplane; Tim Hardin; Creedence Clearwater Revival; Joan Baez; Janis Joplin; the Who; Sly and the Family Stone; Santana; Canned Heat; Jimi Hendrix and the Grateful Dead, all rocked Yasgur's Pond that weekend. Country Joe hollered his Fish Chant to the moon.

Such a choir, so many Woodstock hymns she could have been singing, but one and only one song came chain smoking out of my sister's room that week, over and over, alpha to omega, incessant. They left her no choice. They took her new diary and all of her books. When she asked about her mail, MC said that that Elsbeth's youngest, the one with manners, had checked for her every day, and maybe she wasn't as popular as she thought she was. When Jordan started to yell, Dad took her radio. MC went for the record player, 'This piece of junk they gave you for having such a big mouth.' Jordan got there first. Like my tackle box, she sat on it. When MC picked up the red suitcase record case, Jordan lost it, screaming at her to leave it alone, that it wasn't hers to take. That it never had been. MC blinked. 'Fine. Keep it. But these?' From shoulder height she dumped Jordan's pristine singles onto the floor. 'These you bought with our money. I'll take them.'

That left one choice, one hit with a bullet left behind on the player's spool. In hindsight, you can call that song everything we should have: a clue, a nose-thumbing, a warm-up, a plea, an SOS, a dress rehearsal, an incantation, a swan song, a death rattle, a dirge, a threnody, a last rite, a pibroch. I called it none of the above. I called it pure BS: 'Oh sugar! Do, do, do ... '

(Once upon a time I knew a girl who stood alone at a kitchen window each night until dark, her hands awash in dirty Melmac, watching a game she couldn't play, ordered into bystander exile by her own body and by her not-quite-wicked and Almost-step mother.

When it grew too dark to see the other children, she could still hear them laughing and knew they were laughing at her, at her not-quite-good-enough, not-quite-one-of-us face at the window. A laughter that only orphans and gypsy changelings and ugly stepchildren and possibly cageling bears can hear. And now she'd been told she deserved to face that laughter for a whole day, and not just any day, the best day, the day of the big game: the Balsam Lake Regatta. What were you thinking, Cinderella? Of course the likes of you can't go to the Moon Ball! Remember that? Remember that calendar held safe in hand? Those circles, hearts and stars? Didn't you ask yourself, 'Why does a regatta rate right up there with Burton the Beloved?' Bear with me.)

The St. John's Anglican Church Balsam Lake Regatta had been held in our bay and run by our family since March Year One, that's 1929. Every summer the *Fenelon Gazette* praised it as the longest running regatta in the Kawartha Lakes, and the summer of '69 was its fortieth anniversary. So yes, Jordan had a typical teenage fear of missing the party, but it was more that that. It was about missing out while being seen, about being exiled without an exit, about the public humiliation of not being in the credits of Dad's best summer film and knowing you'd have to watch it a hundred times anyway.

You see, every living parishioner and local attended our regatta, even the non-librarian Missy Peace, whom we counted among the living but gave us cause for pause. It kept the church title, but it had long since expanded beyond the congregation. Hezzy's family, Mrs. Miller, all the locals came, even Kronk, drinking God-knows-what-but-won't-be-smelling out of a bottomless Coke bottle. Mom spent much of every regatta insisting he be thrown off her property. We ignored her. Especially on Regatta Day, it was March property, not hers. And on the Submersion Baptism version of March Sunday, the rule of full attendance reigned. If a few curious Trenters wandered up, Buds in one hand and smokes in the other, even they weren't asked to leave. It wouldn't have looked good in front of the *Gazette*. If a regular didn't show, that would have been big news. So to be a no-show on display, to be caged, gawked at, pitied and heckled, when the likes of Kronk and Trenters roamed and won prizes at will, well, she'd have seen the fingers pointing long after they'd stopped.

But it went beyond wounded pride. Sure, Marches always placed first, second, third and sometimes all three in every race. And yes, it was our day to show off our bay and our beach, to feel pride of place because the speakers were hooked up to our cottage, to stand taller because trophies gleamed on our picnic table, because our front lawn held some two hundred cheering people. But at the heart of it beat another word: 'home.' For one full day, the world looked right at you and saw just another March child. Gypsy Sue became 'Miss March' or 'Tommy's girl.' For one full day our Cinderella could wear the glass slippers and dance. She could bask in the warmth of a real March thaw. She didn't have to pretend. Just as herself, she could pass; she could pass for one of us.

So somewhere over the school year, perhaps during a lesson gone well at the Alderwood Pool, perhaps watching me bring home yet another hockey trophy, she began to wonder. By March she was a believer and by June a fanatic. Her deep belief in regatta magic has been kept from you not because it's pathological but because it's pathetic, a logic that could only come from a child, one who, despite her genius, was still such a needy kid. It went like this: If you feel at home on regatta day, than maybe, just maybe, you could really belong, for good and forever. How? If they give you a solid gold medal. If they all see you getting it. When you win and only if you win. Then you can hold your head high and you can march, March!

So, my sister – who in her entire life had entered regatta event zero, who had publicly pooh-poohed the regatta at every possible opportunity and spent years calling it 'the hockeygatta,' who except for bowling had displayed the athletic aspirations of an earthworm – that sister had been in training, in secret, all year long, for the most prestigious race, the biggest home run and home free of all: the Cross-the-Bay Swim. She'd thrown every cautionary Scottish proverb to the wind and should have known better. They all advised against it: when you're a foot behind the foremost, you don't wonder at your old shoes before you've gotten new ones. Never swim faster than your shoes. She goes long barefoot who waits for dead men's shoes and she who lives on hope has a slim diet. And we should have remembered one for her: glasses and lasses are bruckle ware. Fragile. Easily broken.

WHAT DOES IT TAKE

Our regatta had every kind of kiddie event under the sun – which as a teacher I now recognize as the easiest way to give awards to as many little ones as possible – dog-paddle with- and without-life-jacket races, underwater races, backstroke races, sidestroke races, all divided by age and gender to make it the 1960s version of fair. Adults had rowing races, single and double canoe and kayak races and, my favourite, the pie-plate race. (For you regatta virgins out there, that's a canoe race with pie-plates for paddles. To move at all, you have to scoop like a whirling dervish and most of the water, like the proverbial comic pie, lands in your partner's face.) Good clean fun. The uncles owned this event. Some tanked-up bevy of them always won; except last summer when Hezzy, OB and NOB stole it by inches. This year the uncles smelled blood and the pie-plate race trophy they only half-jokingly called the Manly Cup. To anyone over ten, however, these events, despite their entertainment value, were but warm-up acts. The headliner plays last.

The Teen Cross-the-Bay Swim. Ages fourteen to sixteen. Boys and girls race together, but win separately. Why? Tradition? A rite of passage? Same difference at that distance? Who knows? Maybe the elders couldn't be bothered to run two long swims. Whatever the reason, the officials, a.k.a. the uncles, simply herded everyone onto Grandma's dock, pointed at Peace's Point and blew the whistle. Then they jumped too, into every available rowboat and canoe, to follow. (No motor boats, given an unfortunate accident about two years ago when in all the commotion a knee kissed a propeller, but that's another story.) We still needed boats because kids got hauled out, some of them crying. It's farther than it looks, a good half-mile, and rough, especially mid-current. The first girl and the first boy get pulled into the gleaming white boat that guards the finish line, *Excalibur*, the only horsepower allowed.

They stand on its seats, their winning hands joined high in the air, as Uncle H spins a victory lap around the bay. Before all of March, they each receive a medal, gold, theirs to keep, and a trophy: a golden loving cup, the shiniest, last and best dessert waiting to be served from our picnic table. You can keep it for one night, clutch it like a teddy, but you're not sorry to see it go because the very next day it gets sent into Fenelon to be engraved with your name. On Sunday it goes to church, to be installed with great ceremony in its permanent home, a shimmering glass case across from children's choir loft. For all the years of her life, when Jordan lifted her eyes to sing, she saw the Holy Grail. Proof positive. Positive proof eternal.

What possessed her to join the quest? What made her think she stood a chance? She was up against the aquatic equivalents of Sir Lancelot: rich, healthy, professionally trained sixteen-year-old cousins who had been jousting in pools and coming home with favours since they could walk. Maybe she figured that since she'd been fostered like Arthur, she could reveal herself by similar prowess. But Arthur grew up a country kid, like Hezzy's grandsons, who baled hay before breakfast. How did she get it in her head that she could beat any of them? Beats me. It's not like she confided in yours truly. I found out by accident.

Go back. Set the dials for the morning of that first Sunday, June 29, before the stoning of Yogi that afternoon, before it became Kronk Sunday, and here's what you'll see: me, returning from my run and spying Jordan, tucked into a corner on Grandma's back porch, no Grand in sight.

There she sat, nose to nose with Derwood, calmly having pre-church tea and cookies and, worse, listening to him as if his opinions mattered, leaning in puppy-eyed as if he mattered to her. One tight twosome, far too engrossed in the map before them to notice the likes of me. And to add insult to injury, it was my fishing map, the mariner's map she gave me, my guide to circles within circles on the lake, little round buoys and giant whorled thumbprints indicating currents and depths. Stolen from my tackle box – my locked tackle box. Once a thief, always a thief. I should've remembered that. I snuck up close.

'Dexter and Grayden both say the trick is not to go out too fast. To stay shore-side of the competition and use them as a buffer. Let them take the wind and waves and get tired doing it. But I won't get too close, or they'll slow me down.'

'How can they do that?' She smiled up at him.

'They generate undertow. You know, the same as in the Olympics. Certain lanes of the pool are slower than others.'

'Okay, so is your strategy the same in any weather?'

'Yep. When Gray won, it was dead calm, but last year when Dex won, for the second time, he had to fight a bay full of whitecaps. Dex says I've just got to stick to the March Boys' Plan and it's all mine this year.'

'What about the choppy cross-current, here, dead centre? When she won, Chrissy switched to sidestroke facing the shore, so as not to swallow water.' Derwood looked at her sideways but could only see an inch past his own nose. She winked at him.

'Naw, that's dumb girl strategy. I go underwater. For five minutes dead centre, I surface as little as possible.'

'Won't you get winded?'

'We're talking about me here, little cuz, not you. I don't even know why Uncle T is letting you try.' He hoovered another cookie, shoving it whole. Chunks spattered. 'Just try not to be the first one pulled out, okay? Try not to make us any more asham– '

Grandma reappeared and Derwood stopped mid-word. I took it as my cue to cut out likewise. What a retard! She'd just pumped him for every scintilla of strategy that he or any of his much-medalled brothers had ever used, and he never had clue one.

But I did. And so I watched her. I'd been watching her all summer and no, I didn't tell you, but enough already – I'm telling you now. She'd tried to hide it, but you can't fool an athlete who trains every day. She kept finding excuses to swim farther and longer. Remember those lengths to the rock pile? So painfully transparent. Her claim to a daily skinny-dip? Well, that was a double cover-up, pardon the puny pun. I'd return from my run to find her suit on the line, still dripping. Unless the secret to Grandma's prize-winning rhubarb was that you had to weed it in a wet swimsuit, Jordan had been crossing the bay at the one hour she could hide doing so, at dawn. Had she been caught, she'd have been teased to death and not just by me.

I'll give her this much: if I was the March hare, running around with a clock right in front of my face and still late to the party, she was as stubborn as a March tortoise. She trained every single day. In July she swam in an electrical storm, with whitecaps a foot high, with no boat to be seen, let alone one spotting her. Hell, no one even knew my stupid lightning-bait sister was out there. Time to rat on her for her own good, to be virtuous and save her sorry life. Then I noticed Grandma's canoe wasn't where we'd left it after night trawling. I squinted; I spotted a sliver of grey wood in the churning grey waves. So BS had a new accomplice, a new confidant, a new sidekick. She obviously had no further reason to keep kicking yours truly.

And so on that Monday morning, August 11, when I watched her give Mom lip, waste our precious sugar and flounce back into her room like she needed nobody and nothing, when she had the gall to wink at me like she'd already won, to wink at me the way she'd winked at Derwood, that's when my slow boat finally docked. But not in China. China's real. In reality most things make some kind of sense. Let's call the game in my head 'When Green Lands.' It was a harbour I knew to be unsafe, but at that point I not only didn't care, I longed for a deck-clearing brawl. She wasn't pressing me into service again. I docked, tied myself up tight and convinced myself my line could hold. I cast out my lure and reeled in lies and red herrings twenty-plenty. As I've confessed already, I know it now for my lowest moment of that down and dirty summer, as a triumph of error, envy and malevolent stupidity. Let me spell it out for you in crystal green persuasion: from this sentence on your mildly unreliable, sometimes unsympathetic narrator has jettisoned all sibling sympathy and become not just unreliable, but downright hostile. Sorocidal even. Thank you, Snagglepuss.

Because I'd been had. It was all BS, every damn bit of it. A con. A pack of lies. Each engineered for one purpose: to cheat me of my rightful regatta win, to breed every unfair advantage her devious little mind could spawn. A snow job by a whack job. Take Helter Skelter, the first case in point. When the parents didn't pin the dead Scout on her, she needed a quick Plan B. The hurling and the hurdling? Plan B. It got her exactly what she wanted. For the next five days she could sneak out at dawn to train and spend the rest of her day reclining like the Queen of Sheba. Why? To rest and concentrate before her big race. Why? Because she wanted to stick me with a week of double chores. Why? So I'd be worn out. Why? Because someone who is physically exhausted is easier to brainwash. Because she didn't want two gold medals in the family. Because she didn't want to share victory and knew there was only one way to make that happen – she had to make me want to lose. Me. Mr. Track Star. Mr. Hockey Star. Want to lose. Not to his better – to a ridiculous little girl.

And it almost worked. All summer she'd been jerking my strings, playing me as if I were Tommy the Retard, or the stupid puppet brother, Double Doody, manipulating my pity so successfully that I'm sure she fully expected that come race day I'd happily play Sherman, fall behind and hand Her Bespectacled Genius my medal. Had anything been the whole truth and nothing but the truth? No, I told myself. She figured she was Tarzan, that her story was the only truth necessary. I took myself out on the dock to befriend my fury.

'That's all she is,' I told the waves, 'just BS.' I dug down and kept going, 'Just Adopted Sister. Just Almost Sister. Just Bar Sinister. Just Bull Shit, Baby Sister.' I let those words come winging out of my mouth and presto, everything she'd ever said or done that whole summer long became crystal fucking clear. Here's the wholly holey story I knit myself:

Take all that secret wood chopping. I saw her axe-wielding for exactly what it was: weight training, a BS attempt to build upper body strength to compensate for the puny rest of her. I could've shown her a better regimen, but hey, it's not like she asked my opinion. It was one thing not to tell me in the first place and quite another to lie to my face, to serve me crapped-up cover stories about rape and nightmares. A liar is faithless, 100 percent.

Take that dirty movie. I bet she made it up on the spot after joking around that day in Fenelon. I bet she wasn't upset when she upset the canoe. I bet she complimented herself on her fine acting skills. She wanted what she wanted and she used me to get it. She wanted running shoes. She wanted to be a regular March chicken, one without distinctive footprints for reasons obvious. And how could she swear I'd never hold her under by the hair again? Because she'd planned it. That's why she didn't buy those yellow barrettes. How do you get short hair for a big race when you know your mother will never let you cut it? A little emotional blackmail and presto! MC feels so guilty that you can cut it off yourself, throw it in your pregnant mother's face and never get called on it. Good one. And the best BS of all? The B movie so good it almost sold me? The Baby Ginny Blockbuster, the I'm-Next-To-Disappear Tear-Jerker. Some jerk I was. All a pile of piñata.

Isn't it astounding what we can tell ourselves makes sense, when we desperately want it to do so? I should have listened to myself. I was the one who warned her that if you look for something hard enough you'll eventually find it whether it's there or not, who accused her of taking the bare bones of a story and fleshing them out in such a way that they inevitably took on the aspect of her attitude. And then I did likewise. I made it all seem probable. I looked at random numbers and convinced myself they were palindromes, saw patterns where there were none. I told myself I had to hand it to her, that it took real brains to manufacture a fake diary, to lure me to the tree house and leave it behind. To leave me out of it, knowing I'd get pissed off and chuck it. To know Derwood would find it. She'd been jerking his strings all summer too. Those acronyms really had looked like her writing. Letters? What letters? Mom had been right all along. And to think I nearly fell for it, all of it, hook, line and sister. Hard to say which one of us was crazier.

Forty years later I've gained considerable empathy for the strain it took to do just once what she had to do all her life – create life from the barest of bones – but on that morning, I knew such prestidigitation to be both warping and exhausting and simply didn't care.

I consoled myself with fury, told myself that I could spit out the paddle and walk away, whereas she'd lost her head. She was one girlie Hamlet, one crazy fox who made herself nuts, a fox in a yellow baby dress with a lame act to boot, but with abacus eyes and razor white teeth aimed straight at my March gonads. Insert impressed here; I was halfway hoping the little vixen would win. Insert incensed here. I was halfway hoping the lying little bitch would get creamed. Both were true; one was truer than the other. Of two ills, choose the least.

But of course a parallel universe isn't planet Earth. Three days later, on Thursday, August 14, when Grandma came to call bearing a pot of mint tea and a tinfoil tray of homemade butter tarts, she didn't get past the screen door. Nobody home but us chickens. Grandma made the mistake of saying that she hadn't seen her favourite granddaughter for days. Mom stabbed her gold shoe into the screen and said Jordan didn't deserve to be anybody's favourite. Grandma dropped her voice to a whisper. 'For pity's sake, Caroline, talk to the child! She thinks she's going straight to Hell. Perhaps some reassurance?'

MC snorted. She said that Hell was a March creation, not hers, that the child was so full of her own self-pity that the last thing she needed was someone else feeling sorry for her. When Grandma persisted, MC pulled rank. She leaned out the door and pointed up at her Scottie dog, rusted but still on guard. 'Do you see that sign? Just because you say jump at the other six cottages, Madam Marchport, doesn't mean you can waltz in here and tell me how to raise my daughter. This is *my* house. I'm going to put *my* foot down *and keep it down!*'

When Grandma urged Mom to at least let her in to give Jordan something to eat, MC lost it. 'It's your God sending a bastard child to Hell, a place she needs neither company nor baked goods! The tarts can stay on the counter until she apologizes. Thank-you-oh-so-very-much-goodbye!' Stilettos dug in and jaws clamped shut.

As I said, in the end we all betrayed her. Even Grandma caved. She stood at the door for a bit, but eventually walked back to March One. Don't be too hard on her, what choice did she have? At least she came to the door. Dad, on the other hand, had plenty of choices. What did he do? He developed an urgent need to walk the dog. He whistled for Balsam, who had spent much of the week lying outside Jordan's door, as loyal as Greyfriar's Bobby, the little Scottie dog who lay for years on his master's grave. Dad whistled again. Balsam whined, hesitated and then bounded out the back door.

What did I do? I warned you that you'd hate me at the end. I went into my room and closed the door. I stood at my dresser watching the reflection of the tall, good-looking, well-tanned athletic kid in front of me as he combed his straight, dark hair. 'Good one,' he whispered. 'Serves her right.' He shrugged. 'Once a bastard, always a bastard.' And when I smiled, Mirror Boy smiled back. It was legitimately easy for him to call her the b-word. He was tired of being a gopher; he was a March and only taking what was rightfully his.

This is the first page of a five-page letter she pushed under my door, one without an envelope or a bottle, but containing a buoyant wish just as urgent:

'What does it take to become a bastard? To really feel in your heart that you are one? It's that one time, after all the other incidental times you've heard it, spoken in jest, in anger, in casual conversation – you bastard, that bastard, lucky bastard, little bastard, you lucky little bastard, old bastard, dumb bastard, fat bastard, heartless bastard, stupid insensitive bastard, dirt rotten slimy bastard, shifty bastard, horny bastard, perverted bastard, goddamned bastard – that you realize that you mean you. That you're a swear word. You're the expletive not deleted. Is MC is right – give a dog an ill name and you have hanged him for sure?'

I glanced at that much of it, smiled, recreased its folds and pushed it right back. Good one. Yes, I'm one sick bastard. Tab F. That's me.

HAZEL #100

In 1955, the 23rd of June was humid, dry and crisp with drought, pounding with rain, and colder than a witch's tit. My mother went into labour at whatever time it was, wherever she was. Her water broke at the Lindsay Cleaners and Dyers Laundromat, in church, on a rock at Marie Curtis Park, while feeding the chickens, while bowling, and on a chipped toilet seat in the third cubicle from the left in the washroom of Fran's Restaurant. Her contractions were all of twenty-three minutes and only twenty-three seconds apart.

She walked the seven city blocks to St. Mike's Hospital all by herself. She rode the Queen streetcar with her chattering bowling team, all six Tam O'Shanters, in town for an all-girls tourney. She took the subway for the first and last time, sitting alone, beside her furious husband, an elderly Chinese woman with a bag of mouldy purple vegetables, a bottle-blonde prostitute from Bracebridge, and a Boy Scout with a seeing-eye dog named Calvin. Arguing non-stop, Mumsie, Ma, Mam, Momma, Marmee, Mother, Janie, Kevin, Margaret, Gladys and Angus drove her down from the farm in a horse trailer. Walter, Howard, Tommy and Kronk rushed her to St. Mike's in their Oldsmobile Ford Morris Minor Firebird. She checked in. Nurses gave her knowing and superior and catty and kind and pitying looks. They tried not to look at her at all.

During labour, somebody and nobody held her hand. Since my mother valued and despised Scottish tradition, and since they couldn't put a real axe under her hospital bed, Mumsie, Ma, Gladys, Janie, Margaret and Grandma brought a little charm-bracelet axe with them and slid it under her pillow to cut the pain. My mother smiled at their thoughtfulness and told them to fuck off. JFK, Angus, Walter, her Da, Kronk, her doctor and an unnamed orderly with a chipped tooth all paced in the waiting room. Meg, Jo, Beth and Amy looked up from their knitting and smiled. Nobody came; nobody waited. Nobody brought her a goddamn thing.

It was a hard, fast natural labour, over in three short hours, and a two-day ordeal, the last ten hours of which she was too heavily sedated to remember. She came to and asked for me, and asked for a cigarette, and asked to die.

I was born pink, bleating like a baby lamb. I was born attached, my arms wrapped around a dead twin, a gelatinous lump they scraped into a rusty garbage can, correctly expecting no one to notice or to care. I was born blue. My mother, believing it the will of Jesus, begged the doctor not to revive me. He hesitated and I kicked him. I was born dead. They put me in the garbage can, but when a clumsy Italian janitor kicked it over and the mewling wasn't an easily drowned kit, he said he'd rat on them if they didn't take me out.

My Birth Moment was recorded for posterity at 12:01 a.m., 9:26 a.m., 4:37 p.m., breakfast time, lunchtime, early, mid- and late afternoon, suppertime, bedtime, the best of times, the worst of times, any and no time at all. My grandmother took my picture and my mother has it still. My great-grandparents sketched a painting they would later entitle *Northern Madonna and Child*. When my mother tried to take a picture with the Brownie camera she'd smuggled into the hospital in her new red suitcase, her husband, not my father, threw it to the floor and trampled it. At my mother's request, there is no photographic evidence we were ever in the same room.

My mother held me, rocked me, fed me, kissed every finger and toe, sang me an ancient Celtic lullaby and howled like Boudica when they pried me from her arms. My electroshocked mother dressed me in a little yellow doll's dress, snapped my empty locket shut, kissed my cheek and passed me to the first available nurse. Under doctor's orders, they wouldn't let her hold me; the nurses told her and themselves that it really was in everyone's best interests. Three times, they tried to hand me to her and she said, 'Take that fuck-ugly little bastard away.' A public health nurse shoplifted a yellow dress from Eaton's Bargain Basement. A Filipina night nurse filched a dead child's locket from the Lost and Found.

Every year on the 23rd of June my mother pours over her Hurricane Hazel scrapbook and cries for her one true love and a greater loss: the child kidnapped from her arms. She secretly drives by my house. On the 23rd of June when I am ten, twenty, thirty, forty, fifty, sixty, seventy, eight, ninety and one hundred years old, she puts an ad in the personals of the *Toronto Star*, the *Telegram*, the *Globe and Mail* and the *Fenelon Gazette*: 'Desperately Seeking Susan.' Every 23rd of June, she closes her eyes and whispers thank goodness for small blessings. Someone else's mom thanks God for electroshock and three healthy sons. Every year on the 23rd of June, my sister, born in 1956, gives two seconds' thought to my mother's deathbed confession in 1969; she looks at the phone and looks away. Every year on June 23rd, my mother drinks and dopes herself to a place beyond regret and well past memory. For my mother, for all the remaining days of her life, the 23rd of June is just another summer's day.

BABY I LOVE YOU

'There really is no reason for an older child to love the new baby who is at best a novelty and at worst an interloper and an enemy. Step-children whose relationships in the family might be shaky anyway may need extra help and reassurance. Even the adolescent girl with her growing desire to be a woman may be unconsciously envious of her mother's new parenthood.' – Dr. Benjamin Spock

I don't know what MC expected to accomplish when she read this to Jordan that night. I guess she gets points for trying, even if her abortive nurturing came far too late and entailed labour lasting less than three minutes.

For five days she'd done nothing; she'd knocked, left food outside the prison door and left. For five days the door never opened until the rap-tap-taps faded. On the night before the regatta, however, MC, bearing Saturday's supper, tapped her heels on point, not away, and when the door opened, jammed it with a pointed white shoe. 'May I come in, dear?' She perched on the bed without an answer, looked directly at her daughter and – I'll give her this much – snapped straight at the paddle in the room.

'I've been reading my Dr. Spock, dear. You know how you're so good at catching frogs? Something that, well, boys are usually good at? He says you catch them because on some level you're afraid of them, that you want to be powerful and unafraid, like a boy.' My sister sat, as still as Gandhi. 'Well? Is it true, dear?' I bet BS wanted to say that the woman who had once uttered the stupidest words ever spoken about a caged mammal had just gone one better about free amphibians, but to my surprise she played the girl game: she nodded.

'I thought so, Trixie-Pixie.' MC patted her hand. 'Good girl. Confessed faults are half mended.' She motioned to start eating.

'Dr. Spock says your recent bad behaviour – he'd call it aggressive and masculine, dear – is called acting out. He says older children are often jealous,' she folded her hands over her stomach, 'when new babies come on the scene.'

Jordan developed an urgent need to swallow creamed corn. Anything to keep her mouth occupied so that words didn't come out of it. Mom took silence as affirmation.

'Well now, that's it, isn't it? Don't you worry, dear, nothing will change.' Mom didn't seem to know which sleeve of her pearl-buttoned sweater was uneven, so she pulled on both. 'Perhaps you'll even enjoy helping with your brand-new brother or sister?'

Daylight will peep through the smallest of holes. Jordan crossed her cutlery, wiped her mouth and folded her napkin. She put plate to the floor and uttered three perfectly imperfect little words: 'Like last time?'

'My goodness! Look at that, done already?' Mom made a grab for Canadiana Brown and made for the door. 'I'll just take this – '

'Mother, you heard me! I said, *like last time?*'

Mom stopped, and I think it truly was for sorry. She returned to her daughter's bedside. 'Yes, I heard you.' She sank back down as if her air had been vacuumed out. 'I didn't think you remembered. I've spent a lot of time hoping you didn't ... For your sake.'

'Really? Or for yours? Virginia is my sister! Who'd forget that – besides you?'

'So that's it.' Mom buttoned her sweater bottom to top and held on to the pearl at her throat. 'That's what you've been thinking all these years.' She stood up. A quaver shook her voice. 'You may not believe this, dear, but the hardest thing I ever had to do was send that sweet child back when Dr. Riley said I couldn't both carry a baby and raise one.'

'Good one! Obviously the right choice, seeing how you ended up with neither.'

A moment of silence spins out between two damaged people in a small grey cottage on Balsam Lake. Those who believe themselves injured are eager to inflict injury. Arsenals of words, alert and at the ready, hover overhead. Then sounds so sharp and quick I thought she was being slapped. No, a staccato of stilettos, hail that couldn't cross linoleum fast enough.

'Confiding in you, dear? My mistake. But hear this.' Mother gripped the door knob and stared back into the room at the fourteen-year-old on the bed. 'A turn well done is soon done. It's time to grow up, to end all this poor-little-me quiddling nonsense and start acting like a young lady.' Her voice was rail on snow, the quaver flash-frozen. 'We told you she was your sister because we wanted you to think of her as one.'

She crossed her arms. 'But I can't believe that someone who's as smart as you purport to be actually believed it. She was just one of the hundreds of little mistakes that get dumped off at Children's Aid every day. A complete unwanted nobody, much like yourself.' She yanked on the door. 'So stop punishing me for the loss of a sister who was never yours in the first place.' She exited, pulled the door and spoke through the gap. 'Your new standing orders, Private March? Forget her. She's forgotten you long ago.' She closed the door and hissed through it. 'And face it, dear. She's no more related to you than I am.'

Jordan copied down the new CHUM Top 30 by hand that night, a desperate dictation from a fading Miracle, reproduced in the tiny script of the genuine article, a final effort to live with an unreasonable facsimile, when with every letter, she longed for the real thing. Here it is, her CHUM Chart #655, August 16, 1969. In the margin she wrote, 'The first shall be last and the last shall be first.' Please note them both:

THIS WEEK	LAST WEEK	ARTIST	TRACK
1	1	The Archies	Sugar Sugar
2	2	Cat Mother & the All Night News Boys	Good Old Rock 'N Roll
3	1	Zager & Evans	In the Year 2525
4	4	Neil Diamond	Sweet Caroline
5	7	Tony Joe White	Polk Salad Annie
6	6	Stevie Wonder	My Cherie Amour
7	8	Shannon	Abergavenny
8	5	Andy Kim	Baby I Love You
9	11	The Guess Who	Laughing

10	13	Jackie DeShannon	Put a Little Love in Your Heart
11	17	Johnny Cash	A Boy Named Sue
12	15	The Rolling Stones	Honky Tonk Woman
13	14	Ray Stevens	Along Came Jones
14	9	Roy Clark	Yesterday When I Was Young
15	10	Johnny Adams	Reconsider Me
16	12	Kenny Rogers	Ruby Don't Take Your Love to Town
17	18	Duke Baxter	Everybody Knows Matilda
18	22	The Letterman	Hurt So Bad
19	21	The Youngbloods	Get Together
20	23	Creedence Clearwater Revival	Green River
21	28	Bob Dylan	Lay Lady Lay
22	25	The Fifth Dimension	Workin' on a Groovy Thing
23	16	Blood, Sweat & Tears	Spinning Wheel
24	24	The Happenings	Where Do I Go/Be-In (Hare Krishna)
25	26	The Box Tops	Soul Deep
26	19	Jr. Walker & the All Stars	What Does It Take
27	30	John Lennon	Give Peace a Chance
28	0	Crosby, Stills, Nash & Young	Marrakesh Express
29	0	The Grass Roots	I'd Wait a Million Years
30	0	Underground Sunshine	Birthday

MY CHERIE AMOUR

August 17, 1969. The fifth Sunday. The Balsam Lake Regatta. No one was surprised when Uncle H pulled Derwood out first, but when a little yellow bathing suit surfaced right behind him, you could've knocked all of March over with that proverbial feather. They'd left her in the addition with the dog. She'd raced without blessing or permission. She'd been expressly forbidden to open the screen door.

Later they found a big blue Maple Leafs towel on the dock. She'd used it as a cover and Derwood as a rabbit. She didn't have to beat him, just match him. Yes, even her interest in my big race had been self-serving. She stole my strategy and Derwood's drive, because her end always justifies the mean. And now, chuck all you Farley Marches, she'd won.

There is no cinematic evidence, but legend has it that Auntie E went running round the side of our cottage to tell the parentulas. They, who were on the deck having tea with Aunt May, are alleged to have burst out laughing. 'Good one, Elsbeth!' they apparently said.

I say 'apparently' because I wasn't there. I was nowhere to be seen. I was, in fact, waiting on my sister like one pig waits on another, in the one place I figured no one, least of all her, would ever look for me: Derwood's bunkie. He'd given me the idea that morning on my run when I spotted him up ahead of me on the dam road. It wasn't the first time. Whenever he'd copied me before, I'd turned and gone the other way. But that morning, I could hear more than his feet. He was running and talking, punching the air as he galloped along. Good one. I ran up behind him. He kept just out of arm's reach and kept talking. Unable to punch or trip him, I'll admit that I slowed my stride. And after a while, truth be told, it wasn't half bad. At least he could keep up. It was almost company, except for the noise. He wouldn't shut up.

'They were all empty, see? Except for the charts. Those girls, they don't send her word one, and they send the charts only because she pays them. They stopped 'cause someone,' he jingled his pockets, 'made off with the dimes. Must be that retard son of Hezzy's.' He smiled. 'I reckon NOB got a few of them. I told him he needs a few to buy bait from Kronk. Told him the best time for fishing is lunch. I give him a chocolate bar and he gives me the mail. Guess it's true.' I stumbled as MC left his mouth, 'A full purse never lacks friends.'

He wouldn't stop bragging. On and on about how he'd beat her good, about how she was going to get hers all over again when he won the Big Race. How when he won, he'd give somebody some of those dimes, if that somebody would just flip the switch in his bunkie that linked up to the regatta loudspeakers. He'd recorded a special song on his new guitar for his award ceremony. Then I got it. A friend in need indeed. He was making a wish. The nerve of a canal horse. Sick of the sound of him, just to shut him up, I nodded. Anything for a quiet life.

But alone in his bunkie I wasn't sure of anything anymore. My sibling bruise throbbed, because just as he'd predicted there he was, standing tall in *Excalibur*, one shining wet knight crowned by his own hand, and waving that hand, working the crowd as a proud uncle carved a victory lap. Where was Jordan? Uncle H made her sit in the back of the boat. Of course he did. The best an Almost ever gets is an Almost win. You can't run faster than your shoes. We won't let you. Later he'd claim it was for her own good, so she didn't lose her balance and fall overboard, but I knew better and I'm sure she did. He was playing After Me You Come First, for his own good. If her win wasn't going to count, he didn't want to be seen endorsing its legitimacy. And so on the day, the one she'd wished for and worked for and dreamed about for months, when she'd earned the right to stand with a child of March as his equal, instead my sister got a fine view of a full-blooded March boy's damp rear end. And ergo, so did I.

And here's what I saw: no matter how despicable Derwood was, and no matter what medal they did or didn't give my sibling better half, in the long run his kind would always come first. He was a liar, a thief, a blackmailer, a torturer of animals and little girls and quite possibly the next Charles Manson, but it didn't matter. He was blood kin. His clan would always break out the bagpipes. He'd get a hero's welcome and a home-free. One of the Almost lightning bolts that missed me water-skiing split my chest with perfect aim – that's what she'd stolen from me. This Mirror Boy could be on her side or on his. Not the same difference.

I still don't know how he did it. Maybe he got the idea from all the cords we used to set up Jordan's record player on the dock. Maybe Dex was in on it; he DJed school dances and knew plenty-twenty about the electronics of sound systems. Anyway, I stood in Derwood's bunkie admiring his locked aluminum door, his privacy, his guitar and the Medusa of cords swarming out of the first profes-sional cassette recorder I'd ever seen. They sprang out his window clear onto our front lawn where at this very moment he was getting his medal and BS was about to get hers.

Should I use a thief to catch one? Does one good turn deserve worse? The cassette was loaded, cued and ready. 'What the hey,' I figured. 'Better the day, better the deed. He's already won.' I reached for the switch. 'Here goes nothing.' Maybe he'd put it on a timer. Or on remote control. Or maybe I'm in denial, but I swear to this day that as I reached for it, it all but flipped itself. I'll never know for sure. And neither will you. Loud, so much louder than ever conceiv-ably necessary, a voice came thundering back across the lawn: 'Hazel #1 and Counting ...'

HAZEL #1 AND COUNTING

*N*on-Identifying *Information for the infant child born as Susan Gail Johnston*

You were born on June 23, 1955, at St. Michael's Hospital, in Toronto, birth time unknown. Your birth weight was most likely 7 lbs (although also on record is another document listing your birth weight as 5.5 lbs). You went directly from hospital to a private foster home, which had been recommended to your natural mother by a public health nurse. In August 1955 you came into the care of the Children's Aid Society wearing a yellow hand-smocked dress and a silver locket. You were placed in one of our foster homes. The following November you were rushed to the Hospital for Sick Children with acute bronchitis. You were discharged from hospital in December and placed in a second foster home. (There is no explanation recorded as to why you could not return to your first foster home.) A month later your second foster mother had to request your removal as her children had been injured in a car accident and needed all her attention. You were moved to another foster home but in April 1956 again went to the hospital for investigation of fibrocystic disease. After a week there you went to Thistletown Hospital, a convalescent centre. You were discharged from there to another foster home in May 1956. The following October you were readmitted to hospital for further tests for fibrocystic disease as the April tests were said to be incomplete. All tests proved negative and in November you were returned to your foster home. Eventually, you were placed with Mr. and Mrs. March for adoption.

Your natural mother is described as in her mid-twenties, of medium height with a slender build, hazel eyes, a fair, freckled complexion and straight brown hair. Her worker found her to be a very tense, anxious person who found it difficult to make deep and satisfying relationships with people, although she could get along on a superficial level with business associates. She found it extremely difficult to discuss her present situation or even acknowledge that she was pregnant. Her manner of speech and action was very thoughtful and pronounced. She enjoyed debating and public speaking as well as more domestic pursuits such as crocheting, sewing, reading and some bowling.

She began school at five and completed Grade 11 at age sixteen, followed by a year's commercial training. She was a bright student in the top half of her class all through school. She was a conforming child who tried hard to please but did not take part in extra-curricular activities. After leaving school she worked as a stenographer. A routine psychological testing showed her to be of bright-normal intelligence. Her physical health was good but since high school she had experienced serious emotional difficulties resulting in depression and insomnia.

She was the eldest of two children whose parents separated when she was a young child. Her mother is of Scottish origin, but born in Canada. She had a Grade 8 education plus one year of normal school and taught school at one time. She was interested in keeping up her home and also did excellent painting. She is described as tall with auburn hair. She suffered from nerves and is described as a tense, unhappy woman who placed a great deal of responsibility on her eldest daughter. She dominated your natural mother who spent her life trying to make up to her mother for the father leaving the home. Your natural mother did not know much about her father except that he was born in Canada of Scottish descent and was a farmer. He died after the family separated. The cause of his death is not known. Your mother's sister is said to have had excellent health and enjoyed hunting, painting, basketball and swimming. An outgoing, carefree girl who was happily married.

Your natural mother came to the Children's Aid a few months prior to your birth. She explained she was pregnant by a man whom she had dated a few times but could not remember anything about the circumstances leading to the pregnancy. She had been hospitalized for depression and insomnia and received numerous shock treatments which had affected her memory. Since then she had met and married another man. Her husband knew of the pregnancy and they had married earlier than planned on the condition that she place you for adoption. The husband felt he could not accept another man's child and that it would place too great a strain on the marriage. The Society did work with them for several months in an attempt to see if they might reconsider, but it became apparent that your natural mother was very dependent upon her husband and both were becoming increasingly upset at the delay. You were therefore made a Permanent Ward of the Society in January 1956.

The only information concerning your natural father was that he was thought to be employed as a bricklayer. The Society made several attempts to interview your natural father but messages left with his mother were not acknowledged. We do not know if he was aware of the pregnancy. Your mother's husband was of Scottish origin and worked in a bank. He was very protective of your natural mother and anxious to have your future settled so that they could begin a new life elsewhere.

A letter is on file from the hospital where your natural mother received therapy, stating that she had recovered when she left and that it was felt her condition would not affect your mental health. From the date of her admission it would appear that she was not pregnant during her hospitalization. On reading the entire record I am left with the impression of a very unhappy, emotionally fragile woman who could not accept the situation in which she found herself and was at the same time trying desperately to protect a new marriage. She felt it would be selfish and unfair to keep you under the circumstances.

And the written version, the one I ignored in the tree, the worn typed pages currently splayed out on Derwood's bed, had marginalia. Of course it did. On the last page. More of the tiny unsisterlike script I'd first seen in her version of 'Polk Salad Annie':

Upon reading the perceptions of the lowly employee freely reading my entire record (and no, I cannot accept any situation in which it is illegal or improper for me to read it myself), I am left with the following impression. It would be selfish and unfair of me to keep it from myself under the circumstances:

Daddy was a rapist, skip to my lou.
Mummy was a nut case, skip to my lou.
And baby was made of the stuff of those two.
Skip to my lou, my darling!

SUGAR SUGAR

Sunday, August 17, 4:30 p.m. By the time she got to Yogi, we were half a million strong. It wasn't enough. She left her music on the kitchen counter where the butter tarts had been, propped up against a red case of eternally dancing shoes. From the screen door, it looked like nothing more than her handmade CHUM Chart. But when I stepped to the sink and took it in hand, I noticed her note, added – of course it was – in the tiniest of marginalia. So that it wasn't caught by a kitchen breeze, she used a paperweight, a perfectly executed Plasticine bear:

> Gone to feed Yogi. Hogs and Fishes, Jordan May Susan Gail Johnston March. P.S. 'Righteous acts proceed from pure love without hope of reward or fear of punishment and all virtuous acts to be righteous must proceed directly or indirectly from charity.'

What did I do? I blinked. The mirror image of her Arrival Protocol. I opened my mouth and read aloud, 'CHUM Chart #655, #1 'Sugar Sugar' by The Archies, #2 … ' And I kept reading. But when I hit lucky #13, presto – it didn't free the lame or find the lost, and Aunt May and MC are lost beyond magic – but it freed my feet: 'Along Came Jones.'

There are moments when all the pieces of your life fly together, moments of pristine clarity, and that was mine. That's why I'd decided not to swim. Because I was Jones the Heroic not Sherman the Hesitant. I was an athlete, long, lean and lanky, made to run to the rescue of my Sweet Sue, born to save her. That's why I'd snuck out night after night, why I drove myself to better my time each time: I'd been in training for this moment for all my life. I could find it blind. I could get there a hundred times faster than Jordan. Cut to the crux – I'd get there first.

To this day it plays and replays in my mind like one slow-motion snuff film, an otherworldly underwater ballet, a dance of death wish complete with soundtrack. One stupid yellow sundress draped over a rusting silver mailbox. One bear cage complete with bear.

Wearing nothing but a locket, a Miracle and a pair of wet orthopedic oxfords, my sister stood naked in the afternoon sun. She's what you can't see if you haven't got a camera or a gun. She unlocked the cage and dropped the key. It glinted gold, but she couldn't see it. She's blinded by silver, an empty silver mailbox, her silver self griping a tinfoil tray, silver duct tape dangling between her hand and a Miracle, and the sliver of silver malice in her mother's eyes.

Tarts wobbled in her hand. She's chanting. Perhaps the Venite-found-on-page-thirteen: 'From hence he shall come to judge the quick and the dead'? I couldn't hear her for Balsam, reared up against the cage, his muzzle yowling to the moon. I pulled closer. Not chanting. Singing. And dancing. Edging in. 'I'm gonna make your life so sweet.' She squashed a tart on her forehead, took a step. 'Pour a little sugar on it, baby.' Crushed another to her chest, another step. 'Oh sugar, oh honey, honey.' Flattened one on her left shoulder. 'You are my candy, girl,' and smashed a fourth on her right, 'and you've got me wanting you!'

Yogi lifted her snout and sniffed. She reared up on two legs, salivating. Clasping claws o'erhead, she stomped in a circle. With opened arms, she approached the human honey before her. Balsam leapt into the cage, soaring up like Superman, and Yogi swatted him like a fly, felled him with one swoop of her paw. My feet a blur, I grabbed the corner pole and whipped round it. Seven paces. Nothing for Underdog. I'd make it.

In the last split of a second, I saw Derwood. He and his medal were pounding pavement, feet flashing faster than I ever believed he could run. For some reason, I couldn't hear him. He made no sound. Instead I heard my mother: the devil's boots don't creak. A breath away, his arms outstretched, the shit-faced little spawn was going to get there first and end her story his way. Over my dead body.

Jordan saw us both and hesitated; her left shoe wavered in the air. Then she looked right at me. She winked. 'Oh, do, do, do, do.' Derwood launched a flying tackle as my feet left the ground. His hands hit mine. Our thrusts collided. And together we shoved my baby sister into the starving arms of an Almost dancing bear.

THE FENELON GAZETTE

A Rosedale Tragedy
by Miss Minnie McKelvie

It is with sincere sadness that this reporter relates the tragic story of the death of one Jordan May March, age but fourteen, in the picturesque hamlet of Rosedale, just north of our fair town. So many Feneloners have driven north on Hwy. 35 to see 'Yogi' at Kronkowski's Bait and Bakery. Who would have dreamed that the big pet teddy bear beloved by so many innocent children would one day take the life of an innocent child? Her death marked a sad end to an otherwise joyful historic family and community celebration: the fortieth anniversary of the St. John's Anglican Balsam Lake Regatta, attended by this reporter and hundreds more.

Details remain sketchy, but it appears that on Sunday, August 19, an enraged 'Yogi' escaped by methods unknown and attacked the March girl as she was doing nothing more than so many of us have done – feeding him treats. Her best friend and cousin, Derwood March, age fifteen, who had just won the Boys' medal for the Cross-the-Bay Swim, arrived first on the scene. 'I tried so hard to pull my cousin away, but that bloody bear, he was just too strong!' One can only imagine the heartbreak of this courageous young man!

Jordan, known to all as Jordy, is described as a quiet, traditional girl who excelled in school but did not partake in extracurricular activities. She enjoyed public speaking and those all-but-lost womanly arts of knitting and crochet. Given a childhood birth defect, she wore Foster's Orthopedic Shoes, a mere size two, and walked with a limp, which no doubt accounted for her inability to run from the bear when he attacked her.

She was the adopted daughter and only child of Thomas and Caroline March, a family name well known in the Rosedale area since the 1920s when the paternal grandfather,

Rev. Cranston March, began his summer parish as The Founding Minister at St. John's. No immediate family could be reached for comment, but Jordy's loving namesake, Great Aunt May March, spoke for all. 'A lovely, well-mannered Christian girl. Our family's chosen child. We here at Marchport will miss her more than words can say.'

A passing local, Hezekiah Gale, became the local hero when he shot the crazed bear – thankfully before anyone else became its victim! Victoria County Police have yet to determine if charges will be laid against Mr. Kronkowski, whose whereabouts at the time of the accident remain in question. A routine rabies test will be conducted. Final resting arrangements for Miss March were pending at press time, although church elders confirm that she has been assigned the second Sunday in August as a permanent memorial in her family church. On that date, the Children's Hymn will always be her fitting favourite, 'When He Cometh.' Donations can be made to her favourite charity, the March of Dimes.

Our thoughts and prayers go out to the March family, especially to Mrs. March, now under a doctor's care, expecting the birth of twins. It is hoped that new life will be of some consolation in this, their time of tragic loss. On your behalf, this reporter sends them all the very best of wishes from their many friends here in Fenelon Falls, our Jewel of the Kawarthas. Tarnished today, but ready, willing and able to bravely shine tomorrow! Please note that the St. John's Children's Choir practice and the traditional End of Summer Ladies' Tea will go ahead as planned next Thursday and Sunday respectively.

IN THE YEAR 2525

So I suppose you have some questions. Since we began this old-time movie with Mr. Lightfoot, I'll end it by admitting I'm Tab G. I'm the ghost from Jordan's wishing well. The kind that only gets set free once you see me in all my fetching glory. As Reverend S would say, 'Here endeth the lesson.'

You're right of course; imaginary friends, even imaginary big brothers, can't live on once their imaginer is dead. They can't ghost-write whole novels, particularly post-mortem. I know that, but Jordan didn't. The line between dead and alive was necessarily blurred for her; she scripted a long and happy life for me before ending her own. Saw me win a teaching scholarship. Saw me marry Wendy, honeymoon in Inverness and become the father of twins, Susan and Virginia. Found me an old house on the hill in Leaskdale and a new high school on Frenchman's Bay. Watched as I taught my children to swim in Balsam Lake. Alone in the moonlight, I'd see her hair on the waves: 'Promise. When you've stopped being angry, you'll write us down.' I knew I owed her, but for years I quiddled. I told her I knew numbers not words. She smiled. 'Both make palin-dromes. Both reach solutions.' So I promised.

And now I owe you an explanation, or perhaps more than one. But first I'm wondering how you feel. Are you shouting the current synonym for 'What the cluck'? Experiencing that strangely respect-ful 'Holy shit!' of being punked, blindsided, hoodwinked and had? I'll admit that I both respect and resent an unexpected movie twist or big reveal, and I bet you never saw me coming. Puns intended. Oh well, nobody sees everything. So she had a rainy-day friend. Plenty of lonely-onlys have them. No fault, no foul. Hunger is a good kitchen. Necessity hath no law. Unable to stop the rain, she made a big umbrella, a sheltering alter ego, a real live fit and full-blooded March boy. A BB who belonged in March in ways she never could. Her missing sibling link. Who'd blame her for wanting one who couldn't be disappeared? If I couldn't save her from that fate at least I tried, or I guess I should say, at least she did.

'Then it's all lies?' A good first review question. Yes and no. Of course and of course not. Please observe the object you hold in your hands. It's an invention, a setting of the dials by this Sherman for his Way Back. Please check the epigraphs. I didn't include 'A Salty Dog' just to be clever. I wanted you to be so. This salty dog is so much more and nothing more than a semen's log. (BS would have loved that one.) Its witness is my own hand. And my hand is also hers. So if you got attached to sidekick me after being asked not to, that's your doing. If you solved some of it and had to be taught the rest, math and life are like that. Enough said. But I grew up believing bannocks are better than no bread and I can't blame a hungry girl for feeding herself.

If you blame me for misfeeding you, then ask yourself honestly why you weren't smarter than the average bear, weren't enough of a Sherlock to catch the obvious scent of piñata – that a boy without a name was at best an Almost boy? And please don't ask now – you can think me as obdurate as Rumpelstiltskin but I still won't tell you my name, assuming I had one or knew it myself. I saw what Jordan let me see. I knew what she let me know. You can't get blood out of a dead kid. And if this bothers you, please remember two things: I'm not real and I'm not you. There are real people out there who never know their own first names, who watch the very real yarn of their lives unravel and die unknitted. And it never stops for sorry. But I do. And I am sorry to have deceived you. In my defence, I'm sure we both knew to expect a bit of fiction when you pull up your stool and sit down.

Too little mea culpa for you? I'm tempted to say tough titties. Like adoption, fiction follows no rules of disclosure. I don't have to tell you squat, let alone confess invention. I hinted twenty-plenty. Do your review. Start at hockey camp, Aunt May's Almost birthday present. All of Jordan's second versions were dead giveaways, obvious products of a BS imagination. Think about it. Did anyone else ever speak to me or about me? Jogging with Derwood? Review that too. That was BS ending the last lie and her last tie. Didn't you wonder why a fifty-something man still sounded fifteen, a not-very-masculine fifteen at that? Or did you set up the tabs in your binder with the blind faith of Fox Mulder from *The X-Files*, with his poster as your metaphoric cover page? 'I want to believe.'

Let's put it this way. There's abundant dishonesty in this story, but if your calculations of it begin and end with me, you won't pass the course. When BS made me, she used but thishful winking and kept me in her head. Her birth certificate had been altered; she simply returned the favour when she found mine next to her adoption papers in Mom's desk. Baby Boy March, February 29, 1954. Change stillborn to still born. Insert space here, not even a letter, just one tiny breathing space, one gasp of air, and presto, a real live boy! No harm done. Hey, next to Casper, I'm the friendliest ghost you know. (At least until the last episode.) But when the courts made her, they robbed Peter to pay Paul. Her own minuend, they spliced her to a living three-year-old, one procured by state-sanctioned kidnapping. Real harm done. Her ghosts were far from friendly. My parents, complicit in this unfilmed crime, caged their rechristened trophy in Almost, and when she proved both slower than molasses and faster than they were, locked all the doors. Convinced they'd done Such a Good Thing for a Motherless Child, they felt entitled to feed her penny-pinched crap or nothing at all. And all those upstanding bystanders? I promise, we'll come back to you later.

'But what was true?' Well, you won't be able to drag your net along the bottom of this tale and catch every clam. The guitar? The trailer park? The diary and the regatta? Who really did what in the summer of '69? These are some difficult multiple choices. I did warn you:

A. Jordan did? I did? We both did?
B. Our author? All of us? None of us?
C. What things? What summer? Did some, all, or none of it happen?
D. Did she/I/we/you/Yogi/our author/all of us imagine it?
E. Insert some, none, or all of the above here.

Yes, it's more riddles than answers. But hey, that's always what you risk if you let the teacher keep talking once the projector's unplugged: bonus questions. Like this one, Jordan's all-important Should Question, rephrased from Robert Frost: 'We dance around the secret and suppose, but the secret sits in the middle and knows.' In this book, secrets remain so: to Jordan, to me, to our author and, most fittingly, to you. When you put this book down, when Yogi put Jordan down, or vice versa depending on your perspective, what should you know for sure? I'll add this one up for you: less than one whole. Less than that which makes us whole. Some wholly holey knitting. Jordan's see-through plaid. Her Almost tartan. Welcome to kiltless.

With due respect, it's time for a moment's metacognition: what makes you think you're entitled to more? What's so special about you? Why should you get one easily unravelled, single, substantiated storyline? Jordan got the recursive wuthering heights of a hurricane. A wind with a woman's name, but not her mother's name. Fiction her only fact, the uncertainty of multiple choices for certain. No one to ask or tell. Undercover under covers, both bedtime story and nightmare, she murmured her story herself. A lullaby of improvised whispers, of small consolation. Less than one and always Almost two? Now that's the loneliest number.

'But wasn't she just plain crazy? Borderline schizophrenic?' I can see you're getting exasperated. So let's make a new start, because as I'm sure you know by now in this memoir there's no such thing as a beginning. So go ahead. Grab a tail end, start tale winding. Loop fact and fiction together. Hold the improbable yarns of Back Then, and Way Back, and Now, all in your hand at once. Imagine not having what every person, every religion and every culture has had since the days we found fire – a creation story. Now imagine having to knit yours alone and in secret when you are but a child.

In her position, with needles poised over a blank slate, what purls would you dive for? When your life is reduced to story, why not do the telling? Why not tell a good one, a finely spun yarn? If you are made of lies, why not knit some whoppers? Think big. You need more than baby booties. You need all the clothes you'll ever wear. You need language enough to cover the shame of vast nakedness. You need a home, an entire personal landscape and a full tree of relatives. If you still think an adoptee's loss begins and ends with her birth mother, go back to knit forward; you've dropped some stitches. Hundreds of them. Pick up your hundreds lost and knit them warm. And to yarn over between fact and fiction, craft a Wayback Machine and make it cast off with a well-knit boy who's not named Sue. Now that's some knitting!

Could you do all that and keep your sanity? Isn't the real insanity that we made a child try? It's far too easy to write her off as just another messed-up teen, one who talked to a boy who died before she was born, and for that matter, before he was. Let's face it: she's no crazier than Mackenzie King or than devoted Catholics who, thanks to rebels like Fenelon, speak directly to dead saints and saviours. Adoptees are binary by definition, embodying dualities that the rest of us monorails don't get to judge. Two names, two birth certificates, two families, two histories? That's not their fault. That's iatrogenic illness, adoption-induced schizophrenia. It's a bloody miracle they're not all lunatics. When push comes to shove, there's only one difference between crazy and not – a witness. She had one. She had me.

But I'm the narrator, not the protagonist. I'll never know it as lived experience. I only got close enough to make some pretty arrogant assumptions. And most of you, dear gazers, are probably the same. It seldom, if ever, occurs to people like us that adopted babies become adopted adults, that when you inherit the wind you die in it. We're the sheltered kids in After-School Specials, those to the bloodline born, those with maybe ten seconds of breezy teen angst: 'Hey, maybe I'm adopted!' We've got someone to ask and once reassured we're not, we insert a hurricane of relief here.

Now imagine Hurricane Hazel loss. Imagine loss is the air you breathe. Face incessant reminders: TV, movies, books, religion, conversation, language itself and yes, even cartoons. To handle all that, I submit that it's not crazy to have an imaginary friend, as long as you know they are so. I wasn't in her diary; she never spoke my name, not even to Grand. It's better to eat with a knife than want for a spoon. Let's just say she was saner than March. Saner than a man who films everything and sees nothing, or a woman who insists that her clearly limping daughter walks-just-fine-thank-you-if-only-she'd-pick-up-her-lazy-fat-feet. If like any victim of child kidnapping, Jordan refused to forget, isn't that an act of self-defence? Her kidnappers played mind games, said to survive she'd have to feign death. She remembered in secret, clung to memory alone and unconfirmed. Cogito ergo sum. Since Susie and I don't have corpses or graves or anniversaries commemorating our deaths, it is sane, ergo, to believe we are still alive.

'But you were never born!' Please don't yell; I can hear you. (Evidence, yet again, that I must be alive.) Lots of live people aren't on birth certificates: your mother, for instance. Her name has likely been changed since. And Jordan May March was not of woman born; she began on paper, as an Order of Adoption. Her birth certificate was posthumous, stolen from Susie and forged by a judge. She began at the whim of his pen and judged it equally whimsical to pen me. No baby pictures of me? So what? None of her either. She's the only one who remembers either of our baby-hoods. If life begins when you come to live with those who raise you, then I can begin when she raised me. If $a = b$ then $b = a$. Insert sauce for the gander here. That's not crazy; it's two equally cooked geese. Same difference.

'But only crazy people kill themselves!' Are you sure about that answer? I'm not. Maybe Jordan defied Jiminy. Maybe when she couldn't stop him from whispering in her ear, noosing herself with her hair was a dress rehearsal. Maybe death was a wish her heart made, when she was wide awake. Do I approve? Hell no. I deliber-ately didn't share the details of how a real live girl dances with a starving bear. But if you can cause that kind of pain, then I'm willing to accept that you need to end a greater one.

'But she hesitated! She changed her mind!' Really? MC would say that a wise man wavers; only a fool is fixed. Maybe in the last split of a second my sister proved herself a tad more sentient than the aver-age soup turtle? I could point out that confusion is in itself probable evidence of sanity, but you already know that. And you'd have to retract crazy to see her as sane enough to change her mind. Why the ethical contortions? Are you reaching around for an escape hatch, to pump quotation fingers around 'a tragic accident'? That would be a crime. So she hesitated. Maybe she savoured the moment. Maybe she who hesitates is found.

'But she found death – you're a murderer!' Eureka! I wondered when you'd get round to naming me. Look, I won't get all existential on you, but ask yourself why I called it my one clean moment in a dirty summer? Given who I am, I can't act alone. Her death can't be on my hands without being by hers. Consider this version: having no control over fictions forced upon her, she wrote her own ending. She had the guts to say, 'Insert this ending, my ending, here.'

Derwood, he's a stone-cold killer, but at worst I'm her inner Dr. Kevorkian. I'm grateful that when she couldn't bear it, she asked me to help her bear it. Puns more than barely intended. Insert grins here. Hers, mine and hopefully yours.

It's so fitting. All of Peabody's Improbable Histories ended likewise. My puny BS would chase you down and not let you up until you appreciated all its punny layers. She'd get out her diary: 'Bear is more than a fur-bearing mammal. It's something difficult to tolerate or endure. To support or carry, to be characterized or marked by something and more hopefully, to produce or give birth to, as in to bear fruit, or a child. It means to conduct or carry yourself, to head in a chosen direction, or to use something to force a desired outcome.' So, after bearing for years that which became unbearable, she took her bearings, chose not to bear it further and bore a course using two boys and a bear to bring a more bearable end to bear. To bear fruit, for hope to be born(e), you stayed to bear witness. Ergo, you're just as crazy as the rest of us.

Let me sum it up. I'm not real in the visceral world, but I'm quite real to myself, thank you very much. If I've done my job as narrator, sympathetic or not, reliable or not, I'm also real to you. You've been listening to my disembodied voice, to a real dead boy, scouting out a yarn for pages on end. If writers are off kilter by definition, what does that make readers like you, who voluntarily enter their wordy asylums? It makes you one crazy witness. Because you saw it all: the yellow Miracle, the poo piñata, the pink diary and the silver locket. You read the signs better than we did: Jordan crossing herself in a benediction of butter tarts. Kronk's sign, dripping red from inception, a portent none of us saw but I bet those of you with halfway decent English teachers noticed. I wrote the voice-over, but you made the movie, kept the binder updated in your head. You keep listening, even now when you've been told I don't exist. Where is my voice coming from? The WABAC? The eye of a hurricane? Forget crazy – you must be nuts.

Are you sane enough to answer your Seminal Question: 'Who's to blame?' Got your shining right answer? I promised you one. Just do the math. Factor it all in. Blaming Jordan is worse than useless, though you wouldn't be the first to blame the victim. Part marks for according part blame to the March family, the government and the times. Real harm; real foul. But put the saddle on the right horse or you're stuffing the wrong bear. Yogi's not the worst villain here; neither is MC, Kronk nor Derwood. They're all petty criminals in a larger crime. Blame is more like everyday life than some people want it to be. I said we'd come back to you bystanders. I told you your turn at regret would come. It takes a village to shame a child. And, dear audience, as long as you stand outside her cage staring in, there is no such thing as neutral. By definition, a bystander stands by and lets hurt happen.

But my sister was no tourist. March didn't give her the last word, but I'm glad to say she took it anyway. Jordan's last play, the final testament of her will, was quite logically a hybrid version of When Fenelon Falls and hide-and-seek, a bequest hidden safely under her bed next to her old journal, one she'd clearly intended Mom to find in post-mortem postscript. One single yellow envelope containing seven things my sister knew her mother would have to take in hand: seven shredded relics of a beloved, and the last remains of a ticket to a miracle. All sealed up and tucked into a worn red Bible with one revised Gaelic proverb inscribed: 'When Fenelon Falls, there's one for sorrow, two for joy. Three for a girl, four for a boy. Five for silver. Six for gold. And seven for a secret that's finally been told." This heirloom, this lone legacy, came complete with ribbon, tied with one long lock of snocksnarled auburn curls.

But that's not all the answer you deserve. A story is always bigger than the book that holds it. This Sherman knows that a way back demands and portends a way forward. At the start of this tale, you were just a bystander. You watched as we wrenched a skeleton to its broken feet and made it dance. We split open a rattling cage of bone and pushed as many of you in as far as we could. And though we'll never hear bagpipes, your informed company is Miracle enough. If our shortage of Scottish lore is permanent, and Jordan keeps her bar sinister, and loss is the only kilt we'll ever wear, it is still our name and our game. Our sharing of silver. I'm proud to have been a second set of imperfectly perfect feet. Together our wholly hybrid furiously knitting selves made our Clan of Almost. Our Almost Clan.

So close your binder. If conventions of fact and fiction don't add up to answers here, if we are left boxed and caged by them, then let's suspend them. Let's insert a willing suspension of new belief here.

Thoreau said, 'It takes two to speak the truth – one to speak it and one to hear it.' Jordan and Yogi, BS and BB, author and character, you and me, author and audience, we're all Tabs A and B. We create the twosomes we need. Coupling. It's not crazy; it's human. The need to hold and be held. To behold and be beholden. To be holding a beloved hand for 'Auld Lang Syne.' I promise. I'll always come running to fetch you.

You're still here? What the Sam Hill for? The movie's over and the pibroch's been piped. Oh, I get it – you're waiting for a conventional ending. You think if you stick around, somebody will keep talking – although you probably didn't expect it to be me – and you're hoping that as storytellers are wont to do, we'll fill in the blanks. Tenterhooks are not tender hooks, are they? Maybe you still think you have the right to closure, to a cathartic denouement? Perhaps you expect credits and a moving obituary? Okay, I'll bite:

1. Grandma, she died. And so, of course, did Balsam. My claws are not toes.

2. Derwood joined the army. If his extra-curricular activities get exposed, that's another uniform he won't do proud. If he's as tormented as the archetypal guilty slave owner, ask yourself how much consolation that is to a dead slave. Or to me.

3. Hezzy? My murderer got a medal. They took it away when they realized maybe it wasn't quite legal to drive about with a loaded shotgun bouncing around on the seat of your uninsured and uninsurable pre-war pick up. Caused quite a scandal.

4. A heartsick Kronk stuffed me and mounted me swinging. Maggots set in and the uncles made him bury me. Tourists still bring butter tarts to my grave. My cage? It's become a garden centre. It sells rocks.

5. Jordan's diary? Derwood always ditched his implements of torture and he sure didn't want to get caught with that one. The second he left Miss Minnie McKelvie, intrepid *Gazette* reporter, he ran straight to his Uncle T's pumphouse, yanked it out from under the rotting mattress of an old blue crib and sank it in the swamp.

6. MC had twins: Thomas and Derwood. No, of course she didn't name them Peter and Paul. They're real live boys.

7. How much of Jordan's Non-Identifying Information reached the Rosedale Regatta before Hezzy traced the cords and broke down the bunkie door? Too much, obviously. Assuming they heard anything at all. Consider these versions: if Brother was a fetch, who flipped the switch? What switch? The switch in Jordan's head? Let's define 'switch': a connection between two live wires. A tree branch used for beating. To exchange one for another, e.g., babies switched at birth. Ergo, a switch: one who has been switched. Maybe even once she won, she realized that silver can never be switched for gold. Maybe the voices that get switched on in our heads in childhood reverberate more enduringly than loudspeakers over lawns.

Single silver bullets are for werewolves; I'm just one dead bear. If you want another human ending, go ahead, cook one up. The chefs of this story are all deliberately leaving you with the ambiguous sustenance we ate for every meal. It left us hungry every time. And yours is but a taste. You're just the reader, a little nibbler. Jordan and I are the protagonists; we bite big. What's a bit of wind and a dead bear between friends? Here's one dead bear's answer:

When this story opened you saw one girl on a dock and one bear in a cage. You'll see so many of us now, all equally caged, our suns setting and our hair aflame. Myth and martyrdom aren't so ridiculous this late in the story, are they? So many cages and altars of blood, so many Almosts, burnt like (s)witches for not belonging, for a crime not their own. How long does it take to burn alive? A lifetime. Do you see all the waiting pyres? We do. And we long to change them.

So for the sake of all us Almosts out there, both ursine and human, let's grant that wish. Blood has written enough of this story. We won't let it have this ending too. That sounds just like Jordan's Grand. If she'd seen Jordan one last time, what would she have said? 'Child, all good stories come full circle.' She'd have made some tea. She'd have said, 'Dancing down to the bone, however painful, always shakes the skeleton clean. It births that little human marvel called hope.'

So once upon a summertime, for just long enough to learn from it, you knew a hungry bear and a hungrier girl. We fed on each other and, quite naturally, we died. We had little choice. But you, dear reader, have many. You've held this book in hand, jumped on our wishes and ridden them through. What will you do next?

Consider this version: it's sunset on Balsam Lake, insert today's date here. Insert yourself. Of course you're in this story; you've known it all along. You're living TABS: Temporarily Able Bodies. Transformed Almost Bastards. Truly Almost Bears. And there's no time but the present. The second you put this book down, presto, you're a real live soul! The flesh on your skeleton is warm, the music is warming up. It's the moment you've been made for: who names the new and learns the calls can change the game before anyone falls.

It's your turn. You've opened my cage. Together we run down some fresh gravel, past a rusty brown Ford, a Polk Salad patch, and a little grey cottage next to a swamp. Grand was right: sometimes there's no way out but through. You keep running down the path to the dock. You're fetching, but you're no ghost. In a moment we'll all hear you. I'll hear you, a black bear escaping into a black night in July. I'll pause as I pass the tree house, before I slip deep into Hezzy's fields. You don't have to make do with living memory. The cicadas shouldn't answer for you. You don't need the Avengers or Underdog or even an athletic Almost Boy. This time you can choose to listen. In your version, you can answer for yourself.

You've reached her. Mission complete. You've landed right there on the dock. Despite how you've failed us before, we look up at you with hope. The hope that asks us this time to respect the moon, to stand for her and by her, not simply stomp on her, poke in a pole and claim her conquered. It's your choice. Consider that the planet you're standing on, that you stand at all, is home and miracle enough. Be grounded. Feel the weathered boards beneath your feet and raise your eyes into the night sky. Consider the heavens. It's a marvellous night for a moon dance! And you are borne by the greatest engineering device of humankind: a feat of human kindness. So grab your kilt and offer your hand. It's a brand-new reel. Ask our sister the moon to dance. Just ask. Let us add it up. Let us sing out our names. Let us name the new. Just listen. That, and only that, might just change something. Insert hope here.

What do Jordan and Brother think about this last switch? Let's ask them. They began this story after all. It's their baby; they carried it to term, knit its bones and shook its skeleton clean. They should get to put it to bed or birth it anew, depending on your perspective.

Brother would say, 'Asking me is worse than useless. I'm bloody well imaginary!'

Jordan would squint in your direction. 'But you aren't, are you?'

Yes, this story has endless tale ends. Of course your answer is one of them.

Acknowledgments

My first thanks must go to children. To all the Almosts – the orphaned, adopted, abandoned, abused and murdered – thank you for your patience. You never stopped speaking to me, even when I spent years trying not to hear you. To my children: Conor, for embracing the full life Jordan deserved, and Severn, who did what Jordan couldn't: lived and sought justice. To long-ago children, my very real Rosedale cousins, none of whom are Jordan's relatives, except for Jimmy, who inspired Brother's energetic wit and fleetness of foot. To my some 3,500 students in twenty-four years of teaching, you kept me young enough to remember Jordan as I got old enough to understand her. As we built the home called Improv at Pine Ridge Secondary, your joy sustained me and gave me two little words: ghost narrator.

Next I want to thank the searchers from all sides of the adoption triangle I met over the years at Parent Finders. No book about adoption can be written without thanking our angry pioneers: Orphan Voyage, Betty Jean Lifton, Florence Fisher and, more recently, Oprah, and www.bastardnation.com for their decades of storming the silence. So let me break mine. Jordan's Non-identifying Information isn't just fiction and it isn't just hers. It's mine, divulged and published to bring adoption out from under the bushels of sentimentality, religiosity, fear, ignorance and outright lies that we have kept them under. Jordan and I are every unwanted and Almost child: we are both and obviously neither. A problem must be problematized.

And it can't be solved without love. Thank you Louisa May Alcott and my real-life grandmothers: Florence Agnes Pawley Palmer and Ellen Sarah Morgan Stobie. Thank you, 1050 CHUM and CKOC 1150, for championing the unequalled poetry of the sixties; I am so grateful to have been your witness. I thank all my teachers in the name of two: Barry Marynick, my Grade 10 Man in Society teacher at ACI and Craig Simpson, my university mentor and friend. Many thanks to my brave first readers: Dale Nevison, Marianne Froehlich, David Lomax, Cara Sullivan and Alyson Van Beinum.

Special thanks to first editor David Lomax and Christina Lomax for her many kindnesses. I appreciate the past support of Rachel Wyatt, Adel Wiseman, The Banff Centre, the Humber School for Writers, Marc Jarman and Lisa Moore. I am truly grateful for the sustaining friendships of Judy Palmer; Chris, Christina and Thomas Hartley; David Bowlin; Peter Gubbels; Lahring Tribe; Alina Karpova; Nicholas Dipchand and his clan.

Finally, it is with more gratitude than I can ever properly express that I thank the dedicated team at Coach House: Kira Dreimanis, Christina Palassio, Evan Munday, the paragon of publicists, and, of course, the extraordinary Alana Wilcox, who while she actually failed to purge 'actually' and 'of course' from my vocabulary, still took a chance on a little book about a hurricane, a bastard and a bear, and ran full speed into my cage to help me open it to all of you. Never enough said.

P.S. When I began *When Fenelon Falls*, dear reader, I want you to know I lived in a place that made it possible: Leaskdale, Ontario, just as you come down the hill. I could see Lucy Maud Montgomery's house from my kitchen window and hear my mother correcting my father when he called it 'Leaks-dale' as we drove by on the way to the cottage. If you hear 'Polk Salad Annie' when you drive by, perhaps you aren't imagining things either.

Notes

The quotes on pages 77 and 282 are from Dr. Benjamin Spock's *The Common Sense Book of Baby and Child Care.*

Page 79 quotes from Max Ehrmann's 'Desiderata.'

There is a quote on page 90 from Louisa May Alcott's *Little Women.* The passage on pages 207–210 was inspired by this same novel.

Page 129 quotes from Rev. James MacCaffrey's *A History of the Catholic Church from the Renaissance to the French Revolution.*

Page 137 quotes a stage direction from Shakespeare's *The Winter's Tale.*

On page 154, there is a quotation from Watson Kirconnel's *History of County Victoria.*

There is a quote from George Orwell's *1984* on page 187.

The quote on page 195 is from Pearl S. Buck's *What America Means to Me.*

Page 203 quotes Robert Louis Stevenson's 'My Shadow.'

The quote on page 208 is from *Macbeth.*

'Deteriorata' on page 238 was written by Tony Hendra as a parody of Ehrmann's 'Desiderata.'

Page 299 rephrases Robert Frost's 'The Secret Sits.'

The quote on page 305 is from *A Week on the Concord and Merrimack Rivers*, by Henry David Thoreau.

The following songs are quoted by permission of the rightsholders:

'A Salty Dog'
Words by Keith Reid; Music by Gary Brooker
© Copyright 1969 (Renewed) 1971 (Renewed) Onward Music Ltd., London, England
TRO- Essex Music International, Inc., New York, controls all publishing rights for U.S.A. and Canada
Used by Permission

'Polk Salad Annie'
Words and Music by Tony Joe White
© 1968 (Renewed 1996) TEMI COMBINE INC.
All Rights Controlled by COMBINE MUSIC CORP. and Administered by EMI BLACKWOOD MUSIC INC.
All Rights Reserved   International Copyright Secured   Used by Permission
Reprinted by permission of Hal Leonard Corporation

'Put Your Shoes On, Lucy'
By Hank Fort
© Copyright 1947 Bourne Co.
Copyright Renewed
All Rights Reserved International Copyright Secured
ASCAP

About the Author

Like Jordan in *When Fenelon Falls*, **Dorothy Ellen Palmer** was likely conceived during Hurricane Hazel, and was adopted at age three. She grew up in Alderwood near Toronto and spent summers in Ontario's cottage country, just north of Fenelon Falls. In her twenty-three years as a drama/English teacher, Dorothy taught in a Mennonite colony, a four-room schoolhouse in rural Alberta and an adult learning centre attached to a prison. She coaches for the Canadian Improv Games. This is her first novel.

Typeset in Celeste
Printed and bound at the Coach House on bpNichol Lane

Edited and designed by Alana Wilcox
Cover by Ingrid Paulson

Coach House Books
80 bpNichol Lane
Toronto ON   M5S 3J4

416 979 2217
800 367 6360

mail@chbooks.com
www.chbooks.com